A Land *of* Sheltered Promise

Other Books by Jane Kirkpatrick

Novels

Tender Ties Historical Series
A Name of Her Own
Every Fixed Star
Hold Tight the Thread

Kinship and Courage Historical Series
All Together in One Place
No Eye Can See
What Once We Loved

Dreamcatcher Collection
A Sweetness to the Soul
(Winner of the Western Heritage Wrangler Award
for Outstanding Western Novel of 1995)
Love to Water My Soul
A Gathering of Finches
Mystic Sweet Communion

Nonfiction

Homestead, A Memoir
A Simple Gift of Comfort (formerly *A Burden Shared*)

"In her uniquely gifted way, Jane Kirkpatrick has gotten under the skin and shared the heartbeat of life in three very different but significant eras of the Big Muddy Ranch. *A Land of Sheltered Promise* captures the inspiring story of the miraculous transition from a deserted commune to a premier camp for kids whose background is as diverse as the three eras of the story."

—IRAL D. BARRETT, Young Life trustee emeritus

"Like the junipers clinging to the rocky reaches of the Big Muddy Ranch, *A Land of Sheltered Promise* is destined to weather time as a sentry to the ideals of faith, hope, and love. On a swath of obscure Oregon sagebrush that once made international news, author Jane Kirkpatrick weaves three women's stories over a century's time, leaving us the richer for having been reminded of what ultimately endures. If the book sometimes brings to mind Terry Tempest Williams's *Refuge,* it is, in the end, classic Kirkpatrick, a literary blessing as big and wide as the land from which the story unfolds."

—BOB WELCH, author of *American Nightingale*

"Drawing on the lives of actual women in one decade and eleven historical novels, Jane Kirkpatrick has injected unparalleled verisimilitude and depth into an emerging genre: the stories of America's pioneer women. In this work Kirkpatrick moves into the twentieth century and pioneering in a remote, desertlike, 65,000-acre site—Big Muddy Ranch—in eastern Oregon, adjacent to her own 160-acre homestead. Each of her three protagonists, women of diverse ages, eras, and classes, finds herself trapped in an excruciating conflict. Eva, the seventeen-year-old wife of a Big Muddy sheepherder convicted of murder, and daughter of a convicted murderer, waivers between abandoning and supporting her husband. Cora, who came to Big Muddy when it was Rajneeshpuram, a corrupt commune, fails to convince her daughter that she and her child are in grave danger. Jill, a talented graduate student, sorely regrets setting aside her studies to help her husband build a Christian youth camp. As their pain intensifies, each is forced to act on an untested, possibly disastrous, option. What does this Jewish reviewer derive from this and Kirkpatrick's previous novels? In people of all faiths or no apparent faith, growth begins with a desperate step in a new direction."

—HARRIET ROCHLIN, author of *Pioneer Jews: A New Life in the Far West* and the Desert Dwellers Trilogy: *The Reformer's Apprentice, The First Lady of Dos Cacahuates,* and *On Her Way Home*

"I really enjoyed this novel from an author whose work I have come to look forward to and admire. I loved the way she interwove the three stories. Once I started this one, I could not put it down."

—LINDA HALL, author of *Steal Away* and *Chat Room*

"Jane Kirkpatrick's evocative exploration of three pivotal eras on the Big Muddy Ranch offers readers a historical feast. Where others might only see the hardships and challenges of living in this remote, stark desert land, Kirkpatrick sees what a fertile field one's difficulties become for developing patience, perseverance, courage, and faith. Complex characters, shaped by ideas and beliefs that both bind and liberate, experience emotional extremes that mirror the land. Through it all, Kirkpatrick's intimate knowledge of the landscape soars like the craggy pinnacles jutting high above the John Day River and infuses *A Land of Sheltered Promise* with her distinctive voice."

—LINDA LAWRENCE HUNT, author of *Bold Spirit: Helga Estby's Forgotten Walk Across Victorian America*

A Land *of* Sheltered Promise

A Novel Inspired by True Stories of the Big Muddy Ranch

Jane Kirkpatrick
Award-Winning Author of *All Together in One Place*

WaterBrook
Press

A Land of Sheltered Promise
Published by WaterBrook Press
2375 Telstar Drive, Suite 160
Colorado Springs, Colorado 80920
A division of Random House, Inc.

This book is a work of historical fiction based closely on real people and real events. Details that cannot be historically verified are purely products of the author's imagination.

ISBN 1-57856-733-5

Library of Congress Cataloging-in-Publication Data
Kirkpatrick, Jane, 1946–
A land of sheltered promise : a novel inspired by true stories of the Big Muddy Ranch / Jane Kirkpatrick.— 1st ed.
p. cm.
ISBN 1-57856-733-5
1. Women Northwest, Pacific—Fiction. 2. Northwest, Pacific—Fiction. 3. Trials (Murder)—Fiction. 4. Ranch life—Fiction. 5. Cults—Fiction. 6. Camps—Fiction. I. Title.
PS3561.I712L33 2005
813'.54—dc22

2004026690

Printed in the United States of America
2005—First Edition

10 9 8 7 6 5 4 3 2 1

To Madison and Mariah,
who renew faith, hope, and love
within the landscape of my heart.

Cast of Characters

Part I: Faith

Eva Cora Thompson Bruner	wife of Dee Bruner
Dee "D. L." Bruner	sheepherder for the Prineville Land and Livestock Company (later known as the Muddy Ranch or Muddy Station)
**Gillette*	Eva and Dee's daughter
**Mildred*	cook at the Muddy Station
Francis Bruner	Eva's father-in-law, Dee's father
George Barnes	Bruners' attorney
Morrison and Fern Thompson	Eva's aunt and uncle
John Creegan	partner of Tom Reilly, the deceased sheepherder
W. L. Bradshaw	judge
Frank Menefee	prosecuting attorney
Henry Hahn and Leo Fried	owners of the Prineville Land and Livestock Company
Charlie O'Neal	Dee's boss at the Muddy
**Hank*	wrangler at the Muddy
**Harold "Bunzie" Meredith*	Crook County jailer

Part II: Hope

**Cora Swensen*	seeking grandmother from Milwaukee
**Charity/Charita Swensen*	her granddaughter
**Rachel/Razi Swensen*	Sannyasin at Rancho Rajneeshpuram (the Muddy)

**Ma Prem Deepa*	mayor of Rajneesh (formerly Antelope)
**Buckle Smith*	an Indian, Warm Springs tribal member
Bhagwan Shree Rajneesh	East Indian mystic and religious guru
Ma Anand Sheela	leader of several corporate and communal entities for the Bhagwan
Ma Anand Puja	nurse and director of the Pythagoras Clinic and Medical Center at Rancho Rajneeshpuram
**Swami Waleed*	member of the Ranch Peace Force

Part III: Charity

Dennis and Phyllis Washington	donors of the Muddy Ranch to Young Life
**Jill Hartley*	sociology student at Portland State University, wife of Tom
**Tom Hartley*	engineer and Young Life enthusiast
**Isaac and Gail Bartlett*	board members of Young Life
**Charita Swensen*	visitor to the Washington Family Ranch at Wildhorse Canyon (formerly the Muddy Ranch)
Arnold	oldest volunteer at Wildhorse Canyon
**Brad and Molly Jones*	construction manager and his wife
Jon Bowerman	rancher in Antelope
**Susan (Blanket Flower) and Betty (Pretty Baby)*	wife of Bellevue engineer and wife of of San Francisco carpenter, all living and working at Wildhorse Canyon
**Romeo and Juliet (Irene)*	elderly couple in Jill's retirement project
**Mary*	Antelope resident

** denotes fictional or composite character*

We must wait for God, long and meekly, in the wind
and wet, in the thunder and lightning, in the cold
and the dark. Wait, and He will come. He never
comes to those who do not wait.

FREDERICK FABER

1) THE DALLES

2) SHERAR'S BRIDGE

3) SHANIKO

4) ANTELOPE

5) BIG MUDDY RANCH

6) MITCHELL

7) ASHWOOD

8) PRINEVILLE

9) MUDDY STATION RANCH HEADQUARTERS

10) EVA'S HOMESTEAD

11) CURRANT CREEK

12) MUDDY CREEK

- - - - - - -

STAGE ROUTES

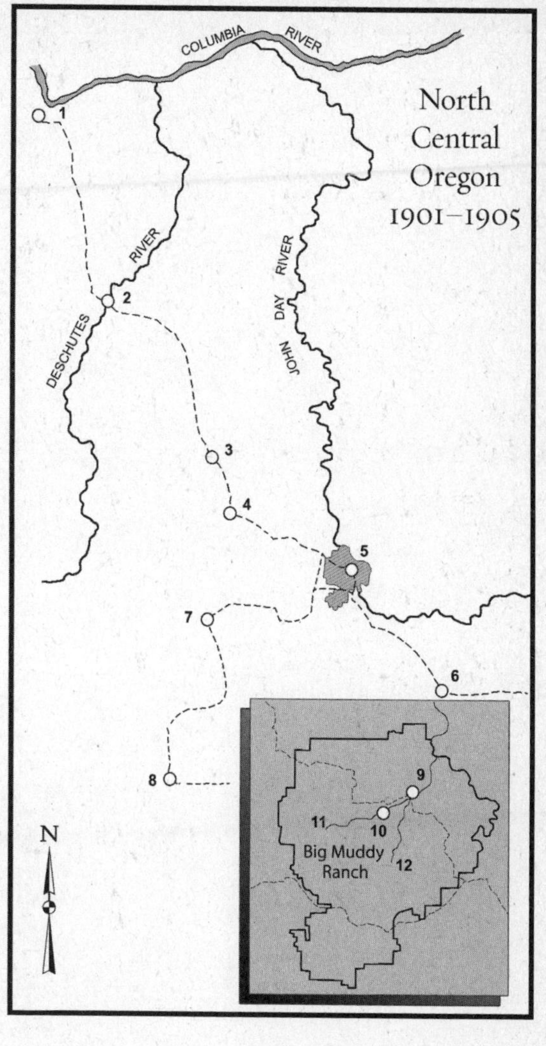

A Land Deposit

Fire and molten rock. Steaming mudflows. Searing vines. Hot lava bakes everything in its path, gouges out craggy parapets and spires, raises rugged cliffs to serve as eagle nests high above the John Day River. In time, people walk, then ride across the landscape. They camp at tiny streams, let their mounts tear at hardy grasses pushing up through ash and smoky-colored soil. Cattle are herded north. Sheep graze. Pinkish rocks surround narrow strips of green; rust- and purple-colored boulders overlook new growth. The land looks inhospitable to some, unchanged through the chain of time. Yet this deposit, stark and desert in demand, offers both protection and the Creator's promise.

Prologue

1887

Like tufts of cottonwood seeds fluffed by winds beside a stream, the tiny dots of white nibble over the purple hyacinth hills. *My hills,* Eva Cora Thompson thinks. *Those are my hills.* She hears a distant crying, raises her eyes to her father in question. "Sheep," her father says and points to the white tufts. "Motherless lambs you're hearing. They make a mournful sound." Eva leans forward, brushing her face against her father's woolen vest. He smells of whiskey and soap. Her mother's cool hand pats Eva's. A large bird whistles above them, dancing with the wind, its shadow a reminder that they aren't alone.

Eva shivers in the icy April breeze despite her sheltered position on the buckboard between her parents. Her father puts his arm around her mother's shoulders, tugging both her and Eva toward him. Chin raised in pride, he pronounces: "Those hills are where we'll make our mark in this grand landscape. The land will help us do that, Cora," her father says. "The land and that Muddy Creek that cuts it and the John Day River that furls like a ribbon along it."

He slaps the reins against the mules' backs, and the wagon totters down the stage road into the valley below. Eva smells the glycerin her mother presses against her lips before running the pasty gel over Eva's. "The air's so dry," her mother complains. Eva hasn't noticed. So much to see, to hear, to feel.

"Who's that?" Eva asks. Her father pulls up the reins and stops. He squints.

"Good eyes," he says. "Looks like root diggers. Hahn said the Indians move through here. It's that time of year. We'll have to find out which roots are edible. Supplement our supper."

"Wild roots?" Eva's mother asks. "Is that safe?"

"They're eating them. First fruits of the land." He smacks his lips to urge the mules on, and the wagon rolls closer to the small gathering.

An old brown woman with a colorful neckerchief wrapped around her head straightens at their approach. She leans against a stick. Each of her children holds a small stick too.

"So many children," Eva's mother whispers. Eva counts: one, two, three, five, seven.

"Hahn says when a parent dies of consumption or meets some other untimely death, aunties and uncles and grandparents fluff the Indian children under their wings."

"I guess they never have any orphans that way."

Her father taps his fingers to his hat. "Morning." The woman clusters the children around her like a hen her chicks. "Looks like a good morning for digging," her father says.

The woman hesitates, then opens up her waist bag. She pulls out stringy-looking roots and offers a handful, open palm, to Eva.

"Go ahead," her father says when Eva looks up at him. "It's a gift of the earth."

Eva takes the roots. She watches the eyes of the children. She looks at the shining faces of her parents. *Here are friends and food and family in the shadow of purple hills.* She's never felt so safe or loved.

It is not a feeling that will last.

Part I

Faith

I will lift up mine eyes unto the hills, from whence cometh my help. My help cometh from the Lord, *which made heaven and earth.*

Psalm 121:1-2, KJV

1

Endurance

1901

Eva Cora Thompson Bruner falters. She's tired. The stagecoach ride across the purple hills to the Prineville, Oregon, courthouse has been long, and dusty pillows of soft earth swirl up to make her cough even though it's spring. Those hills that usually fetch her rest today rise against her, foreboding as the stillness that heralds a mountain storm. She's left her carpetbag at the hotel, no time to freshen. Now she stumbles at the courthouse steps. She lifts her skirt, hem high in case the men have ignored the "No Spitting" signs meant to prevent the dreaded consumption, which takes one's breath away. She's breathless now, but for other reasons.

All these people in front of the imposing building stare at her while she brushes her parasol free of grit. She hasn't slept well since this tragedy began, not that she slept easily before. Whenever her husband leaves their bed, she barely closes her eyes through the night, hoping for his safe return. She is seventeen years old. Today, Eva feels one hundred.

Men in vests with watch bobs sparkling in the spring sunshine step aside, but their wives stare openly. New felt hats sporting breeze-brushed feathers shadow accusing eyes. Or do they pity rather than judge? Eva cannot tell.

She adjusts her white woven-horsehair hat, her gloved fingers feeling the tiny artificial roses that cluster at the brim. Shaped like a large tongue, the overhanging felt shades her eyes. White silk ribbons tickle the back of her bare neck, and she is aware, despite her fear and sadness, that some of the women admire.

She shouldn't be wearing something so fine on an occasion like this, but the hat had been her mother's, and it gives her comfort.

She moves up the first step and then the next, her legs as heavy as the oak trunks felled for the courthouse doors. Her parasol, as long and slim as one of Henry Hahn's cigars, pokes at the stone steps, making tiny scraping sounds. If she's fortunate, accusing eyes will go to that parasol, or to her silk embroidered lisle-lace hose rather than to the ten-year-old cape surrounding her shoulders. She keeps her hems raised, barely exposing her stockings.

The men look away as Eva meets their eyes. If the men return her gaze, she decides, they might reveal their own part in this conspiracy of fools. That's how she thinks of what's happening, as a conspiracy of fools. She wonders if she is the star.

The onlookers part, and Eva walks through them into the dark cool of the courthouse. As her eyes adjust to the wood-paneled interior, she wonders how Dee will look. She hasn't seen him for a month.

He doesn't go by Dee; he never has. "It's a woman's name," he told her once. "A man can't be called by such as that." He calls himself D. L., lets stand the error if someone refers to him as Dean or David. Eva wonders how the newspaper will record his name.

The last time she saw him, April 4, 1901, just a month before, he looked tanned and fit, the smell of sheep and gunpowder melded to his clothes. It had made no sense for him to be there in the shade of the cottonwood trees along Muddy Creek at the Station House. She heard his voice midday when he should have been with his flock, working the dogs, taking sheep to spring pasture.

"Eva! Come out, *ma chérie.*"

She wiped her hands on her apron and pushed against the new screen door of the ranch house, half-happy to see him, half-wary at the surprise. The vein in his neck throbbed, her first warning sign. His left eyebrow lifted.

"What is it?" she asked him. "Who's with the sheep?"

"Call the sheriff, Eva," her husband said, brushing at his pants. He stared at her, that vein throbbing. "Do it," he said when she failed to move.

"What do I say?" Eva asked.

"Tell him I've just killed Tom Reilly."

The courthouse, with its false front, soars two stories above the high desert plateau in the city of Prineville, Oregon. A murder trial brings out the neighbors and witless as well as the merely curious, but only the sturdy and those who rise early have climbed these flights to the circuit court this May day. The rest will read of it in the *Crook County Journal* or the *Antelope Herald.* Eva keeps her fingers gripped around her reticule as though hanging on to it will anchor her taut nerves. She wants to look serene, above the fray. She sends an arrow prayer, as she calls them, high and quick toward the target. *Help me through. Help me through.* Inside, her stomach clenches as it did when, as a child, she watched her mother die. She steps into the courtroom.

The powers behind the Muddy Ranch have provided a legal mind, smartly dressed, dapper. She sees Dee's lawyer, George Barnes, bending near a seated man, his back to her. It's likely Dee, whom George Barnes conceals, or maybe one of the Muddy men of the Land and Livestock Company.

The hush caused by Eva's entrance penetrates Barnes, who lifts his head and turns to her.

The lawyer with his handlebar mustache frowns as his eyes slide down her dress, the cream dress she wore after her wedding reception two years before. She's dressed too proudly, not wearing enough humble. "Dress to please the jury," Barnes told her the one time they'd met. He wanted her to wear black, but the single black dress she owns, a hand-me-down from her aunt, she wore for her wedding. She can't wear it, not to this, not to watch her husband go on trial for murder. Barnes advised, "Look saddened by what your husband's done."

Eva is appalled by what Dee's done. No dress will alter that reality. Her eyes send questions back to Dee as she frowns at him. *How could you?*

She asked him that day they waited for Sheriff Congleton.

"How? How did you kill Tom Reilly?"

Dee sat there, calm, a half-smile creasing his handsome face. His blue eyes wore triumph, their look running icy fingers up her back. She felt her face grow hot, her skin tighten at her temples, her heart begin to throb.

"Was it an accident? What? Tell me."

He looked beyond her, as though seeing in the distance something no one else could see. The vein throbbed at his neck, pushed against his collarless shirt. "Duty," he said, the word hard and cold as old snow.

She sits in this courtroom now for the same reason: It is her duty to be here, her part in a journey begun two years before when she let herself be wooed by D. L. Bruner.

Barnes appears to catch himself. He gives her a polite nod, perhaps remembering that she is but a child. Seventeen, but still a child.

He touches the seated man's shoulders, steps aside. Dee turns to face her.

Eva sees relief, pain, and accusation in Dee's eyes. *How could you? My own wife never comes to see me while I wait out this temporary pause in my rising occupation. Doing my duty as a man should, following orders, and my wife fails to come to see me?*

Eva knows betrayal. She knows it through her father's actions, her mother's weak choices, her husband's unkept promises.

The day Eva met D. L. Bruner, July 4, 1899, music from an oompah band pounded a steady beat for the Independence Day celebration in the park at Dufur, Oregon. The town was once called Fifteen Mile Crossing for the creek of the same name that meandered north fifteen miles to the Columbia River, east of Oregon's Cascade Mountains. Mount Hood shone through fir trees. Eva sat on the grass and arched her neck to see the peak. Exposing the white of her throat, Eva risked her aunt's comments about unladylike behavior, though her aunt rarely had reason to chastise. Orphans wish to please.

Eva leaned back and inhaled the view of Mount Hood. It looked cold, and yet the time she and a friend climbed partway up, she had seen its dips and hollows, which offered springs and wildflowers and warmth of landscape. Down in Dufur, she decided landscapes can deceive as well as nurture.

Beyond her, children squealed at finding frogs; their mothers retreated in quick disgust when the amphibians appeared in pudgy little hands.

"That D. L. Bruner dresses nattily," her aunt Fern said, nodding with her chin toward a man standing off to the side who was not much taller than Eva. "Don't you agree, dear?"

"For a sheepman he's downright formal," Eva's uncle Morrison said. "But I guess he's earned it, working way out there for Hahn and Fried on Muddy Creek. A man's got to dress well when he can." He told Eva, "D. L. tends sheep for the Prineville Land and Livestock Company, the largest landholder in that area."

As though their discussion drew him, D. L. started toward them.

Morrison kept going. "They control thousands of acres for their cattle and sheep. And I do mean *control.*" Morrison hesitated. "A smart-alecky kid, but a hard worker. Been on his own a long time now."

"I'm sure she's heard the stories," her aunt Fern said. "We hired D. L. one summer. You were too young to remember. He's always worked, after his mother...well, after things got hard for them at home. Youngest of six, and mercy me, I can imagine what his mother went through and why she, well..."

"Need any more of my help, Mother?" Morrison asked his wife. "Or am I released?"

"You go ahead. I know you like your horseshoe toss. Eva and I can tend to the food, can't we, dear?"

"Joe Sherar's over there. I'll do business about getting wheat ground at his White River mill," her uncle said.

"Uh-huh," her aunt said. "You know the hardest thing about doing business is remembering to mind your own." She brushed a pie crumb from his vest.

Eva's uncle pecked his wife on the forehead. He was a man not afraid to show affection to his wife in public. Eva liked that about him, that and his willingness to take in an orphan.

Her uncle stepped toward a cluster of men gathering near the horseshoe pit. It was cool for July. Cool for Dufur. Even though Mount Hood rose up to the west and timbered country spread out to the east, Dufur had a dry side marked by hot summer days and nights. Respite came from the rains that plagued farms west, in the Willamette Valley. Eva's mother brought them here after her father's "calamity," as her mother always called the time that followed Eva's joyful, brief memories beside the Muddy.

D. L. swaggered toward Eva and her aunt Fern. He touched his bowler hat. The other men topped their heads with Stetsons or felt hats for which even the unique creases have names. D. L. was different. He wore a dark suit with a tie the color of whipped cream. Just above the stiff collar, a vein throbbed.

"Mrs. Thompson, ma'am," he said, tapping his fingers to the brim but not removing the bowler. "Wanted to take a look at your basket, to make sure I bid on the right one when the time comes."

"Now, D.L., that'd be cheating," her aunt Fern said. She fluttered her eyes. *Is she flirting?* "A fine upstanding man like you knows better. Mercy me, I taught you better than that."

"Cheating, good woman, is when you pour sugar in your beer before betting your friend that your stein will bring more flies than his," D. L. said. He ran his tongue over smooth, unchapped lips before adding, "And you accept the winnings without remorse." He grinned then, and his face lit up, his eyes narrowing with a twinkle in them. Eva considered his features almost feminine and detected an accent of some kind braided through his words. "Only a fool would circumvent a certainty like an early look at a woman's decorated basket," he said. His left eyebrow lifted, and he winked at Eva. She felt her face grow warm as she lowered her eyes. "Besides," he said, "I won't know what's in that food basket, or whether it'll be worthy of the wager or not, so I'm still taking my chances."

He spoke like a man who preferred to take chances. It should have been Eva's alert. It wasn't. She could sugar her thoughts sometimes and only later realize what kinds of discomfort she attracted by such sweet covering up.

All things will be uncovered in this courtroom, Eva decides. *With justice, there is nothing left to chance.* Eva's legs wobble. She finds a bench to sit on; her parasol leans against her cream-colored skirt.

The prosecutor turns to look at her. Eva wonders what this man sees. A square-faced woman with a too-wide nose, too-thick lips, too-full cheeks, an elongated neck. Drab blue eyes, the color of standing water. That's what he should see, trained observer as he's supposed to be. Out-of-proportion is how Eva thinks of herself: wide shoulders, a narrow waist. Eva's father once said she had a mouth wide enough to take a slice of watermelon and still be able to move her tongue around to separate the seeds. Does the prosecutor see such imperfections? Does he care?

Her whole life is out of proportion now. She can't sleep. Her choices frighten her. *How could I have chosen such a man? How could I not have seen the possibilities? Did I so want to go back home that I couldn't see the truth? Sugared thinking. Where was I going before D. L. Bruner took me aside?*

Dee nods ever so slightly to her again, that half-smile making him look overconfident. His vocabulary, larger than one expects of a sheepherder, makes him suspect among the men. He sometimes uses French, calls himself a Frenchie to distinguish himself from Irish herdsmen or Basque. It paints him cocky. She wonders if his lawyer has thought of this, and how the jury will respond when Dee takes the stand. Eva thinks for just a moment that Dee is a small, scared boy using bully tactics to stabilize his life.

Dee lowers his head to listen to something his lawyer says, and in profile Eva sees the close-cropped hair cut clean around his ears, and the wide forehead exposed by horseshoe-shaped openings in a trim brown hairline. Without his hat, the side of his head shows up white. He looks naked without that bowler, older than his twenty-one years and smaller than his five-foot seven-inch frame. More vulnerable, his back now to the gallery. He's hunched over, listening.

The lurch beneath her heart, the sweet pain of seeing one she loves helpless while also harboring outrage toward him, surprises. She presses her long fingers beneath her breast. Her stomach hurts. She aches for him, for his poor choices, for what he's come through, youngest child of six, a mother…well, unavailable for much of his life.

They are orphans, both of them.

These are new thoughts, challenges that did not accompany Eva when she first joined her husband at the Muddy Station. But these courtroom walls, the stares and looks of outrage on the faces of the jury pool now entering tell Eva she has entered a new age that will demand a greater level of endurance. Eva wonders if an orphan like her is capable of such strength. Perhaps. Unlike her mother in the midst of tragedy, at least Eva has chosen to stay here, and this realization gives her a small measure of comfort.

2

STEADINESS

Dee Link Bruner pays attention. He isn't accustomed to such wide chairs, having spent much of his life squatting or on his knees, hovering over sheep. His back is exposed here. He prefers leaning up against a rock cairn, protected from the stealth of unscrupulous sheepherders while watching the dogs and his flock.

Dogs of another kind pant behind him here, dogs dressed as upstanding Crook County citizens. He can smell their sweat on this warm day. He can hear them growl about him, the accused killer, a sheepherder gone wild, they say.

He feels Eva's eyes boring into his back. Is she one of the growlers? No. He can't believe that of his wife, young as she is. She looks tired. This thought irritates. She hasn't had to sit and wait for someone to visit. She's not been inconvenienced by the hours alone in jail, wondering about love and loyalty. She's failed him, never visiting, only talking to his lawyer once. No reason she should be fatigued, none at all. It is his life ebbing away, his future left in someone else's hand, his loneliness, again, that justifies fatigue.

She defies him. She's stood up to him only once before. He recalls it now, his mind trapping him, bringing up painful times from his past to support his present feelings. They hadn't been married long, and he'd come rushing in while they worked to build the main house at the Muddy Station. He'd shouted orders, a man's way, telling her what to do.

"Your poor planning is not my emergency," she snapped.

The other hands laughed. Her boldness and her perceptive eye startled him. His poor thinking had indeed caused the problem. He'd failed to pick up all the precut lumber in Shaniko, as he was ordered to. But she'd always been so yielding, even when he asked her not to speak of things that mattered most to her, her family and her faith. She even stayed away from the little Antelope Church closest to the Muddy Station because he asked it of her. She listened to her husband as a wife should.

Now this, her choice to make him wait.

She's there behind him, where his back's exposed, and he doesn't know if she is covering it for him or if she is a thin sheet of linen as easily torn as that cream-colored dress she wears.

She is there at least, behind him. His father isn't, nor any of his brothers or sisters. His mind runs across the rimrock of emotion. He caps the feelings, doesn't go too deep. She's there. It's all that matters now, her sweet breath filling the space between them.

Then in an instant he is outraged. She never even sent a note to let him know if she would come to stand behind him. No, she's sitting. Maybe that's the halfhearted support she'll offer, not a full support standing tall on his behalf.

That would be fitting. He can name no one in his life who stands for him. He thinks Eva might. He hopes that Henry Hahn and Leo Fried, the owners of the livestock company, will.

His lawyer nudges him, and Dee puts his hands in his lap where scraping at his fingernails will not be noticed. He touches the fine hair that grows on his knuckles. Barnes has told him to be aware of how he sits or looks, that others are reading him like a book, "and we want you to be a good book, boy. A good book." The heavy oak doors open behind the judge's bench, and Dee realizes his front is exposed too as he watches the potential jurors saunter in. Few eyes catch his. Dee wonders if this is a good sign or bad.

"Look respectful now," Barnes whispers, leaning toward Dee.

Respectful? These men who will judge my life, are they worthy of my respect? The coroner's jurors certainly weren't. Not one of those who wandered over the crime site to assist the coroner even asked about gunpowder on Tom Reilly's clothing, or on Dee's striped shirt. How could they ignore such evidence and then question Dee's claim that he shot in self-defense? He didn't think they even looked for residue on Tom's clothing to verify what Dee claimed. Sure, Dee shot Tom, but Tom shot at him first. The man came at him, rifle in hand. What did they expect a man to do?

John Creegan, Tom Reilly's partner and so-called witness, tampered with evidence. The coroner's jury missed that, blind as aging goats. Creegan covered the body with his tent. "To protect it from the coyotes and buzzards," he told the doctors called to do the medical examination. To contaminate it, that's what Creegan intended, to brush off any signs of gunpowder from his fallen comrade. He succeeded, by Dee's reckoning. The justice of the peace appointed the coroner's jury. For one, he chose Garrett Maupin, son of the famous Maupin known for killing the Paiute chief Paulina. Maupin served as if he knew about killing though little about justice. What justice can be found in the hunting down of an Indian warrior trying to keep his land?

Thorn Thornson acted as foreman, that opinionated see-the-world-one-way Scandinavian. What did he find? Reason to bind Dee over for murder in the second degree, not self-defense. Yes, Dee admitted to killing Tom, but not to the other, not to the premeditation of it. His ability to kill does not grow from deliberate calculation. Premeditation escapes him. He acts when urged to. He's always been that way.

Dee shakes his head. Stubborn old Thorn Thornson. All those Scandinavians have heads as hard as bedrock. Eva is Scandinavian, but she spurns stubbornness or strong opinion. She does as he directs, moving with him, taking a job at the Muddy cooking for the cowboys. Even in intimate things, she does as he bids without complaint. Without much passion either, but that's because she's young. She is barely seventeen now; had just turned fifteen when they married. That's why she's confused. Her youth, her inexperience, her immaturity. He must remember that and not judge too harshly. *Judge not lest ye be judged.* The odd phrase of Scripture drifts into his mind. He pushes it away.

Still, Eva failed to visit this past month while he counted rats and roaches in his cell. She spoke but once to his attorney. What kind of argument can the prosecution make of her absence, if they know of it? They probably do. The jailer's wife has a wagging tongue, and she gets news when she brings over the prisoners' meals.

Prisoner. Not for long. Dee has to have faith in that.

At least they won't call Eva to testify to what he said the day of his arrest. She's his wife. And a mere child at that.

The men of the jury pool scrape the high-back chairs on the hardwood floor. New men will decide his future. Dee licks his lips of beaded sweat. Is the room so warm then?

This time his lawyer has some say over who goes and who remains to judge him. Maybe he'll get lucky and Barnes will choose someone who understands the ways of the range, of sheep and cattle, of self-defense and duty. Especially duty.

Dee tries to look calm. He thinks of ponds of water and these men, mere fish swimming around him, curious, harmless. If he lets himself think that they can take his life, his blood will begin to throb at his neck, coursing through his system as though chased by murderous guilt. Maybe his nightmares are related to that, Dee thinks. Maybe they are at that.

He reaches to his neck, imagines Eva touching him there, commenting on that throb. Her touch always stirs him, even touches meant just to reassure. He aches to hold her. It would comfort him. He is a man who spurned comfort until Eva. Her fragile strength drew him. Like a deer's legs, slender and yet firm, she carried him to places he'd never known, places of safety inside a woman's arms.

He shrinks in his chair, young, alone.

Dee looks out the window, tries to imagine being smaller. It's harder to find a slight man guilty, especially when that man acts in self-defense. Tom Reilly towered over him. The jury pool knows this. Barnes is big. The Company sent a big man to make Dee appear younger, smaller, innocent, a man who couldn't think ahead to kill another.

Reilly could think ahead. He's the one who carried the rifle onto the Muddy claim. He's the one who pushed the property lines. He's dead by his own hand, as Dee sees it. *His own hand, not mine.*

Maple trees drop seeds outside the window. Cottonwood buds promise leaves before the month is out, and Dee can hear the clatter of horses pulling carriages through the streets. A simple sound, soothing. Confined inside the Crook County Jail, a place a rat but no one else might thrive in, he hasn't seen trees for a month. In there, he couldn't see the sun or stars, couldn't hear birdsong or even rowdiness pouring forth from Prineville's Longhorn Saloon. He could only imagine. He had never had so much time to sit and think without the distraction of flock or creek or hillside or even a book.

He doesn't want to think now, least of all about his future.

So he looks back at the men being considered for the jury. They cough, look away, await the arrival of the judge. Dee keeps a steady smile on his face. He thinks of Eva, sitting behind him. She's changed in the month since he's seen her last. Her face seems fuller; her eyes have a sad droop, puffy almost. Maybe, Dee thinks, she's been changing all along and Dee Link Bruner hasn't paid attention.

"All rise," the bailiff says, and the hum and murmur of the lookers-on quiet as W. L. Bradshaw takes his seat behind the blood-and-milk-stained judge's bench. A rustle of linen skirts and scrapes of oak chairs mark the standing, then the sitting.

Dee wonders if Eva's wishing now she'd come to see him, to hear his story after he'd been jailed, to see if it had changed. She'd know then what the strategy for defense might be. Instead, she stayed on the Muddy, cooking for the crews, doing what she knew to do, he supposes, maybe trying to put aside her fears like juniper-tree roots, which grip and splay beneath the surface. He resents her choosing separation.

The bailiff reads: "D. L. Bruner is charged with murder, first degree, for the killing of Thomas Reilly." Said that way, bold and cold in the courtroom, evokes gasps from the crowd. Dee works to hide a smirk. What hypocrisy. They all knew the charges before they ever stepped through the door. They wouldn't attend a trial for a man stealing a horse or even a neighbor's argument over an unpaid debt finally brought to court. No, they lust after spectacle, of which he is the center. His father always said a man's a man who lives well with his neighbors and his kin without bringing attention to himself. But Dee wants to be the center of things. Dee smiles. Now he is the center, even if for something a man ought not to grin about. Barnes presses his knee against Dee, frowns. Dee fades his smile. Barnes does not understand. He hopes Eva does.

The judge asks if the prosecution and defense are ready to begin jury selection.

"We are, Judge," Barnes says, and the prosecuting attorney states that he is too.

Eva sits in the public seat, to the right of Dee and behind his lawyer. Sometimes from the corner of his eye, if Dee turns and lays an arm relaxed against the back of the chair, as though he is calm and as comfortable as a man welcoming friends into his dining hall, sometimes then he can look back and glimpse her. He tries to catch her eyes. He sees instead the ribbon of her hat shift with the breeze from the open window, her face shadowed, her eyes downcast, as sad and lonely as a lost lamb. He swallows. He never meant to hurt her. He never thought that doing what he did might hurt the one person he truly loves.

He turns back, ears hot. He notices a carving on the wooden table. Who would have time to carve anything, sitting in this defendant's chair? Barnes says something. He leans in to hear.

"Keep your eyes to the front," Barnes says. "You don't want jurors to think you're playing to the crowd. Look like you take this seriously, as well you should."

Dee complies, his arms now on the table, leaning in with interest. *Be sincere.* But his whole face burns, as though his father has just barked at him about something stupid he has done. The vein throbs.

The opening remarks, even before the jury is selected, come from Frank Menefee, the prosecuting attorney. He brings Hahn and Fried, the owners of the Muddy Ranch, into the fray. "I believe this slaying was a premeditated murder bought and paid for by outside sources for the sole purpose of preventing Thomas Reilly and John Creegan from exercising their rights to run sheep on their deeded land."

A rumble in the courtroom causes the judge to bang his hammer.

Dee thinks Barnes should use this defense. These "outside sources" might be held accountable for Dee's orders.

The state's attorney, Mr. Brink, jumps up and says that none of the officers of the Prineville Land and Livestock Company is on trial. "This is not a trial to determine anything but the guilt or innocence of this man, D. L. Bruner, who is accused of taking the life of Tom Reilly." Dee sees movement from vested men sitting in the gallery. Murmurs rumble through the room. In support or disapproval? Hahn and Fried are big employers, owners of the mercantile in addition to the Prineville Land and Livestock Company. They ship in groceries and supplies from Portland, staples all ranchers in this isolated area need. No one wants to challenge important men invested in this otherwise sparsely settled landscape.

Barnes might still use this tactic, slip it in to remind people that some things happen because of strings pulled by outside hands. Jurors could relate to that. Even the hand of God, who such men as these claim to believe in, causes drought one year and floods the next. Might they then understand his duty, his acts of self-defense?

Tom Reilly was an independent sheepherder, someone challenging the big corporation, the rightness of the established ways. Maybe Barnes could build on that.

Dee looks at the faces of James Cram and D. H. Smith, two potential jurors. Would they see Dee as a man willing to strike down someone challenging the company? Or would they think him capable of premeditated murder, a man drawn to violence by money whiffed beneath his nose?

Tom Reilly's brother is in the courtroom. So is John Creegan, an eyewitness to the account. Dee's a witness too, but what he has to say is self-serving, Barnes tells him. He may not want Dee to testify. Perhaps Barnes could tell the true story with the evidence found when Justice Childers of Ashwood walked the site, picked up shell casings from various distances. Perhaps science could convince jurors when words couldn't.

Dee wants Eva to hear and understand the true story.

Maybe Eva doesn't want him free, maybe that's why she never came to see him. Dee hasn't considered this before. Has this time away from him been balm? Relief for her, abandonment for him? What kind of woman takes respite from her husband's incarceration?

Dee wonders, only briefly, if Tom Reilly's wife has come to watch Dee dangle in the ropes of courtroom justice.

"Though Mr. Fried's and Mr. Hahn's names will be mentioned today," Judge Bradshaw cautions, "they are not on trial here. Mr. D.L. Bruner is on trial for premeditated murder." He coughs, and Dee turns full then to look at Eva. She never raises her eyes to his. She uncrosses her ankles. They look swollen from sitting in the warm May morning. The windows are open. A butterfly makes its way inside and lands on the balustrade separating Dee from the spectators. The butterfly's wings lift and drop, a pulse of breathing in and out. Dee's eyes scan discreetly to see if it has a mate that follows it into this justice hall. Apparently not. It throbs on, a dot of color on the oak, alone.

The day ends with the jurors chosen. Dee stands quickly when the judge pounds his gavel, marking the day's end.

"Can I see her?" Dee asks Barnes as the bailiff snakes his way toward them.

"She hasn't wanted to till now," Barnes says. "I don't want to cause a scene here. Those're reporters."

Dee turns toward Eva. He isn't looking at Barnes now, talking past him, watching Eva stand. She lifts her eyes to his, and through that gaze he knows her love for him is still as strong as always. "She's just a kid," Dee whispers. He smiles. "I'll walk toward her. Head off the bailiff. Grant me one minute. I know she'll talk with me now."

"I don't know—"

"You're my lawyer. It's not the other way around," Dee says.

Barnes scans the room, makes a quick nod, then reaches for the bailiff's hand. "He'll be just a moment. Wants to have a word or two with his wife. The court can grant him that, can't it? How's your daughter feeling? Recovered from her coughing bout?" The bailiff's answer fades behind Dee.

"You came," Dee says, reaching out his hand. He separates his tongue from the words in his heart, not asking why she made him suffer this past month, not saying that he's sorry, so very sorry. Not for what he did, but for her having to endure this. He can make her want to be with him. He can convince her of his innocence if only he has time. He wants to tell her all this, but he smiles instead, reaches for her hand, which clings to the parasol. "It's good to see you came."

Formal. Polite. Easy as a cool glass of water soothing a parched throat. She'll come around, he's sure of it.

"I didn't want to," Eva says as she pulls her hand from his. "It's a long trip from the ranch to Prineville."

"Barnes said the Muddy'll pay for you to stay at the Poindexter Hotel, even pay for your meals at the restaurant there. They serve good fare. It could be like a little vacation for you, not having to cook for the crews."

"Vacation?" Eva's blue eyes, the color of a summer storm, darken as she whispers to him, "You think anything about this could be… fanciful?" Her knuckles grip her parasol, turn white.

"You look lovely as a maiden out for a stroll," Dee says. Stupid words slip out, not what he wants to say. He wants to calm her with pretty words, soothing words. Sometimes they work; sometimes they aggravate.

"I've hardly been a'strolling," Eva says. She lowers her eyes again as the bailiff approaches. Dee can feel the man standing close to him, smells the sweat. He taps Dee on a shoulder that Dee shrugs, then thinks better of it and turns to accept the handcuffs. Over his shoulder he says, "Eva. Please. Come by when the jailer's wife brings supper. You won't be alone. She'll stay while I eat, and we can talk. Please." He doesn't want to sound pathetic, desperate. He needs to be strong for her. "Please, Eva," he says. He hears the catch in his voice before he can swallow it. His eyes tear up as the bailiff leads him out.

3

Abandonment

Eva climbs the hotel stairs, finds her room, then pulls the hatpins and sticks them in the porcelain holder. She adjusts the swinging mirror so it won't tip her hat onto the floor. Before hanging her cape on the wall peg, she checks it for stains. Then she sinks onto the bed, stares at the burgundy swirls in the pattern of the wallpaper. A breeze moves the white lace curtain, and outside she hears the sounds of wagons moving through Prineville, their wheels following an ancient riverbed taken over by the town. Ranchers and sheepherders stop at Elkin's Blacksmith Shop or replenish supplies at Hahn and Fried's General Merchandise store. Some, she supposes, head home only to return tomorrow for the trial.

She has left her Bible in the bedside drawer at the ranch house. She's not read it since the day of Dee's arrest. Her aunt would tell her the writer of the psalms would bring her comfort. But Eva recalls that the psalmist often feels abandoned. She doesn't want to be reminded of God's moving away.

Eva wishes she could go home to the Muddy, to the quiet, though she doesn't sleep well there either. But there is no one she can go home to. She's alone, and that thought takes her back.

"I'll never leave you, *ma chérie,*" Dee told her. He must have read her thoughts to know what she longed for. He sat on her uncle Morrison's porch swing, a chaste distance between them. She heard her aunt Fern washing dishes in the tin-lined sink in the kitchen of their Dufur home. Her aunt could look out at any time to ensure her niece's safety and yet pretend, if noticed, that she was watching the sunset sink below the firs.

"You can't know that," Eva said. "No one can know how long they'll live."

"Sure I can," Dee said. "I'll outlive you. I'm sturdier than you." He grinned.

"A man's days aren't set by his own will," Eva said. She kept her eyes lowered. Talk of God dried her mouth, and mention of such subjects seemed to set Dee's jaw into a stubborn line.

"I'm talking about what we can control," Dee said, pulling his arm from behind her. "I'll never leave you in those times, if you're wise enough to accept my proposal."

Eva never lifted her eyes to his. She wanted reassurance, wanted the fluttering in her heart to be what he, too, felt. But she hesitated. She didn't always think clearly with his breath close enough to mingle with hers. His eyes drew her in like a nectar-filled lily draws bees. She feared that she would drown if she gazed too deeply or too long.

"Don't you doubt it." He patted her knee discreetly, then with his hand he lifted her chin to look into her eyes. He took a quick look behind him, checking on Aunt Fern, and then bent close and whispered in her ear, "Your eyes tell me yes."

She shivered. His confidence both intrigued and clutched at her throat.

"You'll die one day. We all do." She leaned away from him. "My parents did. Are your parents alive?" He never talked much about his family.

"You're right," he said. "We all do, die. Some of us even wait until our hearts stop."

"I don't know that I could stand another separation of someone close to me," she said. "It takes too much to decide to live beyond it."

"You're just a kid. Shouldn't have such thoughts. Kids think they'll live forever."

"I've never thought that," Eva said. She stood, the air close and heavy. His touch could sink her. He could take her back to those hyacinth hills, but what could he want with her, just a child? What did he see in her that she would willingly give?

She watched her uncle walk the open stubble field. Cows licked up kernels of wheat left behind after sheaves had been moved into barns. Yes, she was fifteen years old, but that didn't take away the empty place her parents had left inside her. First her father's sinful wrong-doing in the Silvertooth bar in Antelope, then her mother's death. No one could understand how many nights she lay awake thinking of all she'd lost, of wanting to go back to where life nurtured, when she roamed the hillsides of the Muddy, dug roots, and planted seeds.

"All right, then," Dee said. He reached for Eva's pale hand and gently pulled her to him; her knees touched his on the swing. He rubbed her fingers with his thumb, circular and sweet. "While I live, you will never be without me. I make that promise to you. Excepting when I'm with the flocks, but then my heart will still be in your hands," Dee told her. "These precious, tender hands."

How she wanted to claim that promise! She said instead, "Why me?" and pulled her hand free.

He smiled that almost petulant smile, his thin lips opening a whisper, enough for him to suck in breath. "You're beautiful," he said. "What man wouldn't want to promise never to leave such beauty? It's an easy pledge."

"That's not the answer I hoped for," Eva told him.

"I think I love you," Dee said.

"You think?"

"I know. I judge character well. You'll never forsake me, Eva. We'll be there for each other, for better or for worse, forever and ever."

She'd longed for such a permanent promise. But she wasn't certain if what she saw on Dee's face in that moment of transition was his smile inviting her into the lasting safety of his arms, or just a premonition of a prankish smirk.

That same smile crossed Dee's face when he stood at the end of the jury selection and turned toward her. Eva worries the smile might be taken for arrogance, worries about the consequences of this for herself. Maybe such arrogance brought him to this place.

Why has this happened? Why are we being punished? Her prayerful questions spoken in the nights after the murder, followed by long days of wondering, yielded no answers.

The window breeze touches Eva with chilly fingers. Strange, when the air is so hot. She touches her face, clammy and warm. She wipes at the tears pooling in her ears, turns her face to the pillow slip. She's been crying for days it seems, in between rushes of outrage and fear over what she'll do if Dee's convicted.

She remembers walking beside the John Day River watching an eagle dive for salmon. The bird forced its mighty talons into the fish, but the salmon weighed too much; the bird could not release its grip. They thrashed downriver, both locked together, the eagle underestimating the strength of its prey; the fish destined for certain death as it couldn't toss off its attacker.

Is she the eagle or the fish?

She wishes she sat on the veranda at the Muddy Station, sipping sarsaparilla, eating Mildred's fry bread. Selfish, that's what she is. While her husband sits in a cold jail cell, she dreams of refreshing drinks and food taken in the shade. Lately, half the time she's famished; the other half, merely the thought of food makes her ill.

She gets up, stands before the mirror, and dabs cool water on her eyes. She can't visit Dee looking this bad, her face mottled with red blotches. The blotches are new too. From her tears, she supposes, or from all the work she has to do to keep going, to cook for the ranch crews and still press down the shame deposited by their accusing eyes.

Smells from the hotel's restaurant waft upward. Beefsteak and mutton, fried smelt and pork. Tonight, familiar foods make her stomach churn, and she swallows back nausea. Maybe they'll fix flannel cakes for her, something bland she can eat without syrup. But she'll wait until after she walks across the street to the jail to see her husband.

The nausea passes. She undoes the tiny button rows and hangs her blouse carefully on a hanger. With her washcloth, she dabs at a spot, hoping it won't show in the morning. She'll wear the cream-colored suit the length of the trial. What choice does she have? The skirt she lays carefully on the bed, and she presses it with her hands. The linen will still wrinkle when she wears it tomorrow, but at least some of the creases will be gone. She dabs at her neck with the washcloth, grateful for a room with a bowl and pitcher as well as a chamber pot so she doesn't have to use the privy. She reties the tiny pink ribbon lacing her corset.

After dressing in a simple calico dress, she dons her mother's hat again and pinches her cheeks to give them color. She uses her precious powder to lighten mottled spots at her temples and neck. She'll leave the parasol behind.

These simple acts of getting ready to visit Dee calm her, enable her to hold her head proud walking through the lobby and past the restaurant. She won't be like her mother, who sickened herself to death after learning of what her father did. It will not be like that for Eva. She is strong and self-sufficient.

She waits for horsemen and several wagons to pass before she crosses the dirt street toward the jail. At least no child of hers must live through this time; she thanks God for that. No little three-year-old will pat her mother's shoulder in confusion while her mother weeps. No hunched-over child will wonder why her uncle Morrison and aunt Fern arrive at the Muddy Station to take them from those hyacinth hills, leaving her father and her friends behind. Eva will live through her trial alone, but she will live.

She takes a deep breath and crosses the street.

They serve the prisoners at eight. Dee hopes Eva remembers. They might not let her in past the serving hour. The jailer's salary includes his wife's fixing meals for inmates. For a little extra, a prisoner can even make requests for certain dishes, the adding of a pickled sauce perhaps, or inclusion of potato soup. Dee takes what they serve, grateful for it. He still can't quite believe that Barnes, with all his connections, can't get him released, at least during the trial.

"Too much hostility right now, D. L." Barnes told him yesterday. "Several cowboys quit the Muddy. In protest. Even the *Journal*'s carrying letters about a man's right to shoot a sheepherder coming from another country through here, and that's riled the Sheepherder Association pretty well." Barnes pulls at his mustache. "Taking a man's life is no simple thing, regardless of how one sees property rights."

"Self-defense," Dee said.

"Coor-rect," Barnes said, drawing out the first syllable, making Dee think of Eva's middle name, Cora. "Still, we've some ground to cover before we convince a jury of that, what with the, ah, positioning of the gunshots. Court's got to make it appear that it takes the crime of murder seriously."

"The court should take the crime of pushing boundaries seriously. Clarify what's public land and what isn't. Maybe Tom Reilly and I could have settled our differences peaceful-like if the laws were clearer."

"Coor-rect," Barnes said. "But for now, you'll stay in jail. The jury will know you've done time and maybe see you as having been punished enough. It might weigh on the side of acquittal. We can hope for that."

"They might also see me as someone so dangerous I need to be caged," Dee said. "That won't bode well for me, now will it?"

"I've done what I can," Barnes said. "So sit tight."

Dee has been sitting tight for a month. These last three hours, from the adjournment until now, have been the longest. She'll come. He knows that. She has to. They both need each other.

Still, he wonders as the old Concord clock ticks away to the eight o'clock chime. She hasn't come yet.

The smell hits Eva first. Not the scent of the food the jailer eats with his wife. No, that aroma is nearly pleasing. The pot roast with biscuits and gravy promises to be tasty. It's the smell of something else that troubles, something she can't place.

Her foot catches on a floor nail as she moves forward. "Oh," she says, a small cry. She turns it into a cough, surprised that her throat betrays her presence.

"Welcome, dear," the jailer's wife says. She squints at Eva. The hair braid looped around the woman's head never budges as she nods to her husband. "Your only inmate has a visitor."

Wood floors needing oiling creak as the jailer turns and then stands, pulling a napkin from his shirt collar and hiking up his pants that strain his dark suspenders. "Didn't expect you this late. Supper hour's almost finished. Not sure I can let you see him now." He sounds gruff, but Eva sees soft eyes.

"I wouldn't wish to break the rules," Eva says, backing toward the door.

"Got enough coming through this door that do," the jailer says. He looks at her, must decide she is no hazard. "Well, come along. He hasn't had no visitors but his lawyer, and old George Barnes isn't nearly as pretty as you, nor does he smell as good."

"Harold," his wife says, "the girl doesn't need your commentary on Crook County's legal profession. Have you eaten, dear? You look a mite peaked."

"It's the heat," Eva says. "I wasn't expecting it to be so warm." With her fingers, she pushes air at her face, wishing she'd brought a real fan to hide behind, if nothing else.

"We're in the tropics here in Prineville."

News of the climate exhausts. Eva says, "I'm not hungry, though what you've fixed smells quite good."

"A few herbs and spices of my own choosing," the jailer's wife says. "Not that my usual dinner guests notice. So thanks for that."

Eva looks around, trying to identify the source of the foul scent, the troubled memory. Dizziness threatens to topple her.

The jailer's wife squints closer. "You wouldn't be in a family way, now would you?"

"I..." Eva straightens, sniffs as she's seen her aunt do when offended. *It can't be, can it?* "No, I...certainly not."

"Come along, missus." The jailer leads her into a dark, cool stone room lined with cages. Eva's breath comes in quick bursts. Invisible fists hold her head in a vise. *Is it the jailer's wife's question? The food? The fear?*

Eva swallows. She's transported back to age three. She smells fear knotted with perspiration, memory twisted into pain. She remembers her mother crying while her father stood behind these same jail bars. He reached out for them. She can still smell her father's scent of fear, washed with remorse. She isn't sure she can separate the memory of her father from her husband standing in this place.

Dee doesn't dare reach out to touch her. A feather might shatter her. He decides to talk of little things, help her settle. "How are things at the Muddy? Eva? Are you all right? Do you need a chair? Bunzie, can you bring my wife a chair?"

The jailer leaves Eva leaning against the bars. He returns with a napkin stuck in his shirt. "Here, missus," he says, setting the chair before Dee's cell. He takes Eva's elbow and helps her down.

"I'm fine," Eva says as the man hovers over her. He leaves.

Eva's breathing hard. She scans the tiny rooms. Dee's the only prisoner, so he doesn't know who she's looking at in an empty cell down from his. He looks too. Sees nothing.

"Not the hotel," Dee says to her, "but functional. I have my own bunk without fleas. Bunzie says that's a miracle in itself. My fellow herder bedmates, they got pretty rammish sometimes when we drove the lambs to market and had to share a hotel bed. Got it all to myself here." Could he get a smile from her? Dee sighs. "Not a pretty place, is it?"

"What are you doing here?" She sounds angry. "What am I doing here?" She takes short breaths and keeps shaking her head, her voice tinny and tiny as a child's.

"It's pretty gruesome if you've never been inside a jail before," Dee says. "I'm sorry to be the one to introduce you, but it's no pleasure party for me either."

She looks him in the eye for the first time. "It's not my first visit."

"When'd you come before? I didn't see you."

She reaches to balance herself on the chair by holding the cold metal bars. They're wet and clammy against her hands. She wipes her palms on her skirt. "In here, even the metal sweats," he says. She still seems miles from him. "Eva? You've got to talk with George Barnes." He wonders when she's been inside a jail before.

"I have nothing to tell him," Eva said.

"He can tell you, about the way it was. So you won't hold it against me so hard," he said. "I've missed you, Eva." He reaches through the bars, can't touch her clasped hands that look pale as maggots.

"Are you even sorry?" Eva asks then. "Are you even aware of what your…your…deed has done to our lives?"

"It wasn't my fault, I tell you. Reilly came at me." He stands, paces. "Carried a rifle. I defended myself, that's all. Would you have preferred that he killed me?"

Her eyes fill with tears. "I can't believe you couldn't find another way that would still have Tom alive and you not…in here." She pauses, looks around. "I've been here before," she says. "In this building." Her voice is far away. "My mother brought me here to see my father while he awaited his trial." She stares at Dee now, her face pale. "He killed a man in an Antelope bar." She is shaking, the flounce of her skirt dancing alone. "In self-defense, my father told the jury."

"Why don't I know of this?" A stone has hit Dee's stomach. His heart is pounding. She knows things he doesn't know. She's failed to tell him. "What happened to him?"

"They convicted him," Eva says. "Then sentenced him to life."

4

FIDELITY

Eva stands at the landing in the Poindexter Hotel. It's morning. Another day of uncertainty taunts. Behind her is the closed door of the room paid for by Dee's employer, Henry Hahn. He's her employer, too, though she isn't working now. She isn't tending to her duties. It bothers her, this taking of Hahn's money, and yet without it, she can't afford to stay in Prineville for the duration of the trial.

She's still not hungry. Perhaps the smells of food she hasn't cooked herself spoil her appetite, or maybe the jailer's wife is right. No. She can't think that, not here, not now. Nausea attacks. She heads back to the room but gives up nothing as she buckles over the chamber pot. She wipes her mouth, her hands shaking; she takes a deep breath, then descends the hotel stairs.

Mrs. McDowell, the proprietor of the Poindexter Hotel, lifts her eyes to Eva but does not nod or offer welcome. Eva should perhaps stay in her two-dollar room—one of the better ones—but she wants to use the long-distance phone. Eva needs to call the Muddy Station to see how Mildred is faring. One cook alone will have her hands full with thirty cowboys eating two meals a day. Eva knows that all too well.

From the window Eva sees wagonloads of wool being brought into the new scouring mill. The seeds and twigs caught in the sheep's hair and the heavy lanolin oils will be stripped to save money for the big producers when they ship the wool back east. She hears children laughing on their way to school and sees that life goes on around her even when her world has been arrested in the hush that follows thunder. Eva shakes her head; both she and Dee are arrested.

Eva asks to use the phone and pays her nickel. Mrs. McDowell smiles now, says something about checking in the kitchen, giving Eva privacy. Not that it matters. The operator will stay on the line and report to neighbors any and all of Eva's conversation, regardless of how mundane the topic.

"It's all smooth as cream," Mildred tells Eva across the scratchy line. "A body can cook in a well-organized kitchen. This body's cooked in the other kind, and it's no party then, I tell you that. You've done well getting it all put together. Even alphabetical for your spice tins. I never thought of such a thing."

"I don't know when or for how long I'll—"

"I tell you, we'll do just fine here. How's your D. L. holding up? Was he pleased to see you then? I imagine you've had a chance to talk to him by now. When does he think he'll be out? I tell you, that Hahn should have enough money to get a body released on bail. Cowboys think that's the least his lawyer could do for him. For you, poor thing, out and about all alone."

"He's… It's… They've selected a jury."

"You're sounding tired. Did you get any sleep in that wild town? Did you buy yourself a new hat, Eva? You should, you know. Hats give a body confidence, I tell you. I won't part with mine, and every new one is like a flower that never fades. Try to make some good memories now. Not every bad thing has to stay that way. This'll all be over soon. I tell you, I'm sounding wise as my grandmother every day. What?" Mildred's voice fades, then, "I got to get back to biscuits, honey. You take care. Let us know what's happening. And remember, it wasn't your fault, this whole thing. No sense in more than one person carrying a load of blame, and I imagine D. L.'s weighted heavy as a rock crib."

Eva leans in, pressing the receiver to her ear, clutches the mouthpiece. "Mildred? Hello? Wait." Eva holds emptiness. She wants to hear more soothing words. Nothing troubles Mildred, even being called up from Antelope at the last moment when Eva finally decided to take the stage to Dee. Eva wishes for that kind of mettle. She had it once. Maybe staying away from Dee, to punish him, maybe that takes grit. Or maybe just unspent anger.

She wants Dee free. But even when he is, they'll have to leave the Muddy country, and her dream to be there with her husband, have a family, build their cabin, the dream her parents had before it turned into a nightmare, will disappear like rising mist above the Muddy Creek.

She wonders if Dee does carry any blame for what has happened, for this disruption of their lives. She didn't hear responsibility in his voice last night. Maybe she can't hear remorse through the deafness of her recall. Alone, she enters the restaurant.

George Barnes sits, his waistcoat shrouding a dining-room chair next to him. He writes on a pad of paper while sipping tea. He wears a plaid vest of spring green and yellow, and before she can slip onto a chair out of his sight, he looks up, stands. "Join me, Mrs. Bruner," he says. "Won't you?" He motions to a chair opposite his, moves aside the single tulip in a vase. A flash of light strikes the glass, and Eva looks up to see light bulbs. Luxury, undeserved.

"Did you sleep well?" His face with soft folds breaks into a smile. He might be in his forties, maybe older, though he shows no graying temples. He clasps his hands together, makes a steeple as in that children's finger game. He taps his fingertips as he talks. He wears a wedding band. "Mrs. Bruner?"

The name still surprises Eva, even two years after it changed. She still thinks of herself as Miss Thompson, the girl glad to have lived with her uncle Morrison and aunt Fern, as no one questioned her last name. People accepted her as one who belonged. They didn't know the truth. She never called them *Mama* or *Papa.* Her father and her uncle had been brothers. Were brothers. Death didn't end that binding tie. She's never asked her uncle about how it felt to have a brother convicted as a murderer. She guesses by now Uncle Morrison must have heard about Dee's arrest and trial, read of it in the papers. She hasn't told them, too ashamed to write.

"Mrs. Bruner?" George Barnes repeats.

"The room's lovely," Eva says. "I don't see how I can repay Mr. Hahn, but I will, in time."

"You let Henry Hahn worry about that. He likes to honor men as loyal to him as your husband's been. Charlie O'Neal says he's a good worker, always has been."

"So you think he was ordered to do this…thing? I heard that lawyer say—"

"Mrs. Bruner"—Barnes lowers his voice—"I'm glad we have a chance to talk, to prepare you for events today." He dabs at his mouth with his napkin, then brushes crumbs from his mustache, oiled to fine points at each end. "After the jury's fully seated, there'll be opening arguments. The prosecution begins their case, and they must prove beyond a reasonable doubt that your husband is guilty. You'll hear things today that might not be easy for you to hear, words spoken as though they are truths when they might not be."

"You believe he acted in self-defense?" Eva asks. Self-defense is easier for her to imagine, easier than acknowledging that she works for a man who could order such a thing, that she takes his money for a warm bed and a meal to break her fast.

"The truth, I believe, is somewhere between what your husband recalls and what the prosecution purports. It'll be our job to punch holes into those statements presented by Frank Menefee, the prosecuting attorney, and to present our own truths into those empty spaces well enough that jurors must at least wonder. Your presence in that room means a great deal."

"It's…difficult—"

"Coor-rect," Barnes says. "It takes courage. I hope you'll sit as you did yesterday, behind your husband. Well, maybe a bit more off to the side where he can see you without turning around." He takes a drink of water. "I'm glad you worked out a way to be here. I know it's a busy time—D.L.'s explanation for your not being free enough to visit before now."

"It's always a busy time for a Muddy cook."

"I imagine so."

These past weeks have actually been less busy than usual at the Muddy. Mildred could have easily handled Eva's time away, because the men were out branding, didn't come in for such big meals. Mildred could have single-handedly prepared food for the chuck wagon that traveled out to the men, busy with bawling calves. Mildred will be far busier now. Either Dee didn't remember details of her work, or he fabricated a story his lawyer would accept.

"With so many hands, there are always demands," Eva says, not sure she wants Dee's lawyer to know that Dee lets him believe a falsehood.

"Your presence here brings him comfort," Barnes says.

"Does it?" Eva drops her eyes. "Sometimes I can't tell."

"He's an enigma, your D.L. that's coor-rect. But I know for a fact that he longs to see you, to talk with you. Your being there yesterday means much to our defense. A wife not sitting in support of her accused husband can be interpreted many ways, some not good for us at all."

Eva nods. When a waiter approaches, Barnes orders without asking for her preferences, then continues talking. "I wonder if you could say a few words about D.L.'s state of mind the day of the...accident. I understand he made that call to the sheriff himself, which speaks well for him."

Eva thinks jurors might not agree. A man who takes another's life ought not be so composed he can ring the sheriff and then sit, scraping his fingernails with his pocket knife, his boots crossed at the ankle while he waits to be arrested. Even one of the sheepdogs lay at his feet, calm though away from its flock. If Dee had been agitated, his dog would have been too.

But maybe people manage tragedy uniquely. She hasn't thought of that. Dee sits calm, thinking, sure of himself, even willing to accept the consequences of his actions. Eva tends to prattle in her mind when things go awry. She spins through a dozen thoughts, scenarios, stands up, sits down, wipes her hands on her apron, then returns to what she knows, to boiling potatoes, flouring chicken, frying it crisp.

She'll do anything to keep from thinking of what could happen now that her husband has killed a man. Staying busy at the Muddy helped with that. But now she's here.

"He wanted the sheriff to know what happened, right away."

"D. L. has stepped into the middle of a major social confrontation. Government allocations of land for grazing, arguments between cattle ranchers and sheepherders wanting similar ground—it's a story taking place throughout the West. It's a story been told in Prineville since '95."

"But the Muddy runs both cattle and sheep, so—"

"Here's what happened: Reilly and Creegan took a claim next to land the Muddy herders used for years to move ewes to spring pasture. Reilly pushed his twelve hundred or so ewes down there after lambing. Charlie, Hahn's foreman, told more than one Muddy herder that Reilly would need to be crowded out. So herders crowded their bands up against Creegan and Reilly's claim, nibbling at the piece of land between them and leaving nothing for Reilly's flock. That part of the prosecution's statement is probably truth, about D. L. possibly following orders to crowd."

"I remember Dee saying that Reilly carried a .38-55 Winchester with him and brandished it whenever he met up with another herder."

"Coor-rect. Frightening. Aggressive. All behavior that supports D. L.'s claim of self-defense."

"Does it?" Eva wishes now she'd talked earlier with Barnes. Dee might have told her truths. He'd been recently assigned to that band of sheep, so perhaps he wasn't involved in the "crowding" at all. If Reilly came at him, shooting the independent herder might have been the only way to save himself. Still, Dee borrowed a Smith & Wesson .38 from a ranch hand before he left with his flock, so he must have been aware of potential problems.

Barnes continues. "Reilly and Creegan were in the middle of their lambing season when this all started. First lambing, at that—you know how that can be, a flash-flood showing up on a blue-sky day.

Expect the unexpected. All those young ewes, the cold spring weather we've had, snow still in some of the ravines there..." A clock chimes out the hour, and Barnes stops. "Running late. Please, finish your meal, and I'll see you in the courtroom in a half-hour or so. I'm glad we've had this talk," he says while putting on his coat.

"Me too," Eva says, though she doesn't think she's spoken much. But Barnes's words comfort like a cat, offering warmth with no promise of staying. Here is a reasonable explanation for Dee's behavior. She's been so angry, so humiliated, she hasn't let him tell her facts. *Following orders* didn't mean *kill a man.* Reilly had been threatening. Maybe Dee hadn't meant to kill Tom Reilly. If he had intended murder, why would he come riding back to the Muddy, make a phone call to the sheriff, then just sit, waiting to be arrested?

Yet he never said that day, "I accidentally killed Tom Reilly" nor "There's been an accident." Dee asked her to make the call, and she stood stunned, so he moved to do it, letting her overhear. He spoke with bravado, that same tone he used when he told people that he worked "for Henry Hahn and the Prineville Land and Livestock Company."

So why didn't Dee show more remorse, more horror at what he'd done? He'd taken from this earth a man's life, a woman's husband, a mother's son. Even in the courtroom he didn't hang his head, didn't look worried. He held his head up high, his chin lifted, as though to say he expected not only to be found innocent but also to receive some kind of bonus payment for his efforts.

Eva feels on trial too. Already her husband's actions have changed her life, filled her nights with terror, covered her waking body in perspiration and wondering of what will become of her if Dee is convicted.

Eva's face grows warm; her breath comes in short bursts. She mustn't think these thoughts. There is nothing she can do to alter what has happened. She can only reach for clarity in her thinking so when she acts it will be with conviction.

She hasn't been fair to Dee. She might have explored his side of the story if she had visited him while in jail. But leaving the comfort of the Muddy Station had been too difficult to consider. Now she has to face what Barnes implies, that her absence might have sabotaged his defense.

Make it over into something good, isn't that what Mildred said? Her wise old ways have helped her through the swirls of life. Eva needs to listen.

Eva slices the tender steak the waiter brings her. She takes a bite. She spreads butter on the hard roll, the paste of it against her tongue a rich delight. The salt grains bring juices to her throat. Gratefulness fills her. Her mother might have nodded in approval of her daughter's elegant surroundings, though not the circumstance of her being in them, and certainly not her brazen taking of a meal in the dining room instead of alone in her room as a proper married, grieving woman should.

Eva pushes back her chair, thinks she will push back the bad taste brought on by a father behind iron bars and his absence ever after. She is different from her mother. Eva stands, offers a silent prayer of thanks for the strength at last to stand behind her husband.

5

TRUTH

The trial begins midmorning. The jury's selected and seated. John Creegan, Tom's partner, testifies first. Dee listens, ferrets out the flaws. His heart pounds as John recounts that April day, and for the most part, their stories concur. He agrees that John shouted at him to keep his ewes and wethers away from where John and Tom's sheep lambed.

Dee's flock had no lambing ewes, but mixing herds would separate lambs from mothers, and others would be trampled and die. Dee hadn't planned to push his flock through Reilly's herd. He just meant to crowd him back, use the old public route as though it still belonged to everyone, all free to move their herds across it, just like the Indians they'd first taken it from.

But Tom had made a claim. The land was his now. To prove it, he put birthing ewes in a bad spot. He'd done it as an experiment to provoke.

Dee even agrees with John's account of Tom picking up his rifle and shouting across the narrow canyon where Dee's flock ripped at sparse grass. He had trouble hearing Tom for the wind, but he knew pretty well what Tom likely said, yelling at him to move out, profanities tossed back at John's face by the gusts. That wind forced them to walk a distance to see if they could find a spot requiring less shouting. Dee writes a note to Barnes: *See, I was trying to talk to the man civilly.*

"They talked for maybe ten minutes or so," John tells the court. "Then I sees Tom walking back. He steps five, maybe six paces, and I sees Bruner reach to his pocket and pull his pistol out. He fires one, maybe two shots. The second at Tom's back."

A gasp in the courtroom causes the judge to gavel the gallery quiet.

Not true! Dee writes on the pad and slides it over to Barnes. Just like John to distort things.

Menefee asks what happened next. "Tom dropped his rifle and started running," John says. "Bruner ran after him and picked up Tom's rifle, and he shot at him. Tom kept running, maybe twenty-five yards or so, and Bruner ran after and fired again and missed him. Tom almost made it, but he had a bum knee. Bruner fired a third time. It wasn't enough he missed twice—make that four times, counting his own gun. He wasn't trying to scare Tom, if that's what he tells you. He wanted to kill Tom, and he did. Why, he even dropped to one knee to get a better aim."

"Objection, your honor. It goes to the defendant's intent, which John here can't know," George Barnes says after a smug Menefee sits down.

"Sustained," the judge says.

"How far away were you from all this?" Barnes now begins his examination.

"Maybe a half-mile or so."

"Pretty good eyes for a half-mile, wouldn't you say?"

"I do have good eyes. Ask anyone around here," John says.

"I'm sure patrons of the Silvertooth Saloon would offer excellent corroboration," Barnes says before Menefee can rise to object. "But you couldn't hear what was being said, could you?" Barnes clasps his hands behind his back and rocks on his heels. "You couldn't hear whether Mr. Reilly threatened Mr. Bruner, coor-rect?"

"No, but—"

"Did you see what happened to Mr. Bruner's Smith & Wesson? I'm wondering why Mr. Bruner didn't continue to fire at Mr. Reilly with his own weapon, if he truly intended to kill Tom Reilly."

"Tom was running pretty quick. That Smith & Wesson don't have the range of a Winchester."

"Yet Tom dropped his rifle."

"He was scared, I tell you."

"He might have told Mr. Bruner he was heading back for something bigger, threatening to return to finish Mr. Bruner off. Tom had a bit of a temper, didn't he?"

"Objection!"

"I think it's relevant," says the judge. "You can answer, John."

"I don't know any Irishman who doesn't, but he wouldn't have killed a man. Tom wasn't like that."

"Yet he had threatened sheepherders of the Muddy Ranch on previous occasions, isn't that so? And he was a desperate man, having put all his money into that claim and that flock. Even his brother's money—and yours, though I suppose now the entire flock belongs to you—was at risk. He couldn't afford to be crowded out and lose all those lambs, isn't that right?"

Creegan fidgets. "Maybe. I couldn't say for sure."

"You don't remember Tom threatening other herders, telling them to back off, to stay away from the former public land?"

"Can't say I recall that, no."

"Well, Mr. O'Neal, foreman at the Muddy, will testify that such threats were the very reason he asked D. L. Bruner to run that flock, because he knew D. L. wasn't easily intimidated. A number of other Muddy sheepherders did crowd you, isn't that true? Early in the month?"

"They backed off. It's our land now."

"Yes. They backed off when threatened with Tom Reilly's words and rifle. My point exactly. No more questions, Judge." Barnes sits down.

Dee leans back and smiles. *Good work*, he writes on the pad.

Look contrite, Barnes writes back.

"You didn't have lambs early in the month, isn't that right, Mr. Creegan?" the prosecuting attorney clarifies.

"Right."

"So the defendant's crowding was a terrible thing, not something one sheepherder should do to another as a way of protesting land claims. Crowding first-time ewes and young lambs puts their viability at risk, isn't that so, Mr. Creegan?"

"Viability?"

"They could all die if they were crowded out right after they were born. Tom was just protecting his property, the sheep and his land, wouldn't you say?"

"A man's got a right to do that."

They take a lunch recess, and Dee asks if he can remain in the courtroom for his meal. "I'll stay with him," George Barnes tells the bailiff. "He's not going anywhere."

Behind him, Eva stands. "Stay here, will you Eva?" Dee pats the chair next to him. "Mrs. Meredith'll bring enough for two. She always does."

The jury files out, but Dee sees them watching her. Two reporters stand back, pads in hand. Eva hesitates. *Not now, don't look like you're afraid of me now.* "Let me brush off this chair," Dee says, and he takes his time. Barnes shoos the reporters out. Only Barnes, a bailiff standing at the door, and Eva, the "child-wife," as the newspapers describe her, remain. He hopes Eva hasn't seen the papers. She finally sits.

"Barnes made good points this morning. Tom made threats, and I was just defending myself."

"But once Tom turned away, did you have to pursue him? Why not just let him go?" Eva asks, her hands clasped in her lap.

"He'd be coming back, to kill me or someone else. He said as much when we were shouting at each other over that rock cairn. It had to end sometime. Tom just made it easier, threatening me like that."

"You shot him in the back," Eva whispers. "I didn't know that before."

"Eva, he threatened me. I pulled my pistol and shot at him at close range, to scare him. That'll come out when I testify, and when the coroners report their findings, right George?"

"Well, I don't—"

"But it didn't scare him, it made him mad. He said he was heading back to get more ammunition and he'd return to kill me and shoot my herd. That's what he said, and I believed him. It was either him or me. Can't my own wife believe in me? I got to convince a group of strangers, and I can't even get you to understand?"

He feels that vein in his neck throbbing. The morning session has gone well. Now she plunges him into a rage. *Contain it. She'll come around. It's not like it was before.*

Mrs. Meredith bustles in, carrying her food basket. She hesitates when she sees Eva, a furrow in her forehead. "You're not looking much better this morning. Are you sick? Not my cooking now." Eva shakes her head. "That's right. You didn't eat any. Maybe this stew will hit the spot."

The lunch fare is a little lighter than the dinner meal, and after Mrs. Meredith leaves, Dee comments on that.

Barnes says, "No one wants to see a prisoner eating better than the jury. You haven't eaten anything, Mrs. Bruner," Barnes says.

"She never did eat much," Dee says. "Still she stays plump as a pumpkin." He pats her hand. He wants her to believe in him, to be there for him as a true relative, the way a blood relative should be but better because she's chosen to believe, not been born into it. He wants Eva with him through it all. His mother hasn't ever been. His father isn't now, but Dee expects more of Eva. She takes her vows seriously, even made him take them not before a judge but inside a church, before a crowd of witnesses. "Before God," she'd said, and he knew she meant it.

She can't abandon him, not now. He'll talk of mundane things, to soothe her. "Even with your eating so little, you're looking fit. The Muddy company's paying for good hotel meals for you?"

She looks at her stomach before she speaks, then lifts her eyes, tears spilling, "I...I think I might...what Mrs. Meredith said last night...we might"—then she whispers—"have a child."

They call in another witness, a friend of Tom's who was with the flock that day too. Campbell concurs that Dee fired two shots with Tom's rifle at the back of a departing man, then knelt down and took aim to make the third.

"The landscape is pretty rolling there, isn't it?" Mr. Barnes asks Campbell on cross. "It can be deceptive to the untrained eye."

"I guess so. Only fit for sheep or cattle. Can't farm that country, though Tom did have a homestead claim all right. He had hopes, he and Creegan."

"It would be quite difficult to hit a target at that distance given the landscape's pitch, wouldn't you say?"

"D. L.'s a pretty good shot," Campbell says.

"You've testified he missed several times. And isn't it true that you didn't see anything until those last three shots were fired?"

"Yes."

"So you really don't know what transpired between Mr. Reilly and my client prior to them, do you?"

"Well, no, but—"

"Thank you, Mr. Campbell. No more questions."

Eva thinks Campbell looks dejected, as though he's failed to uphold his end of some bargain. His eyes move to Tom's brother, seated on the far side. Dee looks back at her with an expression on his face she can't name.

Another witness takes the stand, swears truthfulness on the Bible. Eva tries to concentrate on his words. But her hands shake. It's why she's been so tired, what's made the blotches on her face, what's triggered her morning nausea. No wonder fright and confusion overtake her, even when she doesn't let her mind race toward the future of Dee's life. She has another life to consider now. She is worrying for two. Maybe three, since Dee shows so little care about the outcome. He was almost cheerful at lunch.

Maybe that is how he deals with uncertainty and loss. He can't remember much, he once said, about his mother's confinement in an asylum. He was barely six, and his father farmed him out to a neighbor in Silverton. He left just as soon as he turned thirteen and could make it on his own. His whirlwind life never left him in any place fine, and as soon as he could, he'd leave. His father gathered his other sons and daughters to him, giving all a share of his mother's estate. All except Dee. That's when he headed east, working for sheepherders and ranchers and Eva's uncle for a time.

She looks at her lap. Her gloved hands rest beneath a moon of linen. She counts. Three months. She'll have a baby in November. A baby! Would Dee make a good father? A child to care for and support would make him more responsible, perhaps. But he doesn't know how to be a father. He's never had one to show him how. Maybe that was why he tried so hard to please Charlie O'Neal, the foreman. Or Henry Hahn, the owner. Maybe they were the fathers he never had.

Weariness presses her into the chair. The whole process strains her, all the questions with double meanings and the answers that aren't really meant to unveil the truth but to champion a perspective. She still believes what Aunt Fern taught her, that one can't always see what God has in store while in the midst of troubling things. "You have to wait for the dust to clear, and then you'll be amazed at what can happen," her aunt often told her.

"Nothing good came from my father's conviction," Eva said to her. "Mama died of a broken heart, and—"

"And through no fault of your own you were caught up in a flash flood. But it spit you out at a good place, didn't it? Your years with us have been good, haven't they? You didn't get set down in some far-off desert or dropped into a family not capable of loving you as their own, now did you? See, God was looking after you. You just didn't know it then."

Until that day, Eva hadn't realized how much her aunt must have longed for a child, how much she gave to make Eva's time with them a rich and gifted stay. Loving hands wiped away tears, raised her, then let her go to make her own way. Eight years she spent with them, and she would be there still if not for Dee. If not for her headstrong wish to go back to the Muddy country, and for falling in love with Dee in order to do it.

The two coroners testify next, and Barnes gets them to admit they overlooked Tom's clothing and don't know if there was blood on it from a possible facial wound, and they aren't sure that the wound they identified was made by Dee's pistol as he had testified at the coroner's inquest. Tom's clothes are in faraway Antelope along with his body, and no one seems interested in retrieving either for further study. She doesn't know much about this, but it seems like the clothes should be examined for powder burns. Their presence would mean Dee told the truth.

Dee writes something on a pad and slides it over to Barnes. The attorney shakes his head. Eva wonders how long they'll go today arguing about distances between shell casings and whether the shots were random, meant only to frighten. Her stomach finds Mrs. Meredith's stew an unfortunate invader, and Eva swallows back a painful spew. She hopes they finish soon.

"Next witness?" Judge Bradshaw says. "I'd say we have time for one more."

The prosecuting attorney rises. "We call Eva Bruner to the stand."

Did she hear correctly? Eva's heart pounds like a wagon rolling across a wooden bridge. Surely all can hear it!

"Your Honor, I object," Barnes says. "Mrs. Bruner is not prepared to testify. May I approach the bench?"

Barnes doesn't wait for the judge's nod but strides forward, Menefee preening behind him. They exchange quiet words, and then the judge excuses the jury, clears the courtroom. Barnes asks Eva to remain, as the defendant's wife, not as a potential witness.

"She'll be a hostile witness for the prosecution, something the jury won't understand," Barnes says.

"The jury will be fine with this, Mr. Barnes," Menefee insists. "They're a good lot. Prudent as the day is long. Unless of course Mrs. Bruner has something to say that might place your client in bad stead. Surely no wife would share such things."

"She has nothing relevant to add," Barnes says. "She didn't make the phone call to the sheriff. She didn't go with her husband when Deputy Glisan arrested him and handcuffed him to the buckboard.

She didn't attend the coroner's inquest or walk the plot of land. She has no information relevant to this case. Why, she's only seen her husband once since he's been in jail—"

"And isn't that an interesting admission," Menefee says, his pencil tapping at his chin. Eva watches Barnes flinch and step back. "We call her to testify to the temperament of her husband, to let the jury know what kind of man he might be, how impulsive, how cavalier about life and limb. Is he easily roused? What's his judgment like? Perhaps he's good at displaying loyalty to men of influence. Perhaps they keep his rash, thoughtless, hasty behavior in check. His wife was only fifteen when they wed. That alone suggests he's impulsive, a man who can't wait. Does his wife know that side of him? Could he plan for a killing, carry it out? We think so, and we intend to prove it."

"This is not your summary time, Frank," the judge says, his voice a sigh.

Barnes says, "We had no indication they'd be calling Mrs. Bruner. She's in a fragile state."

Menefee scoffs. He jabs the pencil toward his colleague. "Just so you're not surprised again, we are also calling the ex-sheriff of Clackamas County on a relevant incident that took place not long ago. Oh"—he turned to look at Dee—"we'll be calling Bruner's father, too."

"My father?" Dee's chair nearly goes over.

"Sit down, Mr. Bruner," the judge orders.

"Who better should know about his son but the father?" Menefee says. He beams.

Dee's father lives? Eva's palms drip water like the pump back on the Muddy. She longs for the cooling breeze of the John Day River, the safety of the gentle landscape instead of this man-made, confusing place.

6

BELIEF

Eva dreams of landscapes. Flat, gray stones and smoother cinnamon-colored rocks standing upright like table leaves lined up in the Muddy closet. Green lichen floats between her fingers. In the distance, camass patches pull her into a sea of blue and white. She sees an old woman bent to her digging stick, a horse ripping at the grass beside her. Eva approaches but is rushed past into the coolness of the river, the one that receives the Muddy Creek's flow. She floats, her dress pushing outward at the waist, filling with air, with an infant. Sheep and cattle slurp beside her head, so close, the sound muffled as the water fills her ears. Purple lupine spins around her, lifts her, soaring toward the sky. She's lost, confused, mixed up with the hills and rocks and sky.

Suddenly she's watching Mildred quilt pieces of discards. A calico dress. A faded feed sack with pink flowers. Black linen from a funeral dress. "Wedding dress," Mildred says, though Eva hasn't asked. The shapes are all sharp angles or rounded as a melon. "Crazy quilts, they call them," Mildred says. "Organized chaos. But held together just the same." Eva gasps at the beauty. "The stitching." Mildred points to gold threads braided with silver and copper, stitches that make even the faded calico look rich and wanted. "That's what does it. Brings it all together. A body's got to wait for the threads to do their work. Faith's the stitching of the chaos. Here." Mildred throws the quilt at Eva's face.

Eva cannot breathe! She'll suffocate! She struggles and then wakes, breathing like a spent mare. Wobbly, she sits up, then pushes the hotel's crazy quilt aside, first running her fingers over the stitching.

Eva's hand shakes as she holds the teacup in the hotel dining room. She and Barnes are alone. "Is this private enough for you?" Barnes asks her. His eyes remind her of a hound's, drooped and sad. Eva wonders if he has a family who never gets to see him during a trial like this. Maybe he's never married, knowing he must serve at the beck and call of clients. She sees his ring. Perhaps a wife waits for him, loyal, while he talks to a frightened woman over tea.

"I thought it would be more pleasant to meet here than in the lawyer's room at the courthouse," Barnes says. She nods. "I don't know what they'll ask you, but we can speculate." He clears his throat. "Do you have any notions you'd like to share?"

"I don't even know if I believe Dee, Mr. Barnes. Mr. Menefee will stir up my indecision. He'll change it all around." Tears well. "I don't want Dee convicted of something he didn't mean to do. I'm so… angry that we're here, dealing with this. So sad for Tom Reilly's family too."

"Normal state of affairs, Mrs. Bruner." He pulls at his mustache, leans back in his chair, then forward, discreet. "Has D. L. ever given you reason to…fear him? Ever been, you know, rough with you, maybe when he imbibed a bit?"

"He does like his ale, but it makes him…funny," she says. "As for the other…" She hesitates, wondering how much to say. "He pushed me to ride a horse once when I didn't want to, but I wasn't afraid of him, just annoyed. He couldn't see how scared I was." She stirs a maple lump into her tea. "Dee takes risks. I watched him ride across the John Day River when it was in flood stage, just to prove he could. He said it was a 'blast of air to a man's soul,' but if his horse had faltered or he'd been swept off, I'm not sure what would have happened. He can't swim."

"But he's never threatened you or anyone else that you know of?"

She recalls a rumor told at their wedding dance. One of his friends said Dee'd been arrested for striking a man, almost beating him to death. She hadn't taken it seriously because the friend had consumed his weight in ale before he'd told of it, and because Dee was a smallish man, surely not capable of beating another to within inches of his life. *Should I tell Barnes?* "I heard a rumor," Eva says, "about a fight he got into. He bested the other man, I'm told."

"Just a fight?"

Eva nods. "Before we were married. He's never done anything like that since. I think the Muddy hands would have told me. They can't keep a secret."

"Might be the Clackamas County sheriff connection," Barnes says, his eyes moving to a place beyond her head. "I'll check into it. Make a call later. But he's been self-controlled with you?"

"He surprises me at times. He once shoved a baby bullsnake a little closer to my nose than I liked, but I've never been afraid except—" Barnes raises his eyebrow. Eva sighs. "Maybe once. That day of the...of Reilly's death. Dee was agitated when he left, moving from here to there in our room, picking up my hatpins, then putting them down. Charlie had talked with him, but Dee wouldn't tell me what about. And then he left to tend the flock. A few hours later, he walked back, giving me that order to call the sheriff. He seemed so unaware of the magnitude of what he'd done. He cleaned his fingernails. It was as though he was a simmering teapot in the morning, and then the fire went out."

"The five-mile walk back to the Muddy Station gave him time to collect himself, perhaps," Barnes says.

"But still..." She lowers her eyes.

Barnes nods. "What's his relationship with his father?"

Eva catches her breath and exhales. "I didn't think his father was still alive, though now that I think of it, Dee never said as much. Dee said that from the time he was six he'd had no contact with his father. He was dead to Dee. Dee showed me the papers related to his mother's estate settlement, when his father assumed guardianship over his brothers and sisters. Dee is the youngest, just six when his mother was committed. His father farmed. Maybe he couldn't take care of a young child on his own. Or maybe there was something else about Dee that made him decide to leave him with a neighbor."

"Do you know the neighbor's name?"

Eva shakes her head.

"I'm going to give you some possible explanations for Dee's behavior. If you think you can, I'd urge you to incorporate them into your answers to Menefee's questions, so you can shed the most positive light possible on your husband. Do you think that you can do that?"

Eva nods. "I don't want him sent away, I don't. And I feel badly about not coming. I'm just so…confused."

"Just remember to talk to the jury, look into their eyes. Whether Menefee believes you or not doesn't matter. What the jury believes does."

"Were you aware that the Prineville Land and Livestock Company always took their flocks for spring grazing across the canyon that your brother put a homestead claim on?" Menefee is asking Pat Reilly, Tom's brother. It is the third day of the trial. The prosecution has agreed to wait to call Eva and the Clackamas County sheriff and Dee's father.

"It's a free country, don't you know, and the land there looked good for the farming he wanted to be doing in the off-season. Potatoes and all." His brogue thickens, and Dee wonders if he might be playing to Garrett, Lister, and Kibby, a few of the Irish sitting on the jury. How had he, D. L. Bruner, become the outsider? He'd been around longer than the Reillys and worked for the most powerful landholder in the region. Some things just weren't fair.

"The claim was made some months before, was it not?"

"A few. But Muddy knew of it. Tom told more than one herder to step back. He even built a rock cairn to mark the outer boundary."

"But how were these men to take their sheep to grazing then, if not across the established trails, trails used for decades?"

"Around Black Rock," Pat Reilly says.

"Black Rock," Menefee says. "That's a mighty big hill. It would take a flock several days to move around it, and the grazing's not that good for them, now is it?"

"It's a mite out of a man's way, but it's the right way, don't you know. Once a claim's been made, it's legal. He was just doing what was legal. Tom staked his claim fair and square. He lived in a tent till the cabin was built."

"It would take a big operation, like the Muddy, to push against a man's claim, isn't that right?"

Dee waits for Barnes to object. Dee needs a new lawyer—that's what he needs, someone who can handle these Irishmen.

"Your brother's claim is an L-shape, isn't that right, Mr. Reilly?" Barnes asks on cross.

"That's right, don't you know."

"I do know, yes." Barnes continues. "And the crosspiece of that property, if I may show the jury a drawing I've made here"—Barnes raises his eyebrow to the judge, who concurs—"this little crosspiece, the bottom of the L, that's the piece that cuts right across the trail used by the Muddy for maybe twenty years or more, isn't that right?"

"Guess they should have filed on that government piece themselves," Pat says. Dee thinks he sees nods from the Irish jurors.

"Just answer the questions, please. Just beyond that L, that's government land, where sheep or cattle or even picnickers can find safe haven, isn't that right?"

"Don't have much time for picnicking myself," Pat says, and Dee hears a guffaw from someone in the gallery.

"Describe that piece of real estate for me, Mr. Reilly. Could a man set a plow to that spit of ravine that now separates the Muddy from government land? Is it enough land with enough grass on it to be grazed for, say, your interest in Tom's flock of twelve hundred sheep?"

"Wouldn't keep them long, that's sure. It's just a little section. But our sheep were lambing nearby, and D. L. was pushing his ewes and wethers through, and they'd have harmed the flock. Especially those big gelded bucks."

"Your Honor," Barnes says.

"Just answer the questions asked, Mr. Reilly, though you need to give him time, George," notes the judge.

"It wouldn't keep them long," Reilly said.

"Herders could easily move them through your 'little section' and on up to the government land and up to spring grazing in the high country. You don't really need that spit of land for lambing. It's hardly enough for a good-sized garden, but it does limit anyone else's access to the public land."

"Objection." Menefee sighs.

"Is that a question, Mr. Barnes?" the judge asks.

"Can you think of any other use for that L of land than to force someone to go around Black Rock to get to their spring grazing?"

"Tom claimed it fair and square. A man can do what he wants with his own land."

"It does offer the opportunity for intimidation."

"Objection. He's making a statement," says Menefee.

"I withdraw my comment," Barnes says.

Good work, Dee writes on the pad he shoves to Barnes. He'd shown the jury that not all threats were made with a gun. Maybe the Muddy has served him well with Barnes. Dee relaxes and smiles for the first time in twenty-four hours.

Relief bathes Eva. They've called Dee's father, Francis Bruner, to testify first. It gives her time to calm herself, she hopes. She can study this man who sired her husband, see what Dee might become in later years. Maybe she'll come to understand some of Dee's fluctuating demeanors, his confusing vacillation between tenderness and risk, between bullishness and need. She's thought the abandonment of his mother and his father's assumed death stitched these mismatched pieces.

Before her stands Francis Bruner, alive, lean, and lanky. He towers over the bailiff when he puts his hand on the Bible and swears to tell the truth. His shoulders sag as he sits in the witness chair. His longish, well-trimmed hair brushes against his stiff white shirt collar. He has a high forehead, wide, round eyes. Dee must favor his mother.

Barnes stands, objects again that a man who has not seen his son for years can contribute much to the case, but he is overruled, and Menefee begins his questions. The room warms up, and Eva fans herself along with all the other women in the gallery. One takes notes. Will Eva read about herself come morning?

Menefee leads Francis Bruner through a series of questions establishing his identity, and then he asks him how long it's been since he's seen his son.

"About three months," Francis answers.

Eva stops her fan before her mouth to cover her surprise. She looks at Dee, whose head bends over clasped hands on the oak table. Barnes shoves the pad of paper to him, but Dee apparently doesn't notice.

"What were the circumstances of your visit?" Mr. Menefee asks.

"He was incarcerated in the Clackamas County Jail, and he wanted to see me."

"Objection!" Barnes says.

"On what grounds?" the judge asks.

"Prejudicial and irrelevant."

"I'll allow it. It speaks to the state of mind of the defendant. Continue, Mr. Menefee."

"Can you tell us about your visit with your son, Mr. Bruner? Why did he call upon you?"

"He'd gotten into a fight. A major one this time. He wanted my help in getting out."

Eva's mind spins back. Three months. Dee'd been called to Portland, he'd said, by Henry Hahn, to discuss employment issues. He'd be gone for maybe four days. She couldn't go with him. She was needed at the station. She'd be fine. She remembers feeling clingy, wanting to hold him, to keep him from putting a change of clothes into a leather satchel. He'd be back quicker than the twitch of a lamb's tail, he assured her. That night, he'd curled beside her, loved her soundly, then slipped out before dawn, leaving sweet memories behind.

He'd been delayed coming back, but he called her, told her. There was no mention of a jail time, no comment about needing his father. He offered nothing more when he returned, and she was so pleased to have him close again she didn't press for more. Scratches on his knuckles came from faulty tack, he claimed, and a horse that hadn't wanted to be saddled. Had she been a fool to trust her husband? Had she so wanted to live at the Muddy that she lied to herself about her choice of mate?

"The other fights, could you tell the court about those?" Has Eva missed the explanation of the Clackamas County event?

Francis Bruner takes a deep breath. "I'd rather tell you of the most recent one, Mr. Menefee. I think it sums up all the rest. They've all been senseless, unprovoked, in my opinion, but my son has always taken offense where none was intended. This time a man said D. L. took a sip of his ale, and D. L. called the man a liar."

"Hearsay," objects Barnes.

"Overruled. You may continue, Mr. Bruner."

Eva leans forward. Her heart pounds now as she learns things she doesn't really want to know.

"My son's had some training as a pugilist, and though he is of small stature, he is skilled and can be lethal. He bulldogs steers too. He's quite strong." He says this looking directly at the jury. "This time, at Clackamas, the men went outside and had at it. Someone called the police, and D. L. came out of it standing. He was arrested.

The other man was hospitalized." He looked at the jury again. "He still is. My son…my son can be…dangerous."

"But why did he call you? Why not his employer, let's say, someone with influence who might provide an attorney for him?" Menefee asks, walking away and looking at Barnes.

"He always calls me." Francis Bruner's voice cracks then, and his wide eyes grow cloudy with pooling tears. "It's the only time he ever wants to hear from me."

Blood rushes to Dee's face, his fists. He can't keep his feet still. The vein pulsates. He wants to stand up and shout, "Put me on next! Let me tell my story." His father knows nothing about Dee Link Bruner, the man. No one does. No one wants to.

7

Conviction

Eva writes things down now, not sure why, maybe to help herself make sense of what's happening. When she writes, she misses the Muddy Station less. The words come out like prayers she hopes will reach a listening Savior. Her spoken prayers, before she sleeps at night, leave her empty, lost, as though the faith that carried her from childhood no longer buoys but pulls her under, weights her like a sinking stone.

Dee's father has asked me to take a walk with him, to get to know him better. I'm troubled by this request. Reporters lurk at every corner. What will they say of this man who has testified that his son is harmful, perhaps needs to be set aside from others, from me? Shouldn't a father be loyal, never abandon? Shouldn't a wife?

"I'm pleased to meet you, Eva. It is Eva, yes?" Eva nods. They walk beneath elms lining the courthouse perimeter. A few maple trees stand out, a different shade of green. Francis Bruner suggested this place. She is afraid at first that Dee will see them walking. Then she remembers Dee can't see anything from his cell, can't even hear the birds.

What if Dee's convicted, never hears birds again?

"D. L. told me he was married when I saw him...last. He didn't want me to intrude on your life or I'd have come before. And of course the winter lagged on, and getting over the Cascades can prove quite a challenge in the spring, as I'm sure you know. His brothers and sisters will be pleased to know he chose a good wife. At least that's what people have said of you," Mr. Bruner says.

"What people?" Eva asks. "No one here knows me, though I suppose they know of me now."

"Seems some people put up with D. L.'s ways because of you and your sensible head. If he's convicted—and we must face that possibility—I want you to know that you have a home to go to."

"Yes, I do." Eva imagines the hills lifting like petals behind the Muddy ranch house. She thinks of earning enough in the off-season to remain there, to pay for the small room she and Dee now share upstairs. If it happens, she can stay there. She'd have to talk with Hahn and Fried, make them see that keeping her on would help make up for what happened to Dee.

Mr. Bruner says, "There's no sense in your staying way out there in that godforsaken country. You'll just come back with me."

"I have work at the Muddy."

"You can work in Silverton. People won't know your story there." He had Dee's forcefulness, not always listening to what another said. "I've need for a housekeeper and cook, so you can find work right at home if you've a mind to."

"I'm sure my aunt and uncle would take me back should I need somewhere to go, but I don't. Not now."

"Your parents are—"

"Dead. Dee is all I have." She won't tell him about his grandchild she carries in her womb, not yet. "I don't believe he'll be convicted. I have faith that my prayers will be answered. But if he is, I'll stay on at the Muddy."

"I see why Dee chose you. He needs faithful devotion in his life."

"Apparently he didn't receive it from his family," Eva says before remembering that she questions her husband's innocence too.

Mr. Bruner bends to retrieve a maple-seed pod stuck in the boardwalk. "There are many sides to truth," he says. "Just like this seed, fat at one end and a thin wing at the other." He holds it up so she can see through the tiny fibers that form the end of the pod. "The one end makes the other end fly, but they're both part of the same thing."

"I don't know what you're saying," Eva says.

"Prayers are not always answered in the way we wish. My prayer is that my son will be safe, and that he'll harm no more people. He killed a man, Eva. That's a load for a father to carry. I don't know what I could have done to prevent it. But I can make amends, offer the man's kin something good for their lives."

She wants to ask him why he gave Dee away to neighbors. Why didn't he bring in a housekeeper so all his children could be together after their mother was sent away? Dee must have agonized over both the loss of his mother and then the separation from his father and his brothers and sisters. Maybe Dee's outbursts are remnants of that terrible time.

"He's not going to be convicted," Eva says, her square jaw firm.

"He might be better off there, Eva. Away from…temptations. His mother was…volatile too. Maybe that's why I kept bailing him out, because she had so much time with him during such an impressionable age. I should have acted sooner to protect him."

Mr. Bruner drops the maple seed and pulls Eva's arm through his, patting her hand as he does. "Let's face the truth here. Many people might be better off if Dee is convicted. Dee and you included."

Eva pulls her hand from her father-in-law's arm. How has this parent come to wish his son convicted? Mr. Bruner says, "He's going to need a miracle to keep him from confinement."

"Then I'll pray for that," Eva says. She walks back to the hotel alone.

Eva thinks of her mother, how she withered away after her father's conviction, refusing to eat, crying until neither fluid nor food found its way inside her. "A fasting girl," Aunt Fern said, and clucked her tongue at the plates of untouched food. "I've heard of this sort of thing happening, but I never thought it possible to starve to death from grief."

Eva wishes she didn't remember her mother's dying. She wishes she'd been strong enough to keep her mother alive, wishes she'd *been enough* to keep her alive, been someone her mother wanted to live for.

Her father's killing the man named Sherry in that Silvertooth Saloon was an act of passion, it was said, an argument got out of hand. His act sucked her mother into grief. She stepped away from Eva and the world. Within a year of the life conviction, Eva's mother was dead.

"If you want to honor your mother's life," Aunt Fern said as Eva grew older, "you make the best out of bad times. Don't you let yourself get so far from your faith that God can't reach you when He's searching for you hard. When people say, 'There's Cora Thompson's girl. Isn't she a fine one?' you can hold your head up knowing that your parents gave you what they could, and you did your best with it. Do you understand that, child?"

Eva nodded though she didn't understand. Not until now. Like her mother, she's followed a man to a land of promise. Like her mother, she's chosen a man who has killed another. She'll soon have a child to care for. They'll share that journey, too. But unlike her mother, Eva isn't going to disappear. She will survive. She has to. And maybe her belief that God does answer prayers will be enough for the miracle Francis Bruner doesn't think Dee deserves.

Eva arrives at the jail at Dee's mealtime, though she waves away Mrs. Meredith's offer of food. She isn't hungry. She is angry. Francis Bruner's testimony and her walk with him have given her insights into her husband and her own choices as well.

"You lied to me," she says as soon as Bunzie, the jailer, leaves the chair for her to sit on in front of Dee's cell. She hisses the words, not wanting eavesdropping. She hears movement in a cell farther down. She jerks her head.

"Either a rat, or the new inmate's feeling frisky," Dee says. He laughs.

"You let me believe your father was dead."

"He is to me."

"You call a dead person when you're in trouble, when you're in a jail in Clackamas County?"

"I didn't know who else to call. I was trying to get back to you. I knew you don't like to be alone."

"Oh, don't suggest my welfare prompted your act. No, you called on him before you even knew me." She folds her arms over her chest, taps her fingers.

"So you believed him."

Eva leans in, hands on her knees. "Even the Clackamas sheriff testified you showed not the slightest remorse over putting that poor man into a hospital. He's still not out! How do you think that played to the jury? Self-defense? I doubt that. Creegan said you bent down on one knee to steady your aim. No one's going to believe you didn't intend this, Dee. No one."

"He's gotten to you. My father gets to everyone, pushes them around, makes choices for them, and then he wonders why I don't want anything to do with him except as a last resort."

That vein in Dee's neck throbs, but it's his hands gripping the bars Eva stares at. Those knuckles with the fine brown hairs, those fists laid a man out. Perhaps many men. How could she not have seen that in him? What kind of blinders does she wear?

"I'm not talking about your father's actions. I'm talking about yours. You never even told me about hurting that man—or men. You've lied to me."

"I just didn't tell you everything. I was going to do it differently with you. Way out there on the Muddy, what could go wrong there? That's what I thought. I'll just do my job, wrangle horses, start building fences, and run sheep where Charlie tells me to. Come home to you at the end of the season. Would have been fine, too, if it wasn't for Tom Reilly."

Eva spits words out like bullets. "This. Is. Not. Tom. Reilly's. Fault. I. Am. Not. Talking. About. Tom."

"So who are you talking about then?"

"You," Eva says, her anger spent. "And me." A cricket makes its way across the stones. "I saw what I wanted to see, and I wanted to see you and me and a child one day all together, maybe having our own place at the base of those hyacinth hills. I cooked and saved my pennies so we could homestead a place. I saw a little garden and chickens and some sheep of our own. I saw what my mother and father dreamed of the first time they saw Muddy Creek and then lost it by my father's folly. But we could have become one of the independent sheepherders, you and me. We could have made our own way without anyone else telling us what to do."

"How would we have gotten a start on that?" Dee asks.

"My aunt and uncle might have helped us. Your father, he might have lent money for something worthy like that as easily as he put it out for all your...bail."

"Only if he could have controlled what we did with it and where we did it. It wouldn't have been beneath your Muddy hills." He says the last words with a bite, as though the purple ridges that shelter the John Day River are insignificant. Her anger rises again. "Life won't hand you flowers and finery, Eva. You have to make it."

"And what have you made of it? My desire for a home in the shadow of those hills didn't take a man's life. Your father might have put restrictions on a loan, but we'll never have the chance to know that now. You've been too busy doing things your own way. With your knuckles. Keeping secrets. How many other things don't I know about you?"

Quick as a striking snake, he reaches out and grabs her wrists. He holds them close to the bars. "Don't do this, Eva. I need you. My knuckles have never hurt you, and they never will, despite what my father tries to tell you." Her hands sweat, and pinpricks run up and down her spine. "I didn't kill Tom Reilly because I could. I killed him because if I hadn't he would have come and killed me, and the next sheepherder after that." He releases her, and she falls back into the chair. "That's the truth of it."

The hard oak rungs feel firm against her back. "You vowed, Eva, to stay with me through all times. You vowed before your God. You change your mind now, and you'll have more than me to answer to. Think about that when you testify tomorrow. Just think about that." He stands up, then turns his back to her.

Eva informs Barnes that when she tells the court those bad things about Dee, she will present herself as a child, someone whose opinion needn't be given much weight. Dee hopes that's how the jury will see her, as a child. The men lean forward on their chairs. Childlike is no good. Dee writes to Barnes: *Jury can't hear her.*

Could be best, Barnes writes back.

Barnes is right. The jury might not give her soft words the same weight as his father's, blasting them out as though he were God himself passing judgment. Barnes plans to discount all their testimony anyway in his summation, reword what his father and that sheriff and even what Eva says that might work against him, because it doesn't really matter what he's done before. It's this case, Tom Reilly's actions, and Dee's response that matter.

Dee smiles at Eva. He wishes he hadn't grabbed her last night. She looked frightened, and he didn't intend that. She riles him so sometimes, makes him want to punch a board. But never her.

Dark stains beneath her arms show on her cream-colored dress when she places her hand on the Bible and swears to tell the truth. He bets she worries over that, over not appearing her best. He wishes he'd thought to tell Barnes to start an account for her at Hahn and Fried's General Merchandise. A new dress, a new hat—both would grant her confidence, help her remember that life with D.L. Bruner hasn't been so bad.

Maybe the stains bring her sympathy. She's just a kid, a young wife.

"Mrs. Bruner, thank you for being here today," Menefee begins. "I have a few questions for you, and then Mr. Barnes may cross-examine, and then you'll be allowed to return to your chair. Would you like a glass of water?" Eva shakes her head. She wants it to be over, Dee can see that. "Very well. Let's begin. You're the wife of D. L. Bruner, is that right?" Eva nods, and the judge tells her to answer with words.

"Yes," Eva says, "for nearly two years." Dee hopes this goes quickly so Barnes can pick up the pieces and maybe put them back together into some organized sense.

"Thank you. That would have been my next question. Now then, have you ever known your husband to be impulsive, quick to judgment?" Menefee asks.

"He proposed quicker than my guardians might have wished," Eva says. A chuckle flickers through the gallery.

Good answer. Truthful but light.

"Yes, well, I meant in the arena outside of courtship, Mrs. Bruner. Has he ever done something that made you question his judgment?"

"The same," Eva says. "I didn't know why a grown man with a life of his own, working since he was thirteen, would wish to marry someone like me with no experience in life, someone needing to be taken care of. One does wonder about a man's judgment, knowing that."

A couple of the jury members smile and nod. There is a pretty good chance they had fifteen-year-old brides too. Chance for more property to put in their estates, too, with a wife to stake a claim beside her husband's land.

"In no other situation?" Menefee spits those words out. That Eva, she is smarter than Dee thought to annoy Menefee so quickly.

"D— My husband, like most of the ranch hands I've come to know, will ride a wild horse that I think would be better left to graze," Eva says. "He's risked the John Day River in flood stage. But sometimes work demands one take some risks. Even as a ranch cook, there are things I'd rather not have to do, like cook over a fire knowing rattlesnakes might make their way to warmth."

"Yes. Indeed."

She is careful not to use his name. Dee hates that name, is grateful she remembers. He sinks back into the chair.

"Let me try another approach," Menefee says. "Were you surprised when your husband came home to announce that he'd killed Tom Reilly?"

"Stunned," Eva says.

"Could you speak up, please? The jury can't hear you."

"Stunned," Eva repeats after she clears her throat. "I'd never known him to hurt anyone until that day." Her voice almost sings into the courtroom, and she looks straight at the jury.

"So the testimony of Francis Bruner and the sheriff of Clackamas County about his nearly killing a man with his fists was all new to you?" Menefee says this with a smirk, and Dee wants to rise up over the chair and strangle him.

"It was, yes," Eva says.

"What did he say to you that day, D. L. Bruner? What did he confess to you on April 4?"

"He asked me to call the sheriff, because he'd killed Tom Reilly."

"He didn't say he'd 'murdered' Tom Reilly? Or that he'd 'shot' Tom?"

"No. That he'd 'killed' him. He gave me no specifics then."

"And has he since?"

"Only that he killed Tom in self-defense."

"Was he…regretful, your husband, that day?"

"Objection," Barnes stands. "How can she know the state of mind of her husband, Judge?"

"I'll rephrase," Menefee says. "What did he do that day that told you he was either saddened or perhaps surprised that he had killed a man? Or can you recall any behavior to which you put that interpretation?"

"He called the sheriff when I couldn't," Eva says, "as though he understood that was the responsible thing to do. And then he sat down to wait." She hesitates, then breathes in deep. "When Deputy Glisan arrived and handcuffed him to the buckboard, he went willingly, expecting justice to be served. What else would an innocent man do?"

Barnes has no questions for her, so she is dismissed. She walks past the table, and Dee smiles at her, hoping the jury doesn't think ill of him for doing so. He's never been so proud of her. He'll survive this, with a strong woman like that. Choosing her was one good thing he'd done. She'll make a powerful mother for his son.

8

Yearning

During the weekend, Eva sits and prays, remembering her dream. She wonders that she's withstood this trial each night alone in her hotel room. The writing helps, though she still sleeps little. The wallpaper swirls and crazy quilt spinning themselves into worry.

She visits the mercantile to charge pencils and paper. While there, she gazes at books of calico cloth and runs her fingers over a baby carriage made with seasoned maple, the placard reading, "made with fine rattan," and upholstered in "dark peacock blue." Cardinal, wine, bronze, gold, steel blue, or olive can be ordered too. It has a Kinley automatic brake for its sturdy wire wheels and a parasol with fancy scalloped edges. She lets her fingers touch the fringe, then steps away to lift the price tag. She saw it in the Sears and Roebuck catalog last year for $4.95 and thought it extravagant. Far beyond what she could ever pay for. The tag read $8.00. A week's wages. If she's fortunate to keep her Muddy job.

"It's lovely, isn't it?" the proprietor says. "It can be put aside for just a few pennies. You can pick it up when the payment is complete. It's a gift?" he asks.

"No. I mean, yes. It's just something pretty," she says. She lowers her eyes, caught thinking lovely, future-filled thoughts. She returns to the hotel.

Twice now Francis Bruner has waited for her in the dining room for breakfast. On the second day, when she succumbs to his insistence that she break her fast at his table, he orders flannel cakes without her asking. He talks of Silverton, Oregon, where he farms. He tells her bits and pieces about his other children, Dee's brothers and sisters. One attends Saint Mary's Academy. Another farms, like his father. He orders Eva more tea she doesn't want. She should be stronger, tell him that she can order for herself, but she needs to save her strength for the jury's pending verdict. She lets him crowd her.

Monday, Eva dresses in her dark-blue wrapper, aware that the stains on her cream blouse are now too large. She can no longer cover the scent with her lavender powder. Mr. Barnes tells her to buy a new dress, but she doesn't want any more tongues wagging about what she does in town. The newspaper reported that she "boldly walked the streets of Prineville," as if both she and Dee should wait quietly behind bars.

Later today, the defense will begin its case with witnesses like Charlie, who will verify that Tom Reilly made threats, that sheep had crossed that place for years, and that everyone took Tom's claim as a challenge, as Muddy property bordered it on three sides. Dee will take the stand. Eva will just listen and hope the jury gets the case before the day is over.

Eva shakes her head before the mirror. She can't decide where to keep her thoughts. Should she plan for a conviction? Is that disloyalty or common sense?

God is faithful. He grants miracles. She remembers Hebrews chapter eleven to remind herself of God's promises, faithfully kept.

To avoid Francis Bruner, Eva skips breakfast. Her stomach isn't holding food well anyway, so she walks to the courthouse, avoiding puddles deposited by a rain shower in the night. She enters alone to take her seat. Mr. Bruner comes in behind her. He must have seen her walking by the restaurant door.

"Maybe this will all be over today," Mr. Bruner says as he settles in beside her.

Eva gathers up her skirts to stand. She doesn't want Dee to see her sitting beside his father. He'll think she's betrayed him. Before she can move away, Dee enters. He scans the courtroom, his eyes find hers.

He lifts his cuffed hands in a bound wave and nods, then sees his father and his eyes cloud over. He faces front, reminding Eva of a rejected boy, pouting. Dee lets the bailiff take his handcuffs off. He doesn't move until the judge enters and all are asked to stand.

When his turn comes, Dee swaggers to the witness chair, raises his hand to be sworn in. Eva wonders what his words mean as he swears on a Bible he thinks doesn't have anything to say to him. He looks at her before he sits, still wears that mocking smile. She leans forward, longing to hear something she doesn't already know, something with the power to deliver her from wondering into wisdom.

"Let's hear the truth now, since we've been hearing lots of other things in this trial so far," Barnes says after the usual introductions.

"Objection! Summary—"

"Let's move along, George," the judge says.

"Can you tell us what happened a few days before April 4? On the Muddy Ranch, in a conversation with your foreman, Charlie O'Neal."

"Objection," Menefee says.

"It's overruled, Frank. Good grief, you had Charlie on the stand two days ago. Bruner can tell his side of what was said, surely. You can cross. I know you know how to do that."

Menefee sits, his pencil tapping on the table. The judge raises an eyebrow. The tapping stops.

"Charlie said several herders had been threatened by Tom Reilly," Dee begins. "Old Tom was brandishing his rifle under the noses of those herders without much regard for how they took it, except to stay away. He said they couldn't pass across that snip of land and that they'd have to go around Black Rock. It's a good four days to move around there and the possibility of lost sheep, what with coyotes prowling, not to mention the sparse grass. That would put our herds at risk. Tom knew that, of course. That was why he made his claim the way he did. He was deliberate in his intentions, Tom Reilly was."

"Just answer the question, D. L.," Barnes advises.

"Right. Sorry. So Charlie told me that he wanted me to take this herd up and to crowd Tom's flock. They were lambing there on the other part of his claim, so my flock could have messed his up, but not if we just pushed on through like we always had and he'd set his lambing in a safer spot. My boss told me to arm myself 'cause Tom had a temper."

"And did you?"

"Yes, sir. I borrowed a .38 Smith & Wesson from Andy, there." He nods to a ranch hand, hat still on, in the back row of the courtroom. Eva notes as she turns that a number of the Muddy hands are here. Mildred told her a few had quit the Muddy over this incident, believing the stakes were going higher, being asked to crowd or, worse, defend against independent sheepherders that might land a man on trial. Dee continues, "I kept that weapon in my pocket."

"But you don't own a gun?"

"Not a pistol. Just a hunting rifle, that's all."

"So what happened the morning of April 4, 1901?"

"I was moving my herd forward like I'd always done, like I was supposed to. We had maybe fifteen hundred sheep, and the dogs worked hard to keep them moving forward. We got to the end of the ravine, and Tom came acharging across his claim, rifle in hand. We shouted at each other, him telling me to back off, calling me names, me telling him I wasn't doing anything to aggrieve him, and I had to get my sheep to spring pasture. He came toward me then, pointing it right at me." Dee gestures for the jury.

"Did you take that as a threat?"

"Anytime a man points a loaded gun at you, it's a threat, even if he just happens to swing it your way while it's laying snakelike still across his arms," Dee says. "He was asking for trouble, like an Irishman does, thinking he can do whatever he wants, letting the shell casings fall where they may."

Some of the Muddy hands make noises, and the judge gavels them quiet. For the first time she realizes the jury is heavy with Irish names. None from the Muddy or the outlying areas were even in the jury pool, now that she recalls. One or two from Antelope and from Ashwood, neighboring towns, but the bulk came from Prineville and Paulina and Post, little towns populated by independent sheepherders. Irishmen, like Pat and Tom and Creegan.

"What happened next?" Barnes says. "Tell us in your own words."

Eva wonders if Barnes rehearsed Dee, told him not to use big words, the ones that make him sound too smart. The jury might find a man guilty for his word choices.

"Tom patted the side of his rifle and told me, 'I'll fix you!' Well, I knew what that meant. So I grabbed the muzzle. I was pushing it away from me. Man says he's going to fix me, and I take him seriously. So I drew my pistol at the same time, and I fired it to scare him. But he moved forward in the struggle, and my pistol shot grazed his nose. I didn't really notice it until he bent to pick up the rifle. He'd dropped it when I shot the pistol. I saw blood on his nose. The coroners could have seen his bloody nose if they'd been looking, both for gunpowder and for damage caused by a .38. They'd see that I was doing what I did in self-defense." Dee crossed his arms over his chest and twisted his neck as though to free it of the chafing collar.

"I'm sure the coroners did their best, Mr. Bruner," Barnes says. "Now, what happened next? Take your time."

"Reilly said he was going to get more ammo, but he couldn't keep hold of his rifle, and he ran. I picked it up, and while Reilly was running downhill I ejected the live cartridge, I guess. Not thinking. Then I loaded the chamber with another."

"That live shell marks the spot where the two of you were talking, here"—Barnes points to a spot on the big chart of the property that the jury sees—"is that right?"

"Yes, sir. Then I just fired a bunch of rounds in the air, to scare him. I wasn't intending to kill him, I wasn't, though I was prepared to defend myself, I tell you that. And when he shouted that he'd get John's rifle and be back, I figured he was coming to 'fix me.' So I ran forward maybe twenty-five yards and fired, hoping to scare him into staying at his tent, but I missed him on purpose. Then I fired again and missed him then, too. I was going in my head, back and forth, from trying to scare him to keeping him from coming back to fix me. Things got kind of jumbled up. Then he was laying there. I thought he was fooling at first. I mean, he was quite a distance from me by then. I didn't think I could even hit a coyote running that far away. So I assumed his laying there was to lure me up there so he could grab his rifle out of my hands and shoot me. A lot goes through a man's mind when he's been threatened like Tom threatened me."

Mr. Barnes asks a few more questions. Dee lets his shoulders drop. He isn't fidgeting now. Eva thinks he looks…smaller, someone a juryman might take pity on.

Frank Menefee stands to cross-examine. As he lays his pencil on the oak table, the room darkens, and Eva hears the distant rumble of thunder followed by the rush of raindrops against the window panes. A few people scatter to close the windows, and Menefee has to wait, then raise his voice to talk above the downpour.

"Mr. Bruner, we have an eyewitness who says you knelt down on that third shot to take a steady aim to shoot Tom Reilly in the back. A man trying to miss doesn't kneel down to steady his rifle unless he hopes to make the shot, wouldn't you agree?"

"That's one reason, sir," Dee says. He stiffens now.

"You have another?" Menefee says, his eyebrows lifted. "Pray tell me what that might be."

"I was winded, sir. I'd been running, hard, uphill. My flock was threatened. My life was threatened. And I'd just shot a man and grazed his face. I was breathing hard, and I knew I couldn't keep it up, and I didn't know what Tom would do when he came back. So I just got down on one knee to catch myself, to take in a breath."

"And while you were regaining your…wind, you set your rifle to your shoulder, and it just happened to go off and kill Tom Reilly in the back of the head?"

"I was trying to miss him. I needed a steady hold to make sure I didn't hit him. I'm a good shot, but not that good." Dee grins openly now. Eva shudders.

"You'd have us believe that you were steadying your hand *to miss?* Is this really what you're trying to convince the jury of, Mr. Bruner?"

"I was just steadying my hand," Dee says. He nods to the jury with that mocking smile. *He doesn't know what he's doing. He thinks this is all a pointless game, that Barnes through Hahn and Fried's connections will get him off.*

"Well, apparently it wasn't steady enough, Mr. Bruner, because Tom Reilly is dead with what you'd have us believe is a lucky shot from a winded man."

Barnes and Menefee make their summations at the end of the day, and Eva hangs on every word. Judge Bradshaw gives the instructions to the jury May 13. He discusses three possible verdicts, with lengthy explanations for them all.

Eva abbreviates what she hears, to remember. First-degree murder, willful and premeditated. Second-degree murder, purposefully and maliciously carried out in the heat of the moment. Manslaughter, caused by provocation to make it irresistible to kill another. Or innocent, of course. They can find him innocent as well, though Eva doesn't remember the judge saying that.

It's nearly midnight when the jury leaves the courtroom to deliberate and Dee is taken back to jail.

Francis Bruner takes Eva's arm. "It's late," he says. "Let me walk you to the hotel."

"I think Mr. Barnes—"

"He's left with D. L. I'm sure he'd want you looked after. Dee would too."

Eva doesn't really want to walk past the rowdy saloons alone. The storm has passed, and while the air now smells pure and clean as Fels Naphtha soap, the mud that lines the puddles requires some skill in maneuvering. An arm to lean on might be welcome. Should she accept assistance from the enemy?

Eva's brought her reticule. She puts her slippers in it and dons a pair of boots.

"Tiny feet you have, Eva," Mr. Bruner says as she pulls her skirt up just above the mud. He has a way of blending fatherly concerns with the flattery of a manly man. She's heard ranch hands talk about their girls this way when they've forgotten Eva can hear them through the windows in the summer kitchen. She couldn't always understand the words, but the tones give their flirting eyes and licking lips away.

She ignores Francis Bruner's comments, takes his arm firmly to keep it at a distance, then lets him lead her across the street. She wishes she'd waited with Barnes and Dee at the jail. She knows this isn't visiting time, but it's been a strange day all around, what with the trial going so late and the jury just now getting the instructions. She looks up to see the lights burning in the deliberation room. She speeds a prayer their way. *Help them find the truth. Help them find the truth I can believe.*

At the hotel Mr. Bruner says, "You're welcome to wait in my room. It might be hard to be alone through this."

"I don't think—"

"Oh, I caught you, dear." It's the jailer's wife, winded. "The mister sent me. Said Mr. Barnes wanted you to know you can wait at the jail. Accommodations might not be as dapper as the hotel, but spending time with your mister might be nice. I'll bring you back there, if you're wanting."

"Yes," Eva says, "that's exactly what I want."

They play euchre with a deck of cards, Barnes and Dee. The jailer's wife heads home, and a prisoner in a far cell snores on. Eva watches, thinks, then Dee suggests that with the jailer, they could have a poker foursome.

"What have you got to bet?" the jailer says. "I'm not accepting rat scat as chips."

"Keep a tab," Dee says. "I'll pay you when I get out. Eva and I will, won't we, *ma chérie?*"

"D. L.," Barnes says as he deals, "this could come out badly for you. I think we have to consider the—"

"I'm not talking about it," Dee says. "I did what I was supposed to do. What happened was an accident. They can't condemn a man for that."

Eva's thoughts are swirls of worry. The not knowing will soon turn into *what now?* If he's freed, will he want to stay at the Muddy? Will Pat Reilly and his friends try to avenge Tom's death? Family blood demands that kind of loyalty of some. They'd have to leave. Go where? And if he is convicted...what would she do for five or ten or even twenty years without him? Could he get life? Death? She feels her skin grow cold. Not death, surely not death. What would she do then? With each slap of a card she breathes a prayer: *Don't separate my family more; don't separate my family more.*

Dee nods off, and the jailer snores in his own chair, feet outstretched. Only Barnes and Eva stay awake. He pats her clasped hands. "We'll get you through this," he tells her.

At 5:00 a.m. the bailiff comes around to say the jury has a ruling.

"Let's go," Barnes says, pushing against his thighs to stand. He calls Dee awake.

"I have a good feeling about this," Dee tells her. He brushes against her arm and leans to kiss her check before the bailiff puts the handcuffs on and leads him out.

The warmth of his touch lingers as Eva walks to the courthouse. She clings to his optimism and holds her head up, though her eyes feel heavy as wet wool. She should have tried to catch some sleep. Barnes steps back to walk beside her. The lawyer offers her his arm. She tries to put into words the difference that she feels between Barnes's offer of assistance and Dee's father's. Dee might be right. His father might have tried to define their lives too much if he'd been an early part of it. But still, her aunt and uncle could have helped them. She wonders how they are. Her relatives might have helped her build her dream, one she'd never even spoken aloud to Dee until it was too late for him to even do a thing about it.

The jury files in, not looking at her. That's when she knows. They keep their eyes from hers, not because she's a mere woman but because she is the child-wife of a convicted murderer.

9

Certainty

"How will I... How will I live?" Eva says. Her heart hasn't stopped racing since the jury foreman read "guilty of murder in the second degree." She feels faint, and then the judge pronounces the sentence, telling Dee, "You'll spend the rest of your natural life confined."

Life! Her father's sentence. Her husband will go to the same prison near Salem where her father was held until he died. Her world spins like a child's top, wobbling out of control.

Francis Bruner stands beside her before she even moves toward Dee. "You'll come back with me to Silverton," he says.

"I... My things are at the Muddy." She pulls away from him. "I have an obligation—"

"You owe the Muddy nothing," Dee says, turning, hearing.

She doesn't know if he is urging her to return with his father or telling her she needn't worry over the Muddy. His voice grates like sand in the bottom of her slippers.

"They owe me," Dee charges. The vein in his neck throbs. "I did what I did for them. We'll appeal, Eva."

"Did you really try to miss him?" Eva asks, not sure why she bothers now.

"I was winded," Dee snaps. "Resting, that's all. It was a lucky shot at that range."

"An appeal will be costly," Mr. Bruner says.

"Hahn can afford it," Dee says. "You'll start it, Barnes."

"Maybe not," Barnes cautions. "The jury's vote on the first round was apparently eight for murder one and two for murder two with two to acquit. So at least ten of the jurymen believed right off that you lacked sufficient provocation. They believe you thought it through, Dee, and killed a man. We have no grounds to appeal, not really."

"Not even based on that shoddy coroner's jury?"

"Limited," Barnes says.

"You received a good defense, son," Mr. Bruner says. "Now it's time to face up to the consequences of your acts. This is your duty now."

Eva watches a dark and violent look cross her husband's face as he turns his eyes on his father. "I don't need the likes of you telling me what my obligations are or aren't," he says. "I don't need you for anything."

"Dee," she says, "don't—"

"I don't need anything from anyone." He turns his face from her, stares at the ceiling. *Is he blinking back tears?*

"D.L.," Eva begins, but she speaks to stone, and when she touches his arm he jerks away, rattling the chains that hold him.

"Take me to the jail," he tells the bailiff.

Eva is reminded of her uncle's root-cellar door, dark and wide with a blast of cold air hitting her in the face just before it closes against darkness. Dee isn't interested in what happens to her. She's on her own.

Eva considers her options as she moves restlessly around the hotel room packing up her writings and few clothes. She doesn't know when she'll see Dee again. Barnes tells her she must think of herself now.

She can go back to the Muddy, Barnes tells her. She wonders how long that will last before they set her packing with a baby on the way. She can return to her aunt and uncle's farm in Dufur. They'll gather her to hearth and home until her baby comes. But she'd be one of those women who lives off others, cleaning and cooking for people who'd rather do it themselves but permit it in the name of charity.

She'd be an old maid aunt, in a way. A widow of sorts, languishing, abandoned, alone.

She can disappear as her mother did, become one of those fasting girls who refuses food until her body no longer demands it. But that would injure her baby in its sheltered place beneath her heart. For the first time, certainty rises in her: She'll take care of this baby.

Eva brushes her hair, long strokes as she sits at the dressing table, tears springing from her eyes. She can visit Dee more often if she returns to her aunt and uncle or even if she goes with Francis Bruner. She isn't sure Dee will even want to see her. That closed door of a face still flashes a pain as deep as sorrow in her side. She wipes her eyes and sighs.

Dee said nothing to help her know what to do with her life, nothing about being sorry for not being with her now, nothing. Her husband might as well have gotten the death penalty, he is that dead to her.

She catches her breath. She mustn't think that way. He's alive, still flesh and blood, and he is her husband, the father of her child. Miracles do happen. The jury might have erred. She might be called at any moment to return, be told that the jury has a new verdict. There'll be a knock at the door. They miscounted!

She catches a look at herself in the mirror. Drawn cheeks, eyes sunk deep. Brittle brown strands falling long around her tear-blotched face. She's tired, so very tired. She should pray. For what? Her lone image in the mirror mocks her hollow faith.

A knock on her door interrupts. The miracle!

"Who is it?" Eva asks, the brush still in her hand.

"Francis Bruner. I've come to take you home."

On the way from Prineville to Antelope, the stage road passes the Muddy Station, where fresh horses are changed for the long pull up the grade alongside Muddy Creek toward Antelope and beyond. Eva has a little time to talk with Mildred and to pack her other belongings.

"Leave somethin' here," Mildred urges as they stand in one of the second-floor bedrooms of the ranch house. "You'll change your mind about things a hundred times, I tell you. It's the way it is with a woman. She sweeps the hearth with a fast broom when life hands her what your D.L. handed you. When the dust settles, you'll put up that broom and move on. You might well want to do that right here, crazy as it may seem now. You didn't do nothing wrong, you remember that. You weren't sentenced to a life behind those jail bars. A body's got to think of her own future, I tell you. So leave something that'll call you back."

"The hills will call me back," Eva says. And with those words she knows that leaving the purple hills, the craggy rocks, the streams and rivers, may well be harder than saying good-bye to Dee. She starts to cry.

"Oh, sweetie," Mildred scoops her into her arms. "You didn't do nothing wrong. God's awatching. He knows. You go see where D. L. will be. Get some things settled in your mind. Then you come back." She leans in to Eva and whispers, "A body's got to depend on someone reliable, like herself, at a time like this. But you can lean on friends, too."

Eva fears the sobs won't stop. She grieves Dee's actions, her anger toward him, her waiting so long to see him, the loss of all they'd hoped for. All she'd hoped for with him, here.

Mildred pats her back. "It's all right. A body's got to cry some at a time like this to heal." After a while Mildred says, "Take a look around. What can you leave here that'll call you back? What about this?" Mildred points to a bedside table with thin, narrow legs and two small drawers.

"It was my mother's," Eva says.

"Good. I'll keep it safe for you till you come home."

The big woman with a square of apron pinned to the bodice of her wrapper pats Eva's arm as she carries her carpetbag out to the stage. "These dry hills can heal a soul, they can. You're young. You'll get through this. A life without a man around ain't half as bad as some make it out to be. And you got the luxury of saying you're married to send off any unwanted suitors. Oh, I s'pose I'm speaking out of turn here. My Winston says I'm like that some. You forgive me, sweetie, will you? And you write. Don't you lose touch with your Mildred, now. And I'm glad to see you putting on a few pounds."

Eva steps back onto the stage. Francis Bruner pulls himself up behind her. She speaks little as they head toward the town of Antelope. "Looks like some of Bill Brown's horses made their way north," Mr. Bruner says. Eva looks at him. He points out the window to a herd of maybe fifty or sixty horses, grazing. They startle away as the stage rattles its approach. "I hear he had ten thousand of them ranging from Lake County all the way north."

"I wouldn't know," Eva says.

"So many he couldn't keep track of them in a land this big, no fences to hold them. Now they're free for the taking, or so I've heard."

Eva stares at the animals, their dark manes flowing in the wind as they twist and turn, free to roam where they might. *Free.* Something Dee will never be again. Maybe she won't be either.

The route takes them west toward Mount Hood, then down the Bakeoven grade into the hamlet of Sherar's Bridge, across the Deschutes River, then up the other side to Dufur. She'll stop at Dufur and her aunt and uncle's farm and try to decide from there what to do next.

Eva leans out of the Concord stage door and looks back at the rugged purple hills of the Muddy Ranch. A rush of memories rise on the trailing dust. Fifteen and just wedded, rolling in the opposite direction with Dee to make a life there on the Muddy. The stage rolled by sparse trees, not the high fir timbers and pine that clustered around the town of her aunt and uncle. Spots of juniper trees and miles of clustered sage broke up the wide open spaces. They crossed Currant Creek and dipped down into meadowland, natural hayfields irrigated by unseen rivers. She wondered then if the barren hills might not be jealous of the meadow's fertile ways. They crested the grade, and Eva saw even more layers of hillsides shedding shades of pink disrobing at the skyline into blue. Hills like the petals of a fading rose. Purple spilled into pink, then mauve, then magenta, layer upon layer until the craggy rocks above Muddy Creek disappeared into eternity. A black rock mountain rose beside them, and an antelope bounded across the twisting road not far from where a man spilled his blood, murdered. She shivered. It was so beautiful once, and now…

She feels ill. The baby perhaps recognizes her grief. "Oh," Eva says, letting her hand lie on her abdomen.

"Are you all right?" Mr. Bruner asks.

Eva nods. She makes her mind stay with the pleasant thought of her child and her hope it will be a boy. Dee will want a son, to follow in his footsteps, won't he? Hadn't he once said that every Frenchman wants a son to carry on his name? Eva wonders if the world is prepared for another son like Dee. She lowers her eyes, fearful her thoughts can be read on her face. A girl might be easier to raise alone.

Mildred's words come back to her. She's done nothing to be ashamed of, even though Dee has withdrawn his love.

Well, she'd waited a month before coming to see him. She hopes that didn't set the jury on the path they chose. She hopes her words didn't send her husband away.

No, Dee made his choices. Now she would have to make hers.

She hears a meadowlark chirping from a sage as they start the descent into Antelope. A verse comes to her. "I will lift up mine eyes unto the hills, from whence cometh my help. My help cometh from the LORD.… The LORD shall preserve thee from all evil." It is an old verse. Yes, she heard it as a child, her aunt quoting it to her mother.

"Feeling all right?" Mr. Bruner asks. "You look flushed. I can pull the window flap closed." He reaches across her, brushes her shoulder with his elbow.

She puts her hand up to stop him. "I'm fine," she says. "I'm quite sure I can take care of things myself."

Eva turns for one last gaze at the Muddy hills. This landscape called to her from the time she was three. She was sure her life was meant to be here. How has it gone wrong? Perhaps like that crazy quilt of being, the patches of her life are formed by ragged edges of disaster, and the silver threads of faith have all pulled out.

10

Resolve

As the stage approaches her uncle's home in Dufur, Eva remembers. She was barely five the year her mother died. Memories of her mother flutter in and out of her awareness the way the dancer, Loie Fuller, uses colored lights and strands of silk to tempt and taunt. The light of the lantern in her aunt's home flickered while her mother pulled a silk scarf through the air for Eva's joy.

"Of course the strands would be nearly transparent," her mother said, "and the lights would have colored paper over them, to change from red to blue to green while the audience watched."

"You saw her, Mama?" Eva asked, though she knew the answer.

"No!" Her mother switched from bewitching to annoyed. "I'm deprived of such things out here where your father brought me." Darkness crossed her face, and then, as though her aunt had lit the lamp, her mother's face took on a glowing look. "I have a friend, in Milwaukee, who attended Miss Fuller's performance, so I can imagine it." She brushed the silk scarf across Eva's neck. Her mama sighed, then rolled it into a ball and pushed it to the back of a slender dresser drawer. The scent of lavender lifted from the powdered lining. Eva loved lying in her mother's bed, even knowing that at any moment her mother might disappear inside her mind or insist that Eva run to ask Aunt Fern to fix her hot tea, as she was "feeling weepy." That's what she called it.

"Is that Aunt Betsy?" Eva said, trying to keep her mother's look a joyous one.

Her mother nodded. "Not your real aunt, but as good a friend as I have ever had."

A better friend than me? Instead Eva asked, "A better friend than… Papa?"

Her mother bristled. "Your papa betrayed us," she said. "We wouldn't be here in this…this…place if it wasn't for him. I'd be dining at the Rauch Haus every Friday evening in Milwaukee instead of serving field hands who hardly care that they've just been delivered one of the finest German kraut dishes."

"Let's go back to 'Waukee, Mama," Eva said.

"We can't. Not with your father…" Her mother motioned with her hands for Eva to move off the coverlet. Eva looked away, her eyes leaking tears, her mother disappearing into a place Eva wasn't allowed to enter. Her mother sat before her in the flesh, but Eva was alone.

Now, twelve years later, Eva enters the room where she found her mother wasted away one morning. Eva now calls this room her own. It was, until she married Dee. Francis Bruner is downstairs plying his truth, she imagines, trying to convince her relatives that he can best take care of her. Perhaps he can. She must decide.

Mr. Barnes says that Dee will end up at the Salem prison sometime in the next few weeks. The sheriff is waiting until he has another prisoner to transport to make the trip more economical. Barnes will notify her at her aunt and uncle's home, and she can come to see Dee then. "Don't visit until he agrees to see you," Mr. Barnes suggests. "Coor-rect?"

Eva agrees, but will Dee ever?

She can't remember visiting her father at that Salem correctional facility. Vague memories of her mother dressing and putting on a special scent come to her: her mother crying, then melting like a tallow candle to the floor; Eva worrying that her mother's throwing plates outside the kitchen door is because of something Eva's done; her mother disappearing into the sheet, feather pale, her wrists as thin as chicken bones. Eva's tears cloud the vision of this room, a silk scarf of memory transforms her view. Too many sad memories here. She can't come back. She'll go with Francis Bruner, but not for the reasons he's proposed.

"Eva? Come on down, dear. We need to talk."

Eva breathes a prayer as she descends the steps: "Help me sound firm."

The three of them—aunt, uncle, and father-in-law—wait in the parlor. Their eyes rise as one when she approaches. She wears a wrapper tied loosely so as not to bring attention to her changing state.

"Your father-in-law has made a generous offer," her uncle says. "He has a big farm near Silverton, which will be closer to the prison so you can visit Dee. He can afford to keep you—"

"Sit, dear," her aunt says. "You men just jump right into things. We women need a little time, don't we, Eva?"

"I was saying," her uncle says, "he can do for you now while your husband can't. There won't be any state assist for you, Eva. Maybe a judge would grant a divorce decree so you could marry again, have another care for you, but—"

"Divorce?" Eva says. "Dee's my husband."

"In name only now," her father-in-law says. "So unless you're prepared to spend the rest of your life alone, divorce is an option you should consider. Decisiveness at times like this can be the best for all involved." Eva wonders if he justifies the commitment of Dee's mother to an asylum with those words. He continues, "What I offered you in Prineville is an offer I shared with your relatives. I will provide you with a respectable livelihood and a place to live. Until you regain your own respectability."

"I wasn't aware I'd lost it," Eva says.

Aunt Fern leans in. "Your mother struggled with this same thing, Eva. People would walk across the street rather than share the boardwalks with her after they learned what your father did. She agonized over the lonely hours, the weeks of being powerless to change things."

"She looked after me," Eva says. "She was doing something."

"In that she found no peace," her uncle says. Eva flinches. "After a time she saw that you'd be safe with us, and her life became this"—he brushes the air with his wide paw—"this…wispy thread. We worried that we'd brought that upon her, looking after you."

"Maybe if she'd seen that you needed her, she wouldn't have just disappeared, but we…well, we don't want that to happen to you, dear. We want you to find a purpose," her aunt concludes with a nod of her chin.

"You don't want me here?" Eva says.

"Of course we do. It's just people wouldn't have to know your…history there." Her aunt stretches a lace-edged hanky through her hands, over and over.

"It's a sensible thing to do, Eva. People would look well on you for being sensible now, what with your husband having been so…" Her uncle searches for the word.

"Reckless," Eva offers.

"Reckless. You want to appear calm and steady so you can get through this with people thinking highly of you."

"What does it matter what people think of me?" Eva says.

"You have your whole life ahead of you. You don't want to make foolish choices," Mr. Bruner says. "Someday you'll understand that it matters how the world sees you. Dee never did."

She stares at these adults who say they care for her but do not realize that her struggles now are not driven by what strangers think. Yes, she worried over such trivia at the trial, but that is behind her. This is where she sits now. If she begins a journey to please others just to ease the pain, she will waste away as surely as her mother. Perhaps Dee did that, tried to please powerful men until he acted without regard for her or Tom Reilly or himself, to win their approval. Her aunt pats her hand, the lavender sachet tucked at her wrist wafting into memories of her mother. Eva's idea, like Loie Fuller's silks, crystallizes in the clarity and light.

She takes in a deep breath. "I know you have my interest at heart.

You as well, Mr. Bruner. But the most foolish thing I could do now would be to consider a divorce or even commit myself to a course that might seem safe but would keep me from standing on my own. Besides, Mr. Barnes might still get an appeal."

"Oh, dear, you're not hoping for a pardon, are you?" her aunt asks.

"A pardon? No, I just meant Dee has his whole life before him too, and people can change no matter where they are. Isn't that right? And maybe my showing him that I can make my own way, even with a child, will help him see that he has a say in that, making me a stronger person in the end so his life will have meaning too."

"You're expecting a child?" Francis Bruner asks. "Well, that settles it. You must come live with me."

Eva turns to Dee's father. "I told Dee that I wished we had asked you for help earlier in our lives and not just when he was in trouble. Dee said you wouldn't have been willing, and that if you had, you'd have controlled the purse strings tighter than a tether to a cantankerous calf. I need to know if he was right."

Francis Bruner stands, grasps his suspenders as though they are ropes. "What are you asking?"

"Will you help me, us, in the way I think might work for me—without tethers? Or does your offer have but one rope to bind it?"

Eva continues on to Silverton to live with Francis Bruner. He's agreed to her terms. She'll work for him through winter, but in the summer, after the baby comes, she will leave, pursuing her own plans back on the Muddy.

She writes Dee weekly, shares with him the progress of the baby growing. She counts on the promise of that warm being to thaw her husband's frozen heart.

Dee doesn't answer.

Barnes tells her not to visit until he wants her. She waits.

June, July, August. Eva writes to Dee of how her garden grows, of eggs gathered, of supper conversations she has with his father. She speaks of hopeful things, of how she longs to see him, and if he'll write to tell her when she should come, she'll be there within the week.

She sends him paper and pencils. They're returned as items "not receivable by inmates." She remembers at least once or twice her father had written. She remembers her mother's hands shaking with some papers in it.

"Do you know what the prisoners might do all day?" Eva asks her father-in-law as they share an evening meal. Chickens cluck close to the back porch. Eva hears them through the screen door. She likes the comfort of their cooing conversations.

"They have a jute mill," her father-in-law says. "They do the work to run the prison. Laundry. Sweeping. Suppose they have a tailor shop to make those striped uniforms the men all wear. And someone has to cook."

Eva smiles, thinking of her husband rolling dough.

"I sometimes get a prisoner assigned to the farm here," Francis tells her.

"You do?" She's never thought of this. "Do you think—"

"Not one serving life, Eva. They'd never let a lifer out. Those inmates have it hardest I've heard, because they struggle to find hope." He lowers his eyes as Eva brushes wetness from her cheeks, gets up to fill the potato bowl for Francis.

That night, lying with her belly mounded to the ceiling, she decides again. What she must do does not depend on how Dee acts. She thinks this might be true of all relationships, her faith life, too, where answers seem far distant from the questions. She can still pose them, still proceed as though God's heard them. *Lifers have little hope.* She'll hope for all three of them, hope that one day they'll all be back on the Muddy, Dee included. She'll put her faith in that.

It's Thanksgiving, and Eva had hoped to have a child to show Dee, but instead she makes the trip wearing an ever-expanding wrapper and a wide cape that conceals. A matron approaches, pats her through her dress to make sure she doesn't carry contraband. She's deemed acceptable, then waits. The air smells damp and musty. She stands between two gates, and for a brief moment she's behind bars too, both sides locked. When the inner gate opens, Eva follows a man into a tiny room, where she waits again. He may not even come to see her; all the effort of her travel may be a waste.

She puts on a smile when the door opens, but she's unprepared for what she sees. Dee's skin's the color of camass root, his hair brittle and dry as old stems. His shoulders slump, and that mocking smile is missing. He coughs once. He wears a bandage at the edge of his eye, and a stitch looks red at his jaw line.

"Why did you come?" he asks. He doesn't look at her. She doesn't answer, still recovering from the sight of him. "Get on with your life. File for a divorce decree. Desertion's grounds."

"For better or for worse," she whispers. "I made a promise. I just don't know exactly how to carry it out. I thought you could help me figure it."

Dee snorts. "You didn't stand by me for better or worse the whole month I sat and waited in that rat-infested jail in Prineville."

"I…I was scared, Dee. I was thinking of myself then, not you. I didn't realize I could help you by visiting. I'm sorry over that, but now I want to help you. And you can help me too."

"Look at me," he says. He spreads his arms out to take in the room, holds them out for a moment, his eyes to the ceiling. "I can't help anyone. You and everyone else took care of that."

She feels her face get hot. "I didn't put you away," Eva says. "I tried to say what I could to support your claim of self-defense. You just didn't act like Tom's life mattered to you. The jury could see that. I could see that."

"No need to think of it now, is there?" He leans toward her, elbows on the table, looking directly at her for the first time. "It was an accident, Eva. It was." Despair weighs his head down as he looks away.

Eva falters, tugs at the wrapper's ribbon near her throat. "I'm…I'm glad you agreed to see me. I don't know what I'd have done if you'd refused. I'm just waiting for the baby, and then, I don't know, I thought maybe you could help me decide what to do."

"Don't come again." Dee's voice slices through chilled air. The guard stirs in his chair as Dee pushes back from the table. "Don't ask me to make your life for you."

Is he planning to leave me just sitting here?

She doesn't want to cry. She's planned for what to do or say, and it isn't this. She wants to talk of finding things worth living for and wanting him to find that too. "You…you behave as though you have no part in this, no part in your own life. It isn't my fault you're here. Or your father's nor anyone else's. It's what you did. And the rest of us have to pay for it."

He stands. "If I've done such a poor job on my own, why would you even ask me to help you with your life?" To the guard he says, "Take me back."

"No, wait, please." Eva tries to reach out to touch him across the table. Instead she catches the scent of harsh lye soap as he brushes past her. Once again, she's alone.

Gillette Cora Bruner arrives December 1, 1901, three days after Dee and Eva's second wedding anniversary. Her father-in-law has hired a midwife, so Eva has the comfort of a woman's hands to bring her daughter into the world.

The infant's fawn-colored hair caps a tiny face. As the days wear on, her round blue eyes turn brown. Eva holds her in her arms, determined that if she can bring an infant into the world without Dee waiting outside the door, she'll do what she must without him. This tiny being needs her. Eva vows never to fail her, not the way her mother once failed her.

"How did my mother ever decide to just let herself die?" Eva, nursing Gillette, asks her aunt one morning. Her aunt and uncle have made the trek to be introduced to a new baby, despite the threat of snowfall. Gillette has a firm grip and makes sure Eva knows she's awake and thriving. "I can't imagine not wanting to be as much a part of this infant's life as I possibly can."

"She's a spirited one, your Gillette," her aunt Fern says. She's darning socks. "It's good she's got your spunk."

"Dee gave her good things too, Aunt Fern."

"Oh, I know. But you are the strength for that child. You're not wasting. Your mother wasn't herself during that time. She didn't know how to get, oh, redirected after your father—"

"Betrayed us. I know."

Her aunt hesitates, then says, "He wasn't an impulsive man. It was the liquor. No excuse, of course. And witnesses said there was provocation. After his conviction, well, you know what happened. Your mother had a weak constitution."

Eva nods. She lets the baby's fingers wrap around her own, their tiny opening and closing as soft as a butterfly resting on a flower petal thinking of flight. "And my father died...when was that exactly?"

"Oh, there's your father-in-law." Her aunt stands, dropping the yarn from her skirt onto the floor. "We really need to thank him for taking you on, at least for a time, like this."

As her aunt scurries from the room, Eva thinks it odd that she hasn't heard Francis outside the door. But Gillette calls Eva's thoughts to her, and Eva happily complies.

11

EMUNAH

"I appreciate your letting me know where you'll be," Barnes tells Eva. It's spring, and Eva holds her four-month-old baby in her lap, her arm wrapped around the infant's middle, safe and tight. Prineville's winter snows have melted. Shade trees arch over the boardwalks and shade the "No Spitting" signs now in front of the courthouse. The town's been troubled by many consumption cases in the year since the trial.

Eva considered waiting until she settled in before speaking with Mr. Barnes. She didn't need any more men trying to talk her out of this thing she planned. Her father-in-law chided her before finally consenting to help. Her aunt and uncle expressed despair as she outlined details. In the end, they didn't really give her their blessings, but spoke cautionary words: "You can always come back when things get difficult. And they will." They suggest that Eva leave Gillette with them while she pursues her "folly."

Eva refuses. When she steps into the stage, waves good-bye first to Francis, then to her aunt and uncle, a weight lifts. Going toward a place of belonging proves much more joyful than leaving one behind.

She and Gillette rest one night at the Sherar House, then cross the Deschutes River twisting up the bare hill grade toward Shaniko, then down the twisting grade to Antelope. Her heart soars in the openness of landscape. She rides past the Muddy on to Prineville, knowing only a brief time separates her now from the hills that call her home. She must see George Barnes before she answers that landscape.

"In case something happens," Eva tells him, "I want to be sure you can find me. Maybe they'll unearth new evidence. Perhaps there'll be a pardon."

"Mrs. Bruner, who's led you to believe such an unlikely thing? You haven't paid a lawyer money seeking such, now have you?"

Eva shakes her head. "Prayers get answered," she says.

"Oh. That. Well..."

"And it's a better thing to think of an appeal in progress than that Dee'll be there forever. It helps me carry forth my plan."

"Which is?"

"I've borrowed money for supplies from my father-in-law. I intend to pay him back with interest, but I could see no other way."

"Hahn and Fried would help you with whatever it is you're venturing into, I'm sure of it."

"It's best I sever ties with the management of the Muddy." Gillette works her way from under the felt blanket, her brown eyes exploring George Barnes's office. "I honestly don't think Dee would be where he is without the Muddy's influence."

"Now, Mrs. Bruner—"

"I'm not saying Dee isn't responsible for what he did. He is. But the Muddy foreman took advantage of his wish to...serve. Dee's loyalty was misplaced. It's all he ever knew, Mr. Barnes. Trying to please his employers, like they were good fathers. He wanted them to notice him. He crowded. That's what it's called, right? Even provoked violence, because he...felt like an orphan, I suspect. He wanted to belong."

"The West's a violent place, Mrs. Bruner. We've a history of taking what we want. Ask the Indians, they'll tell you."

Gillette coos, and Barnes reaches a fat finger out toward her. The child's eyes moved to his long mustache. "Perhaps if we'd had Gillette sooner, Dee would have seen how much another's life depends on him and walked away from Tom Reilly's threats."

"He had you."

"Yes. But I could have been a better wife."

"Now, Mrs. Bruner, your testimony did not injure your husband. Don't—"

"Oh, I'm not a bad woman, I know that."

Barnes clears his throat. "The Muddy can provide references if needed."

Eva pauses. "There were forces there on the Muddy, things happening that pushed Dee past that point when he might have turned back."

"Forces?"

Eva looks down at her baby again. "It's nothing I can name. Maybe it began with those Indians you mention, with their having been crowded right off their land. Chief Paulina was killed not far from there. Bloodshed followed by takings, now the feuds between sheepherders and cattlemen and homesteaders, too. I've read the papers. Maybe we didn't know how to defend against the forces pushing Dee's life and mine, moving us into extremes, places we wouldn't otherwise go. We didn't know what mattered to us most."

"It wasn't all troubling things that happened there at the Muddy," Barnes says. He nods at Gillette.

"No. Good things came with the bad. But it was a time I've yet to understand the why of. What is the point to a life lived until the age of twenty-one and then spent behind bars? And Tom Reilly's life? How much of his living and dying will even be remembered? And all over ownership of a piece of land."

"You haven't told me yet what you'll be doing. Is your father-in-law funding a millinery shop for you?"

Eva takes a deep breath. She has no need to please him, but she doesn't want another man chortling at her hopes. "I've filed a homestead claim," Eva tells him. "Dee will know that his child and wife stand on our own and make a way for him when that time comes, when he's freed."

"Mrs. Bruner, false hopes are just that. False."

"But what else should I do but keep going toward something? Hoping Dee might share it is better than wasting away, waiting."

George Barnes appraises her. *"Emunah,"* he says. Eva wrinkles her brow in confusion. "A Hebrew word meaning 'to be firm, sure, ready.'

You remind me of that. You appear much stronger than when I saw you last."

"Gillette." She looks at her daughter, rocking forward on Eva's lap. "*Emunah* also gives us the word *amen.* So we'll count on that."

Whenever Eva pushes back the tent flap to step into the morning sun and face her hills, she remembers Dee and says a prayer for him. She thinks of what his day might bring. She talks aloud, asks him what he thinks she should do about that stubborn sagebrush that stands right in the middle of the ground she and Quartz, the mule, plan to dig up for a garden some day.

"So what do you think, husband?" She speaks to the breeze. "One hundred sixty acres of government land. I'll have to haul water up the bank, but Quartz has agreed to be my chauffeur, haven't you, old boy?" She pats the mule's neck. He is a purchase from the Muddy stock, made when she let Mildred know of her return. "The Muddy Creek's running full but staying in its banks. I've picked a safe spot." Conversations with her husband and spoken prayers comfort when she wakes in the night, too, listening to the mournful cries of coyotes or longing for Dee's hand instead of the tiny fingers of Gillette to lay heavy across her breast.

She wishes Dee could see the land she's picked, a butterfly-shaped parcel. She doesn't want to be in the way of the spring movements of the independent sheepherders or the Muddy flocks. A man named Long sold out much of his holdings to the Muddy the year of the shooting, as Eva thinks of it, but left one small unclaimed piece. Two plots of ground are linked by a narrow rise of land, one end bordered by the creek, all land within the shadow of rocky, purple hills. Dee might not have chosen it, but she doesn't dwell on this thought. The things she cannot change, she won't honor with her time. Not when she has months of work to do before she and Gillette roll up the canvas tent she's set beneath a juniper tree and return to Silverton.

She plans to have a cabin built and ready as her year-round home by the time Gillette turns four. Nineteen-o-five has a nice ring to it, and that becomes Eva's target year for true independence.

Her biggest worry is whether she's doing right by her Gillette. She can accomplish more if Gillette stays with her aunt, she knows. But children separated from their parents suffer. Children need kinship, need to be close enough to feel the breath of one who loves them. They thrive when they can watch a mother work, know how to reach her in a time of trouble. Separations can rot the soul. Dee has taught her that. In truth, Eva can't bear the idea of leaving Gillette, though she agrees with her aunt that the child faces unknown risks living out here "alone." Eva trusts she's not alone.

That first spring sets the pattern and the tone. Eva begins by moving a ring of rocks she's discovered near the creek. The symmetry of their arrangement makes her think they serve a purpose. So she replaces them, brings in others until she has a round rock wall that rises to her waist. Then she lays a wide piece of muslin across one half. Beneath it, she places Gillette in the shade, out of the wind that seems to rattle up the ravine, noisy but harmless, like the peddler with his wares who found her one day.

Each day, Eva ties rope around sagebrush roots, then lashes them to Quartz's harness. She dumps the sagebrush along the creekbed, hoping the barrier will collect debris and prevent the creek from flooding its banks when the thunderstorms drop torrents. She reads the landscape, sees signs of high waters in the tall grasses, bent and weighted by tiny clusters of cobwebs and sticks. Along the creek rise junipers with black, sooty trunks. Fires. She plans to build her cabin close enough to the creek to reach water easily in case of fire but not so close to put it at risk of washing away. Each day she seeks the land's clues, taking her toward her goal to live in safety here, and with a promise.

She writes in her little book that she rarely feels alone, returning to this place that called her name. "When troubled, I'll look to the hills for help," she tells Gillette. And so she does.

Eva sends letters to Dee describing what she sees and the work she does, but when she's troubled, she doesn't tell him. She fears such admissions will push him deeper into silence. Neither does she expose the peaceful place developing in her soul as she writes and talks aloud and works this land. She doesn't want to challenge his disbelieving heart, not yet. For now, she records those thoughts separately, then folds the paper, mindful that she's changing for the better even with prayers unanswered. Her husband remains incarcerated. The appeal stagnates. Yet her life shows signs of filling up.

She planned to build the cabin first. But one load of lumber from Shaniko is enough for but a single room, and she really wants two. She lacks resources for two. Francis Bruner stakes her, but she has to pay him back by tending his house through the winters. The twisted junipers that dot the ravines prove useless as a pine-log home. She can use it for the window sills one day, but she needs planed lumber for a secure structure that will resist the winter and the winds. So she and Gillette live in the wagon and the tent, cooking over a low fire until she can afford the second load of lumber.

Three visits mark Eva's journey into strength that season. The first social caller is Mildred. She rides out and invites Eva once again to work with her at the Muddy.

"Your little dresser's still there," she reminds her.

"I'll get it when I have my cabin," Eva tells her.

"It is a pretty spot," Mildred agrees. "And a body's got to be somewhere." Eva serves coffee made from grains kept cool in the shaded stream. "But I worry over you out here alone with that little one. Snakes, black widows, coyotes, cougars—they can all creep up on you when you least expect. You don't even have a dog."

"There are dogs that warn about spiders and snakes?"

"Some do. Usually the ones that survived a snakebite themselves. They get pretty vengeful. Some even been known to kill a rattler.

Maybe you should get yourself a peacock. They screech at intruders something awful."

Eva smiles. "Gillette would love that, and their pretty feathers. Would Sears and Roebuck have them? I wonder how expensive they might be."

"I'll see what I can find," Mildred tells her. "But you'd have to build a shelter for it at night. Could put chickens in there too, though. They can scratch your garden during the day, and you'd rustle them in at sunset. Since you're not wintering here, you could bring them to the ranch until spring when you come back. I'd look after them for you."

"I don't have the money for my lumber yet." Eva sighs. "I don't know where I'd get money for chickens or a peacock."

"This land'll give a body most everything it needs. You rig up a shelter. Maybe use that little rock house you have half started." She nods toward the circle of rocks. "Let me figure out how to get you a couple of laying hens to get you started. You get extra eggs, the Muddy'll buy 'em."

Two weeks later, her second visitor arrives bearing two wooden crates on the back of his horse. "Ma'am," the wrangler says, tipping his hat to her. "Mildred sent these. Says they're four of her best laying hens, and you're to let them peck the day away. Just bring 'em in at sunset." He looks around. "Set 'em over there?" Eva nods. "Keep 'em closed in at first, so they know where to come back to. But if it gets too hot, you got to let them out. Chickens wilt to nothing in the heat." He turns back. "Unlike such as you, ma'am. My name's Hank." He sweeps off his hat and holds it briefly to his chest. "Pleased to meet you."

He's a little older than Eva, this Muddy hand. Tall, he sits the horse well and smiles as he looks at her with eyes the color of wet sand. It's been so long since someone looked at her, inviting her to sink inside. But she is *emunah,* firm, sure, ready.

"Thank you Mr.…Hank," Eva says. "Please, put the crates there, and I'll refill your canteen before you head back."

"Not starved for company, then?"

"My daughter's a fine companion," Eva says as he dismounts.

He carries the chickens to the rock circle. Eva's made a sagebrush-root lane that extends out one side of the shelter. The brown speckled chickens cackle and flutter their wings as they stumble into the sagebrush lane, confined.

Eva thanks Hank, then takes his canteen to the creek and fills it. She hands it back to him and withdraws her hand quickly when his fingers touch hers. She walks to where Gillette's been resting in the tent shade, holds her on her hip.

"You'll need a rooster before long," Hank says.

"Thank you again," Eva says. "And Mildred, too. Tell her I'll pay her back."

"She didn't say nothing to me about payment." He puts his foot in the stirrup, lifts and swings his leg over the saddle. The horse grunts with his weight. "A woman and child out here alone, you sure you're safe at night?"

"We are," Eva says. "The predators I have to worry about usually come in daylight."

Her third visit comes late in the summer. There's been no rain for weeks. Two women wearing calico dresses belted by leather strands, dark calico scarves around their heads, lead a family of children and kick up dust across the sagebrush flat. Eva wonders about the scarves. Most women prefer hats for shade. They are somehow familiar. Maybe it's the way they walk, with one horse carrying their belongings; or perhaps it's the chattering children who grow silent, as polite children do when they see strangers. They move closer and one woman nods in greeting, her sun-darkened skin wrinkled as a walnut. Her skin reminds Eva of the root diggers she met here as a child with her parents. These are different people, surely, from a different band, just moving through, but for a moment Eva feels a link to her happy past.

Eva offers them cool water, and the little children smile and point at Gillette's sunrise-colored hair. "You can touch her if you're gentle," Eva says, not certain they even understand. But they do, and the four children pat at Gillette while Eva holds her.

"Chickens," the second woman says, the one who has yet to smile. She points with her chin to the rock-circle wall. "Where we set our tipi."

"Oh," Eva says. "I…I didn't know. I used it first to shade my baby, while I worked, to keep her safe. I should have realized—"

The smiling woman signals her silence, chides the frowning woman, a sister perhaps, with words Eva can't understand. She turns back. "Children and chickens need tending. I show you how to make a carrier for your baby." She removes her scarf, a length of calico cloth. She folds it, then motions for Eva to place Gillette lying on her back on the scarf. She loosely ties the child into a sling, then lifts her onto Eva's back. "Carry her while you work," the woman says.

"It's perfect," Eva marvels.

"We make a new ring." The smiling woman nods to the rock circle. "This land offers many places for shelter."

Eva says, "I'll share the gathering of rocks."

When those first cold rains of October fall, Eva bundles up her child, harnesses the white mule, and says good-bye to the hills to spend the winter with Francis Bruner. It's what she's agreed to do.

Every other month through the winter rains, she visits Dee, or tries to. Sometimes he won't see her. When he does, he speaks little, never mentioning her letters or what she's doing to change their lives by being on the land. He never asks to see Gillette.

What he does doesn't matter. Like the land she's come to love, she'll stay faithful, calling him back. *Emunah.* Amen.

12

IMPOSSIBILITY

Dee ignores the letters. They stack up beneath his cot. "You get more mail than the president, I'll bet," says his jailer. He sniffs the latest envelope. "This has to be from your sweetie. Whatchya think she's doing out there without you? Bet she's finding something good to keep herself occupied." He sniffs. "Smells pretty." *Moldy* would be Dee's guess. Eva's staying with his father in the same drippy climate he's in. Even the walls are damp. "This one's from Antelope," the jailer notes. "She's getting around, Dee." He emphasizes Dee, won't use D.L.

Dee feels a flash of envy that Eva's traveled there. For a moment he wonders why, but he lets it pass. She has separated from him. He's alone.

"Oh, here's one from Silverton. Likely it's your father. Or maybe one of your brothers. You got brothers? Have they ever written? This is a first, I bet." This jailer's a spiteful man, and Dee ignores him as he does the letters he adds to the stack beneath the bed.

On Sundays, Dee lets himself be led to a room where preachers come. He likes the music but switches off the words. At least the room is different. Bigger. More space to turn around in. New spiders climb the wall. No one wants a thing of him. He can sit, invisible.

But one Sunday he hears a story of an infant set adrift by parents, "for protection." Dee's father claimed that's why Dee's mother was committed; why Dee was placed in other homes. But parents tell children what they will to save their own hides.

The story goes on. The boy grows up, finds favor with powerful people, and then kills a man. Maybe in self-defense, maybe an accident. Hard to know, the preacher says. The man runs, hides. And later returns to do good things, to challenge men who'd once put him in the position where he chose poorly. He rescues hostages, takes them back home. No one remembers what he'd done those years before. "He's pardoned in the eyes of God," the preacher says. "For what he believes and how he acts when called."

Dee grunts at that. Such pardons happen only in fairy tales. The preacher says the man ran but that God still found him and made him turn around. He found love, a family, and a life.

The story stays with Dee while he works at the jute mill, when he chops at weeds and brush to keep a road clear, his leg hampered by a heavy ball chained to him. The man ran but still did well. He still had family. Dee still has family, though he knows little of what they're doing. His own choosing. Maybe he'll read one of Eva's letters.

"I think I have enough this year to build the cabin," Eva says. She stops at Mildred's, this second year on her claim. I've ordered two loads of lumber, and I'd like to hire a wagon and driver from here to haul the second."

"I'm sure the hands will do it for free, for you and that little one there. Isn't she a plump plum?"

Gillette, at eighteen months, waddles like a duck. She's not yet found her footing on the uneven grass that surrounds the Muddy ranch house. She falls often, which she does now. Eva leaps to help, but the child pushes her away to do it all alone.

"Independent little soul." Eva laughs.

"Like her mother. But a body's got to accept a little help from friends. Lot of folks here would like to do something for you."

"I want to pay my way," Eva says. "Be beholden to no one."

"How is D.L. then?" Mildred asks. She stares beyond the boundaries of the Muddy.

"Defeated. He's only agreed to see me three times," Eva says. "He never talks about what I've written, so I don't think he reads the letters. I thought of stopping. But I promised I won't make what I do dependent on what D. L. decides. I won't be like my mother."

"I never knew your mother, honey, but if she didn't accept help from friends, then she was a foolish body. Now you just tell me when the lumber's coming in on the train at Shaniko, and I'll ask Charlie O'Neal if he can't get the boys to bring it down." They sit on the porch in silence, listening to meadowlarks warble. Fragrant sage drifts up. Sweat beads at Eva's lips. Mildred adds, "I'll bring your little table to you. Guess you're not planning to come back to the Muddy."

Mildred and the hands bring the lumber, then stay two days to raise the cabin of two rooms, each with a window cut out to face the distant hills cut by the John Day River. They hang the door on leather hinges. The second day, Mildred sends a wrangler with the chickens, a rooster, and some chicks, and the little table that belongs to Eva. It sits perfect on the yellow pine floor beside the mat that marks Eva's bed.

"You see?" Mildred says as she holds Gillette on her hip that July day. "You give us a fine memory by letting us help you out. Time comes you'll pass this on and give to someone else. That's the way it works here. We all just look after each other."

It hadn't worked that way for Tom Reilly, or for Dee either, but Eva lifts her eyes to the hills and keeps her tongue still. This is a place of extremes. Today the extreme is amazing generosity. A new cabin. Hank keeps his eyes in check, and Eva accepts a gift that warms her like a breeze.

Eva spends winter in the Willamette Valley living with Francis, a hard-working man, opinionated but kind, Eva's come to discover. It may be her imagination, but Dee appears paler to her when she sees him just before Christmas. His hair is thinning. But he also talks more. He asks about Gillette. When Eva pushes her hands into a flannel muff one winter's day as she prepares to leave, Dee says, "I look forward to your visiting. Maybe Gillette could come next time?" It's the best Christmas present she could ask for.

In the third year of Gillette's life, back in the shadow of the hills, Eva shows her daughter how to set a rabbit trap the way Dee once showed her. An abundance of rabbits threatens the garden. Eva knows the rabbits lived there first, but she has to feed her family. Rabbits supplement their staple of beans and rice.

Gillette squeals with curiosity, squatting and following something slithering through the bunch grass. Eva grabs her child, then sighs relief at the bullsnake that so easily masquerades as a rattler. "He's hunting rabbits too," she tells Gillette. "We mustn't fuss with it by following him."

"He hunts?" Gillette asks.

Eva nods. "He's a good snake, but if you see one with a head shaped like this"—Eva makes a triangle with her two hands together—"you leave him alone."

"The good snake is sister to bad snake? They take trips together?"

Eva smiles. "Sometimes good travels with the bad, and yes, we have to sort between them."

This third year, 1904, Eva decides to travel into Antelope to church on Sundays. She sees Mildred there each week. "Do you keep a rifle handy?" Mildred asks her after services one Sunday.

"I've got a pistol."

"There's been some shootings south of here," Mildred says. "Sheepherders killing each other. The owner of the mercantile was shot to death, and folks are saying it's because he knew who slaughtered all those sheep last fall." She shakes her head. "The things a body does to another over such fleeting things as ownership and sheep."

"I don't think I could shoot anyone," Eva says. "Not even in self-defense."

"You got Gillette to think of. You need a rifle. You best let Hank teach you how to fire it."

Eva writes to Dee about Mildred's suggestion. Perhaps potential danger might bring him to respond. *I'll let you decide if I should arm myself,* she writes.

Eva works the soil to enlarge her garden. She plans to raise vegetables to sell in Antelope. Large harvests of potatoes she can take eight miles farther onto the railroad terminus of Shaniko for sale. Her chickens lay sufficient eggs that the Muddy even gets extra now. If she earns enough, next year she can spend the winter here. She feels a stab of guilt that she has a future to look forward to, then outrage that her husband's choices rob her of his presence, twist a joyful moment into pain.

Quartz catches her attention from the small corral she's built with rocks and sagebrush roots. The mule makes a sound that signals a visitor. She turns and sees Hank with a rifle across the saddle pommel. "Morning, ma'am," he says, sweeping his hat off to his chest. His horse stomps impatiently at flies. "Just shot myself a coyote." He puts the rifle back into the scabbard. "Got a letter for you." He pulls a packet from the inside of his shirt. "Picked it up at Antelope. Coming back this way, so thought I'd drop it by."

She reaches for the letter. "You need a good dog, ma'am," Hank says.

"Maybe when I start my flock."

"Could look after Gillette." He nods toward her daughter, carrying rocks and rolling them into the creek.

Hank still holds the letter in his hand, and Eva wonders what might have happened to her aunt, or what her father-in-law wants her to know.

Hank releases it with a slight tug. He grins at her. The letter feels warm in her hand from the heat of Hank's chest, where he'd stowed it.

She ignores his lazy smile, slips her finger beneath the wax seal, and lifts.

It's a letter from her husband.

She wants to read it alone, but Hank remains and Gillette is outside playing, so she sits on the bench beside the house. "Excuse me," she tells Hank.

Remember to only shoot deer or elk in months that have the letter R *in them,* Dee writes. *Hank's a good shot. Let him teach you. Since you asked, I will tell you that knowing how to bring down game is a good thing for any homesteader. I hope you remember how to set snares for rabbits that run thick as swarming bees there. And you need to be careful of the snakes.*

She reads the rest of the letter, folds it with a smile. "So, Hank," she says, "my husband suggests you teach me how to shoot."

Hank pushes his hat up from the brow so she can see his face fully. "Ma'am," he says, "it'll be my pleasure."

Once a week, Hank rides to Eva and Gillette for shooting lessons. They aim at old tins set on craggy rocks beyond Eva's claim. Hank tells her to imagine where the bullet goes, to use her mind as well as her arms to find success. He stands behind her, helping her hold the rifle steady. He tells her to push the wooden stock against her cheek so she can sight with one eye. She has little money to spare for ammunition, so after Hank leaves, she practices with an unloaded rifle.

One day, not long before she knows that she'll be leaving for the winter, Hank holds his arms around her, tight. Today, she's aware of his scent, a mix of oiled leather and lye. She feels an aching in her heart and a longing for a lean and male touch.

He brought a shotgun for her to try. "See if you can hit that bird, that quail there," he says. His fingers brush against her breast as he points. She takes aim and strikes the bird, then shakes free of Hank and steps away.

"Good shot. That one's gone forever," Hank says. "His mate'll have to pair up with another."

She hands the shotgun back. "I probably don't need any more lessons."

"I'm giving it to you," Hank says. "Rifle, too."

"It's too much."

Hank walks to the wagon. He leans against it while he pulls cigarette papers from his pocket. He drops a pinch of tobacco in, rolls, then licks the paper's edge. "The weapons don't come with no strings, if that's what you're worried about."

She drops her eyes. "I made a promise, Hank."

"Kind of empty when he's so far away. And will be his whole life."

"It isn't what he did or does, it's what I do." She looks at him. "Your help is welcomed. But it wouldn't be fair to take your gift. I can buy the rifle over time."

"I'd feel better knowing that you had it. Mildred would too. Taking it would make her happy."

Eva hesitates. Receiving isn't weakness. She wants Dee to accept… "As a favor to Mildred, then. Yes. But just the rifle."

"D. L.'s a lucky man," Hank says. "I bet he don't even know it."

But Eva thinks Dee might, because of something else he'd written in that letter Hank delivered weeks before.

Learn how to catch fish, too, he'd written. *Since you're not far from the John Day River, you can catch salmon in the spring and fall and bass in the summer. Dry the salmon. Indians who come through there know how. Ask them. It'll keep a long time that way and be good for you and Gillette, too. Watch out for the rattlers.*

Eva hasn't mentioned fishing to Dee. She's talked about the garden and the rabbits and Mildred's recommendation that Hank teach her to shoot. But something she'd written made Dee start to think of a future.

Or maybe it wasn't anything she'd said at all, but something changed in him.

An October rain has washed the juniper and sage, leaving behind pungent scents. The wind blows with a bite that promises winter and a drying of wet ground. Eva decides to supplement their food with venison.

This morning, early, sounds wake her. She checks Gillette, who sleeps, then peers outside her window flap to see her cabin surrounded by a herd of mule deer, their large ears and white bottoms distinguishing them from the smaller deer her father-in-law brings home across the mountains in the fall.

The animals move around as though the cabin is a rock. In the stillness, she sees a gray doe, one barren without offspring. Eva quietly reaches for the rifle, hoping to use the window sill to steady her shot.

But the sound of the blast will frighten Gillette, so instead she slips outside.

Her movement sends the animals leaping, disappearing over the ridge that marks the narrow center of her land. They run on up the slope, but she knows they seldom go far before they return to rip at grass. She can pick up their trail in the wet earth even if she can't see them right away.

Eva slips back inside, pulls on a pair of Dee's old pants and boots. Should she wake Gillette and put her in her back sling? Or let her sleep? Eva won't be far away. She lets her sleep.

With the rifle slung over her shoulder, Eva follows the little dry balls of earth spit up against the damp ground by deer hooves. The rain hasn't penetrated deeply. Dust lingers just beneath the surface.

Over the hill, she spots the deer and crouches. She seeks the gray doe with a floppy ear; locates her. When she's within forty yards she sits down, positions the rifle using her knees as a brace, then holds her breath the way Hank's taught her. She squints one eye shut, takes aim, shoots.

The crack against the morning silence clangs into her ears as the deer bolts. She's sure she's heard *cathunk,* the sound of a target, hit. Her heart pounds as she stands, her head ringing from the blast. The doe she aimed for jerks to the side as though hit but then runs along with the others.

She can't have missed her, not with that sound of lead hitting flesh. She can't have! It's dead without knowing, Eva decides, then runs, the rifle at her side. She breathes hard. Over a small rise, she spots the deer again. This time several deer look back toward her, trying to localize the danger. She can hardly steady her gun, she huffs so hard from running uphill. She can see her doe still running, one leg thrown out oddly. She did hit her! Now all she wants is to put the deer out of its misery. If only she can hit her again. The rifle wavers as her arms shake. Eva's gasping so hard she can't hold the weapon still.

In desperation, Eva drops down on one knee to brace her elbow, to steady the gun. She catches sight of the gray doe moving up a farther ridge, past a rock cairn marking someone else's claim.

It's an impossible shot at such a distance with her heart pounding and an open sight and the deer moving randomly. She shoots. She releases her finger from the trigger and waits. She doesn't hear the sound of her bullet hitting the doe, but it drops.

Eva makes her way to the carcass, both saddened that she's taken life yet heartened that she's put it out of its misery after her botched first shot. They'll have enough meat to last them until she and Gillette leave next month. She's had her first successful hunt, and at such a distance, too. She sighs in gratitude. She'll write Dee of it.

She walks the area where she knows the deer dropped. She finds it pushed up against a sage. The animal lies on its side. The first wound, behind the front leg at the upper chest, has hit the lungs. A good clean shot, Hank might have said. But not enough to bring the animal down.

She lifts a back leg to assure herself that the doe has no bag, hasn't been nursing a fawn, and she hasn't. No orphan left behind. Eva's picked her target well. She pulls the animal over, looking for the second shot, hoping she hasn't hit it in the gut and thus ruined good meat.

But there is no second wound, only this first one, and yet the animal ran several hundred yards and fell only after the second shot. Eva looks back to where she stood. She looks back at the deer. The first shot must have brought the deer down; she'd just run until her lungs gave out. Eva realizes it would have been impossible for her to have hit the animal, running as it was in that spot, with her winded and trying to take aim resting her rifle on her knee. If she had, it would have been a lucky shot, an accident to kill at such a distance.

A magpie flies past her and lands in sagebrush beyond. Eva turns to see. A gray rock, out of place here among the sage, catches her eye. Eva walks toward it.

Another deer. Dead. She's killed one by mistake!

Somehow, in her effort to aim carefully, she missed and hit another! An impossible shot, all winded like that, and yet she made it.

Winded. A lucky shot. An accident. Kneeling down so as not to hit Tom Reilly, simply scare him.

Eva feels tears well up. Dee hadn't meant to kill Tom.

Through her tears, she begins the gutting process, tending to the meat of two animals now. Already a buzzard flies overhead. "You'll have to wait." Had Dee claimed initially his shot was accidental? Or only later? Had her husband, so wanting to please, to be accepted, put all his faith in the Muddy's ability to defend him rather than confess early on it was an accident? He'd let a lie speak louder than the truth.

Eva feels rushed now, needs to finish. She must talk to Barnes, someone. Maybe they can reopen the case.

13

Tenacity

Eva hears Gillette, calling, as her child makes her way up the ravine to where she's cleaning the deer. "Up here," Eva says, waving her arms. "Can you come up by yourself?"

"I hurt," Gillette says, and Eva can see now that her child cries.

What has Eva left out she might have gotten into? The lye? A knife? She lifts her child up. "Where does it hurt?"

"Here," Gillette says, and shows a red welt the size of Eva's thumb on her thigh, a tiny black dot in the center.

"Did a bee sting you?" Her aunt spit on mud to put on Eva's bite one time when it started to swell, and all turned out fine. Does Gillette swell? The child's never been stung, so Eva doesn't know.

"No bees. A crawly thing." She motions with her fingers.

Spider! "Was it black or brown?" Did the child even know her colors?

"It hurts, Mama. Sick," she says, then turns her head to throw up. Gillette holds her stomach, and Eva feels her skin, clammy now. She's pale as egg white. She's breathing fast.

Eva wipes the child's face with her shirttail, then runs, the child bouncing against her chest. She lays Gillette on the wagon bed, grabs Quartz. The mule gives no resistance, and she saddles him, runs back for her child, lifts her up, then steps up in the stirrup. "We're going to the Muddy Station. Mommy's going to ask for help."

Mildred's taken over. The doctor out of Antelope's been there and gone. Dandelion poultices and yellow dock tea with sarsaparilla has been ordered, helping lower the fever that racks Gillette's frail frame. Hank's gone back to claim the deer meat, brought it back for jerking. He brings the chickens to the Muddy ranch house too.

In a moment, all is changed.

With a soft wet cloth, Eva cools her daughter's brow.

"I never should have let her be there by herself," Eva confesses. "I should have known."

"Dangers seek a body out," Mildred tells her. "Only so much a body can anticipate. Mostly, you got to trust you're not alone and learn to ask for help. You did that. You didn't leave her like an orphan; you were doing what you thought you should."

As weeks wear on, her illness lessens, Eva remaining at the Muddy. She earns her keep, cooking as she had before, receiving help from Mildred in her daughter's care. She decides to stay through winter, sends a letter to her father-in-law and aunt and uncle; hopes to see George Barnes before the snows fall heavy.

"Since you weren't coming back this winter," her aunt Fern says, "we decided to come here; to be sure you were all right. Such a scare you had. I'm amazed, I tell you. That you could live out there all that time alone. Well, we knew something bad was bound to happen."

"Good things happened too. I'm going to ask George Barnes to have the case reopened. I'm convinced now that Dee didn't mean to kill Tom Reilly. It was an accident."

"Oh, Eva." Her aunt shakes her head. "Well," she sighs, "I guess stranger things have happened. It's certainly been sad for me to think that your mother wasted away before she learned about your father's pardon."

The air stops moving. Eva stops breathing, lets the word *pardon* enter her as new. Her aunt darns a sock over a smooth rock, and the scrape of the needle against the stone shatters the silence.

"What pardon?"

"What?" Her aunt's eyes widen. "Oh. My." Her aunt lays the sock down on her lap. She's always busy, Eva realizes. Always cleaning, tending, covering.

"My father was pardoned? When?"

Her aunt pushes her round glasses to her nose, takes them off. Then, "Just five years after he was convicted, your father received a pardon."

"Why did I never know this?" Gillette starts to whimper as Eva sits straighter in the rocker, her hand still holding Gillette's. "Why didn't you ever tell me?"

"There was provocation in the fight in that Antelope bar where your father took that man's life. The court reconsidered, after a time."

"You said he'd died in prison," Eva accuses.

Her aunt covers her mouth as though it betrays her, her answer muffled. "I don't believe we ever said he'd died there. We just let you...believe it."

Eva hears the fragile sound of her voice and its childlike cry. "Why didn't Papa come back for me?"

Her aunt's crying now, using the sock to wipe her tears. "We thought it was the right thing to do. Your father couldn't really raise a small child alone, and you were settled in with us. You'd already watched your mother die, and we just thought it best you remain in a stable place. Your father agreed. We didn't want you to live with another disappointment in case your father didn't make it on the outside."

Eva tries to imagine her father outside the prison walls, walking and working. Gillette sits up in her bed, tearful. "Mama?" She pats Eva's hand.

"Sh. Sh now."

"John did occasionally send a note from some far-off place where he'd found work. I have those still." She lowers her eyes. "The letters stopped after a year or so." She reaches for Eva. "What we did was probably wrong, but we didn't want to raise false hopes."

"False hopes? But I needed something to believe in." Gillette cries so hard now she hiccups, the sound returning Eva to her. She lifts the child onto her lap. As Gillette calms, Eva pats her back, her face pressed into Eva's breast.

Eva tries to name the feeling that pushes against her throat and makes her want to cry in outrage. *Betrayal.* She's been betrayed by the people who loved her first.

She carries Gillette outside, breathes in clear air. Chickens cluck beneath the ranch house porch. The sharp scent of juniper carried on the breeze causes her to lift her eyes toward the hills.

Eva wonders if she should mention to Dee her efforts to reopen the case. She wonders if she should mention her father's pardon. Either might give him hope. But the news might discourage him too. Maybe instead she'll plead with George Barnes, convince him the investigation was lax, that if they'd truly walked the site where the shooting occurred, they'd know that Dee's claim is true. Or could be. Dee wanted to scare Tom, and instead had made a shot few could make even with practice. He'd been convicted mostly by his attitude. Dee'd gotten life for being loyal and naive.

Pardon. The word tastes like sweet honey on her lips. A pardon will redeem Dee's life and salve the wounds of her own.

She needs cash to hire George Barnes again. Or maybe she can hire a Portland lawyer, someone who might have ties to the Muddy. She'll renegotiate the loan she's taken from Dee's father. She'll write letters, badger lawyers, scour the papers for pardons, even locate a copy of her father's at the courthouse.

It occurs to Eva that she's learned how to wait by doing what she can in the meantime. Would she have found such strength if she'd known her father had been freed?

In February of 1905, Eva makes the trek to the Salem penitentiary. She hears someone coughing as they walk toward the small room where she waits. She told Dee in a letter about the day she shot the deer by mistake and realized that Tom Reilly's death had been an accident, one brought on by Dee's fiery nature, one that could have been avoided, but one that was accidental nonetheless. His letters to her since ring of sadness. *How different I would be if I was with you now,* he wrote. *I'd look after you and Gillette as faithful as any husband could. A man has time to think in here, to read some, too, in books. I've looked at what makes up a man with all his whines and foibles. I was born with other ways to make my mark, and I confounded those. Nearly confounded you, too, but you're strong, Eva. Stronger than me. I can say I have a wife who never failed me. Few men can say such things, especially after what I did to you.*

It is that last bit that warms her heart. He's forgiven her. Maybe soon she can forgive herself.

The cough grows closer, and Eva stands, her hands inside a rabbit muff. The room is always chilly, and she wonders if the cells are equally cold. She's nervous, anxious about how he'll look after all this time. It's been almost a year. Gillette's recovery has kept her from these visits. Will she still sink into his eyes?

The man who walks through the door weighs less than Eva. He's wrist-bone thin with skin pasty as bleached flour, yet shadowed gray. His cheekbones sink like dry ravines, and Eva says, as gently as she can for someone so close to death, "You must have the wrong room. I'm waiting for my husband, D. L. Bruner." She looks at the guard, who holds a handkerchief to his mouth. Has he been coughing? "I believe this gentleman must have family waiting for him in another room."

"It's me, Eva," Dee says.

She squints. Yes, the wide forehead, the horseshoe-shaped hairline, those eyes...it is her husband. But he's so thin, so unbearably thin. She moves toward him. He put his hands up to stop her.

"I have tuberculosis. Don't come close. Keep your hand over your mouth when you're talking so as not to breathe my air."

"But I have...have to touch you," she says.

"You can get it too and give it to Gillette," he says. "That's why I didn't want her here. Never want her here again. You, I just want to look upon your face one last time. I figured I could keep you from me. Keep you safe that way."

"Dee, please." She reaches out, her fingers stroke his hand. In that moment his shoulders slump. She feels the callus on the side of his palm. Perhaps he works—worked—in the sewing factory, pushing a needle through cloth. She imagines her husband working, not this reality of a man with eyes so hollow that only emptiness looks out.

She hears him groan and brings her thoughts back to his face. He curls a finger around hers. "It is good to touch you, Eva. And I can stay awhile to talk if you sit back. Don't come closer. Promise you'll wash your hands as soon as you leave." He croaks a terrible cough as he pulls his hand free. She marvels at his discipline as he sits, holding a handkerchief now over his own mouth.

She pulls a lace-edged handkerchief from her reticule, and between the two, muffled words of comfort fill the otherwise chilly room.

Tuberculosis. Dee will probably die before she can get his case reopened. Her face flushes with anger toward her aunt; she lets the feeling pass. Maybe all things do work for good. If she had known of the real possibility of a pardon, she'd have spent her time just hoping, believing in what a judge could bring about. Because she knew no other way, she let herself be wooed back to the Muddy, built a life, became stronger, drawing comfort from the landscape and her faith. Only a pardon can save him now.

She's contacted Portland lawyers to no avail. She's gone back to the Muddy to be with Gillette, then she's tried again to talk with George Barnes. Her job on this May day in Prineville is to convince the lawyer to seek a pardon. She prays he won't just see her as a crazy wife batting at stars, hoping one falls in her lap.

A horse trots beside the wagon as she and Gillette head into Prineville. During her stay at the Muddy ranch, Eva participated in the wild-horse roundup, cooking, taking her wages in an old horse already broke to ride. She'll sell the horse to pay George Barnes.

It strikes Eva as the dust rises up behind the mule that a way has been made for her to have nearly all she needs in life. She cooks again at the Muddy, which pays for their small room on the second floor of the ranch house and keeps her and Gillette in staples. She's made payments to her father-in-law. She records her thoughts on change and faith and puts the pages nightly into the drawer once used by her mother. She writes to Dee, and though he writes little back now, she knows it's because he's ill and has so little strength.

Gillette has become the jewel of the ranch hands who long for children and grandchildren to spoil. They nod with approval at the quartz rocks Gillette finds and calls "my diamonds." And while Eva misses the frame house on her own claim, the shadows of the Muddy hills protect and offer riches beyond measure.

Horse dung dots the streets of Prineville. People scowl at each other, and Eva notes a tension she hasn't seen here before, even during the trial. She's read of recent murders, sheepherders being killed along with their flocks as cattlemen claim overgrazing. Crowding, still crowding.

"A governor makes such decisions," George Barnes tells her as she asks about the pardon. "But usually it's for lesser crimes than… Should we be talking about such things in front of your child?"

"I know everything," Gillette says.

"I'll just bet you do," he says. He hands her a lead pencil and paper. The child reaches her chubby fingers to take his offering, then curtseys an awkward thank-you to him. "You can write me a letter," he tells her. "Coor-rect?"

"I write to Daddy, too," she says. "He's in a sill. He can't get the window open to get out."

Barnes smiles. Eva says, "Tell them about the poor investigation. Let the governor know there were extenuating circumstances. Provocation. That's what my father's pardon was based on."

"That argument carried no weight with the jury, Mrs. Bruner."

"Oh, I know, but they were involved in a way, a part of the atmosphere. Part of the landscape, really. The governor will lack that kind of...passion. You could emphasize Dee's illness."

"I don't think Governor Chamberlain will much care about the poor fate of a murd—" He looks again at Gillette. "A man imprisoned in a sill."

"But tuberculosis is so contagious. Might we convince him that Dee could infect other inmates and that he's"—Eva stops herself, takes a deep breath before continuing—"that he's likely to die anyway, so why not release him to his family? The governor must get letters from others hoping their sons and husbands won't fall ill while they serve their time. This could be something he tells them he's done, for the health of other inmates."

George Barnes pulls on his mustache. "Coor-rect. Save the state the expense of treatment, too. I believe you may have something there," he says. "Those inmates can't vote, but their families can. Don't get your hopes up, now. Faith in the impossible is still impossible."

14

MIRACLE

Her garden produces, though not well. At the end of her workdays at the Muddy and on her days off, she and Gillette ride Quartz to the cabin, then haul buckets of water from the creek to nourish the potatoes. A once-a-week watering will produce putrid little things, but they can be eaten. She's sold the crop in advance to the Muddy Ranch. She'll keep some for herself to juice, as Mildred tells her such a liquid provides good cure "for the consumptive body." If by some miracle Dee does receive a pardon, she wants him to have all the potato juice his body will take.

Today as they ride up, she notices horses staked near the cabin. Children scramble over the rock circle. It's Many Scarves, what Eva has called the Indian woman since she gave her scarf to Eva to carry Gillette when she was a baby.

"We have riches now," Many Scarves tells her. "Two horses. And my sister takes a husband, so we have company when we travel." Her face is brown as the bread Mildred makes. "Your wall falls down."

Eva surveys the rock circle. It won't foil the weasels and raccoons anymore. Already, weeds threaten these structures so hopefully raised. Without regular tending of the cabin, it looks as though no one has ever lived there. Long grasses grow up to clog the windows. Tumbleweeds crowd against the door. Cobwebs reign.

"I take the broom to the spiders," Many Scarves says. "You're here to stay now?"

"Thank you for the sweeping," Eva says. "And no. I'm staying at the Muddy. Working there. My daughter got bitten by a spider, and I needed help."

The woman grunts approval.

Without steady effort to keep the place up, Dee won't have anything to come back to. Few signs of her bold steps onto the trail of faith remain. Only steady effort will preserve what she's built.

She wishes in that moment with an aching heart that Dee could at least see this place, know the comfort of it. She yearns for some sacred confirmation that she has prepared this place for him.

Gillette and one of the Indian boys her age drag small buckets of water, splashing themselves before pouring the water into the trough around each potato mound. They find more sparkling rocks. Eva cherishes Gillette, her "diamond," and the experience of being tended well by her aunt and uncle as she grew. She even has evidence of her father-in-law's stilted affection, and Mildred, and yes, even the Muddy wranglers willing to sustain her. Her hope for the future leans on that past. And today she's been greeted by friends who promise to sweep her hearth of webs.

"First fruits," her sister says. "The roots are."

"We're first fruits of the land," Many Scarves corrects. "We came from the dust to be formed by the Creator's hand."

People as first fruits. It is a new thought for Eva, and she remembers that first fruits are what God loves most.

"Stay for a while at my cabin," Eva says. "When I go back to work, you stay here. It will help me."

"Oh no. This was never a staying place for us, always a resting and root-digging place." Eva must look disappointed, for Many Scarves adds words to soothe Eva, keep her worrying not about the past or future. "We'll stay...until we go."

Eva's rifle has been steady through the fall. What meat she doesn't jerk, she places in heavy brine that could float eggs. To the brine now,

Eva adds molasses and a bottle of ale for flavoring, content that before long, she and Gillette will have enough to get through the winter at this site, their home. She's already put money down on a pressure cooker, so next year she'll have Mason jars lining her shelves. She's buried a garlic plant that surprised her by producing thick cloves, which she's hung in strings in the bedroom she and Gillette share. She thinks she might have enough to trade away until Mildred informs her that juiced garlic is good for the lungs too.

She'll take some when she visits Dee. She's decided she'll see him at least once more before winter sets in.

Once more. She thinks of his last days. Will Dee want to keep living with consumption? Or get better but be forever stuck behind bars? She hasn't considered that before. Perhaps death isn't the worst part of living; perhaps being separated, lost, and alone is. How should she pray for him? For healing? For release? She doesn't know. She lifts her eyes to the hills.

On a September day long after Many Scarves and her family moved on, while Eva and Gillette dig up potatoes, George Barnes rides out, leading the horse Eva left in payment earlier that summer. She knows then, as she spies the horse, that he's failed to secure Dee's release. He said if he wasn't successful, he would keep neither horse nor cash.

But as he approaches, Eva sees his smile, wide beneath the long mustache. Her heart thumps loud like Many Scarves's drum. "Gillette," she calls, "come greet Mr. Barnes. He gave you the writing tools, remember?" Her daughter scratches at her thin legs as she limps forward. The long skirt Mildred made for her of a coarse grain sack catches at Gillette's ankles.

"I have grand news, Mrs. Bruner, Miss Gillette," George Barnes says, tipping his bowler to her. Gillette giggles. "Or at least I believe you'll see it as such. How it finally comes out, only God knows."

He steps down from his horse, unwinds the lead rope from her horse, and hands it to Eva.

"But you said you'd give her back only if you weren't successful. How can that be good news?"

"I have in my hand," George Barnes says, pulling a thick letter from his saddle pack, "that which confirms the fatality of your husband's condition. He is dying of tuberculosis, Mrs. Bruner." Eva nods. "But he has also been pardoned."

"Your idea for how to approach the governor won the day," George Barnes tells her as she serves him sarsaparilla. "So you have to take the horse back. A man can't take payment for an idea that wasn't his, now can he?"

"Not a man of integrity," she says, "which you surely are." Her head spins with the joy of the news. "Your father's coming home, Gillette!"

"Here it is," George Barnes says, handing the papers to Eva. Her fingers shake as she reads.

> Whereas, D.L. Bruner, was by the Circuit Court of the State of Oregon for the County of Crook, at the May (1901) Term thereof, convicted of the crime of murder and sentenced by the Judge of said Court to a term of life in the Oregon State Penitentiary,
>
> And Whereas, the Prison Physician certifies in writing that he has tuberculosis and will in all probability die in a short while, and that his incarceration in prison and confinement in the hospital where he now is will seriously endanger the health of the inmates of the Prison,
>
> And Whereas his relatives are willing to take him and care for him during his serious illness.

> Now therefore, in the view of the foregoing premises, and by virtue of the authority in me vested as Governor of the State of Oregon, I, Geo. E. Chamberlain, Governor, do hereby give and grant unto the said D.L. Bruner, a full pardon, restoring to him all the rights and privileges heretofore enjoyed by him under the laws of this State.
>
> IN TESTIMONY WHEREOF, I have hereunto set my hand and caused the Seal of the State of Oregon to be hereunto affixed this 7th day of September, A.D. 1905.

It's signed by the governor himself with a seal raised into the paper.

Gillette tugs on her mother's dress. "Why are you crying, Mama? Mama? Don't cry. You made her cry, Mr. Barnes."

"Sh," she tells Gillette. "These are good tears. I cry when prayers are answered too."

"You should bring him here," Francis Bruner says when Eva shows him the pardon later that month. "I can help you take care of him."

"The drier weather east of the mountains will be better for him, I'm sure of it."

"At least wait until spring. You're here now. Gillette is settled into her room. It will be much better for the three of you here."

"My hope has always come from those hills," Eva says.

"Then leave Gillette. No reason to expose the child to such a grave illness."

"We wouldn't want to be without her," she says. "And who's to say she might not get consumption from people here? It seems to be everywhere."

"My point. Why expose her to someone you know has the disease?"

"I'll leave it up to Dee," she says, with the prayer that Dee could get well without making anyone else ill.

Eva lets her father-in-law come with her to pick Dee up from the penitentiary. They make a bed of blankets in a covered buggy and attempt to leave Gillette with a neighbor. But the child screams she wants to see her father "open his sill" and doesn't stop crying until they agree to bring her.

Eva ties a handkerchief around her daughter's mouth, another around her own when they enter the infirmary of the prison to take Dee home. "I'm Many Scarves too, Mama," Gillette says. *Does Gillette remember her father?* She holds back, clinging to her mother's skirts.

Eva's tears wet her facecloth as Dee lifts his arms to his father's neck to be carried out, frail as a babe. She carries out a small box of letters—the ones she sent him. Maybe she can't make him well. Does she have the right to deprive her father-in-law of his last days with his son?

But the hills seek her, and she believes with all her heart that Dee needs to make his peace with that place where he took another's life. He needs forgiveness for acting foolishly. But who hasn't acted foolishly? She married a man she hardly knew, led more by the memory of those hills than an understanding of her vows. She sought past pleasures and almost missed the promise of present moments. She acted without clarity when she separated herself from Dee before the trial, a choice that may have even led to his conviction. She failed to protect Gillette, who walks now with a limp. Gillette has to live with the consequences of what Eva's done too, just as everyone does, even the management of the Muddy. Hahn and Fried in the quiet of their beds at night might wonder if they are culpable for wanting every piece of land they can acquire, and for crowding others off because they could. Each is responsible for the choices made on life's journey.

But she hears a call to return to the Muddy, end their separation from the strength offered there. She wants to see Dee in their cabin, looking out the window at his daughter; Gillette, with a memory of her father and her mother in a place where faith and loyalty brought spiritual healing and maybe even more.

"I'll take him home," Eva tells Francis that evening. Dee's breathing rattles, but his eyelids remain still. Eva believes he's resting well.

"Stubbornness does not become you," Francis tells her.

"It's kept me going," Eva says.

"He might not survive the journey."

"October and even November can be beautiful along the Muddy. And dry. Here it will rain, you know it will, and that won't help his fever or his breathing. He'll be isolated at the cabin, not infect anyone else. Gillette could even stay with Mildred if we decide that's best. Besides, I have a cache of potato juice and garlic, both of which will build his strength." She hesitates. "Or at least allow him to die in some comfort."

"Does he want to go?"

Eva looks at him. "Yes," she whispers, "he does. I think he needs to be reconciled to himself there. Maybe even see Tom's brother, if he gets well enough."

After a time of silence Francis says, "Then I'll come with you." The fire he stares into has burned low in the hearth. "You're strong. You've proved me wrong, surviving alone. But it isn't good for you to be there alone; not with Dee needing so much."

"I'll consider it," she says, lifting Gillette to put the child to bed.

The words she puts herself to sleep with, the words that give her comfort, come from a psalm. "I will both lay me down in peace, and sleep: for thou, LORD, only makest me dwell in safety." In the morning, after her first good night of rest in years, she asks Dee to decide.

"Are you awake?" She speaks behind the muffle of her handkerchief.

Dee groans but opens his eyes. "Am I dreaming?" he asks. "Or have I died and against all odds ended up in heaven?"

Eva smiles. She lowers the handkerchief so he can see her, then replaces it. "No angel, just human flesh."

Dee reaches for her hand, stops himself. "Soft flesh," he says. "Good flesh." His words are interrupted by a cough, and he turns his face aside. "I haven't thanked you. The pardon."

"It's a miracle. It is. In the midst of all the bad things that happened, you and I and Gillette have received a miracle." She brings a basin of water and washes his face, then his hands. "Your father wants to come with us when I take you home to the claim. If you want to go there."

"To make things happen his way?"

"He's been…helpful, Dee. He has. He needs healing time too. But if you think he might not be, then we can do this alone, just you and me and Gillette. Or we can stay here. Until you're better."

"I won't get better," Dee says. "Not here."

Eva nods, continues to wash her husband's throat, his bony shoulders. "I think it's your father's way of saying he's sorry. That he gave you up. Maybe that's why he helped you those other times when you were jailed, though it didn't really help." Dee coughs, and she hands him a spittle bowl. "You'd be giving him a gift by letting him come with us," she says.

"Let him come," Dee says after the coughing ceases. "I have little to give anyone. Guess I need to give what I can."

Five-year-old Gillette stands at her grandfather's side as he fixes garlic compresses for Dee's chest. Except for the beds and table and chairs, their things remain at the Muddy ranch house. Eva remembers only later that her letters to God, as she thinks of her papers, are still in the bedside dresser left at the Muddy ranch house. She'll get them later. She has little time to write now as she tends to Dee.

November turns into snowy December, but with each passing day, with the juices of potatoes, the press of garlic, fresh eggs, venison, and gifts of Muddy beef and mutton, Dee Bruner becomes stronger until one day in the spring, when the Muddy sheepherders move their flocks past the garden plot Eva has relined with rocks, Dee looks up at the sound of the bleating. He sits with his back against the cabin wall, a stick between his knees for balance. A crazy-quilt robe is draped around his shoulders. Eva bends over the potato mounds she readies for planting. Dee calls to her, and she stands, shading her eyes with her hands.

"Someday we'll have us some sheep," Dee says as Eva approaches. She smiles at his hopes for the future. Her heart soars. He's risen to where she always hoped he'd be.

"It's a heavy proposition, getting into sheep with so little land to feed 'em on. It'll put you into conflict, son," Francis Bruner says as he steps out of the cabin, wiping his hands. The scent of lye soap greets her.

Eva waits for Dee to bristle. Instead he says, "You're probably right, Dad, but it's still worth considering. A man has to keep considering things, don't you think? He's got to have a little faith that things can be different. The man who invented the wheel must have taken quite a beating from those who believed in pull and drag."

Francis Bruner laughs. "You've a point there."

Dee points to the flock in the distance. "Is that John Creegan? Tom's old partner? He always had that limp. Gillette's walk reminds me of it."

"Do you want me to find out?" his father asks.

Dee hesitates. "When they come back in the fall. I think this place will have made me strong enough that I could walk to them then," Dee says. "They might trust my…regret."

"Papa, come look," Gillette calls out to him. "All of you come here. Now."

Eva smiles at her daughter's insistence. She hopes that some of the bossiness turns into tenacity one day. The three of them make their way toward whatever treasure Gillette will share. Eva imagines a bullsnake or a wayward frog.

Instead Gillette points to a flash of color. "Look," she says, "spiny red flowers."

"Cacti," Francis says, bending down. "Strange place to find them."

"They're beautiful," Eva says, the hem of her dress brushing dust as she squats. Five red blooms spur out of one; three and four open on an adjoining plant, forming the cluster. "I've never noticed them before. So unexpected."

"Miraculous," Dee says.

Eva watches her husband's eyes turn back toward the sheep. She sees the purple hills rise behind him. *I will lift up mine eyes unto the hills, from whence cometh my help.* She's read and reread that psalm, always delights when the pastor at the Antelope church lifts those words along with the promise of how God preserves and keeps. The short psalm repeats those words. *He that keepeth thee will not slumber... The Lord shall preserve thee from all evil...preserve thy going out and thy coming in from this time forth, and even for evermore.* He keeps and protects orphans and misfits and repentant murderers, bringing them into the strength of the shadows of his hills.

Dee wobbles against his stick. He's thin as a grass reed, still weak as an orphan lamb. He isn't well, but he's better. And no one else has fallen ill, while the land has given up gifts of healing prepared by loving hands.

That psalmist might have been asking a question, wondering where his help would come from. But it isn't a question, Eva decides as she helps Dee back to his chair beside the cabin. Faith isn't a question, it's a statement. It isn't the hills that offer help, but the Creator of them who loves so much. Where there is such great love, miracles sprout like blooming cacti in unexpected places.

She watches a miracle. Not of a husband healed of consumption—at least not yet—but of a son and father carrying on a conversation like two friends; of a daughter hugging her father's knees and begging him to show her how to ride the old horse, how to ride into her future, before she scampers off toward the creek; of a wife standing beside her husband, amazed at his changed heart and her own.

"You're smiling, husband," Eva says. She brushes Dee's thinning hair as his head rests against the cabin's walls, his eyes closed.

"Thinking of a story I heard in Salem. Of a man who dreamed of a ladder with angels going up and down to heaven. The Lord stood at the top and told the man he'd return him to that land one day." Dee laughs. "When he woke up he said, 'God is in this place and I did not know it.' "

Eva Cora Thompson Bruner watches a hawk lift, then land on the rocks and wonders if this is what the Antelope pastor means when he urges "conversion." He calls it a turning around, finding a transforming faith that keeps and preserves. She has experienced this change, a change that challenges her to more, whether in the presence of others or all alone, whether she sees God answer her prayers or learns she must wait. For this is what Eva believes has happened to them all in this barren, dusty landscape: not only a pardon, but a conversion. Now there is a miracle indeed.

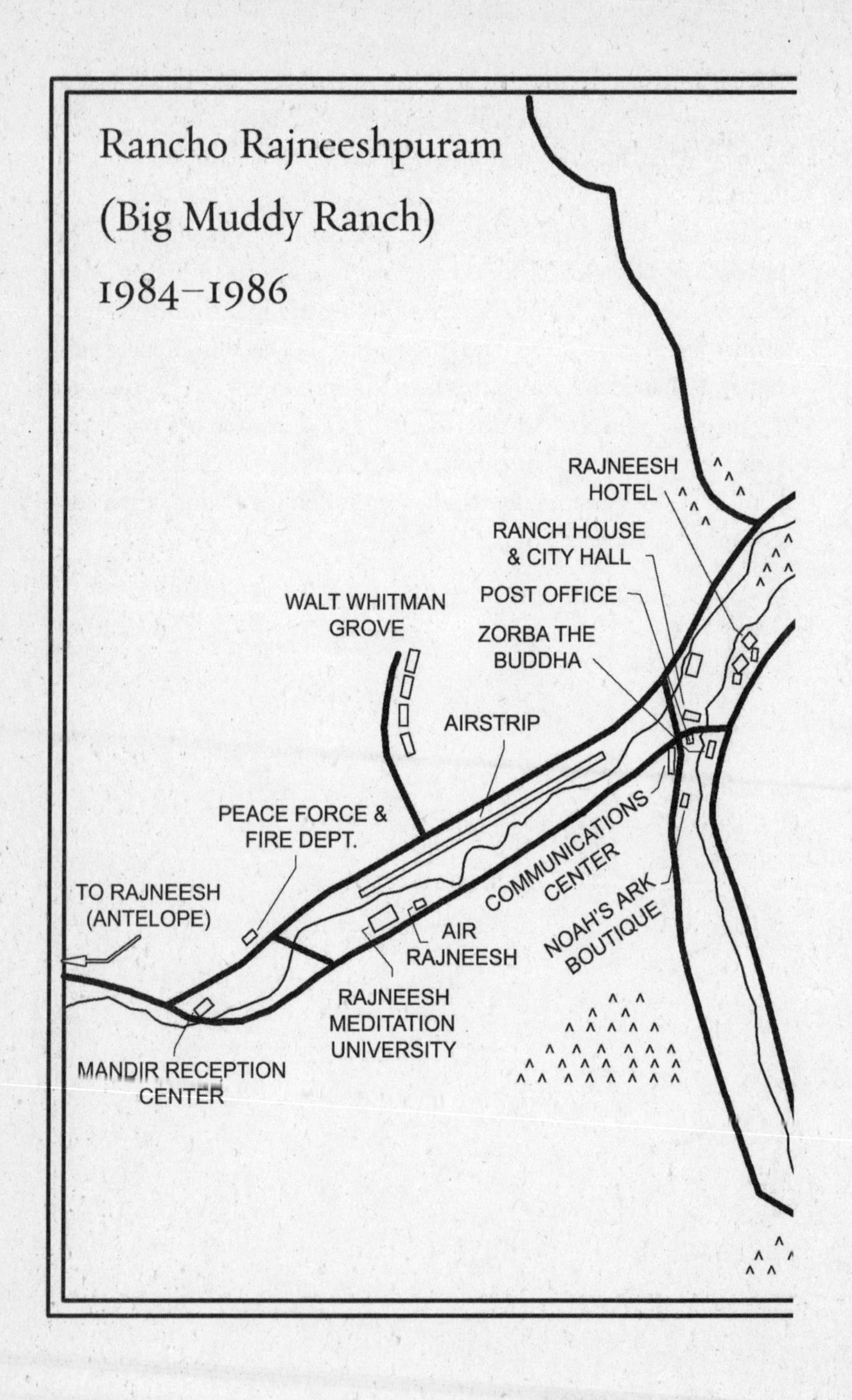
Rancho Rajneeshpuram
(Big Muddy Ranch)
1984–1986
RAJNEESH HOTEL
RANCH HOUSE & CITY HALL
POST OFFICE
ZORBA THE BUDDHA
WALT WHITMAN GROVE
AIRSTRIP
PEACE FORCE & FIRE DEPT.
TO RAJNEESH (ANTELOPE)
COMMUNICATIONS CENTER
NOAH'S ARK BOUTIQUE
AIR RAJNEESH
RAJNEESH MEDITATION UNIVERSITY
MANDIR RECEPTION CENTER

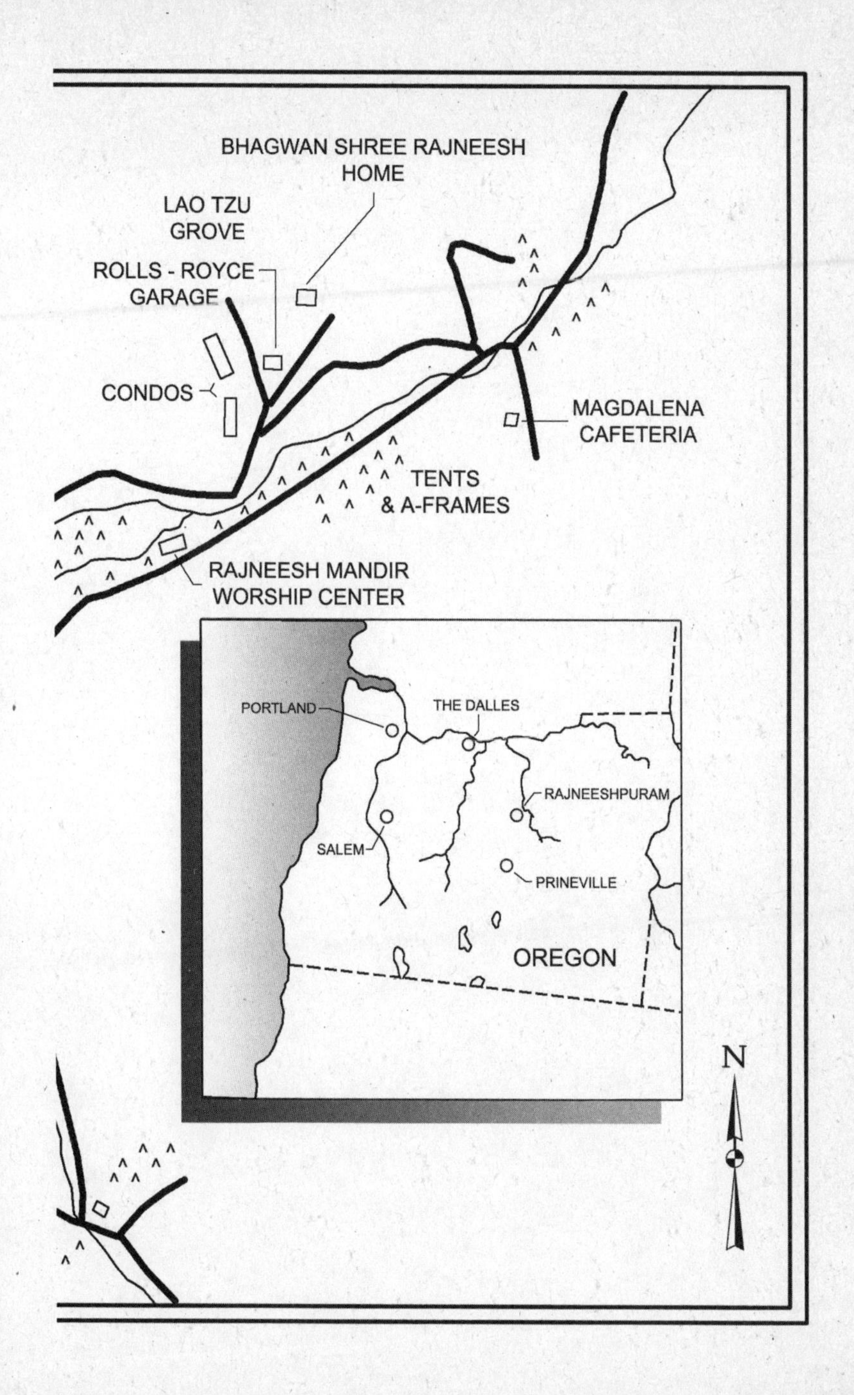
BHAGWAN SHREE RAJNEESH HOME
LAO TZU GROVE
ROLLS - ROYCE GARAGE
CONDOS
MAGDALENA CAFETERIA
TENTS & A-FRAMES
RAJNEESH MANDIR WORSHIP CENTER
PORTLAND
THE DALLES
RAJNEESHPURAM
SALEM
PRINEVILLE
OREGON
N

A Land Deposit

The Indians called it ceded land, given up to others but still claimed for gathering roots, hunting deer, making sacred journeys to the rocks baked pink and purple by volcanic fires. Through the years, sheep grazed, nibbled low the tender grasses, fought with cattle for the land's resources. Herds of deer, antelope, and, later, elk browsed their way across Black Rock, down craggy ridges and ravines, and slurped water from the tiny creeks. The John Day River widened its meander, and men brought wild horses in. They let the landscape tend the horses, then took the yield, young mustangs, rounding them up each spring, herding them for sale. The cowboys pushed them to corrals and profited from the increase. Wind buffeted the people who wrestled lives from white-ash soil and worked for the Muddy. Some said the land was ravaged and abused those eighty years; others said it merely rested, waited.

Part II

Hope

"For I know the plans I have for you,"
declares the LORD, *"plans to prosper*
you and not to harm you, plans to
give you hope and a future."

Jeremiah 29:11, NIV

15

Expectation

June 1984

The child opens her eyes. Why isn't her mother with her?

She leaves her mat, runs barefoot between rows of canvas tents that rise like the bug bites stinging the surface of her legs. Her callused feet do not notice the stickers and sharp stones. The tents all look alike. The rows are all the same. Pinpricks of blood dot wooden steps as she stretches on tiptoes to peer into a tent window slot. Inside the darkened place she hears muffled voices and then giggles. "Beloved, do you want to join us?" A man laughs. "No? Then run along." She ducks down. It's not her mother's voice, not her mother's scent. Where is her mother?

Mother might need me to keep her safe.

Music floats above the canvas city, lifting to the purple hills surrounding. Dust coughs up from sandaled feet of thousands of Sannyasins clad in orange, maroon, pink, and red, colors of the sunset, walking arm in arm, no room between them for her, a child.

A helicopter chops above her. The child remembers! Flower petals will start falling soon, announcing the Bhagwan's arrival! That's where she'll find her, in the crowd of followers celebrating as god drives by them in his long silver car. She'll find her mother bowing, smiling.

She hurries toward the dusty roadway, pushes forward through the red-clad legs. She worries, hopes. Will she recognize her mother? It's been days since she has seen her, days since she's been held safely in someone's arms.

Cora Swensen hopes the driver's on time and can find her amid this mass of red and orange and business suits deplaning at the Portland, Oregon, airport. She hopes she's made the right decision, coming here. She hopes she'll have the strength to do what she's come to do. Then just as quickly, she wonders who she is to be making such a choice. She adjusts her leather shoulder bag and lifts her reading glasses from her nose and lets them hang on beaded chains. "Oh, sorry, love," a red-clad woman says and smiles as she brushes past Cora. The plane was half-full of these sunset-clad men and women all headed for "the ranch," they say when Cora asks. No child among them, just smiling adults.

At the gate, she listens for her paged name as she walks to the baggage claim. She checks her Seiko watch. She wishes Olaf had come with her. She grabs her Yves Saint Laurent tapestry bags from the moving belt, then scans the aisle. A man with an acorn-colored face framed by two thin braids approaches, walking fast. He wears a blue headband. He holds a card with her name on it. *My husband's hired an Indian to drive me? How western of him.* Her driver wears jeans, cowboy boots. That's right. She's in cowboy country, having left urban Milwaukee behind.

Don't you go western on us now. She recalls the refrain of her mother and, before her, Nana Betsy. Nana's best friend Cora "went western" in the early 1900s, marrying some man who took her into Oregon, then brought her trouble. Nana's Cora bore a child, then her husband whisked her away to a remote ranch called the Muddy, where they dredged themselves a living. The name itself suggested something murky. Within months, he killed a man, then died in jail. Nana's friend chose insanity or something like it before she died. Nana never saw her friend again.

In Cora's family, "don't go western" means "don't take any chances, or you'll end up neglected and abused, just as Cora Thompson did." Cora often wondered what happened to that other Cora's child.

"Mrs. Swensen?" the Indian asks. He straightens a large silver belt buckle nestled under a round belly. Something about roping is lettered in the silver. "My apologies for being late, ma'am. Our smoke signals don't have the Swiss workings of your Seiko, aay." He grins wide. "Had another delivery to make. Let's head on south." His words are slow and steady. When he bends to pick up her luggage she sees his headband is a silk scarf.

In the parking lot, Cora strides forward; he moves ahead to a Bronco with the logo "Indian Pony Transport," opens her door. She steps up, her tailored pants still creased despite the travel.

"How long a trip is it?" Cora asks when he settles himself in.

"Three, three and a half hours by these ponies." He grins at her in the rearview mirror. "Course, you could fly right in there in a Learjet if you know the right people. The Bhagwan's got his DC-3s coming and going out of there."

"And miss this chance to see the country my daughter's chosen?" *Miss the time to figure out just how to do what I must?*

"It could take longer, depending on how many flats I get. And I need to stop at the rez for just a minute. They expecting you?"

"No," Cora says. "No one knows I'm coming."

"They won't let you past security without a reason. There aren't any accommodations for uninvited guests," he says. "The festival—"

"Oh, I have a reason," Cora says. "Besides, it's a city, isn't it? I read that, that they've built this city of tents and townhouses in the middle of some godforsaken desert. Surely a city has a hotel of some kind for its guests."

"They have a hotel, all right. But getting in requires a special invitation, or they consider it trespassing." He eases the Bronco through traffic, heads southwest toward Mount Hood. "Their city's just the public road, sort of like a long snake. If you step off it you can get bit. Walk on private property, and those Uzis'll poke you back to the public part. Lots of legal things related to that. But you can always pay your five hundred a week for a sleeping bag and the use of a tent. Or get a motel in Madras."

"*Mad*-res?" Cora asks. "On the map I thought it was an East Indian name. *Mah*-dress, like the cloth."

"Think *crazy,* that kind of *Mad*-res."

"We'll forget Madras," she says. "It might be best for my daughter to think I have no other place to stay except with her and my granddaughter. And that I have no way back until I call for you. You do understand that I expect you to come back for us?" She hopes it will be *us.* He nods.

Cora pulls her compact out, puts lipstick on. She meant to bleach the dark roots of her hair before she left, but after the news accounts of escalation, this journey became urgent.

While they drive, he points out the changing landscape as city suburbs give way to mountains of fir trees marching like soldiers down steep ridges. A white-capped mountain looms before them, then disappears as they cross deep chasms, speed across wide plains, and wind down through "the rez," as he calls it, the Warm Springs Indian Reservation. "This is where I live," he tells her. He stops before a concrete building, runs inside, then returns with a red cooler. "It's some culture they're growing for the bird operation at the ranch," he tells Cora. "They do research on their poultry production, hoping to avoid salmonella poisonings."

They drive on, cut across a twisting side road, head north through dry lands. The air conditioner hums. "What are they called, those trees?" Cora points.

"Junipers," her driver says. "Hardy. They can live through quite a drought. They ratchet to water."

Hardy. Yes. Able to endure during a wilderness time, even in the troubled West.

"Can't grow much of anything here without water brought in from the mountains. It's alpine desert. My people walked across it, digging for roots, hunting and picking chokecherries. Later, sheep and cattle kept the grasses down, but now there're farms raising irrigated crops. Out where you're going, they say they've got sixty acres of lettuce and tomatoes and a vineyard and whatnot. Got quite a system for growing food for all those people. Course, they've gouged the ground to do it. Looks like a giant cat box in places, all dug up."

"You go there often?"

"Enough. This is their busiest time of year. Big religious festival. People like jackrabbits hopping around. Red rabbits, aay." He grins. "The Bhagwan told his followers that when he died there'd be the biggest party ever, so they've flown in Sannyasins from all over the world this year, because this might be the time."

"Religious festival," Cora says. She hears disdain roll off her Episcopalian-trained tongue. She inhales. She'll have to watch how she speaks to her daughter about "religious" interests. Cora's way of talking always sets Rachel off. Not ideal for the most important conversations she'll ever have with her child. She can't make a mistake. Again. She has to be successful this time. The Jonestown deaths, the news reports of brewing hostilities, that Sheela woman's horrible statements on national TV threatening violence, filmstrips of followers toting guns. This so-called festival might just be a cup of poison disguised as water to quench a thirst.

Her granddaughter is in danger. Cora knows it, feels responsible in part.

She blinks back tears as she gazes out the window. How could her daughter toss aside her life for a guru called Bhagwan? Rachel doesn't just call him that, "blessed one" in Sanskrit; she breathes the word as though he is a god. Cora shakes her head, wipes at her cheeks with her fingertips. Her daughter's gone western, just like Nana's friend.

"How many therapists does it take to change a light bulb? Only one, but the light bulb really has to want to change." Ma Prem Deepa smiles as her audience claps. She's a doughy woman, and the magenta shirt and slacks she wears remind Ma Prem Razi of Santa Claus this night. Razi laughs. The joke opening each Antelope City Council meeting is now an ordinance, a law proposed by Mayor Deepa, approved with only one dissenting vote, the only member that day not dressed in sunset hues. Razi corrects herself. This isn't Antelope anymore. Ma Prem Deepa is the mayor of Rajneesh, a sister city to Rancho Rajneeshpuram, the Bhagwan's home along the Muddy Creek and John Day River. Ma Razi's home is there too. Antelope's name change will be made official when the council votes later this summer, but everyone knows it now as Rajneesh.

Ma Razi loves to laugh, and having a city council required to open with a joke is a wonderful thing. Her mother, a strait-laced Episcopalian, rarely laughs. Until Razi took Sannyas in Poona, India, three years before, her laugh stayed dormant, deep inside herself, never spinning into the open. But here, in land once neglected and as destitute as she, Razi knows shelter. She's beginning to trust herself. Her hope is to detach from the world and better serve Bhagwan, to have no material obligations, to simply live and be. She serves the Rajneeshpuram mission to build a city with such glory, so unlikely in this desert place, that all who see it will be amazed. Learning by experience, not memory, is what Bhagwan encourages, so here she's free at last to pursue her path of meaning. Even the daily choice of clothes no longer troubles. She wears red, the color of sunset, the color of power.

Razi pushes her dark hair behind her ears and clasps her hands together in a tentlike *namaste*, the Hindu prayer position used when greeting others, as when the Bhagwan passes by in one of his Rolls-Royces. The *mala* around her neck taps lightly against her breast as she bends, then straightens. She closes her eyes in joy, then opens them. She looks at her hands. She doesn't chew her nails anymore. Life here has changed her in so many important ways.

If she is troubled, ever, it means she has unfinished business from her childhood she must tend to. She must own all her problems now, cease to flee them. Razi envies her child, who runs free without rules or limits, who shares a hundred mothers on this ranch.

The mayor nods her head at Razi, smiles. The joke is meant for her, she knows. Ma Razi spends her days in the meditation center, leading guests in dynamic therapies. Since Razi's been leading them, there've been no injuries as they'd had in Poona. People expressed intense feelings through rapid breathing, then collapsing, rather than through aggressiveness and pain. Paying clients and Bhagwan's books pay their bills. Those and gifts. Loving gifts. Mayor Deepa is a therapist too, though she has little time for therapy now. Ma Razi wishes she'd met the mayor back when they had the names given by their mothers, when Razi was Rachel Swensen, studying to be a psychologist. Razi would have laughed more then, she suspects, if she'd known the mayor.

Now they laugh together as they move toward enlightenment through detachment and the worship of their work. In Poona, India, where they met, the friendship flowered swift and sure and did not falter even after Ma Prem Deepa learned Ma Razi had a child. Few children inhabit any ashram, even the ones in London or Australia, but here at the ranch, there are hardly any.

Ma Razi remembers when she asked her mother to keep Charita. Her face burns with the memory. Her mother accused her. "A child mustn't be neglected by her own mother," she said. How ironic, those words coming from her mother's mouth.

Ma Razi likes watching the mayor maneuver the increasing hostilities bubbling like a thick stew among local residents of Antelope. Rajneesh. A small cow town that once housed a Silvertooth Saloon, where it's rumored a man was shot to death. Now the saloon boasts the name Zorba the Buddha Café. It's all so joyful, this creating something new out of the rubble of what was. Even the names at the ranch make Razi giggle. Sheela lives at Jesus Grove. Her mother would be offended by that, as though the name *Jesus* should not be used for something so mundane.

But then, her mother would be lost here among the people who gift Razi with such insights. *Why do I even think about my mother?*

A man stands in the back of the church, which is now used as a city hall. Ma Prem Deepa has moved the meetings from the school, "where there is negativity," to this church once given by the Episcopalians to the cow-town residents to use for public meetings. Ma

Prem Deepa says a church is a better place to deliberate, even though it puts a bitter taste in the locals' stew. Their narrow minds never considered the building could serve a different religious group. Razi sees the new council deliberating where an altar once stood as a pleasant kind of power play pushed beneath the noses of the locals. The man asks a question, and the mayor makes a joke. He persists, wonders about the ownership of the building. Antelope residents tried to give the building back to the Episcopal diocese, disliking the Rajneeshees' "abuse" of it.

"We are appealing that decision," she tells him. "And perhaps the appeals will appeal to you." Laughter. "Tonight, though, we are celebrating the decision by Oregon's Land Conservation and Development Council to refuse to halt development at our sister city, Rancho Rajneeshpuram." Spontaneous applause. "So our appeals have been heard, and our city will bloom on the desert."

"Like cacti with spines," Razi hears an Antelope resident mutter.

Mayor Deepa is a powerful woman. She made the offer to Oregon State to give back the town of Antelope in exchange for land permits to allow the ranch to become a true city, even though it sits on agricultural lands. Krishna Deva, the mayor of Rancho Rajneeshpuram, concurred, but the state balked. With this new ruling, the Sannyasins will have both cities, will keep building on the ranch, though they'd never stopped. They will continue receiving the state and federal funds they deserve while that land-use group, 1000 Friends of Oregon, appeals to the state land board. Meanwhile, Sannyasins will complete the printing center to distribute the Bhagwan's worldwide missives. The state lost its chance to rescue Antelope and return it to these angry old people when they failed to accept Ma Prem Deepa's offer and chose instead to wait for lawsuits to worm their way through land-use committees and courts. Sheela was wise to choose such a state where efforts to preserve farmland make it easier for the Bhagwan's lawyers to display their brilliance by confounding.

All things in the universe move well with the Bhagwan at the center. "This commune is an experiment to provoke God," he told them once. They must expect amazing things to happen. Ma Razi has never felt so expectant, hopeful, and secure.

"What about your request for permission to search visitors with trained dogs?" This from a reporter. "Will that continue? Are you going to start requiring that for people coming to Antelope—"

"Rajneesh," the mayor corrects, her pointer finger held to the air.

"—for people coming here, too, to get sniffed like at the Muddy ranch?"

"You are all such slow learners," the mayor says, a big smile on her face. "It isn't the Muddy ranch. It is the incorporated city of Rancho Rajneeshpuram. But you know this. You just try to upset us. But we don't get upset easily." She smiles, ignores, then moves on to another item.

Ma Razi hopes to learn from such a model, such a mentor as the mayor is.

The mayor says, "The beautifully trained peace force at Rajneeshpuram has indicated a willingness to provide protection to those of us here at Rajneesh. And we are all in need of that, aren't we?" More spontaneous applause from those dressed in red. "They are trained by the State Police Academy, but they know how to use their weapons for peaceful measures. They are all beloveds. All those in favor of accepting their contract terms, please stand on one foot."

Ma Razi laughs. She is in the audience, but audience members can vote too, though their votes are not recorded. A Sannyasin on one leg makes a joke about being a flamingo, and several flap their arms. Ma Razi joins them, laughing. She looks down at her bare feet to keep her balance. She needs a pedicure; the red polish is chipped.

A local resident, steaming, shouts, "This city don't need no protection from the so-called peace force shining lights in bedroom windows all night so people can't sleep. We don't need no Rajneeshees walking in uninvited, showing up in our gardens. They ain't pulling weeds in there, that's sure. Who'll pay for this protection? You're mixing church and state to have a religious group carrying weapons to 'protect.' Ha! Nothing but intimidation. As my pappy used to say, 'You can put your boots into the oven, but they still ain't biscuits when you take 'em out.'"

"Uzi, uzi, coo," the mayor mocks. "No whining."

The man stands, his ruddy face as purple as an eggplant, his fists wads of outrage. Ma Razi feels a pinch of worry, wondering if the man might attack. He's old, and the aged resist change. But he only mutters words of disgust and knocks his chair over. He has to move sideways through the press of people to reach the door, his face awash with scowl. The old man pulls open the door. He jerks his Western hat over his white hair and nearly slips when he steps out.

Ma Razi feels a twinge of something she can't name. He's older than her father. Perhaps he worked the land, or came to retire in Antelope, a one-street town where deer and sometimes elk browse in the yards at night. She's heard that some residents fear poisonings and won't even eat their own vegetables from their gardens anymore. How silly. One man even put up a sign in his yard that said, "Better dead than red."

Ma Razi turns back to the mayor. How fanciful minds can get when they wander without the Bhagwan's guiding wisdom. Anyone who'd allow good lettuce or tomatoes to dry up and rot because of some silly fear does not deserve respect. She heard about the county judge in Madras who fell ill after a meeting with ranch leaders, but that was coincidence. The universe is filled with coincidences. There is no all-knowing God who cares about individual lives, except Bhagwan. These old people in Rajneesh must learn this.

A few more agenda items and then the meeting ends. The mayor motions for Razi to come to the front table while she disperses the reporters and some of the guests. "Thanks for waiting to drive me back to the ranch," the mayor finally says. "That road's so crooked, and when I'm tired at night I could fall asleep or hit an elk or cow."

"I'm pleased to serve," Razi says. She is so happy here, so filled with joy.

The mayor smiles. "Is Charita staying here at the kids' bunkhouse, or are we taking her back to the ranch with us?"

"Charita? Oh. I'm not certain." *Where is my daughter tonight?*

Buckle, as he calls himself, is a barrel of information. He describes the spot where each day Bhagwan drives one of his Rolls-Royces to, sends someone in for a soda pop, then turns back toward the ranch. He tells her of the target range where peace officers practice shooting at silhouettes of men. A county official got sick mysteriously. "Lots of times people can't come out for building inspection because the Rajneeshees' heavy equipment breaks down right in the middle of the road. Takes 'em quite a while to get it fixed, aay."

"Where do they keep the children?" Cora asks.

"Kids? Can't say I've seen any the times I've been there," Buckle says.

"Is there a school for them?"

"Not summertime." He seems thoughtful. "There must be some there."

They cross a bridge, drive past an "Antelope" sign. "Antelope," Cora says, just then aware she's laid a family story on the surface of her own. "Antelope…there was a murder here years ago."

"More than one," Buckle says. "Lots of extreme things happened here. My great uncle, Chief Maupin, got murdered near that ranch." He stops his vehicle short on Maupin Street, facing a crowd of people standing before a church. "From the looks of those peace officers and residents crowding each other, we could just have another."

"Crowding. That's a western term?"

"Just means pushing all the limits to get what you want. How long are you planning to stay, ma'am?"

"As long as my crowding takes."

16

ANTICIPATION

They pull up in front of the Zorba the Buddha Café, right across the street from a double-wide trailer marked "Mandir Reception Center." Cora stands to stretch her legs a bit, gather time to think through the cobwebs of fatigue. She hears raised voices coming from the gathering. Sitar music floats out through an open window. She'd like a soda pop, but the café's closed. It's nearly 8:00 p.m. They have thirty minutes more, Buckle tells her, before they reach the ranch. Thirty more minutes to figure out what to say to her daughter.

Cora hasn't had a lick of exercise today, no Jazzercise, no swimming at the club. For a moment she imagines Olaf running. No, he wouldn't be running now. It's two hours later in Milwaukee, and besides, his knee's swollen.

The smell of someone's dinner cooking comes to her on the hot air. She takes off her sweater. Birdsong rings clear, and she hears laughter pour out of an open window.

"We'd best get permission to proceed," Buckle tells her, pointing with his chin.

Cora sighs, then starts across the narrow street. She stops when she sees an animal—no, a child—crouched down in the pansies. "Hello," she says.

The child turns. "Sh. We're playing hide-and-seek." The boy needs a haircut.

"It's so late," Cora says.

"No, it's not," the child says. A child who challenges an adult.

Interesting. He's wearing a shade of fuchsia, though the setting sun casts a golden hue to his face, now turned to Cora.

"Won't your mother wonder where you are?"

The child looks at her with blank ash eyes.

"Ollie ollie oxen free!" Another child jumps at the ash-eyed boy from around the reception center, and he squeals a high-pitched surprise.

Cora guesses they're maybe five or six. Possibly seven, Charity's age.

"Do you know a child named Charity Swensen?"

"Does she live at the ranch?" the second boy asks. "I just got here from Australia."

"Did you? That's a long way to travel."

"I come by meself. Well, with other mates. Our parents comed last week."

"She has green eyes," Cora says. "She's a really pretty little girl." *Is she still?* Cora hasn't seen Charity since she was four, three years before.

"Don't know no Charity," the child needing a haircut says. "I'm going to ask Bhagwan for my new name."

"Me mum got her name a long time ago. It means *calm water.* There's a lake at the ranch, and we float on it. Do you like to float?" Both children seem interested in her attention. Cora looks around for adults. Three scarlet-clad people sit on stone steps of a house farther up the street. These children probably belong to one of them. An argument is still going on near the church, but the voices have lowered. Police lights on a Bronco flash.

"Where'd you come from?" the boy asks.

"Milwaukee. It's in Wisconsin."

The child shows no recognition.

"We study English and math," the Australian boy tells her. "Did you come for the festival? You're not wearing your mala with the Bhagwan's picture on it. I bet you forgot." He grins. "Me mum gots me a cowboy hat to wear."

"Mrs. Swensen," Buckle walks up behind her. She nods.

She supposes she's avoiding this first contact, this opportunity to learn whether her daughter will even let her see Charity. Her mind flashes to the arguments—no, she mustn't think of those now. Cora's therapist tells her it is wasted effort to consider the future or hold on to past decisions. When she visits those memories she brings their troubles to the present. Avoidance is a good defense mechanism, her therapist tells her, but she can't afford that anymore. She has to tell herself the truth.

"Is he your lover?" the ash-eyed boy asks, pointing to Buckle as Cora walks up the ramp.

"My what?! No. He's… He drove me here. It's been pleasant talking with you," she tells the boys.

"Can we go with you?"

"You need a ride home?" Buckle asks.

"We'll go wherever you're going," the Australian says. "You go to the ranch?"

"But don't you have a place? I mean, aren't your parents going to come and get you?"

The ash-eyed child pulls at his Superman T-shirt and blows his nose into it. Then he bends for a handful of sand, which he grinds into the wetness of the shirt. The other boy says to him, "She won't take us. Let's go to the bunks. Or play another game first." The two grab hands and run off, disappearing into darkness.

Cora knocks on the door, troubled by the children's strange independence wrapped in waifish looks. A cheerful looking young woman in her twenties interrupts her thoughts, smiling at Cora through a screen door. Crickets have begun to sing. Cora tells her she wants to visit her daughter, Rachel Swensen. The girl turns to several others inside, says something Cora can't hear.

"Oh, Ma Prem Razi, you mean, yes?"

"Yes." She wants to forget that disgusting name. "That's right. I'm her mother."

"Ooh," the woman says. She wears a maroon sarong and is thin as a fountain pen. "Come inside, and we'll see if we can find her for you. Leave your shoes, love," she says.

Cora sees the rows of sandals outside the door. "You know, I think I'll just wait out here. I feel a little more comfortable with my shoes on."

"This is not a problem," the Sannyasin chirps.

The children continue to hover and hide in the bushes; more have joined the two. Cora loved hide-and-seek as a child. She relished that little rush of wondering whether she'd be discovered before she ran toward safety, shouting, "Ollie ollie oxen free."

Whatever did that mean? *Ollie ollie oxen free.* Sometimes people said things over and over without ever thinking of the meaning. Like the liturgy, the familiar prayers and scriptures. "You shall know the truth, and the truth shall make you free." She wants to be free now. Free of this anxiety about her daughter and grandchild. Free of the worry over this strange cult her daughter has chosen. How could Rachel have abandoned her upbringing, all the hopefulness of the Christian faith, for this, this way that isn't even Buddhist. Buddhists take issue with the Bhagwan too, according to the *Milwaukee Journal.* They cite the Bhagwan's practices as dangerous, especially the therapies. The Bhagwan is a charismatic leader who's convinced thousands to give up their wealth for what? For life in this desolate place?

Cora raised her daughter to be a clear thinker, sent her to private schools to become a leader, not to drift into…this. A cult with its own rituals and symbols and language and rules and requirements, a cult where everyone must think the same or leave.

Cora and Buckle wait, watching as the peace-force Bronco with a searchlight turns down the street they're on. Red-clad people from the confrontation at the church walk toward them. In the police Bronco, a man holds his head in the backseat. Two pink-clothed officers sit in front.

"A rather arresting color, pink," Cora says.

"But if you're carrying an Uzi, who argues with you?" Buckle says.

"What are you doing here?"

Cora turns around, hears the hostility before recognizing the speaker.

"Seeking you, Rachel. And Charity, too. Where is she?" Razi's mother asks.

"She's back at the ranch. I'm sure."

"They were calling ahead to see if they could find you."

"This is your mother?" The mayor approaches. "Welcome. We're pleased you can join your daughter for the festival. If you had let us know you were coming, we could have prepared a special place for you."

Razi fingers her mala. She doesn't want her mother's presence to ruin the growing closeness with the inner circle she's developed, beginning with the mayor. She introduces her mother to Ma Prem Deepa and adds, "The mayor is the head of the commune too."

"I thought that was this Sheela person," her mother says.

Razi cringes. "Ma Anand Sheela is the head of Rajneesh Foundation International. The commune, the ranch, is separate. We're a very large, complex organization, Mother."

"Let me see what we can find for you to stay," the mayor says and steps inside the reception center.

"Why didn't you let me know you were coming?"

"Would you have welcomed me?"

"I'd have told you that now is not the best time. I'd have encouraged a different date to visit."

"Would you? I suspect you'd have thrown away my letters. You haven't answered any since you've been back in the States. How is Charity?"

"Charita is fine. Happy. Healthy. As I am, Mother, if you cared to notice."

"Charita? You've changed—"

"You must go out to the ranch with your daughter," the mayor says, stepping back out into the twilight. "What a joy for a mother and daughter to have time together. Can you drive Ma Razi out to the ranch?" She looks at the Indian driver.

"But you're tired, and the road—"

"It's all right, Razi. Families need time with each other," the mayor says. "I'll stay in town. It will allow me to converse with the residents here." She rubs Ma Razi's back in a circular motion, soothing the tension settling there. The mayor's hand is warm and healing.

Maybe it will be all right. Maybe she and her mother won't get into one of their arguments with the driver able to hear everything. Her mother is conscious of what other people think. Perhaps she has just come for a visit. Ma Razi has been lax in writing to her, but her mother fails to understand what she's about now. Ever since she took Sannyas, her mother's letters rail against her. It's better to stay silent. Her father must have told her she was back in the States. Ma Razi sighs. The eighteen miles between here and the ranch stretch before her, long. The mayor signals them to wait, goes inside again, and Razi hears laughter. She wishes she'd been asked to stay and play. Now she'll practice distraction, the detachment that the mayor and Ma Anand Sheela and Krishna Deeva and the other leaders use so well. Her mother will visit and then go home. But her timing, coming here...perhaps the timing is divine, light on an idea germinating in Razi's mind.

The mayor returns. "I'll radio to the checkpoint to let you through. Will you leave now?"

"Yes, ma'am," the driver says.

"It should take you about twenty-five minutes to reach the first checkpoint. Please stop, but they'll wave you through when they see Ma Razi." The mayor's smile warms Razi.

"Or come alooking for us if we're late," the driver says.

"We wouldn't want you to be abandoned way out there on the gravel road at night," the mayor says. She is so gracious, this woman. "It would be a sadness to be so lost," the mayor says and smiles. To Razi she adds, "There's room for you to join your mother at Jesus Grove tonight."

"Sheela has approved it?" A mix of dread and anticipation fills Razi. She hadn't yet believed the Bhagwan's personal adviser would know her name, let alone suggest she stay at her private compound. The dread is that she'll be alone there with her mother.

"She wants to give you this reward, Razi. Something special given in advance."

"Advance of what?"

"Too many questions, Razi. Just accept the gift."

"And Charity?" her mother asks.

"You can see her in the morning," the mayor says before Razi can think to speak.

Her daughter slips behind the front seat, pulls the seat belt on, then crosses her arms. Cora takes the passenger seat while Buckle starts up the vehicle. Her daughter doesn't want to talk, gives one-word answers to simple questions: *How are you? Have I inconvenienced you, running into you here?* She's afraid to ask anything more complex, though a thousand questions burn. They turn off the pavement onto a gravel road, wind up twisting grades, then reach a hilltop with a sweeping panorama, where Buckle stops.

"Always liked this view," he says. "At sunset, it can't be beat."

The hills beyond rise up in shades of brown and purple, shimmering metallic mauve and faded rose. A bowl of land falls away below, dotted with juniper trees and sagebrush and worn-out grasses cut by tiny streams. A rush of sadness overtakes Cora, staring at these foreboding hills. Perhaps it is a trick of the setting sun, or only the culmination of the day's tension and fatigue. Close to the road, old craggy rocks dribble, broken like neglected stone walls in the old parts of Milwaukee. In the distance, spires of rock with pinched tops rise up like English castle turrets holding caged prisoners for execution. Cora feels as cold as death's last breath.

"All that you can see," Rachel says with joy, "belongs to Rajneeshpuram. Sixty-four thousand acres. Fourteen miles of river frontage along the John Day. The Muddy Creek flows out of there toward the ranch. Currant Creek runs that way too."

"They say a sheepherder murdered a man there nearly a hundred years ago," Buckle says. "Blood-stained sage. Crowding over sheep. A young girl, his wife, involved somehow, or so the story goes. A bad time."

"Takes away a little of the splendor in those grasses," Cora says.

Rachel's joyful tone fades only slightly. "You always find the negative, Mother. Ma Anand Sheela, the Bhagwan's closest adviser, found this place for him in 1981," Rachel says. Her voice carries an awe-struck tenor, as though recounting a mystical, miraculous encounter. "Sheela bought it the moment she saw it. It was a ravaged place. Thousands of acres had been overgrazed by sheep and cattle. Sheela heard the land ache with the abuse, but she saw its potential. She recognized its promise."

Her daughter talks like a public relations tape.

"The Bhagwan came to restore the land that reminds him of Poona," she continues. "Sheela brought him here for his health, and he has improved. This is a healing place, and in return we are healing a land that has been raped and neglected." Rachel fingers the mala she wears around her neck the way she once rubbed the cross necklace given to her on the occasion of her Christian confirmation. "You know about neglect, Mother."

Buckle puts the truck in gear; they drive the grade toward the ranch as darkness presses down on silence.

"You see him, then, this Bhagwan?" Cora asks finally.

"When he's in his Rolls-Royce. All work stops so we can worship him as he drives by. It is a privilege to await the passage of someone so great."

"You worship an old man who won't talk," Cora says before she can stop herself.

"And you worship someone you can't even see," Rachel says. *Is that a quaver in her voice?* "Besides, the Bhagwan's talking again. He answers many things for me, Mother. Questions Father Pennington never could."

"Rachel—"

"Episcopalians don't have the answers," Rachel continues, her voice rising. "They only pretend to."

"I don't think... Let's not talk about that now." Cora takes a deep breath, turns around to face her daughter. "I came to see Charity. And you, of course. That's all I want for now."

"Of course," her daughter says, her face featureless in the darkness. "And you always get what you want."

17

Prospect

Cora wakes, not rested. The tension of yesterday wakes with her. Guards at each checkpoint pushed gun barrels toward the windows until they recognized Rachel, then waved them on. Cora raised the Jonestown issue, and Rachel scoffed at her. "We're under siege here from government forces, from dominating elected officials and old people set in their ways. We're no threat to anyone."

They saw a road sign: "Essentially a one-lane road." Cora wondered if it is a one-way road as well. They passed a lake, the moonbeam like a yellow ribbon splitting the center of it as if defining the extremes of this place: a land ravaged and being restored, a place where people gave up their wealth then worked long hours for free.

At last, they drove beneath an old ranch portal now framed with the Rajneesh symbol of two birds, necks entwined, reaching for the sun. Cora shivered. They drove beneath an octagonal building set on the hillside that Rachel called a water tower, though it looked more like a guardhouse. Cora imagined red-clad men with binoculars looking out through the window slits, their guns prepared to shoot. Cora swallowed. *What have I gotten myself into?*

An old ranch house sat behind a split-rail fence with a sign that read "City Hall." Buckle crossed a creek, turned left past a bunkhouse toward a well-built single-story structure. "Sheela's place," Buckle said.

"Jesus Grove," Rachel corrected.

Beside it sat two large double-wides connected to the wood structure. Rachel said they were Sheela's custom-designed homes: all bedrooms and living area, no kitchen. "Everyone eats at the Magdalena Cafeteria and Food Tents," Rachel said when Cora raised her eyebrows.

They walked up the cedar decking, through the french doors, and into a hallway. Through a second set of doors, the home opened wide into a tastefully decorated living area. Cora took in the soft couches, the Oriental rugs woven in mauves and purples, the teak tables holding sleek vases of flowers.

Rachel showed her mother to a room down a hall off the living area. "Will you stay here too?" Cora asked.

"I'll get you settled in, then see you in the morning," Rachel said, evasive, secretive, as she disappeared. Cora fell exhausted into bed, her last thoughts prayers for her daughter and grandchild.

Only this morning does she remember to pray for Olaf's knee, or that she needs to send up petitions for herself.

She should call him, tell her husband they've arrived, but it's still early there. It's 8:00 a.m. at home now, 6:00 here. There's no phone on the desk or beside the bed. She opens the drapes. Through the window of her well-apportioned room, Cora views a bare ridge dotted with people out early, their profiles thin pencils painted against a sky as blue as Lake Michigan on a still summer day. She closed the window in the night when cool air rolled in. "This is high desert," Buckle told her when he carried her luggage to the room. "It can drop to freezing at night, even in June."

Cora dresses. She'll walk on her own to see if she can find her granddaughter. Cora wants to learn everything she can about what her daughter's gotten herself into, so she can make her case to get Charity out. She's given herself until the end of September, well past the festival time. She hopes to bring Charity back to start a new school year in Milwaukee. If Rachel does not give her up willingly, she'll employ legal means, maybe have her daughter declared an unfit parent. Hasn't she already gathered some evidence of that in less than twenty-four hours here? Why, Rachel doesn't even know where her daughter is.

She sits down at the desk to make notes. She shakes the pen. No ink, of all the times! She looks in the drawer for another. She doubts she'll find any Bibles placed by the Gideons in these drawers. Of course not, but she finds a pen. It's a Cross brand, known for quality. The Sannyasins do not neglect amenities, then, only people.

She unpacks her own Bible and places it in the open. Perhaps she can lift it against the presence she feels here the way she's seen crosses raised in B movies against vampires. Cora smiles wryly. She doesn't believe in vampires or evil spirits. She leaves the Bible out just the same.

Her note complete, she walks to the private bath for a last look at herself before venturing out. Cora's dark slacks and white top appear out of place, she decides. She should buy something in that red color so she won't stand out. With no mala or wrist bracelet, however, chances are she'll be pegged as a guest no matter what she wears.

She misses her morning paper and news programs. Perhaps they'll have a paper at the hotel Buckle mentioned. She slips on her white sandals and heads toward the door.

A gentle knock stops her.

"Madam would like chocolate or coffee or tea?" Cora opens the door to a tiny crimson-clad woman. Music full of sitars and Hindu singing greets her, piped into the hallway. A pleasant jasmine fragrance moves past her as she steps back to let the woman in.

"I thought I'd take a walk. Perhaps get some breakfast," Cora says. "Have you seen my daughter, Rachel?"

"Ma Prem Razi asks that I bring you a breakfast here. She will join you if you permit."

"And her daughter?"

"Charita sleeps well. She has places to go when she awakes."

Cora follows her back into the room as the woman places the tray on the desk. "Have you been here long?" she asks. Olaf told her that the invisible people one encounters in a company provide better insights into what's happening than management.

"For more than a year," the woman says. She has finely etched facial features. "I was in Leeds for two years before that."

"And what do you do here?"

"I'm a server," she says. "It is *wunderbar.*" The accent is German. "Some of us do laundry, some clean, some make furniture or teach children or tend chickens and spinach plants, and some of us make sure each room everywhere has soap and fresh towels. My room, too, is fresh when I come home after a long day." She leans into Cora then and whispers. "It is like having a good wife. Someone to do all tidy work while we do work of our hearts." She smiles.

"And serving me breakfast is the work of your heart?"

"It is, madam." The girl lifts her eyes heavenward, and her face is beatific, as though she's seen a saint. "*Bitte.* Please. Have tea now."

"You're up early, Mother," Rachel says as she enters. "Jet lag, perhaps?"

"Or the music," Cora says. "Who could sleep through that?" *Why do I bait her so? It won't help.* She's here to make it easy for Rachel to give Charity up. Sarcasm will get her nowhere. Even her therapist tells her that her repressed anger, her inability to face the grief of her own heart, is spent on others in sarcasm and gets her nothing of what she desires.

The serving girl bows and backs out as Rachel thanks her.

"We could eat out in the dining area if you'd like," Rachel says. "There's a little more room, and you could meet some of the other guests."

"I did plan on my morning devotionals. After a walk," she says. "Is Charity still sleeping then, Rachel?"

"Mother." Her daughter sighs as she sinks onto the corner of the bed already made up by the server. "While you're here, I'd like you to call me by my name, Razi. Others won't know who you refer to—"

"The serving girl knew exactly who I meant when I called you Rachel."

"It would please me, Mother. It doesn't mean you approve of who I am or what I do. It's just a…courtesy. You'd grant it to anyone you cared about, maybe someone who wanted to be called Suzanne after years of being known as Sue."

True. Cora has honored that kind of request before. "I'll try," she says.

"Trying is a cop-out, Mother," Rachel snaps.

"It's never good enough, is it?"

Rachel sighs. She touches her mother's hand. It's the first physical contact Cora's had with her daughter in nearly five years. She feels a pain like a bee sting to her heart.

"Rachel," Cora says, placing her hand over her daughter's. "I—"

"I'll take *try* for now. I want us to both live through this." Rachel pulls her hand away.

"Rach—Razi. What does it mean?"

Rachel hesitates, then says, *"Secretive."*

"It doesn't fit you, you know. You've never been secretive. In fact, your father and I often wished you were a little less obvious with your life. We didn't need to know about all those escapades you participated in at the university, all those things you exposed Charity to, taking her to those football games when she was, what—just a month old?" Rachel remains silent. "I guess I hoped this was one of those... fleeting things." She swings her hand to take in the room, the picture of the white-bearded Bhagwan on the wall, the hills filling the window. "We hoped it was a little adventure you'd get over."

"Love isn't something to 'get over,' Mother. I'm committed to the work of the Bhagwan. Here, I'm allowed to do all the things I want to do in my profession. I'm challenged in ways I never was outside, and I'm happy here. Don't you want me to be happy?"

"I think you're being...duped, Rach—Razi."

A dark look flickers across her daughter's face, but then she smiles. "Spend some time with us here, and see if you still feel this way."

"How long will I be allowed to remain?" Cora asks.

Her daughter bites her lip. "How long do you want to stay?"

"Oh, I'm not sure. Through the festival."

"Any longer and you'll have to stay at the hotel, I'd guess. The accommodations here are for Sheela's special guests and reporters, people of influence. I don't know if they'll have any more tents you could rent. We've set up thousands, but we're expecting fifteen thousand people. You're privileged to be here."

"I couldn't stay at your place?"

Rachel looks out the window. "I don't think that would work out. No. Besides, I'm staying in the tents during the festival. It's...better for my work."

"And Charity?"

"Charita. It means Charity, so it shouldn't be too hard for you to remember, Mother. Or should I call you Cora, *mother* being such an evocative word?"

She, too, moved easily between sweet and sarcastic.

"She stays where the other children stay," Rachel says. "She's happy, Mother. Secure. This is her home. It's where she belongs. Here. With me. Just as you told me, what—maybe five years ago?"

Cora's heart pounds harder even while it sinks.

The child sits swinging her legs at a table near the window in the expansive lobby area of Jesus Grove. She holds a piece of toast covered with a purple jam. Buckle sits across from her, and he stands as soon as Razi and Cora walk in. He nods his head. "Morning, ma'am, Mrs. Swensen," he says. His hair is shiny black and long, held back today by a folded black headband. "Morning's fit for a chief," he says and smiles at Razi. "Your daughter here invited me to breakfast. Kid's a good judge of character, aay."

"He reminds me of Rajiid, Mama."

Razi frowns. She doesn't like the idea of this man eating breakfast with her daughter, but Charita's eaten breakfast with men who woke up on the other side of Razi when the three shared Razi's bed. "Hospitality here is valued," Razi says. "It's a beautiful morning. I'm glad Charita asked you to join her for breakfast."

Charita leaves the toast and comes running to her mother, throws her arms tight around Razi's legs. Razi pats her shoulders, strokes her red-blond hair, and watches as her mother steps forward and bends down beside her child. Charita doesn't withdraw. She looks with curiosity.

"Charity? Is that you? Do you remember me?"

"Nana?"

Razi tries to see what her mother sees: a pretty child with porcelain skin standing on sturdy brown legs, wearing a pink Bugs Bunny T-shirt covered with berry stains. A typical child.

She releases her mother in an instant and grabs at her grandmother's pants. The word *abandonment* comes into Razi's head.

"Oh, Charita, careful!" Razi tells her, pulling her back. No telling what her mother will do if Charita messes up those tailored slacks. "What do you have on your fingers?"

"It's..." She turns to Buckle.

"Jam. Huckleberry jam," he says. "My grandmother makes it. She picks them berries herself. I always have jars of it in the rig. A fast meal on the ready: a loaf of bread, a jug of spring water, and hand-picked huckleberries."

Her mother lifts a napkin from the table and wipes away the dark smudges on her pants, smiles as she wipes at Charita's tiny fingers. Maybe her mother has loosened up a bit about dirt. She'd see plenty of it here and before long exchange her little high-heel sandals for something more practical in this dust. Just not bare feet. Razi smiles to herself over that image. Weeds with stickers are everywhere. Then she notices that Charita's sandals have been left behind somewhere.

"You didn't make it back to Warm Springs last night," her mother is talking to Buckle. She holds Charita's hand. The child swings it wildly back and forth.

"Your daughter said I could stay at the hotel and arranged it. I could have spent the night in my sleeping bag, though. But a bed's welcome, and I thank you for that." He says this to Razi and tips his hand to his forehead, showing off the green visitor bracelet he's been given. Her mother will need one too.

"You've stayed here before," her mother says.

"In a tipi covered with tule mats. Not all that unlike those." He points his chin toward the rush mats lining the outside of the Oriental rug. "My grandparents met on this land, a long time ago. I spent my summers here growing up. Shot my first deer right out there." He points toward a grove of fruit trees. "We rounded up cattle on the flat beside the river; wild horses in the ravines. I even tended sheep one summer along Currant Creek. Mostly went with my grandmother and her sisters. They liked their scarves." He touches the headband made of a colorful cloth. "Handed down from their grandmothers and aunties. Lots of memories, aay. We ranged across this land a long time ago."

"Activities that overgrazed and wore out the land," Razi says. "We've had to do a great deal of work to repair it. You'll see some of that good work, Mother. On the tour."

"Bringing fifteen thousand people to party has a tendency to deplete the land a mite too," Buckle says. He bites off a piece of toast.

"Maybe you could show me around," her mother says to Buckle. "You can point out what used to be from what now is."

"I'd be pleased to—"

"I've arranged for you to join a tour at ten, mother. I think that would be better."

"Do you? Well, whatever you say, Rach—Razi. But can't it wait? I've just now gotten to see my granddaughter. Unless she can go too."

"I can go," Charita says. "My carer-person said I could do what I wanted today."

"You may not. Shati is coming to get you. You got up very early this morning."

"I was looking for you."

Buckle swallows the last of his bread. "I'd best be getting on my way, let you ladies to your duties. I've got more festivalgoers to pick up in Portland." He moves toward the french doors.

"Can I get a newspaper anywhere here?" her mother asks. "Or could you pick one up for me? I'd be so grateful."

"Sure enough," he says. "I'll bring it later this week. Do I drop it here?"

"For now," Razi says. To her mother she adds, "When Shati gets here to look after Charita, we can go to the mall and you can pick up a *Rajneesh Times.* It'll have the latest news."

"Not exactly objective," her mother says, then adds, "but thank you for suggesting it."

Buckle leaves the women then, and Razi feels that uncomfortable stirring she always does when left alone with her mother.

"I'd like time with my granddaughter. Must I go on the 'arranged' tour?"

"I want you to see what we're doing here, Mother. So you won't be worried about us. Charita's well-supervised, truly."

"And this morning, when she wandered outside and invited a stranger in to breakfast?"

"That's a coincidence."

Her mother purses her lips. "I noticed that children playing last evening were dressed in your colors. Aren't there any local children in Antelope—I mean Rajneesh—for her to play with? Does she have no normal friends, then?"

Razi steps over the baited word and watches her mother spread huckleberry jam onto a piece of dry toast. "They chose to send their children all the way into Madras rather than allow our teachers to teach them," she says. "It's a sign of their discrimination, Mother. We welcome people, but they push us away, send bombs to our hotels, isolate their children from us. We want to be a part of the larger community. Why, we even have a new program..." She stops herself. It isn't something she's supposed to talk about, at least not yet. They need more resources to make it work. "The children have each other and the finest of teachers. Your grandchild is blooming, Mother. Can't you see that?"

Razi hopes her mother hasn't read about the fiasco over the school. The board was taken over by Rajneesh residents, and after agreeing to set aside surplus funds to pay for the Antelope children to attend schools in Madras, they instead used the fifty thousand dollars as their own. That action bothers Razi, though she supposes it's better than taxing the Antelope people, which they could do now. Still, the angry look on the faces of the women at the school board meetings stays with Razi. They only wanted the best for their children. It's unfortunate they can't see that they have the best in such highly educated Rajneesh teachers.

Charita has gone back to the table and wears a sticky smile. "She does look like a typical child this morning. She reminds me a lot of you at that age, only your favorite jam was strawberry. I hope I can buy film at your little mall," her mother adds. "I'd love to get a picture of you two, jam and all."

Razi decides to take this memory of her mother's as one positive step forward. It's all in the timing, this reeducation of nonbelievers, and making insightful choices that will send her mother on her way when the time is right. Razi's load will be lightened when her mother leaves, especially if that happens before Razi lets any secret slip out.

18

Distraction

Cora walks in silence with her daughter to the "tour bus." Charita's gone skipping off with this "carer-person," but the child looks pale as a potato chip and just as fragile. Two blue spots below her eyes suggest food allergies or some other nutritional deficiency. Cora can't remember the name, but she's read about them in *Good Housekeeping* magazine. The child's perfectly formed ears peek out like pixie points between greasy strings of hair. She may be eating often at the Magdalena Cafeteria and Food Tents, whatever those are, but she isn't healthy by any means. And Cora can't get anything from Rachel about where the child spends her days—or nights.

Cora tells herself she'll take copious notes when she gets back from the tour. She wants to understand the organization, to know how best to confront her daughter with what she's doing with her and Charity's lives. Maybe she'll report to Olaf. She wishes he were here, but then she didn't ask him to come. Not that he would have. As they walk the dusty path lined with tiny white flowers, Rachel waves at workers heading out in Rajneesh buses or stops to hug her many friends, and Cora notes the many beautiful people here, mostly Caucasian, mostly in their twenties or early thirties. Everyone they meet smiles. Men with well-kept long hair and beards nod their heads, and women with shiny, flowing tresses down slender backs give Rachel hugs and kisses, chattering like junior-high-school girlfriends. They'd have touched Cora, too, but she keeps her arms folded over her chest or brings her hanky to her runny nose, which causes them to change their minds, though not their demeanor. The dust is thick on her feet, and she assumes this is why her nose began running as soon as she left the air-conditioned Jesus Grove. "We're so glad you're here!" the Sannyasins warble when her daughter introduces her. Club Med. The giddiness reminds Cora of Club Med.

She and Rachel cross Muddy Creek toward a sign reading "County Road" and head toward Noah's Ark Boutique.

Cora stops to identify a rhythmic pounding. She frowns. "Building, Mother. We're doing so much building here. It goes on even while guests arrive for the festival." Between the ranch house city hall and the Mandir Meditation Center, regiments of tents stand at attention to the hills like soldiers in perfect German order.

Everyone appears to know everyone. Questions are asked without the proper grammar, assuming subjects as pronouns. "What did they decide?" might be answered with "We can finish it," with everyone except Cora apparently knowing who's decided what and which buildings—or events—will be completed. Handclapping follows the exchanges as though joy is the natural state and these pronouncements call for additional celebration. Cora wonders if such cheer is due to the large number of festivalgoers or if this is the status quo. Or perhaps it is a show for her, to spotlight their happiness for the mother of a Sannyasin not yet wearing any wristband.

The landscape itself challenges. The bare hills, the gouged-out ravines, the hardy, twisted trees, all speak of the land's authority. But the people, the orderly dwellings, tidy paths lined by white stones, all sing that the land's been tamed by the followers of an Indian mystic. Cora wonders which message of the land is more true.

Row after row of tents with wooden floors dot the ravines, and dusty vehicles drive by taking people to work sites, Rachel tells her, or taking worshipers to various meditation classes. The *Rajneesh Times* they pick up includes an aerial shot that makes the complex look like tract housing built following World War II. Nearly two thousand permanent residents are self-sufficient, Rachel says, and will provide the services for the thirteen thousand visitors expected by week's end.

Laughter rises from the phone banks they pass, where people chat, then spray bottles of disinfectant against the mouthpiece.

"AIDS prevention," her daughter says when Cora asks. "The Bhagwan announced earlier this year that two-thirds of the world's population will die of AIDS. So we do what we can to prevent it. Ronald Reagan will do nothing. Other world leaders are blind to this need. Only Bhagwan understands. New people who wish to live here are set aside in a safe place until they're declared clean. Even the festivalgoers submit to health exams to prove they're not carrying any sexually transmitted diseases. You'll have to have an exam too, Mother."

"Oh please, Rachel. Must we talk of such things here, in public? And how can you begin to think you and Charity are safe from such a rampageous disease if you're surrounded by people with no self-discipline."

"It's not about self-discipline. It's about loving safely."

Cora waves her into silence. They'll discuss these sexual matters later. But she has no intention of submitting to any kind of medical exam.

They pass the Omar Khayyám Casino near the boutiques. "It now stays open an hour later so Sheela can gamble. Sheela loves to gamble," Rachel says. She looks around as though waiting for someone. "There should be a tour ready soon. The Twinkies know all the details."

"Can't you show me around? What's a Twinkie?"

"A tour leader. And—"

"I'd like to see things from your perspective."

"Well..." Rachel decides to wave down a dust-laden Chevy. The driver gets out and happily helps Rachel in. "All right. Get in, Mother. You'll find out then how what we're doing here will truly change the world."

Cora finds her chest tightening as her daughter points out the communications center "with phone banks to keep us connected worldwide"; the hotel, a grand structure "with a central courtyard with pools and ponds for meditative times"; the meditation center "that's really a greenhouse" with room enough for at least four basketball courts—Cora is certain of that. Rachel leads her inside, where a stone altar rises. The expansive building later will be "filled with worshipers." Catwalks crisscross overhead, and when Cora asks what they're for, her daughter mumbles something about "armed protection" during festival worship sessions. Cora wonders what kind of worship requires armed protection but doesn't ask aloud. She wants no animosity. She must be intentional for success.

Near the John Day River, about a half-mile from the meditation center, her daughter shows her irrigated vineyards and calf barns "managed by a former psychiatrist," and acres of strawberry and vegetable gardens tended by dozens of red-clad people bent under the sun, pulling at weeds. A helicopter hovering overhead veers off. "Security," Rachel explains. She describes the "hydroponics system" that helps raise the food supply that serves "three hundred at a time" in the cafeteria. "Additional people brought in from work sites by buses are served under tent awnings. All eat fresh vegetables and eggs and dairy products grown and processed by our own hands."

They stop to use the cafeteria rest rooms. A sign near the doors reads, "If it's yellow, let it mellow, if it's brown, flush it down."

"There are water problems?" Cora asks.

"We conserve," someone nearby answers, but Cora isn't convinced. "We wash our hands with alcohol before eating, so we save water that way, too."

"It's part of the AIDS prevention, Mother. The alcohol."

"Where does your water come from?" she asks as they drive the dusty car back to the Grove.

"Wells, Mother. Dozens of them sunk at great expense. We have wells we haven't even used yet. We have plenty of water in reservoirs, too, and we're not stealing it from the aquifers as some of the local ranchers contend. That's just one more story they've drummed up to be angry about. If they weren't so ignorant, they'd find out how to do things in a better way. We have a sophisticated water and sewage system."

"Free labor has some advantages I suspect old ranchers don't have," Cora says. "And unlimited funds. All these gardens, vineyards…this place is an Eden," she says, then wishes she hasn't used that term.

"Sheela has helped us find ways to acquire funds, and new people, from Hollywood, have brought resources to the Bhagwan's work. Thus the work is blessed." Her daughter wears that glassy-eyed look again. "There's the burial site of a European prince who became enlightened here. He left a large bequest to the work before he died. We were able to build the crematorium."

"You need that?"

"To be enlightened—to be able to step outside of ourselves and watch our own deaths, then be reunited in another life—this is the deepest desire of all who follow the Bhagwan."

"To watch yourself die," Cora whispers.

"To die to self so self can be reborn. The Bhagwan says all birth comes from either desire or compassion. He offers us both." Her daughter turns away. "It is all necessary for our purpose here."

"And what is that, exactly?" Cora asks. She pushes her reading glasses up on her nose to peer into her daughter's eyes.

"We have three purposes." Rachel pauses as though considering how much she dares to share with this "unborn" soul.

"We wish to build a city, a great and wonderful city for all humanity to see the possibilities of living in harmony with the land and with each other. Can't you see what we've already done to improve this landscape? We intend only restoration, redemption for the depleted soil. Second, we're archiving the world's great books on microfilm. All of them, so we might have a complete library of wisdom."

"A library? That's impressive," Cora says.

"Our most popular book sales at the ranch right now, after the Bhagwan's titles, are Louis L'Amour titles," Rachel says. "But that's because we are all so new to the West and need an introduction from another kind of master."

"You're collecting Westerns."

"A library, Mother. Of classics. Of physics and geometry and botany. Whatever we feel people will draw sustenance from in the new future."

"Knowledge is good," her mother says. "But no religious books? Nothing on the arts?"

"Charita's teachers have doctoral degrees in all sorts of specialties, but only English and science are taught. All other knowledge comes through experience. Our third purpose is to finish our underground city, a place of refuge."

"Refuge from what?"

"Within fifteen years the end of the world will come, Mother. And those who survive in our underground city, with a library of all human knowledge, will be able to start a new civilization led by the Bhagwan's teachings. We have so little time," she says, "and so much to do. These lawsuits and arguments with Immigration and the State of Oregon and 1000 Friends, they hamper our true mission. We must have protection, make this the safest place in the world so we can begin the world anew."

"Oh, Rachel, you really believe in this, don't you?" Rachel stares. "What have you gotten yourself into?"

"How are babies handled here?" Cora asks Rachel at the food tent that evening. Rachel meets her as planned, but there's no sign of Charita. The question has been gnawing at Cora all day as she was left alone to wander about. "With so many young people running around half-clad, I imagine you'll have quite a population explosion before long."

Her daughter pauses, then recites what sounds like a public relations answer. "We have no medical facilities for delivering babies here." A freckle-faced woman sitting next to her giggles, pokes with an elbow at the handsome young man sitting beside her. *Adolescents. Pretty people, but adolescents every one.*

"You have doctors running calf barns, and I'd guess at least a dozen midwives. And didn't you say there was a clinic, where I'm to have a physical? Does the Bhagwan not welcome children then? How else will his following increase?"

"We have much to do, and children can interfere with the work here," her daughter says. She won't look at Cora, but she hasn't since this morning. "They are a distraction. Speaking of which, I need to go to work now."

"Now? It's late."

"I have things to do, Mother. To make your stay more pleasant."

"But where's Charity…Charita?"

"I'll be bringing Charita by. I'm to move you to a condo. You and Charita. Sheela's arranged it for us."

"You'll be there too?"

"Don't sound so disappointed, Mother."

"But I'm not. Rachel, I'd like time with you, I would."

"That would be new."

"Is it so bad to be with your own mother?"

"You never wanted to be with me when I was growing up. You didn't even want Charita around, as I remember."

"I've changed since then."

"I guess we'll have a chance to find out."

Cora hesitates. Her daughter needs encouragement from her. It's so hard to give. "It's kind of you to have thought of this. I appreciate it, I really do."

"It was Sheela's idea. Apparently she's…noticed you. Go back to the Grove and wait for me, will you? I need to explain to someone why I won't be spending tonight in his company."

Cora ponders her daughter's words as she follows the paths back to the Grove. This woman Sheela, who insulted people on national television, has somehow taken an interest in her presence. Cora doesn't welcome that kind of attention. Something good might come of it, perhaps more time with Rachel, but it concerns her. She hopes to slip Charity out. Her daughter's apparent willingness to please this woman by doing something she clearly wouldn't otherwise do worries Cora too. Rachel was a bright and thoughtful student through the years. She was always her own thinker, headstrong even, until making this Bhagwan connection. Well, maybe those qualities brought her their share of trouble too. She married young, against Cora and Olaf's wishes, but she completed school despite being pregnant with Charity. They made a terrible mistake in indulging their daughter, paying for her schooling, her trips to Europe and the East. Rachel's husband divorced her the year after her graduation, not such a bad thing, but then she became engaged to this cult. Olaf believed she'd grow out of it if they left her alone. Instead, she morphed into some kind of automaton with this thinking about end times and destruction and her total neglect of Charity. Neglectful and even abusive, that's how the commune's red buildings on the once-beautiful landscape appear to her. Probably to Buckle's memory, too, if she understands well the story of his people's losses.

She doesn't want to think about neglectful things; she wants to make amends.

The end of the world is coming? These red-clad children will save civilization? Her daughter has gone mad! Fifteen years, she's said, before some cataclysmic event will put an end to everything. Cora has read nothing about such predictions in all the research she's done on this cult. It does explain the urgency, the apparent disregard for rules and regulations. Instead of being good neighbors, good citizens of Oregon while building and gaining acceptance, they crowd, to use Buckle's term. Why care if people agree with them or if they win friends? They're on a mission. They'll crowd out anyone who gets in their way.

But such crowding puts them at risk too. That's why all the guns. Charity, this sweet, innocent child, is put at risk by a mother who believes she'll rescue the world through Uzis and isolation. Cora must be careful not to antagonize her daughter. If she can, she'll convince Rachel to let Charity go, for Charity's sake.

If that doesn't work, she'll simply whisk her granddaughter away.

Music drifts up from the boutique area. Other followers worship at Rajneesh Mandir, the large complex that might be a greenhouse—or might not. The shopping area near the ranch house also houses telemarketers, who sell worldwide the Bhagwan's books and items like T-shirts and sun visors imprinted with "Die to Self." *Self-indulgent* comes to mind, and yet the people Cora has met have all been friendly. Maybe because she's an outsider. Perhaps she'll gain a truer vision of what goes on here on this ranch if she wears shades of sunset.

She steps onto the deck of the boutique and smells the incense filling the warm night. Lovely people sip ginger tea at deck tables. Festival guests, not workers, Cora imagines. Customers using Rajneesh dollars exchange scrip as Cora runs her hands over the soft fabrics draped on hangers. Maybe she'll buy a loose pair of Sun & Sand brand pants to fit in here and still use for lounging back in Milwaukee. The darker colors will help hide the dirt that attaches to her white pants like Charity's little huckleberry fingers. It's a practical purchase. The dry heat makes her face itch. Maybe she'll buy Rajneesh lotion bottled in red.

Or is she violating personal beliefs by purchasing sunset colors?

"It's just lotion or a pair of pants," she says aloud.

She feels a tug against her pant leg. She steps back, curious, and parts the clothing on the circular rack.

"Charity." Cora squats down. "What are you doing in here?" She pulls a thread caught in the child's tangled hair, holds the pointed little chin in the palm of her hand.

"It's the best place to play, Nana." The child's green eyes are big as boulders. "It's warm at night too. Even when it's cold outside. I sleep real good in here, if they don't know I'm lost."

"Oh, Charity," Cora says as she pulls the child to her breast.

19

LACK

Razi's on her way to take her mother and daughter to the condo, just as Sheela wishes. Sheela's interest in Razi's comfort unsettles, especially since she recommended Charita be included. Perhaps Razi's success as a meditation leader has brought her higher in Sheela's esteem. She's told Razi she'll be called upon for a special task. She's being groomed for something big. But can that be, someone as unworthy as Razi is?

The condo is located in one of the remote ravines below Lao Tzu Grove, where the Bhagwan has his compound. It's two stories, a frame structure rather than a tent, though all are built to be easily moved should a state or county inspector question whether the buildings are permanent or temporary or have the proper permits. Razi smiles. Sheela's team is wise. She's even had tunnels dug to harbor people while inspectors or state lawyers check estimates of population. Only so many are supposed to be here, except during festivals. The tunnels serve as escape routes, too. Razi notices no one asks what they might be escaping from. Questions aren't encouraged, defined as negativity.

Sheela's approaching with her entourage. Razi's heart rate increases. Will she stop to talk to her, here, in public, near the restaurant? Her eyes drop. Razi wishes that Sheela wouldn't wear the .357 magnum pistol strapped to her hip. The peace force carries sufficient guns. Wearing the pistol gives the impression that the peace force is inadequate or, worse, that Sheela's in some special danger. She passes by. Sheela always has an audience, but then no one leaves the ranch alone these days. When did that start? Razi can't remember. She considers herself privileged to be alone this evening. Maybe there's time to find Rajiid, a man she met two weeks ago who came in for the festival, time yet to enjoy the evening.

But no, she must find Charita and take her and her mother to the condo, get them settled.

She hopes her mother won't see Sheela's weapon. She doesn't want any distractions from what she must speak of tonight. Sheela can't know this, but placing Razi in a private place with her mother will offer her the chance she needs. Razi will surprise Sheela, offer new resources to serve Bhagwan, if she's successful with her mother. She approached her father months ago, but he was noncommittal. Still, her mother's come. The two events must somehow be related.

Now if only she can find her child.

Cora sweeps the grubby child into her arms. Doesn't anyone notice these children; doesn't anyone care how they spend their time? She starts to carry Charity out the door and sees the boutique manager approaching from the side. "She's my nana," Charity says. The blond woman steps back, bows, and smiles. Charity waves back. At least some adult is prepared to question a stranger dressed in white slacks and yellow top trying to carry a child away.

Outside, the two walk hand in hand toward Jesus Grove, and Charity chatters, asking if her nana might read her a story when they get back to the Grove.

"As many as you'd like," Cora says. "After your bath. Would you like me to trim your fingernails? You might not scratch yourself so much."

Charity nods and rubs at the tiny nicks on her face. "Mama's busy, but she says she'll cut them. And my hair, too. Will she mind if you do that, Nana?"

"I'll explain if she does."

Inside their room, Cora strips the shorts and shirt from the child while the tub water runs. *How does the laundry get back to the children?* She lays out clothes for Charity brought as gifts. A shorts set, the color of spring green. She helps her step in. Bug bites cover Charity's slender legs, and the bottoms of her feet are leatherlike, brown and tough. Cora picks a tiny pointed seed from Charity's heel. It leaves a reddish puncture spot, as though infected.

"That's a goat head, Nana," Charity says, and with two tiny fingers lifts it from Cora's hand and flicks the spiny seed into the wastebasket.

"Didn't you feel that in your foot?" Cora asks. "It's very sharp, Charity."

"I'm tough," Charity says. "My name is Charita, Nana. Don't you remember?"

Cora nods. She wants to win this child's loyalty and will call her anything she wants. "Charita. That sounds Spanish. I bet it means the same thing as Charity. Your name means giving, and love."

The child splashes. "Do you have toys, Nana?"

"I'm afraid not. Do you have some where you stay?"

"We put them in the baskets, all together. Everybody shares." She motions with her finger for Cora to bend closer. The child reaches her wet arms around Cora's neck, then whispers in her ear, warm water dripping onto Cora's throat. "I don't like to share everything, especially not my mama."

"Who do you share her with?" Cora asks, whispering into her granddaughter's wet ear.

"Rajiid. And sometimes other men wake up with us in her bed." She sits back and splashes. "It's good I'm here to take care of her. Do you know where she is now?"

Razi checks at the Children's Room, located in one of the condos composed of eight bedrooms, a playroom, and baths. She finds empty bunk beds, toys piled in willow baskets neatly stacked. The kids must all be out enjoying the early evening, visiting with the new arrivals flown in from Leeds and beyond. Some will be without their parents, who've not yet made transport. These will be exploring, finding out what good things the ranch offers creative kids. If school were in session, it would be easier to find her daughter. Still, Razi admires her child's independence and ability to educate herself through experiences at hand. Bhagwan has said that children understand the "giving up to all"; here they aren't restrained by early parental regimenting, where parents interrupt their learning from experience. Parents interfere when they say, "Don't go near the water" or "Don't throw rocks." The consequences of such actions bring immediate wisdom to a child. Razi's mother was right to insist she take Charita with her to the ashram in India as a toddler, even though her mother spoke from selfish interests. She didn't want to bother raising her grandchild while Razi went off to India. She was too busy, always too busy.

Razi walks along Muddy Creek. Several boys pick up shiny rocks and throw them. She hears the plop of stone in water. Two girls huddle over tree frogs. She asks, but none has seen Charita. She makes her way toward the food tents. Perhaps her child is hungry, but they're not serving now. Charita knows the schedule. Music floats from loudspeakers that can be heard throughout the ranch. She turns back. Charita might be looking through the festival tents for her. She'll find Charita there and maybe Rajiid, too. Or maybe Charita's just gone back to Jesus Grove in search of her nana.

Razi heads there next, thinking as she walks. She can be of greater service to Bhagwan if she follows through on her idea: The time has come for her to ask for her large trust fund, early. Her mother's presence is but another sign. Sheela's said the Bhagwan needs fresh resources. Calls have been made to Sannyasins around the world, requesting their presence at this Master's Day Festival of 1984 and their consideration in making a gift to the effort here. Sheela gives loving reminders to everyone to seek resources wherever they might find them. Most recently, she stared at Razi as she spoke, though there were thousands in the crowd.

Razi looks up. Sheela's left the restaurant and is heading with her entourage toward the casino. She doesn't notice Razi as she stands in the shadows of the ranch house. Sheela's dressed in red slacks with a holster and belt at her narrow waist. Puja, the head of the medical treatment center, walks with her. Razi doesn't like Puja. Well, it's not dislike. It isn't healthy to dislike anyone, but she reminds her of Big Nurse in a Ken Kesey novel she read years before, always with a smiling face but with her hands full of power or hypodermic needles. When she makes a point, her almond eyes slither into slits as sharp as razors. But no harm can come to Sheela while Puja is around, and she does manage the AIDS protection project and ensures all new Sannyasins are free of disease.

Razi doesn't want to think of the possibility of something happening to Sheela, the Bhagwan's closest adviser. Sometimes, when she hears rumors about disagreements among the inner circle or when the Wild Geese, as the defectors are known, fly away, Razi feels a gnawing in her stomach, and she worries about the stability of this grand effort to create a new world. Sheela holds it together. Sheela makes sure nothing is neglected.

And yet Sheela also provokes. On *Nightline* she ordered elderly residents from Antelope to "shut up" and called them bigots.

Maybe Sheela wears the pistol to provoke, but whom? Only Sannyasins and those who love the Bhagwan see it here. Well, the television cameras arrive often. And more and more state and county officials try to enter to inspect records or see if building permits have been properly executed. Maybe she challenges all authority by wearing the .357.

Razi shivers in the cooling dusk. She refers to the weapon by the slicker name .357, as though guns are commonplace. Is that how violence happens, slowly, as the outrageous transforms unnoticeably into something everyday?

Razi's heard new rumors about the outside dangers too. The Rajneesh hotel bombing in Portland started it. Now, some days, she hears gunshots from the deep ravines. Sheela's purchased more weapons and trained 150 more peace-force members. They walk around carrying Uzi carbines and Galil assault rifles with sniffer dogs leashed to their sides.

Peace in Hebrew means "nothing missing, nothing broken." Razi turns this over in her mind and concludes the peace force offers reassurance.

But her friend Waleed, one of the peace officers, says they spent twenty-five thousand dollars last month alone on ammunition, practicing to improve their accuracy. *Aiming at what?* Waleed told Razi that once the festival starts, armed guards will stand spaced fifty feet apart during morning *satsongs* at the Mandir Meditation Center.

"Whatever for?" Razi asked him.

"To protect the worshipers and Bhagwan," he said. "Now that the Bhagwan is giving *satsongs* again, everyone will want to hear him. He'll be vulnerable to danger."

"From who? Everyone here wants to be here. Everyone gets screened. Anyone who wants to leave can leave. Isn't that what the Bhagwan's always said?"

"That was before," Waleed told her. His voice held annoyance.

"Before what?"

He shrugged his shoulders. Then, after a pause, as though he hadn't had to think of an answer before he said, "Before all the challenges by the courts, and those old ones at Antelope. And those religious fanatics in Madras."

Razi shook her head. "Those old people are harmless, beaten down already. They wouldn't set foot out here to harm anyone."

"It isn't always wise to speak against the way things are here, Razi," Waleed said, one eyebrow lifted. She quieted. He was right. The Baptists, who chanted opposition when the Bhagwan made his daily trip to town, are no supporters of their efforts here. They might send spies. But the Baptists worked out an agreement to stop chanting, and the Bhagwan agreed to drive his Rolls-Royce only as far as the Willowdale Café instead of all the way into Madras. The district attorney helped negotiate that agreement, which was a sign of conciliation, a willingness to find a way to live peaceably as neighbors.

Right after the agreement was reached, the district attorney became violently ill with a very rare infection. He almost died. A helicopter took him to the hospital in Bend and saved his life. The Rajneesh doctor had been in the Madras hospital when they brought the D.A. in, and he said he'd never seen anything like it, such a rapid loss of blood pressure, such a plunge toward death. Preposterous rumors spread that the Rajneesh had something to do with that. If any intentional poisoning had gone on, it would have targeted the Rajneeshees, not some helpful government official.

Still, if people think the Rajneeshees caused the man's injury, "they" might plan some uprising against them. It has happened in other places, innocents attacked. Maybe the poisoning had been staged to provoke outsiders into attacking them at the ranch!

Razi takes a deep breath. She shouldn't let her thoughts race away. She needs to be calm, to let her mother see her as a competent adult capable of making decisions about her own future and her own resources.

She wishes she had someone safe to talk to. Waleed sometimes is, but he takes questions as complaints, and she can't afford to be seen as negative. Negative people are reassigned to tasks like cleaning huge pans at the Magdalena Food Tents, one of the few tasks rotated every week, as it demands so much. Rajiid she hardly knows. He is only someone warm who shares her bed some nights.

Maybe she'll call her father again. She's here, near the phone banks, a sign. She'll just call and talk. Not so much about what's happening here, but just to let him know how she is doing. She's been lax in keeping him posted. Only once has she called, and then to talk about the trust. In her effort to avoid the criticism of her mother, she often blocks her father from her life as well.

Razi sprays the mouthpiece with disinfectant. Her mother nearly had a fit when she saw this earlier. But the people must take all precautions against an AIDS outbreak. They even have a means of isolating people if need be in cabins in one of the far ravines, to protect the community while treating those with illnesses.

She dials. Hears the phone ring behind a series of strange clicks. They're so far outside civilization, even the phone lines groan in protest.

Stars shine above her like tiny agates at the shoreline of the ridges bordering the sea of sky. A slice of moon smiles at her. As the phone rings she feels that rise of anticipation hoping she'll hear her father's voice. She's dialed the direct line into his office. He often works late.

"Hello?"

"Daddy? It's me, Razi…ah, Rachel."

"Who? I can't hear you very well. Who is this, please?"

"Your daughter, Rachel." She hates to shout, might interrupt another laughing couple who spray a mouthpiece two phones down. A tiny whirlwind lifts sand, and she blinks and closes her eyes.

"Rachel. Oh, Rachel, of course, how are you?"

"I'm fine, Daddy. How are you?" She wipes at the water in her eyes.

"Fine, fine. Busy as usual. How's your mother?"

"She made the trip well."

"Good, good. She's been worried about Charity. And you, of course."

"Of course."

A pause then, "So how is Charity doing? Oh, you call her Charita, right?"

"Great, Daddy. She loves it here, she really does. She's all tanned and brown as a beetle."

"That's good then. She'll enjoy visiting next summer."

"Visiting? Did you say you'd come to visit?" Clicking sounds again. "I'd like that, Daddy. It's been a long time."

"My knee gives me fits," he says. "Or I'd have come with your mother—"

"Would you?"

"—to bring Charita back. We're looking forward to having her here."

Static interrupts his words. Razi thinks she hasn't heard him right. "What makes you think Charita's coming to Milwaukee?"

"It's not a good place for her there. Too dangerous. The news is full of it."

"It isn't anything like that, Daddy. I wish you could come and see what we're doing here."

"I thought this was all settled," he says. "That's why your mother came out, to get Charity."

"That's why she's here?"

"Why, yes. Your mother said you'd already agreed to let Charity go."

20

Wilderness

Cora wraps the child in plush pink towels, rubs her slender body dry. She's ticklish at her rib cage, and her laughter sounds like rippling water. Cora dresses her in a nightshirt that says *Milwaukee Brewers* with a baseball on it. For the first time, the word *brewer* seems unfitting for a child of seven, but she'll only sleep in it. Cora puts a salve on the puncture wound and vows to take Charity to that Pythagoras Clinic in the morning. Blood poisoning comes easily to a child.

Cora bought a children's book at the airport before she left but wonders now if it might be too scary. Charity sees the colorful cover with the beastly looking characters and begs Cora to please read. "My mama doesn't have time to read," Charity says. "She works very hard. Did you read to my mama when she was little, or did she read to you?"

Cora feels a regretful twinge. "Sometimes. She learned to read herself quite young."

"I can read," Charity says. "Not big words with 'ings' and 'eds' in them, but little words. See, there's *the,* right there." She points to the title. Cora begins to read *Where the Wild Things Are,* strangely comforted by the words.

She's certainly where the wild things are. This landscape fits that description: the barren hills, the rounded ridges that rise up from the John Day River, the sand and snakes and dust and even little goat heads, weeds that poke and easily infect. Of course, from her daughter's perspective, it's a safe wilderness, not counting the snakes and spiders. Everyone believes the same things here, participates in similar exercises, shares a unifying purpose. There's little discord, at least none on the surface. The Bhagwan is idealized. In his silence, he can become whatever they want him to be: a distant, loving sage, a demanding leader, even a jokester according to the book *Drunk on the Divine,* which Cora purchased at the bookstore. Her daughter can love this man and avoid the day-to-day give-and-take that a real relationship between lovers demands. Cora suspects that her daughter seeks safety and separation. And she's found both here with the Bhagwan, where the wild things are.

But Charity hasn't found it, Cora thinks. The tiny cuts, the splintered hair, all tell of too much time alone, away from loving care. She eats well. And she doesn't look as though anyone physically harms her. She doesn't look quite as pale tonight as yesterday, but the clean pink facial skin can't mask a kind of emptiness in the child's eyes, an emptiness Cora can remember. She kisses Charity's hair, aches as the child leans into her.

The door to the bedroom flies open.

"You need to leave, Mother."

Cora bolts upright, the book dropping to the floor. "You scared me half to death."

"Such…deception."

"I didn't know how to find you to tell you Charity…Charita was here."

"This is not about finding Charita, Mother. It's about your plan to steal my daughter from me. What right do you have to even think you could do a better job of raising her?"

"Wait," Cora says. She tries to quell the pounding of her heart. "Let's go in the other room. There's no reason—"

"Charita is old enough to know how conniving her nana is," Rachel says.

"Perhaps I did mislead you into thinking I was here just to visit, but I had your best interests at heart. I truly did. I was going to bring it up. I just wanted us to have some time together before I did. And I am interested in how you're living here, I am. Your tour was fascinating. I'm reading interesting things." She points to the Bhagwan's books on the bedside stand.

However had Rachel found out? Olaf! She must have called her father, or he called her. No, he wouldn't go to the bother. Receiving a phone call here requires a fair amount of effort. Why, she's only seen the phone banks out there in the middle of town, not a single phone in any of the rooms she's been in, just at that telemarketing center.

"Daddy said it was all decided. You told him I'd agreed!"

Cora pulls the reading glasses from her nose. "Well, I hoped you would agree. I might have let him think that we'd worked it out, but I just knew you'd be reasonable once I arrived here."

"She's my child! I'd never let her come to any harm. That you would even think that—"

"That's just it, Rachel. Razi. I know you wouldn't *intend* harm to her, but you're all wrapped up in this, this place, the work here, your...inner growth, your devotion and seeking. Intention has nothing to do with it, really. Neglect has many faces. You rarely see your daughter, from what I can tell. Other people fix her food, wash her clothes, even read to her at night. She's starved for affection. No one is a stranger to her; she just talks to anyone. She apparently stays out as late as she wants. Her life isn't...normal."

"And my upbringing was, I suppose," her daughter challenges. She stands with her arms crossed over her chest, her fingernails gouged into her flesh. Cora reaches out to touch her, but her daughter retreats as though threatened by a snake. Rachel's eyes brim with tears, and red blotches flower her neck the way they always do when she's upset and unable to really say what she wants. She's never outgrown that. "I suppose having a mother busy with her clubs and hollow church functions so *her* child came home to an empty house after school and fixed my own snacks and got myself up even when you were home, I suppose that's normal. And when you were there, which wasn't much, you hovered over my every move, making sure I chose just the right clothes to wear so I wouldn't make you look bad, making sure I always 'tried a little bit harder, dear,' reminding me—*lovingly*—whenever I made a mistake or took a chance that 'I wasn't raised that way.' Did you even notice me when I wasn't performing?"

Cora sinks back onto the bed. She's aware that Charity huddles, her arms hugging a pillow. Two red spots stain her cheeks. "It's all right, Charita. Your mama and I are just talking."

"Don't patronize my daughter." Rachel brushes at Cora's hand that pats Charity's knees. "She knows as well as I do that this is outrage, not 'just talking.' She's smarter than you think."

"Well, I'm taking this outrage to another room," Cora says and stands. "You're welcome to come with me."

Cora strides to the soft couches in the L-shaped living area, her bare feet caressed by the thick carpet, her heart still pounding as she prays for time, for words. Where has all this...venom come from? Has Cora really been such a poor mother? So distant? Rachel makes it sound as though she raised herself.

"This wasn't the way I wanted to talk about Charity," Cora says when her daughter plops into the chair across from her, arms still folded over her chest. "I know you love Charity; of course you do." She clasps and unclasps her manicured nails. "She's a charming, delightful child who wouldn't be that way without you, without what you've given her through these years. But things are different now. She has different needs."

"No. She. Doesn't. She's with her mother where her mother wants her to be, facing a good, safe future here. I'll meet her needs as I always have. You have no right to judge me. I did what you wanted me to do years ago, so you have no say in how it's come out. None."

"You're busy here. You said so yourself. And you're right, I have no say. But I'd like to be a part of Charity's life. Let me take her. She has no steady male to influence her here, and your father could be that for her now that John is, well, hasn't been available."

"You can say it, Mother. Now that John is incarcerated. Yes, there's another thing I did wrong, marrying a man you found to be less than adequate who turned out to be just as you said, inadequate. Criminal."

"You came to your senses," Cora says, regretting the words the second they leave her mouth. Her daughter's eyes spill over with tears. She jabs at her cheeks to brush them away, and suddenly Cora wants to wrap her arms around this child of hers, wrap herself around Rachel the way these hills wrap around the canyon, protectively. She wants to lift Rachel up into her arms, be the valley she'll come to for refuge, the shelter from all that happened before with John, with whoever else has hurt her. Instead, she's just another goat head in her daughter's life, provoking and inflaming sensitive skin.

"Look," Cora says. She unfolds her hands, lays her palms out on her knees. "Why don't we go get something to eat? It's been a long day, and I don't think all that well on an empty stomach. I can't leave here 'just like that' anyway. You know that. Will Sheela even allow it? I thought she'd made some special arrangements for the condo. I wouldn't want to…spurn her hospitality. And I do want to spend some time with Charity. Please."

Rachel's fingers twitch against her arm the way a cat's tail does as it sits watching a mouse hole. "You won't try to steal her from me?"

"I've been reading that the Bhagwan doesn't like having children around. It could be helpful for your work here, if Charity came back to Milwaukee."

"She is my daughter," Rachel says. "She's not an orphan, Mother. She has me."

"I know that," Cora says. "But we're all orphans in a way, looking for that perfection in our parents, feeling neglected and abused and even abandoned when we don't find it. Some of us carry it into adulthood."

Rachel's shoulders sag, and she drops her arms. "I doubt you ever felt abandoned by Nana."

"Don't be so sure about that." Rachel stares at her mother, waiting. "She'd tell you, if she were alive, that I went western once, made some foolish choices. In return"—Cora makes her voice light, trying to omit the pain still there—"she left you a large trust fund and excluded me. She turned me into a barrier, the high ridge you'll have to scale until you turn thirty."

In the morning they establish a wary peace while moving Cora's suitcases and a few of Rachel's personal possessions into a nicely furnished condo up a distant canyon. The red buildings stand two stories tall and like Monopoly game hotels, scrunched close together, at least four in a cluster marked by covered porches Rachel calls decks. The abode is larger than Cora expected, at least eight bedrooms: four upstairs, four down. Up the stairway, she sees that a futon and elegantly shaped brass lamp top the open stairwell.

"Charita and I will sleep in this one," Rachel says, taking the room to the right of the stairwell. "That one's the same size." She points to the room directly across from the one she chooses.

"Will Rajiid sleep with us tonight, Mama?"

"Maybe Charita would like to share Nana's room," Cora says.

"That would be better. At least for tonight," Rachel says when Charita sticks her lower lip out in protest. Cora hears voices coming from a room near the back, and the sound of a clothes dryer. They must be servers, she decides when the voices disappear as she's unpacking.

Rachel leaves to lead her meditations, and a carer-person, as they call the children's servers, along with three other children, takes Charity to the river to float on inner tubes. Cora's not invited. At least the child will be protected. Cora finds herself with an unsupervised afternoon.

It occurs to Cora that the trust fund might be the bargaining chip she can trade for Charity.

Does that make me a terrible person? She writes this in her journal, a necessary outlet she discovers that morning after reading in Psalms. She lied to her husband, telling him Rachel had already agreed. Well, she let him think that, though she didn't actually say it aloud. *What kind of wife am I? What kind of mother, to have raised a daughter who might take money for her child?* And yet if Cora releases the funds, they'll only go into this...this cult of self-deception. *What kind of mother would relegate her daughter to such mercenary hands? Is that not neglect?* Her granddaughter's future is worth whatever it might take, but in making such a trade, does she condemn her own child to disaster, possibly even death? Does that make Cora any better a mother than her daughter? So much to consider. Her thinking's getting muddled. She ought to talk with Olaf, see if he's annoyed with her, apologize for her misleading.

She walks down the stone-lined path, then out toward the airstrip and reception center where she signs up for a tour to see if she can clarify for herself what this commune is: camp or occupation.

The Twinkie tour guide raves about the Rajneesh conservation practices. "Huge herds of deer and elk find a place here on this divine land," she says. She identifies the many trees planted to shade both residences and streams "to protect the fish." She points out sagebrush and cut juniper trees lining the banks of Muddy Creek "so when the water runs high, debris will collect along the side in the tree branches and the soil will not erode." She has an accent with lovely, lilting words.

"Won't all the tree cutting and digging *cause* erosion?" Cora asks.

"Oh no. We employ the best practices here as we create new, healthy land. Vida is well trained, and he ensures that we do everything better than it could be done anywhere else. We have a compost that forms new earth, and we mix this with the neglected ground that required many acres just to feed a single cow. Now we have rich soil. See, we do everything. Even make soil." People laugh.

The idea of creating soil amuses Cora, too. It sounds like something her neighbor in Milwaukee mentioned when Cora complained about the foul smell arising from an old oil drum in his backyard. He'd made a compost drum by following directions in that hippie magazine *Mother Earth News.* He did have healthy soil for his tomatoes the next year, but it was hardly new, just reformed. There's nothing new under the sun. She read that in Ecclesiastes.

A few others on the tour ask questions too. She wonders if an older couple said to be visiting their son might like to spend time with her later. She tries to talk with them at the stop in front of the post office, but the Twinkie reprimands her as though she's in the seventh grade. "Others won't be able to hear if we all talk at once, yes?" Cora nods and feels her face flush. After that, the couple always has other touring Sannyasins between them and Cora. *A pariah gets identified quickly here.*

The Twinkie points out sorting areas for bottles and cans and paper, and a special site for items that have been in contact with "bodily fluids." "Even sewing needles are doused with alcohol. For cleanliness," the Twinkie adds, then quickly moves on to another subject before Cora can pursue what threaded needles have to do with bodily fluids.

An attractive man dressed in a burgundy business suit leans into Cora. "It does seem that cleanliness is the order of the day here, with bottles of disinfectant set about, wouldn't you say?" His accent is British, his hair gray. He wears a gold-framed mala on a long string of ebony beads.

"You noticed that too? Even on the bus someone can disinfect their hands."

"Yet most everyone wears freshly laundered clothes, and showering doesn't seem to be a problem either." He smiles at her, his eyes moving down her frame. "Everyone looks scrubbed clean." He takes a deep breath through his nose. "You've certainly come from a refreshing place." Cora feels her cheeks grow hot. He smells of a scent Cora thinks is called patchouli. She sniffed it in the men's section at the boutique, thinking she might buy some for Olaf.

"My daughter says they've plenty of water here, though there are some disturbing signs at the Magdalena Cafeteria."

"Sh," warns the Twinkie, and Cora is relieved to have a reason to be silent.

"If I were to come here," someone asks, "would I do what I had done in the larger world, or would I be assigned something new?"

"We would decide what was best for you," the Twinkie says.

"We? Who would 'we' be?"

"Your fellow Sannyasins, who look out for your interests in light of the Bhagwan's guidance and your own journey to enlightenment."

"It would be a committee decision?"

"What did you do before coming here?" another woman asks the Twinkie.

"I owned a designer boutique in Brasilia," she says. "But when I came here it was to find true happiness in service to Bhagwan." She smiles as she says his name. "Though he would not say it was to serve him, but to discover ourselves that we are here. And from that we will transform the world at this Buddhafield."

"That's the religion then?" a man not dressed in red asks. He's taking notes, and Cora assumes he's a reporter. If so, then all the descriptions the Twinkie is giving might be less candid than Cora hoped.

The religion question appears to fluster the Twinkie, and she says the commune is not a religion, though there are religious practices. "The Bhagwan is a holy man, but his is a nonreligious religion. We can believe what we wish. Here are the bird operations," the Twinkie says. She chatters on, and Cora is aware that the gray-haired man is standing across from her now. He smiles, and Cora wonders at the racing of her heart.

The Twinkie says the bird operations house both laying hens and pullets. In another area she points at large ostrichlike birds called emus, which, like the many peacocks strutting around, "help protect against the snakes. We may also have a large enough herd to market emu meat, which is both tasty and healthy. It is another way we wish to integrate with the larger community and dispel the myth that we are isolated and contrary. We are a happy place, good neighbors."

The armed guards who patrol the streets and a second helicopter overhead drown out some of what she says. "We have all our own eggs too," she continues after the helicopter moves on. "This is a wonderful thing that we provide so much of the food to feed our residents and guests. We even do special research to improve the health of our poultry, and in this way we avoid problems with salmonella that sometimes plagues large egg operations. We will share our knowledge with the world to benefit mankind. We have thought of everything."

The bus takes them past various housing developments hidden by trees and hills. The Twinkie assures them there are enough A-frames and cabin-tents for the many guests in ravines, known as Gautam the Buddha Grove and Walt Whitman Grove. "The Bhagwan lives in that compound." Cora spies a sliver of manicured lawn behind newly planted trees, huge stone pillars, and a high security fence. "Words of Buddha are inscribed on the pillars," she notes. "Bodhisattva Sheela's home was custom manufactured with no kitchen. We all eat together." Cora can't believe the leaders eat with the common people, and she wants to ask her what the title *bodhisattva* means, but the Twinkie no longer makes any eye contact with Cora. But every time she looks across the circle, the gray-haired gentleman does.

"Where does that path go?" someone asks.

"This is off limits except to residents," the Twinkie says. "It leads to the crematorium where we had a beautiful ceremony last August."

Cora remembers what Rachel said about the crematorium and wonders if the Twinkie will tell her the same thing. "With so few residents here year-round, why would you need a crematorium?" she asks.

"We are a complete city," the Twinkie says irritably. "With an airstrip and transportation company and an electrical generator and a sewage and water system and even a university. We coordinate all the work of other ashrams around the world, and many Sannyasins from those centers are drawn here because the Bhagwan is here. Why wouldn't we want to have everything a person would need for their entire lives, including the end of their earthly life?" Her dark eyes flash.

Everything they need. Except a way to deliver babies.

"Everything we do here is as it should be," the Twinkie says over the microphone as she pulls rubber gloves from her hands and tosses them aside. They return to the reception center to end the tour.

"Would you care to have some oolong tea?" the gray-haired man asks as Cora waits for the Twinkie's final chirping blurb.

The Twinkie says, "The Divine has blessed this place with the Bhagwan's presence, and everything that happens here is part of the Divine's plan."

"I'd enjoy your company," the gray-haired man says. He has agate-colored eyes, and Cora's palms sweat as she notices them.

"You need to return to the reception center," the Twinkie says as she walks through the dispersing tour group toward Cora and the gray-haired man, her cheerful lilt gone. "You have no wristband. I'm surprised you have gotten through the checkpoints without one. I should not have let you on the tour. You must go now. A peace officer and his dog will take you." A guard seems to materialize next to Cora out of nowhere.

Cora's relieved to be rescued from the muddle of the gray-haired man and her racing heart, but unsettled. She follows the German shepherd and his gun-toting master, wondering if Rachel has reneged on their truce and found a way to send her mother home.

21

INATTENTION

"Mother, what are you doing here?" Rachel stands naked at the bedroom door. She hikes a hand towel over her breasts, then seems to think again, lowers it, holding it loosely at her side.

"I…just came back. I had to get a wristband." Cora shows her the green plastic bracelet. "And they drew blood. At your Pythagoras Clinic. Disgusting process. My, it's warm in here."

"Just a precaution," a man says. "The physical." He walks from the bathroom toward Rachel and stands behind her drying his face with a towel that hangs down, barely covering the front of him. Both of them have wet hair. "You must be Razi's mother?" He lowers the towel. "I'm Rajiid."

At least Charita's at the river.

"I didn't realize you had company."

"We left our sandals outside the door. All you had to do was look."

"Yes. I should have. I…" Cora ignores the man's hand he reaches out in greeting. "Oh, I [illegible]" She casts about for someplace safe to rest her eyes.

"Hey, love, where's the soap?" A young woman sings from upstairs. Cora hears a man's voice mumbling as well. The woman squeals in delight, and both bound naked down the steps, stop when they see Cora, and smile, don't even bother to look embarrassed. They glide on down the steps, and the girl lights a vanilla-scented candle in the hallway. The man with her stands and smirks.

"How many people are…here? I thought you had your sessions this afternoon."

"They'll spend the night in their room, if that's what you're worried about, Mother."

"We won't keep you awake, love," the smirking man says. *Their room?*

"I'm not worried. I just…don't you think you should get dressed? All of you."

"It's how we arrived in this world. Just the way God made us," Razi says.

"And poor choices made us understand that we should cover up. Charita shouldn't be exposed to—"

"Nana." A small voice demands. "Did you bring me a present?" Charita stands, hands on hips, at Cora's bedroom door. *At least the child has clothes on.*

"It's the human body, Mother. Made in God's image. Nothing to be embarrassed about."

Cora feels her face grow warm. She looks away, thinks better, says, "Charita, I didn't get you a present, but if you want to come along with me now, we'll stop at the mall and see what we can find."

"Can I keep what you get me, as my very own?" She glares at her mother.

"Yes," Cora answers for her. "You shouldn't have to share everything that matters."

Charity stomps down the steps, then fast-walks along the stone-lined path toward the shopping area. "Wait," Cora says, and the child slows. Cora's mind's a muddle. The heat of anger warms her cheeks. Her daughter's lack of regard for what a child should see and not see, of how little she must care for herself to let strangers walk naked around her daughter, let alone herself, weighs on her. What has happened to Rachel?

Cora passes Charity, slows when the girl complains. "My foot hurts, Nana."

"Does it? Let me see." She looks at Charity's heel. A small black line thin as a spider's leg marks the back of her calf. Of course. She neglected to take the child to the clinic. She's no better than Rachel. The carer-person hadn't noticed it either.

"Bad things are happening here," Cora says as she settles Charity onto her hip and heads toward the clinic. She and Rachel must finish last night's conversation and come to resolution. She doesn't see how Charity's remaining here can be good for this child at all, especially not with this nakedness business. Being here isn't even good for Cora, as she's forgetting important things like tending to this child's infection. Even worse, Cora's aware that the attention of that gray-haired man on the tour stirred strange, unwelcome feelings in her.

As though she's willed him into her presence, a car pulls up beside her, driven by that man. "Can I offer you a lift then?" Cora hesitates, then nods. She wants Charity seen as soon as possible, and surely this man won't try anything with a child along.

"The kids?" he says when Cora makes small talk as he drives. "I'm told most live at the other town, Rajneesh. They don't come out here much at all except in the summer. In our ashram, there's a building for them, lots of bunks. Kids love bunk beds, don't you, love?" He smiles at Charity.

"I like my own wide bed I have at Nana and Mama's," Charity says.

"Your own wide bed. Well, that's something," he says and reaches over Charity's head to rest his hand on Cora's shoulder. His hand feels hot as flame.

"And Mama won't let anyone stay overnight with us while Nana's here. She told me, she did."

"The clinic's that way," Cora says, leaning forward, out from under the hand. She points to one of the red-stained buildings beyond a wide row of tents. "I appreciate your giving us a lift."

"You might have to go on into Madras," he says. "I can wait and drive you if you'd like." *He's just being kind. He must have some authority here to have access to a car.*

"We'll pick up some antibiotics. That should do it," she says cheerfully. "I can't imagine we'll need anything more."

"I'll look for you during the festival, then, love. You never know what you might need."

While they wait to see a doctor, Cora struggles. Has she done something to entice the man? Should she care that he flirts? Flirtation's harmless. All Europeans do it, or so she's heard. She's done nothing wrong. Neither has he. It was a touch of friendship. Yet her cheeks warm in the way that once followed Olaf's touch.

The waiting room smells of antiseptic. Posters of Bhagwan look down on them with searing eyes. Servers bring out tea, and Cora takes a cup, the flavor refreshing on her tongue. Charity leans against her, dozing, and Cora picks up another of the Bhagwan's books. She wants to use the Bhagwan's own words to convince her daughter that being right with the Bhagwan means surrendering Charity to her. *Devotion is the highest form of love,* she reads. *Devotion is a kind of madness.... Devotion is the art of dying, of drowning one's self. It is not the art of seeking God but of losing one's self. In seeking God, the ego remains as it is; the seeker remains as he is.* Just reading the words troubles her, all the talk about dying or drowning as part of devotion. Cora pictures the lake.

No, she can't think that.

The Bhagwan contradicts himself. He does require devotion. That's what all these young people are doing here, devoting their lives to him under his rules of what to wear, how to live, even what their therapy and occupations should be. And yet he claims they live in freedom. And what is the point of seeking if "the seeker remains as he is?" Doesn't God transform human beings? Isn't that the whole point of devotion? *The Bhagwan abuses the loyalty of his followers, takes advantage of them for his own reward.*

She paws through more pages, more accounts of people finding their way to this Bhagwan. He says nothing of children. Perhaps the omission speaks loudest. The glossary at the end might be helpful, but the only thing she takes away from it is the definition of Sannyasins—*to take Sannyas, to detach from the world, to become a disciple of Bhagwan.* She closes the book and watches as a butterfly lands on a yellow flower blooming outside the window.

She read once that agents trained to spot counterfeit money study the "real thing," for hours or days, before they're ever shown the counterfeit bills. One has to know the "real thing" in order to identify what isn't.

Cora is annoyed with herself that she can't articulate the "real thing" well. She doesn't know how to counter the Bhagwan's teachings or even Rachel's words. That brief interchange over nudity distresses. She pulls Charity closer. Cora's faith is childlike, elementary, she decides. Maybe she's in over her head, trying to talk about God with a daughter who's chosen to surrender to Bhagwan. Cora certainly hasn't devoted her life so completely to her own faith. In fact, she's neglected her faith journey for some time.

She sees that now, and sadness creeps across her heart. She's neglected it though she's attended church each Sunday. Abused it the way the landscape here has been abused, tall grazing grasses stripped and replaced by thousands of flimsy tents and gaping sites dotted with dressed-up condos. She should read the Scriptures more; but she can hardly call on the Bible to support her when she's been so miserly with her attention to it for so many years.

She recalls a poem she read years before by the German poet Rilke, about God sending each person "out beyond their recall, going to the limits of their longing." Maybe she's been led here not only to rescue her grandchild, but to learn to think differently, to be pushed beyond the routines that abuse her own spiritual journey, that numb her spiritual sensitivity. Maybe she is here to go out beyond her recall into a wilderness where her own faith requires her attention so she can be transformed.

The doctor has kind eyes. He checks Charity, gives her a sucker, and cleans the wound. He gives her a shot, and she is brave. He hands Cora pills.

Outside, Cora nods at various people they encounter as they walk slowly to the mall. It doesn't seem like fifteen thousand people have gathered. The festival is scheduled to start tomorrow; surely the guests would have arrived by now. Already Cora is exhausted.

"Bhagwan will drive by soon, Nana," Charity says. "See the helicopter?"

She hears the chopper hovering. Sannyasins suddenly move as one to line the road on either side, their hands in the namaste position. Armed guards riding on the front fender of advance vehicles show off their carbines, glaring. The look of joyous awe on the faces of the onlookers makes Cora ache. It's as though they're in a trance. Little shouts of joy burst from their lips. Some toss flower petals at this man with a white beard and small wool cap on his head despite the warm weather. The car prowls through his adoring throng.

What is it about him that makes so many people give up everything to follow? Intelligent people. Otherwise discerning people. What has he promised them? Carefree living? But they work long hours. And look at the armor; he's unapproachable. No common person comes within fifty feet of him, except when he's inside his Rolls-Royce. Even then, bodyguards scan the crowd for crazy outsiders who might hurt him. Cora feels like a target in her brown slacks and ivory blouse. She lifts Charity to her hip. *The child's so thin!*

His followers do not notice her, they simply adore him. Only the peace force focuses on something other than Bhagwan. Peace force. Even the protection is a contradiction.

They're arguing again, this time on the outside deck. Music piped in from the Mandir Meditation Center rises over the open area and floats onto their condo nestled in the ravine. The evening promises to be warm and pleasant, if only her mother will stop haranguing. Her mother makes a canyon from a rut. Razi does feel badly that she didn't see Charita's infected foot, but the girl is getting medication now.

"She's fine. Children get slivers, bug bites, all kinds of things. Even in Milwaukee. It's part of growing up, Mother. You've just forgotten."

"She's being exposed to all kinds of things she shouldn't ever see, and especially not at this young age. I'm… Perhaps she and I should stay at Jesus Grove during the festival. Give you and your friends… privacy."

"This is what's been arranged. It's a privilege to be here. You want time with Charita, this is where it'll be."

"If not the clinic," her mother snaps.

Razi sighs. "You didn't notice it either, and when you did you took care of it. If the carer had seen it, she'd have tended it. We're communal, Mother. Charita has lots of mommies. And things happen. It's not the end of the world."

"No, that's fifteen years away, isn't that what you said?"

"We called a truce until after the festival at least, didn't we? Let's try to find a way to just endure each other's company until then. If you can't do that, maybe you should just go home."

"No, no. You're right. I was just frightened for her, that's all. Blood poisoning is terribly painful. And she's so little. She isn't getting enough nutrition—"

"Mother, please."

Razi hears the vehicle first and turns. The Indian driver gets out. Buckle, that's his name. He holds a newspaper. She motions him onto the deck.

"You remembered my paper," her mother says.

"Aay, Mrs. S., I did. This place makes news. The *Oregonian* reporter's got comments by locals about the impact of fifteen thousand festivalgoers on this landscape. A couple of Sannyasins say this will be a special festival as the Master's having 'trouble staying in his body.'" Her mother looks a question at Razi. "Means it might be the very last time people get to see him," Buckle says. "Explains why everyone's traveling from far away to be here at this little spot beside Muddy Creek."

Her mother finds the article, reads aloud. "'From a press release of Rajneesh Foundation International urging people to attend the festival...to show these idiotic politicians that their fear is not going to stop the work of the Rajneeshees.' How loving is that?"

"Another shot fired into the hills," Buckle says.

"I'll get my money. Thank you for remembering the paper," her mother says and leaves despite Buckle's protest. Razi offers him iced tea, which he declines, asks for water instead.

He sits on the wooden railing. They listen in silence to the music until Buckle says, "I wish the Harvey family still lived in the old ranch house. I always stopped for coffee with them, when you folks first came here. There were fewer guardhouses then."

Razi remembers the Harveys. The former ranch manager hasn't come to mind for several months. "He was going to teach Charita how to ride," she says.

"Never even knew they were leaving. Miss the kids," Buckle tells her.

"Did you know the Harveys well?" She hopes her mother will hurry back. She's not comfortable conversing with non-Sannyasin men. Too intimate; too revealing.

"We gathered up wild horses together. He knew all the old stories of this place along with some of the hands from Prineville and Madras and Antelope." As long as he talks, she's fine. "My people have their own history here. And I have my own story." He looks at her as though deciding whether to say something more. "About two years ago, after Sheela first came here, an old cowboy from Eugene called me up and said he'd had a vision about this place. He said it ought to be a home for orphan boys or displaced kids. He wanted me to come up here with him and pray for the land, that God might bring that about one day."

"Did you?"

"Did. Drove up with our horse trailer, and your people wouldn't let us in, so we took a side road, and the way just opened up because the gate wasn't locked. The road was muddy slick like driving on intestines, but we made it, and no one pursued us. We rode our horses to the top of the ridge overlooking the ranch, spent the whole day. Strangest thing I've ever done. My grandmother and her sisters would have been proud that I'd spent a day praying to redeem this land."

Why is everyone so critical of what we've built here? "Does it need to be redeemed? Look at how beautiful we've made what used to be dry, barren grasses."

"That cowboy used the word all day long, like he was collecting on a promise or saving something from a worse fate. My grandmother always said *redeem* had to do with the price of changing a person's heart."

"We're doing fine by this land," Razi defends.

He nods politely, lets her have the last word. He glances down at the newspaper. "Looks like some of your folks are thumbing their noses at Oregon's politicians. With the election in the fall, you might not want to antagonize the commissioners who've been good to you. Even a guy with limited education like me knows not to aggravate a herd of bulls by throwing rocks at them, aay, especially when the fence between you is made of legal paper."

Razi will take this over talk of redemption and land being made into children's camps. "I think sometimes our leaders go a little far," she says. "But they're wiser than I am. I'm just a faithful follower. My mother must be minting those coins for your paper."

"It's only thirty-five cents. Tell Mrs. S. it's on me, and I don't charge for delivery. I best get back on my ponies there"—he nods with his chin toward his car—"and head home." He takes the deck steps two at a time, then stops. "Did you say Bob Harvey was going to teach Charita to ride?" Razi nods. "I could do that for you, if you'd like. Course, whoever's managing the stables could show her, if they have horse sense."

"I think the coordinators pressed the new stable manager into that because he took his other job too seriously. He worked in the medical laboratory with Puja, but he was…reassigned." She is saying too much. "I'd have to get permission," she says. "To use the horses and the paddock area."

He nods, walks slowly down the steps. She rubs her arms. It's cold. She feels suddenly lonely. She could invite him to stay. Rajiid is staying in his tent tonight, and she'd like a diversion from her mother's judging eyes. It is a long drive back for him. A part of her fears he might accept her offer; another part fears he wouldn't.

"Maybe after the festival," he says then, turning back to her at the bottom step. "I can come back and teach her then. I gotta be going now."

"Yes," Razi says, relieved. His grin is wide, and he straightens his headband. Yellow today. "Good then. I'll see you in a few weeks."

She likes the idea of seeing him again, and she's glad she didn't try to fill in a lonely place with the touch of a stranger. She'll deal first with the emptiness between her and her mother.

22

ATTENTION

Razi sits in the back of the coordinator's meeting with Ma Anand Sheela reigning at her living room's throne, legs curled under her like a kitten on the cushions. Razi's invitation to be present at this July meeting, included in the small inner circle, is a high honor, especially considering the failure of the festival. Only half of the projected fifteen thousand people attended. There were no incidents, nothing to warrant trouble, but fewer had enrolled in the lucrative month-long therapy sessions than planned, and even fewer presented alms on behalf of the needs of the Buddhafield.

Rajneesh Mayor Ma Prem Deepa says it isn't failure, but rather a challenge. "Fewer people came in support," she says. "So we are challenged to spread the word of Bhagwan's needs. We must work harder now, another kind of joy." The mayor sits close to the front on the pillow-covered floor, looking up at Sheela.

Razi's palms grow wet with the effort of making herself small in this hallowed place. She imagines this is what it's like to sit in the presence of the Bhagwan, sitting here at the feet of one closest to him. Incense perfumes the air. A soft morning breeze lifts a meadowlark's warble through the screened windows. Razi blows against the oolong tea she cradles, then tastes, her eyes focused on the dark liquid rather than on the leopard-black eyes of Sheela. Razi pushes her dark hair behind her ears so it won't dip into her mug. She wipes her palms on her sunset-colored jersey pants.

This meeting did not begin with jokes. Instead, the chief lawyer updated them on the various lawsuits involving the land, the city, and the permit process, as well as one against Sheela by a former Antelope resident for libel and Sheela's countersuit. Sheela, however, jokes about these and the "little worms" that brought them all.

The head of the Rajneesh Modern Car Collection Trust discusses acquisition of Rolls-Royce number seventy-five, and each Sannyasin present smiles and applauds with the pads of their fingers, making the sound of rain. Individual units of the Rajneesh Neo-Sannyas International Commune provide reports, including the Buddhafield Transport Bus Line, and the community infrastructure coordinator, who discusses the successful sewage disposal during the Master's Day Festival. Rajneesh Investment Corporation, Rajneesh Foundation International (the church), the Institute for Therapy (of which Razi is currently an assistant), the international commune, the medical corporation, legal services, the financial trust, the humanities trust, the World Celebrations Committee, even the Rajneesh Travel Service all provide updates. Ma Prem Deeva provides a report of the city of Rajneesh, as does the mayor of the incorporated city of Rancho Rajneeshpuram. Like a talisman, everyone who speaks of Rajneeshpuram precedes the word *city* with *incorporated* in an almost reverential tone, as though saying it will make it so.

"We will implement our larger plan, then," Sheela says when each coordinator finishes. Murmuring ensues, and Sheela raises her small hand dismissively, gold bracelet glinting in the morning sun. She silences the others. "I will tell you which one," she says. "One at a time, like a little dance we'll do, yes? We begin with the need to win the election for commissioners this fall. These silly Oregonians have almost no restriction on who can vote in an election as long as they 'intend' to become a resident. We have many good intentions," she says to laughter. She silences them again with a wave of her hand. "We have two and one half months to accomplish this, but all depends on the success of the incorporated city being recognized by the county. This can happen if we have the right people as commissioners. Then we can continue to access the federal and state funds we are entitled to and thus build our city, even though our individual support has lessened. That is merely the ebb and flow of the universe. The tides will change before long, but we will be the moon to cause the change. These ignorant Oregonians are still jumping their cows over that moon, thinking it nothing but a children's rhyme."

Everyone laughs. "We will all participate," she says, casting her cat-wide eyes around the room, stopping on Razi. "Even those who believe they have less to offer than others. Even those who think sometimes that their leaders go a little far." Razi feels herself blush with the warmth of Sheela's recognition and with confusion. Weren't those the very words she'd said to Buckle?

"The Share-a-Home project is what we will implement. It involves all of us. Public relations will get many calls about this once the ads appear in the paper. The vultures of journalists will have a joy with this, but we will point out to them the humanitarian nature of this effort, rescuing people from harsh city streets before the winter. We must recruit five thousand at least in order to have a sufficient number of voters."

"The costs for this project will be substantial," one of the coordinators says. "Getting them here, controlling them, the numbers needed—"

"We have need of resources!" Sheela screams the words.

"Perhaps one less Rolls-Royce—"

"I will tolerate no weakness," Sheela says. Her words hiss in the direction of whoever dared to suggest one less Rolls-Royce. The Bhagwan hisses too, drawing out each syllable as though stretching it to a breaking point. "The Bhagwan will have what he needs," Sheela announces.

"We'll need more than five thousand homeless voters," one of the lawyers says, his fingers at a calculator. "There are seven thousand registered voters in the county. We'll have to have more than that to elect our candidate."

"This is our last opportunity," Sheela says, her voice high as a hungry cat. "Without an infusion of financial resources, our work here is doomed. To acquire them, we must become an incorporated city, or they will never let us alone. You see how they challenge. You see how they treat us like dung. Are we dung? No! We are chosen." She pulls the red silk sari from her shoulders, revealing her slender arms. No .357 at her hip today. "It is all worked out." She's calm again. "Five thousand is all we will need." She smiles at Puja, the nurse, whose hair is drawn back into a severe bun, pulling her almond eyes tight. She sits with her legs folded under her too. "Are there other objections?" Sheela asks. "Let us hear them." Her eyes scan the now-silent room.

"Razi," Sheela finally says, "you will coordinate the phone banks used by Sannyasins to solicit funds for this special one-time project." Ma Prem Deepa smiles at her. Razi swells and listens. She is part of the trusted inner circle not just for this meeting but for the future! They will bring in five thousand homeless people, provide them with food, shelter, and health care, and invite them to register to vote. Right up until the last day of the election, they can register to vote. It is the Oregon way. "The Rajneesh way is to take advantage of their silly loopholes," Sheela says to the applause of finger pads.

The discussion complete, Sheela prepares to dismiss the group. She scans the room once more, taking them all in, drinking from their faces as though from a single pool of refreshment. "All resources are valued. Any worship through work is desired and loved by the Bhagwan. I will tell him of all your efforts. Remember," she says, "any treasure is important." She flashes a diamond necklace tucked inside her magenta blouse and pulls it out for all to see. "Even my husband's gift of love to me. I will toss it out to still the tides of the moon." Everyone claps their fingers. "But," she says, her eyes stopping on Razi at last, "American dollars can be converted most quickly."

Can Sheela possibly know of her trust fund? She doesn't see how.

"Remain behind, Ma Prem Razi," Sheela says, raising her ring-weighted hand. Now Razi's heart does pound with hope, though she can't tell by the way Sheela looks at her if she's pleased or upset.

They've survived the festival without argument, and Cora believes it's because she's chosen to be happy rather than right. If she doesn't contradict or correct her daughter, all goes well. She tells herself she isn't being weak by not confronting Razi about the disturbing things she sees and hears. Instead, she's buying time, gaining strength for her final move, whatever that might be.

Charity sits in a pile of white, beachlike sand not far from one of the dirt roads she and Cora have walked along this morning. Why there's a pile of beach sand in the middle of this desolate country, Cora cannot fathom. A wisp of cobweb cloud sweeps across the sky. Cora settles beneath a juniper tree, the fallen foliage making a soft bed once she brushes away the purple berries. She leans back, watches while Charity makes her sand castles. She'll write in her journal. She takes out her pen, then something red catches her eye. She gets up to look at the flash of color in the shade of another juniper.

Barrel cacti, in bloom.

Surely these aren't native. Cacti in Oregon are as out of place as an East Indian guru. As out of place as her once worldly and vivacious daughter in this harsh, high-desert land.

Rachel was quite a catch as a teenager, outgoing and flirtatious. Olaf always enjoyed his daughter and her animated stories of the young men she teased, then discarded. He chided Cora when she pointed out that such flirtations could lead to trouble. Someone might take their daughter seriously and plot revenge, or assume she was older, or worse, take advantage of her. Men have minimal control of their impulses; at least that has been Cora's experience. But Olaf said he thought Rachel both lovely and wise and able to take care of herself. "My women are good, strong women," Olaf was fond of saying.

But when Rachel latched onto several different older boys and at age sixteen brought home a man in his midtwenties, Olaf finally intervened and sent Rachel to an all-girls boarding school.

With a level of guilt, Cora realizes as she writes in her journal that she didn't mind Rachel being away. Her daughter came home most weekends and school breaks, holidays and summers, so it wasn't that she didn't have time with her daughter, she did. But Rachel was right about Cora's clubs, her community commitments, taking her time. Perhaps she had neglected Rachel. With Rachel at school, Cora could pursue her passions. She earned an art degree but was never paid for using it. Instead, she devoted hours to the local theater group, building sets and sewing elaborate costumes for full-blown productions with lights and music and choreographed scenes. There, Cora pursued her passions at the expense of her child. She winces.

In the intervening years, Rachel honed her skills. She completed high school, moved on to college. Her flirtations had engaged her to John, a suave young man with intellectual promise but few practical goals. Rachel wooed Olaf's consent. They married, and Olaf set them up with a house, a new car, and an allowance while they attended college. Cora still thinks that a mistake. Every young marriage needed the challenge of working together, overcoming barriers to accomplish mutual goals, and they had stripped the couple of that. John soon dropped out of school. Rachel became pregnant, and with time on his hands while Rachel attended classes, John made poor choices, neglecting his wife and his studies. Rachel turned to religion. An Eastern religion. Olaf paid for her first trip to India.

Today, Cora sees in her daughter an older woman, harder, leaner, and not attached to worldly affection. She wonders how much different detachment is from neglect, really. Perhaps it is a way to ease the pain of being overlooked.

Charity tires of sand play, and they walk slowly back to the condo, the child pointing at rocks. "Doesn't that one look like a face, Nana?" She shivers. "It's a wild thing." She bends to pick wildflowers that wilt in her hot hands.

At the phone banks, Cora decides to try Olaf while Charity shows her limp flowers to Sannyasins passing by. Cora sees that she's no longer limping as she giggles with the adults.

Olaf answers. He sounds pleased to hear from her, but he chastises her too about misleading him into thinking everything was arranged for "Charity's return."

"Escape, you mean," Cora says.

"Ya. Escape, though maybe it's not so bad there as what the press says. I don't hear from you so often, so it must be all right sometimes. I wonder if maybe you've met someone there to take care of you."

"Don't be ridiculous." She hasn't seen the gray-haired man since the festival ended, and while she feels a little regret not to have shared an iced tea with him, she is also greatly relieved. "I didn't think you'd want to be bothered," she tells him. "And I have to stand outside to call. Or get a ride to Antelope to a pay phone."

"Ya, and you didn't want me to scold you for your white lie." The phone crackles.

"I don't think I ever said outright that Rachel had agreed to let Charity come with me. I thought Rachel would see that it was best for Charity."

"Charita, she calls the child."

"Yes. I try to remember. I don't want to antagonize her or make poor Charity—Charita—have to choose between us." She waves at her granddaughter, who turns at the sound of her name.

"How long will you stay?"

"Now that the festival is over, we'll have our talk. I can't just run with her like I thought I might have to." Cora lowers her voice as a Sannyasin picks up the phone next to her. "There are guards everywhere," she whispers now. "And they've got a cadre of Madison Avenue lawyers who'd chase me down, I'm sure. I don't think there's enough evidence to say that she is physically abused or neglected. The things I've seen sound...mundane when I write them out," she explains.

"So maybe you don't think she should come back with you?"

"Oh no, I don't have any question in my mind that she needs to be"—the Sannyasin next to her glances up—"somewhere else." She turns her back to the other phones. "This is no place for a child. It's the one thing the Bhagwan and I can agree on. She's allowed to run free, set her own schedule, do whatever she wants when she wants to.

That's neglect, isn't it, not helping a child learn the limits of living, not supporting her through her choices? But I also know she'll be devastated without her mother. She worries about her, Olaf. She takes care of Rachel in little ways. Runs to get her pills. Puts washcloths on her forehead. It's like Charity's the mother and Rachel's the child."

"She used to worry over you, Rachel did."

"No. I never noticed that," Cora protests.

"Ya. She ran for your aspirin when you held your head. She reminded you to color your hair."

Cora laughs. "I don't think it's the same. I want Charity out of here, away from the influences here, the undercurrents and innuendos. But the thing is, I want Rachel out too, Olaf. Even though she's a grown woman, I want her free of this...bondage they have her in. I wish you were here. You could describe it maybe. They're worried about the end of the world, and that makes me anxious about how far they might go to get what they want. Did you hear me? The phone has such a loud hum at my end. Anyway, that Sheela even wears a .357 magnum. Charity told me that. Imagine, a child knowing about that sort of thing. But I can't haul Rachel out of here against her will any more than I can take Charity out if Rachel protests." The line clicks. "Olaf?"

"Ya, I'm here."

"Nothing fits. There are contradictions. They say they've plenty of water but post rules about flushing toilets. And they report having plenty of money—and they're spending it—there are bulldozers and huge trucks and building going on all the time. And yet Rachel says the commune is losing money."

"Nothing good then," Olaf says.

She pauses. "I saw barrel cacti today, blooming red. Isn't that strange?"

"You want me to come there?"

"It would take so much time from your work." His offer brings such relief, yet she can't bring herself to ask for his help. "And your knee. The plane trip would be hard on it."

A pause. "You'll do well, then. You make good decisions, Cora."

Cora sighs. Yes, she does. But sometimes it would be better not to have to make them alone.

"Do you have something to tell us, Razi?" Sheela asks. Puja has stayed behind, and Razi is aware that the nurse listens without smiling.

"To tell you? I…am grateful to be helping with the Share-a-Home project."

"You have a trust."

How does she know? Did Razi ever mention it to the mayor? Maybe.

"My mother is the executor. I don't know if I can get the funds released early, but I'll get it all in two years, all five hundred thousand dollars."

Sheela is as motionless as a stalking jaguar waiting to pounce. "It will help with the homeless program. Perhaps you could offer your mother your child in return for the release of the funds. You might consider it."

Razi knows this for certain: She's never mentioned to anyone her mother's wish to take Charita back with her. The Bhagwan must be clairvoyant, have special powers to know what's happening. Or perhaps the phones are tapped. But why eavesdrop on their most loyal followers?

"Unless you think your leaders go a little far."

"No, I—"

"We have another task for you as well. You can handle more than one assignment, yes, a woman as wise as you?"

23

SECRETS

Everyone knows of Razi's role now. They nod to her with new respect as she makes her way to the condo at the end of the day. She arranges transportation and accommodations for the homeless people; that's her new responsibility. The new recruits will arrive using the Rajneesh Travel Service, which will arrange for bus tickets from Atlanta, New York, Chicago, Milwaukee, Los Angeles, Denver, and a dozen other urban centers. They expect the biggest influx at the end of September, which gives Razi the rest of July, August, and September to rise to the occasion. Razi suggests they subcontract additional transportation, as they did for the festival, to bring people from Portland and Seattle. She thinks of Buckle. She hasn't seen him for several weeks now with all the activity. Charita even asks about him. She doesn't wonder where Rajiid went.

The plan is to house the homeless in A-frames built for the festival and construct additional ones as needed. The structures have wooden floors and walls, are easily moved to remote canyons. They've been moved out of the way, some to deep ravines. Electricians will run wires to them. Bathing and other water needs will be provided as they were at the festival, at a central place. Food could be a problem. They don't have enough workers now to feed many immigrants for longer than a few weeks. New recruits will have to step up, become workers. But Puja, the medical director, insists on a decontamination schedule and AIDS testing for all new arrivals; she'll not allow them to mingle with the residents for at least two weeks. So they'll need to be fed and kept busy while they hang around doing nothing. The lack of structure could be a problem. Some homeless have emotional problems, have lived with years of stress and strain. Coming here could aggravate them. Razi knows this. She has no solution yet.

"There will be infiltrators," one of the coordinators says at the morning meeting. "Imposters."

Sheela nods. "If anyone tries to hurt our new people, there will be blood. We are capable of disarming them, not just of their sneaky ways but of their ability to tell others of what they think they see, but don't see. They are all blind, all those outside of us. They are blind, and we have our ways," she says. "If they try to infiltrate us, we will have a rude surprise for them."

Another coordinator mentions again the numbers of voters needed. Sheela, with a tiny bit of spittle on the corner of her mouth, says with manufactured sweetness, "I will show you why you do not have to worry. You trust me."

Razi has no idea what Sheela has in mind, but she will leave the running of things to those who do it best. They are dealing with high-profile people: a U.S. attorney named Turner, who threatens to have the Bhagwan deported, and the Attorney General of Oregon, Dave Frohnmayer, who filed the original suit challenging the constitutionality of the "city." Both threaten the success of the commune, and most of the discussion this morning is about them, and about a disciple suing them for taking funds from her account against her will.

Razi didn't know a disciple could have an account in her own name. She listens. Apparently, some people keep their money in their own names but authorize the Bhagwan's access. She wonders if some of the Hollywood crowd who live near the Bahgwan's compound have such separate accounts. Perhaps she can keep her account separate, convince her mother that the money would be used only if necessary prior to her thirtieth birthday.

This rare evening, Razi is free to do whatever she wishes. In all the commune condos, fresh laundered clothes are put away by someone else, on shelves marked with tiny labels placed there by someone else. *It's like having a wife.* All the maintenance duties of a relationship—cooking, cleaning, paying bills—the things that bogged down her and John all those years before, are all attended to here. They wouldn't have argued over who should take out the garbage or whether he remembered to pay the diaper service. Such details are remembered by someone who loves to do that kind of work, as worship.

Would John be in her life now if he'd come with her to Poona? Razi doubts it. He didn't commit to anything for long. Someday Charita will ask more about him, but for now, it's good to let her think he's dead. He is to them, so dead to the world, to life, to what might have been if only he had followed the Bhagwan.

Actually, she wonders why Charita doesn't ask about him. Maybe all that time with her nana distracts her from her usual questions. Her mother spends hours with Charita, time Razi would have liked as a child. She hears them laughing together. The two go for walks by the river, play cards on the grass in front of the Mandir Center, their backs against warm rocks. Razi hasn't mentioned the rattlesnakes killed near the center. No need to mention a problem taken care of by someone else.

Often now, work goes late into the evenings, with huge lights shining on preparations for the new arrivals and new developments in the underground city. That work of a secretive nature is better done at night when the newspaper and television reporters are fast asleep in their visitors' rooms and the peace force can ensure their safety.

Razi works at night now too, though her mother suspects she's partying. Razi can tell by the look on her face, if her mother opens her bedroom door when Razi comes in. Charita sleeps with her nana now. But Razi is in service. She's marrying immigrants with citizens so they can remain in the United States. Some people do find true love here, or mated love, as Razi likes to think of it, because love is everywhere in the Buddhafield. But many who want to live in Rajneeshpuram aren't citizens. The Immigration and Naturalization Service has sent investigators. Sometimes the checkpoint guards alert her, and dozens are ushered into the underground tunnels to wait.

After such close calls, Razi has learned to make sure when she marries a couple that they can tell each other's stories—where they've met and their families and favorite foods and plans for their future together—the things a couple would know before the wedding. Unless they marry in Las Vegas, Razi thinks, where she found John. Being married to an American citizen stabilizes the residents. The American spouse will serve in the commune and register to vote. There were six weddings during the festival. Razi performs at least one a week, often in the evening after the workday ends.

Charita attended the wedding today, and her mother as well. Tonight, her mother rankles her. Razi needs to talk about trust, her mother says, not vows and the mixture of ritual and invention. "Those marriages sound like something out of that movie *Star Wars.*"

"I don't see that movie, Nana," Charita says.

"Well it's quite a fantasy, let me tell you," her mother says. "Lots of mumbo jumbo that isn't fitting for a marriage."

"Mumble jumble, mumble jumbo," Charita chatters. Then she says, "Read this book, Nana." Charita hands her Katherine Paterson's *The Bridge to Teribithia.* Cora tries to remember if she's ever read this book. Olaf was the one to read to Rachel. Olaf was the true parent. Olaf stuck the books in her luggage when Cora wasn't looking. She reads the back cover. A story about friendship and loss. Wasn't that what life was about, building relationships, then learning to let them go? Olaf told her that he kept children's books at his office. His staff thought they were for the offspring of clients bored by their wait, but he kept them for himself, he said. "Children aren't so patient with authors who take three hundred pages to make their case," he noted. "A children's author knows how to go directly to the soul and has only thirty or forty pages to make the journey."

"The soul," Cora remembers telling her husband, "where healing is needed."

"Not now," Razi says.

"Yes. Let's read now," Cora counters, glad to put her mind on something besides holds that hurt the heart.

After Cora finishes, Charita asks, "Is that story true, Nana?"

"Well, there might have been a few things that got changed when people told that story to their children. But in my heart, I know it's a story you can trust."

Razi says, "Time for bed."

"You never send me to bed. I always get to decide."

"Not tonight."

Charita scowls, then asks, "Can I sleep in your bed?"

Razi nods, and Charita lets her mother tuck her into bed.

"I sleep with you, Mama. No one else tonight."

"Right," Razi says. "Your nana and I will be right across the hall if you need us."

"I don't remember your having a divinity degree," her mother says after Razi sinks into the chair in her mother's room. Razi tries to remember if her mother ever read a story to her. "Aren't you worried about the INS?"

Razi centers a flower vase on the end table. She brushes some of the tiny black seeds that have dropped and pushes them into the trash. "You don't need a degree, Mother. Just a license, and there isn't much to that. It's a pleasant thing to do, to be with people who are joyous and want to stay that way. If it doesn't work out..." She shrugs. "A legal divorce is easy here. No fault. And Bhagwan tells us not to stay where we are not wanted."

"Marriage as a way to get to know someone," her mother says. "Now there's a twist."

"Arranged marriages worked exactly that way. Years ago."

"Yes, but I believe both parties understood that the goal was permanence, long-term commitment, not the dating-game mentality."

"Dating game?"

"You must have been out of the country," her mother says. She sits with her legs crossed over the ottoman, her arms clasped behind her head. She looks relaxed. Now is the time.

"It is an honor to officiate at the weddings. And it has been an honor to lead the dynamic meditations. And, Mother, I have a new honor. I am in charge of soliciting the funds for the new Share-a-Home project. You've heard of it?"

"Oh yes. From your father."

"Daddy called you?" *Why does that sting?*

"I called him. I try to, once a week, though those phones crackle. Have you noticed that?"

"He told you about Share-a-Home?"

"He didn't know it had that name. He saw the ads, and frankly, Rachel, we're both a bit worried about those kinds of people coming here. I don't think it'll be safe for Charita or you, I don't."

"You don't even know what kinds of people will be here." *Calm, be calm now.* "Sheela took my suggestion that we have recruiters go to the cities, to screen them for true interest before spending the money to bring them out. Like a job interview. Only the finalists get to live here."

"I didn't know that. That'll be good. You offered a good idea."

Despite not wanting to, Razi beams.

"Your father also told me the last time we talked that you want the trust fund early."

Razi feels her heart pound. The palms of her hands moisten instantly. Her mother has lowered her arms and stares at Razi now, focused and intent. She's had her hair dyed. No, she is letting it grow out to a natural pewter gray, a color that flatters her narrow face. *Focus, focus.* Razi hugs herself, holding her arms against her chest. "Daddy said it wasn't up to him, that you'd have to make the final decision because Nana left the management up to you."

"Yes, she did."

"I always thought that was strange, with Daddy so good at numbers and investments. Nana knew Daddy was skilled with finances, didn't she?"

"She did." Her mother leans back now and closes her eyes. For the first time Razi thinks her mother looks old; moments before she looked so…vital. "Perhaps she hoped we'd be linked together that way, having to confront each other about money, if nothing else. She was always troubled by our…separation."

"You told her we didn't get along?"

"*We* didn't get along, your nana and me," her mother says. She gazes at her daughter now. "But I suppose the real reason was that she wanted kin in control of the trust, Rachel. And Olaf is not your kin."

Razi frowns. "Daddy is not—"

"Your father." Her mother closes her eyes again. "I should have told you earlier. It is one of many things I neglected to do."

Razi's world is swirling. "Why tell me now?"

"Because I want you to know that none of us is perfect. If I've led you to believe I wanted you to be perfect, then I was wrong, so very wrong. Worse, if you believe I only loved you when you 'performed,' then I seek your forgiveness. I never had it from my mother, and I don't want to carry on that sort of tradition."

Rachel's puzzled look reminds Cora of Charita's. We are our mothers' daughters. She wonders if she should tell Rachel that against her mother's wishes, Cora hitched her way across the country toward sunny San Diego. Just out of college, she skipped the grand party her mother had planned for her. Instead, she partied in paradise, giving her heart and innocence to a Navy man before he sailed away to Korea. She never heard from him again.

When she realized she was pregnant, she crawled back home and let her mother make a match for her with a droll but reliable second-generation Scandinavian named Olaf Swensen. She began right then to disappear, to become the woman her mother expected, the one Olaf deserved. But even then, when she might have made amends, her mother sealed the separation by setting up the trust to exclude Cora.

"You never told me about Daddy," Rachel says. "Why didn't you ever tell me?"

"Olaf was always your father in the best sense of the word."

They both hear the door open and turn. Charita stands there in her purple nightdress. Rachel looks over at Charita. "Go upstairs and get me my headache pills, will you, love?"

"Are you sick, Mama?"

"A little. Hurry along for me now."

When the child is out of sight, Rachel says, "John isn't Charity's father either."

Cora isn't sure she's heard right. "What?"

"Sh. Not so loud."

"But who is—"

Rachel looks down at the knuckles of her hand holding the mala, her fingers rubbing the 108 beads, her thumb circling the face of the Bhagwan. "I'm not sure. I chose Bhagwan as her spiritual father, just as he is mine."

Tears try to wash away the pain in Cora's eyes, her head. Have the sins of one generation truly passed on to another?

"You suffered through that alone?" Cora says. "I'm so sorry you couldn't tell me."

"Not alone, Mother. John stayed with me. But it got to be too much for him." She looked up warily. "Daddy knew."

Cora manages a wry laugh and wipes her eyes with her handkerchief. "Olaf knew? He never told me."

"I didn't want him to. It would have been one more thing on your list of sins I'd committed," Rachel says. "A list I thought long enough."

All those times it seemed the two of them conspired to exclude her, Cora told herself she was only imagining things. But she'd been telling herself the truth. Her husband and daughter shared a special bond, a secret kept to protect. Whatever their motives, she'd been left out. How tragic that her daughter couldn't bring her greatest needs to her own mother.

Olaf, Olaf. A father holding both secrets in his heart, hoping to protect the two women he loved most.

"I'm sorry," Cora says. "Sorry I couldn't be there for you when you needed me."

"You could amend that now, Mother," Razi says. "By releasing the trust fund early."

Cora takes the blow, returns it. "Never. You'd only use it for Bhagwan."

"It is my money, isn't it? My choice?"

"Yes, but—"

"What if I let you take Charita? What then, Mother? Wouldn't that be a storybook-perfect ending?"

In the morning, Cora wakes before the sun. Rachel's perfect ending dances in her head like too much caffeine, leading to chaotic rather than clear thinking. She turns on the light, picks up another book Olaf's packed. Children's Bible stories. She opens it at random. Joseph's coat of many colors. A boy betrayed, a father grieving, nasty siblings lying in wait. He was a brassy boy, bragging and making sure his older brothers knew their father loved him best. The brassiness served him later in a foreign court. It helped assure him that his dreams had meaning and that if he trusted God, his life would have meaning too. He didn't know how, but he had hope.

This man must have faced lonely days, a victim of jealousy, of false accusations, sold and imprisoned. But the separation from all he knew allowed his relationship with God to change, and in the end, Joseph forgave his brothers, engaged in a reunion, too.

Reunion. How Cora longs for that, to end the hurt, the disappointment, the neglect. She steps out on the deck with the book as the sun begins to rise. The hills seem to wrap themselves around her. What has she done? What kind of mothering resulted in this, a daughter so devoted to a false god that she would give up her own child to a woman she resents? And for money. Maybe Razi hopes Olaf will wield the greater influence in Charity's life, and that Cora's presence will be merely incidental.

"What are you doing, Nana?" Charity walks sleepy-eyed onto the deck. She smells of vanilla, a scented soap the laundress uses on all their clothes.

"Reading," Cora says.

"What's it about?" Charity cranes her neck toward the book, pushes on the pages to see the colored pictures.

"It's about a father and his sons and feeling lost and then finding each other again."

"A happy story," Charity says. "I like happy stories. How'd they get lost?"

"They weren't paying attention," Cora says. "At least the boy named Joseph wasn't, and neither were his brothers. They weren't very nice to him, but then he was kind of a smarty boy, bragging a lot."

"Zahir is like that. I kick him in the chins."

"I suppose that would be one way to bring a high and mighty boy down." Cora smiles. "Though it would have consequences."

"What's consequences?"

"What happens, good or bad, after we make a choice."

"How'd they find him, that boy?"

"They were led to him by…" She wants to say, "led by God," but she isn't sure what that word means to Charity. The Bhagwan is called a god. "Joseph was hopeful. He believed that the God he followed would keep him safe and look after him, and eventually, if it was meant to be, God would help him find his family again. He used the time when he was alone to get closer to God. It took quite a few years of consequences before everything worked out."

"Is that a story I can trust too?"

"Yes. It's really true."

"Is Joseph's God your God, Nana, or is it Mama's?"

So she distinguishes.

"Joseph and I share the same one," Cora says. She kisses the child's forehead. "And I'm hoping that your mama knows Him too. Her mother—that's me—I wasn't a very good teacher when she was growing up." She hugs Charity to her as the girl climbs onto her lap. "But I want you to know Joseph's God too. He's the One you can put your trust in, no matter where you are."

"Mama's still waiting for things to work out, I guess," Charity says.

"As are we all," Cora says.

24

BEHOLD

Razi is throwing up. Perhaps it's something she's eaten. More likely, she's sick from having posed the bargaining of her daughter. *What kind of mother am I?* She's sick from worry that they won't be ready for the homeless, who will arrive soon. She's sick from noticing that some of the people usually at the morning meeting with Sheela are missing, like the man who questioned the number of homeless they'd need to vote in order to win the election. When she asked, Puja said, "Those people are getting needed rest."

After the meeting, Sheela stopped Razi and told her she'd done well to broach the subject of the trust with her mother, so now she knows for certain the condo is bugged. "For security," her friend Waleed of the peace force told her when she mentioned it. "You've nothing to hide, so don't worry."

Razi steadies herself against the counter, splashes cold water on her face. She's been ordered to participate this morning in a tour with the three county commissioners. Sheela and Puja are part of the tour, and Razi will act as server as needed. There's to be no mention of the SAH, as the Share-a-Home project is now known. No mention of bringing more people, though word will spread soon enough as full buses drive through the region even though the festival is over. They're pushing the laws. Only a few "agriculture employees" are legal residents.

Puja's knocking on the condo door to pick her up. Razi throws up again and wonders if that's being recorded too.

She's relieved that Puja asks no questions. The August day is hot, and Razi hopes that the thunderheads building in the west might bring rain and a cooling to the ranch. They've had little rain since the festival. The commissioners are shown the limited settlements described as "staff housing," though the earth shows scars left by thousands of tent platforms. They are not shown the SAH A-frame building areas, the decontamination areas, or the "rest areas" where Razi thinks those who question Sheela are "resting." Two of the commissioners spar with Sheela, questioning each thing she says. The third is silent, and Razi wonders if his silence is agreement or if, like her, he is wary of how words are used, even his own. The bus gets hotter, and Puja offers water throughout the day.

They all ride with the commissioners on the tour bus out to the reception center. Razi recognizes Buckle's Bronco and is surprised by the lift to her heart. She looks for him, sees him changing a tire. The commissioners' cars appear to ripple under the hot sun. The high rocks on either side of the area act as ovens holding the heat in.

"Flat tire," one of the commissioners says, and he isn't speaking of Buckle's. The county car has a flat too. Large yellow flowers with black centers wilt beside the road. No birds sing in this sultry heat.

Puja motions Razi to follow her and slips into the reception center as the men, including reporters, hover around the tire. "Flat as an elk's bladder," Razi hears Buckle say.

"Take these out to our elected officials," Puja says, carrying two tall glasses of water with ice out from the small kitchen area. "Make sure Commissioners Hulse and Mathew have these," she says. "I'll bring one for the other."

Waleed arrives in his peace-force vehicle. He helps change the tire. Everyone is cheerful except for the commissioners, who appear anxious to leave now. Reporters keep making notes, trying to find juniper shade, which keeps them too far from the hot parking lot. Buckle approaches Razi and mentions the riding lessons for Charita. She's forgotten but nods and suggests that he return with her when she's finished here. His hair is braided. He's wearing a green scarf as his headband, darkened by sweat. He likes color in his headbands.

She thinks of him as Rainbow Man. She needs to concentrate. She hands the commissioners their water.

They're about to head back when Razi hears a groan. She turns to see Commissioner Hulse collapse. "Is it the heat?" Puja asks. "It's very hot." Then Commissioner Mathew also holds his stomach and falls to his knees. He vomits. Sheela orders Waleed to take them to the clinic, but Commissioner Hulse is nearly unconscious, so Waleed says to put them into the Rajneesh peace-force vehicle and race them to the hospital in Madras. Razi wonders why they didn't fly them in the chopper, but she doesn't say it aloud. The third commissioner stands stunned but not ill. His hand holding the water glass shakes as they finish changing his tire on the Wasco County car. His tie is loose. He gets in and drives off.

"Didn't the commissioners come to see the buildings, to see if you're sticking with the permit process?" a reporter asks Sheela. "They've a legal right to do that, don't they?"

"Commissioner Hulse came to harass us, as all government officials come here for this reason," Sheela says. "Now he's sick. This is providential." She smiles then, puts a hand on her hip to show off the .357. She grins to Puja, the medical director, with an almost gleeful look. The taller of the two laughs outright.

"Kind of interesting that wherever two or three of you are gathered, trouble happens," notes one of the testy reporters. Razi has heard him challenge them before. "Like that D.A. Didn't he almost die when your medical people were standing right there? He drank cold water too."

"If he has contaminated water, it is from his own office in Madras," Puja snaps. "We have work to do and can't be bothered with these questions that suggest we are in some way responsible for the illnesses of Wasco County."

"That was Jefferson County. The D.A. was from Jefferson County. I'm sure you'd want to be correct," the reporter says.

"The weak constitutions of these Oregonians are coming to fruit," Ma Anand Sheela says to the remaining reporters.

"What do you think caused their illness?" another reporter persists.

"Divine retribution," Puja says. She smiles and pats Razi's shoulder as she walks by as though she is a supportive friend.

Something is happening to Cora here, something she can't explain. She's shared unspoken confidences with her daughter, revealed secrets harbored close to her heart for years, spilled them out as though they are recipes she's eager to share.

With a fresh cup of coffee left by the server, Cora steps out onto the small deck. Rachel's gone "touring," she says, with elected officials. Her daughter seems pleased to be included in "important work," the very work Cora finds most alarming. The closer Rachel gets to the powers that be, the more vulnerable she is.

Charita naps, something new for her. Cora's accustomed to thinking of her granddaughter as Charita now, likes the uniqueness of the name that makes her think of a happy, perky bird. The child's soft breathing whispers like a cello sighing in the background. Cora hears bird sounds, the occasional squawk of a peacock. She tries not to think that the peacocks are there to ward off snakes and instead imagines their beauty. The afternoon lies silent in the shadow of the rimrocks.

Why did she tell Rachel these secrets? Is she losing her mind in this place where everything routine is chucked for red clothes and surrender?

"It isn't surrender," Rachel keeps assuring her. "We make our own judgments."

Yet what Cora sees are well-educated people, intelligent people, who have done that, surrendered their will to that of the Bhagwan or his associates. She even overheard someone say, "If Bhagwan asked me to kill myself, I would do it. If he asked me to kill someone else, I would do it." Cora wasn't able to see the woman sitting behind the magenta bougainvillea who spoke, but the words pierced her heart.

She told Olaf what she's heard.

"There are many who think like that there?" he asked.

"I don't know. But with these new people coming, well, I just worry."

He told her what he's heard of the homeless project through the nightly news. Though he handles corporate legal cases now, he's had experience as a public defender. He knows that sometimes homeless people turn to crazy thinking that can result in harm to anyone stumbling across their path. Bringing total strangers in while being obsessed with keeping others out seems absurd. Another contradiction.

Cora likes talking with her husband on the phone, even about the difficult issues. They both listen to each other. She wonders why that doesn't happen when they're at home, each with a book or magazine in their lap in the evening, a Brighton clock ticking in the silence.

"Do you think we could win a lawsuit, if I just left here with Charita? Rachel will challenge us."

"We could fight good," he says.

She supposes she knew mothers back in Wisconsin who had even less time with their parents than Charita has with Rachel, what with T-ball practice and band and ballet. Any judge would pronounce the child precocious and apparently well-tended. No, the only way Charita would come back with her for good would be if Rachel allowed it—or came too.

"Don't risk yourself, Cora. I want you home safe, ya."

"This is such a strange state, allowing people to register even up to election day! Why, anyone could come up with a name, even choose one from a cemetery." Perhaps her nana had been right: Going western could well mean the leaving of one's senses.

She decides that's what happened when she told Rachel about Olaf. She'd gone western.

Something good came of that, though. She and Rachel made a phone call together to Olaf, telling him that the family secrets had been shared. "Good enough," Olaf says. That was all. A man who had kept quiet for nearly thirty years, and all he could find to say was, "Good enough."

If she leaves without Charita, Cora thinks her heart will break. She's never loved anyone the way she's come to love that child. Quick-witted. Kind. Curious. All the things a child should be. When she plays with the few other children, she's neither bossy nor scared. She looks at the world as though it's hers, but not hers alone.

But to give money for this place and relegate her daughter to its chambers—could she do that? Lose one child to save another?

She writes the word *hope* in her journal. The psalms have become friends to her. Here, in the most unlikely of places, in a mystic's commune, out of her routine, she speaks prayers not at all like those she says at home, rote and memorized. She has conversations more than prayers. And while she doesn't hear any audible response, the word *behold* has come to her more than once, as though God seeks her attention.

Behold, the wicked brings forth iniquity.... I will praise the Lord. Why should she behold something wicked that will produce more wickedness? *Behold.* She wants the word to make her think of Christmas and the birth of a child. *Behold, I bring you good tidings of great joy.*

There is much to behold here, she supposes. The landscape appears depleted, yet it offers up small treasures that speak of the promise of faith. Tiny white flowers flourish in the dust. Butterflies of inordinate beauty flutter orange and black. She even saw, near the river, a snake that moved along the dark rocks like a living string of emeralds, a row of rattles as the clasp. She'd caught her breath, been startled by its presence. *Behold.* The wicked. A green rattlesnake. It slithered away, leaving her to wonder that she'd beheld life in a place of death.

I will praise the Lord. Therein lies the true hope. Not to ignore the evil and injustice in the world, but to notice it and do what one can to relieve it, by placing hope in the Lord.

No evil shall befall you, nor shall any plague come near your dwelling. This one, too, troubles her. Evil does befall people. The people from Antelope would say evil fell upon them and a plague has seeped into their dwellings. Do they have hope it will one day be better? Even her own grandchild's been exposed to things that might harm her forever, unless someone acts.

Unless someone intervenes.

Cora feels a sob rise up from somewhere deep inside her. She finds a tissue, blows her nose. Rachel has yet to demand a final word on the finances, but she must know there's a way around the trust. Cora and Olaf could put up the money now for Rachel to pay back when the trust matures. Would she do that? Perhaps, if Rachel and not the commune retains control over the money.

But would it matter, if Cora could take Charita away from this place? She's heard that the daughter of the congressman who was gunned down in Jonestown lives here as a Sannyasin. What veiled truth does that young woman tell herself to help her set aside her father's memory and risk living here? What veils cloud Rachel's eyes? If only Cora could lift them. If only she could bring them both home.

A bird with an unusual warble chirps her to attention. The sound is followed by the sight of Razi, who walks more stoop-shouldered than Cora has ever seen.

"You keep a journal?" Razi asks as she steps onto the deck.

"Since I've been here." Cora moves her hand over the words.

"I wasn't going to read it," Razi says. "Buckle is meeting me at the stable. I need to take a break, then get Charita." She holds a glass of water and takes a drink. "Here's what I'm thinking. I'd like you and... Olaf to loan me money against the trust. I could pay it back when I'm thirty. That way, I'd have it now when I need it, and you'd be assured of getting it back."

"There's no assurance that the commune won't try to transfer the money out of your account. Some European woman sued over that."

"That suit hasn't been settled yet."

"Oh? I thought a judgment of 1.7 million had been awarded her. It was in the paper."

Razi looks confused. "I... No one's said that." She drinks the glass of water, looks at it, then sets it down. "The lawyers could draw it up so that wouldn't happen. Daddy could help set it up. I wouldn't cheat you. You know that. It's just a legal thing," Razi continues. "Nana wanted me to have the money to do with as I saw fit. These people who'll come here will need so much. We don't have the resources anymore, Mother. You saw how few came to the festival."

"Maybe it's a sign that you're to leave," Cora says. "That the commune will be closing down."

Razi laughs at that. "This is my life. The money will make Charita's life easier because my life will be easier here, with enough resources to help the homeless. Residents. Don't you want to help Charita?"

"Yes," Cora whispers. Her chest feels heavy and tight. "I want to help her more than anything. You, too. That's why you should both come back with me."

Razi shakes her head. "You think you have the energy to keep up with her when you get back to Milwaukee, but here you've had all sorts of help you won't acknowledge. No cooking. No cleaning. No sewing. Just playing with Charita or resting or walking, whatever you want. You have no distractions. You can be attentive to her here. She's a bright, happy child. You know she is."

"A lot of the time, yes."

"The money will ensure greater happiness for her here. The commune will flourish. We'll settle these lawsuits and refocus on the work Bhagwan wants of us. A refuge for when—"

"So your offer to...exchange, that's off the table now?"

"Yes." She rubs the wooden railing. "I mean, no. If you'll advance me the money, I won't have to be in that position, of making an exchange. You have to consider this. Ask Daddy...Olaf."

"You don't have to call him Olaf." Cora reaches out to touch her daughter's hair. She wants to stroke the side of her cheek. *Behold!* A daughter. A woman of beauty. *A child of my own.* Rachel leans away, a movement as subtle as a butterfly's breathing. "He's your father, and he loves you too."

"Too, Mother?"

"I do love you," Cora says. She's been neglectful with these words.

"Then you'll release the funds early?"

"Only if you and Charita both come home with me."

"You're s'posed to teach me to ride," Charita says. "What took you so long?"

"Nothing subtle about this kid, is there?" Buckle says to Razi as he laughs. "You're tired of this grown-up talk."

"Well, will you?" They've walked to the corral. Razi's perspiring in the heat.

"Be my pleasure. Didn't mean to neglect a pretty girl like you, aay," Buckle says. He clicks his cowboy-boot heels together, makes a little bow. "You're not worried about falling off now, are you?" he asks Charita as he lifts her onto the saddle.

"I'm tough. You'll come back again, won't you?"

"Hey," he says. "We're here now. Don't you be worrying about the next time before this time's up."

"Okay," Charita says.

"You do what I say, and I think we'll be fine," Buckle says.

"Am I gonna die?" Charita asks.

"I sure hope not, at least not on my watch."

"What an odd thing for you to say, Charita," Razi tells her.

"Nana says we all gots to die one day. I don't want to be doing it today."

"Me neither," Buckle says.

"Careful with Mama too? 'Cause I don't want her going away."

"Oh, especially with her," he says, catching Razi's eye.

A dusty car drives up the road, stops, and a Sannyasin steps out. "Love," the woman barks to Razi, "you're wanted at Jesus Grove. Now."

"You have been given special privileges," Sheela tells Razi. A hummingbird flutters against the window behind the Bhagwan's adviser. "Look at me," Sheela says, raising her silk sarong around her shoulders. Her voice sounds sharp as a tiger's tooth against bone.

Have I done something wrong? Not pushed enough for the money?

"The condo for me and my mother and daughter has been a generous gift. Have I not thanked you enough?"

"Yes, and so close to the meditation center."

"My mother will be leaving soon."

"Alone?" Sheela lifts a sculptured eyebrow.

"We're...negotiating."

"Yes. When you are asked, you will have the honor of repaying these privileges. You will do what is asked by Bhagwan, through my words to you, yes?"

Sheela has the deepest, most hypnotizing eyes, nearly as compelling as Bhagwan's.

"Whatever I can do," Razi says. "It is my life to give back to Bhagwan."

"We understand each other then," Sheela purrs. Her countenance flickers from chastisement to charm.

Razi feels relief wash over her. At least they can't listen in on her heart, know how much she struggles with the exchange for her daughter.

"We have something more for you to do. You must be ready at a moment's notice to make a little trip away from here. Not for long, but for very important work. It will be easier if you don't have your child to worry over. To decline will tell us you are weary and needing rest, a reassignment. Are you weary?"

"No," Razi says. "I'll do what you ask. I'll never tire. I've found my bliss here."

25

SECURITY

The first busload of Share-a-Home guests arrives the first week in September. Razi's in charge of the initial crew once they clear decontamination. Razi meets the bus and smiles as each new person steps off, bewildered looks on their faces as they squint at the brilliant September sun. They already have their "invited" wrist tags, a different color from those of guests who "pay" or "fellowship."

"Welcome to the incorporated city of Rajneeshpuram," Razi hears a Twinkie say. "This is your new guide, Razi. She will take you to your residence for the next two weeks."

A tall man with a long beard and an eye that stays shut glares at her with the other. "A woman gonna take care of us?"

Belligerence often accompanies fear and uncertainty, so Razi steps over it to speak to what isn't said. "It must be very challenging to come so far to such a strange place. Have you ever been to Oregon before?" Her old counseling skills will serve her well here.

"If I had I wouldn't be here now," he says. He scans the rocky ridgeline, kicks at the stickery, tumbling weeds that a gust of wind blows toward him. Razi notices, too, that since the festival the usual manicured areas have been neglected. Groundskeeping requires vigilance, and the workers have been intent on readying A-frames and other, more important things.

Another man pushes up behind him. He wears faded jeans and two long-sleeve shirts and a vest, as well as a wool hat pulled down nearly to his eyes. He has bathroom thongs for shoes. "She's got the food then?" he asks.

"Yes," Razi says. "I have food. We'll go together to the site where you'll be staying. Just for two weeks. You can eat there."

"The ad said food and shelter and women if we wanted. And doctoring, too," another man says. He has heavy eyebrows and broken teeth. "I got a bad toothache. You got a dentist?"

Several women gaze into the clear blue sky. Though they look frightened, they also look curious, unlike the men.

"You married?" the broken-tooth man asks.

"Me? No," Razi says. "Except to my work."

"Like a nun she is," the tall skinny one cackles, wiggling his good eyelid.

"I like them unsullied," the broken-tooth man says.

"No kids anywhere." One of the women scans the area. "What kind of a place has no kids? Is this the outer limits? Are we on earth? Are all the children dead?" She's flapping her hands in front of her face. "What happened to them?" Another bus pulls in, unloads. "I got to have kids around."

"You ain't had a kid around for years," a man with her says. They might be a husband and wife, or perhaps a brother and sister. But they seem harmless compared to the broken-tooth man who fidgets and cranes his head to look around as though he is an emu catching the scent of something good.

"We were promised the Hilton," the broken-tooth man says, his voice rising like the wind blowing dust around them. "We were promised good accommodations."

"But not a Hilton," Razi says. She must maintain control so the man doesn't lose his. "You'll have temporary places to stay that are comfortable, out of the wind. And then you'll move into an A-frame house, like the ones you see there." Razi points across from the airport. By now the broken-tooth man is highly agitated. Razi thinks of radioing Waleed, but she doesn't want to appear weak.

"I have clothing for you, for after your showers. I'm sure you're tired and would like to clean up," she says.

"I want to see children. Oh, Billy, what did you bring me to?"

"Shut up," Billy says. Then to Razi, "Where's the grub and the clothes? You taking us, or do we walk?"

"Follow me," Razi says, though she doesn't really like the idea of turning her back on the lot.

Something hard hits her on the back.

"Billy!" the woman says. "Don't throw rocks."

Razi turns. Billy's moved close behind her. "Violence is not tolerated here, love." She pulls packets of cashews from a fanny pack. "I'll trade your rock for food," Razi says, her gift out. Billy raises his arm as though to strike her. Razi matches his stare. He puts his hand down. She fills his palm with a tiny nut packet.

"Steaks. You better serve me steaks."

They'll need more supervision, more help, more food. It's the only way this program can work. She'll have to get the money from her mother.

Cora wonders if she should contact Buckle to prepare a time for them to leave, put him on alert. Maybe she should write to Olaf, have him call Buckle, since their phone lines here are always broken up with chirps and crackles. But she is not sure all the letters she sends reach her husband; sometimes Olaf doesn't seem to know of incidents she's written of when she talks to him.

She wants to wait until after the election, when this Share-a-Home project will surely be unveiled for what it is, an effort to thwart the system. Should she give Rachel until then to come to her senses, or simply risk a night flight out with the child?

They'd probably see her leave, even at night. Everyone's working longer hours, and when they return to the condo at night, Cora hears few giggles as they climb the stairs. Perhaps sleep has become their siren, replacing sex.

Razi arrives later, later than usual. Charita shoots from her bed at the mere sound of her mother's voice. "Where have you been?" the child asks. "I can't sleep until you get home."

Razi laughs at her, tussles her hair. "Oh, love, you sound like your nana when I stayed out too late on a date. Remember, Mother?"

Razi winces as she sits. "Here, love." She pats her lap, and Charita plunges in like a puppy into a pond. "Oh, careful."

"Are you all right, Mama? Want a soda pop?"

Razi glances at her mother. "I'm just tired, and yes, that'd be sweet."

"What's your day been like?" Cora asks as Charita heads to the fridge in the widened area at the top of the stairs. Cora makes small talk as she lights a lavender incense stick.

Razi's silent. Then, "Do you really want to know?" Cora nods. "Interesting," Razi says at last. She takes a drink of the soda Charita hands her. The child leans her head against her mother's chest. She strokes her mother's arm. "I used some of my old skills."

"Counseling?"

"Hardly. These people aren't ready for words. They need their basic needs met."

"That's why they're here though, right? Because they're homeless and have been neglected."

Razi narrows her eyes at her mother. "Yes. It's a gift to them, but we also hope they'll become permanent residents."

"So they can vote."

Razi nods. "Getting them to fill out the forms has been..." She searches for the word.

"Interesting?" Cora says.

Razi nods. She leans forward to set the soda pop down, then winces.

"What's wrong?"

"I'm fine. Just sore. One of the new residents…used his feet today, to make his point against my hip."

"Did you report him?"

"I'm in charge, Mother."

"Oh, Rachel, how I wish I knew how to help you. It's a terrible price you're paying. You have independence, yes, but you seem blind to me, blinded by this passion of yours."

"You never had a passion like this, Mother, so you don't know how one can consume."

Cora stays silent. She remembers Rachel's father. But that was a passion that didn't sustain. Maybe her daughter is right. But she does have a focus now: keeping Charita safe. As she watches the child stroke her mother's hair to bring her comfort, it becomes clearer that whether Charita wants to go with Cora or not, leaving will be that child's only hope to grow up safe so she'll discover a true passion of her own.

Razi thinks that coming to the meditation center will give her peace. Usually, the chanting and music calm her frenzied thoughts. Tonight, she watches the Bhagwan dressed in white leaning back into his chair set on the altar, a high promontory made of lava rock in the center of the stage. Several hundred Sannyasins sway to the music, and Razi gives in to the movements, lets the *hoo-hoo-hoo* of the meditation replace her worrisome thoughts, which flee into dry desert air. Her fingers tingle, her head feels light. She's dizzy. She falls to her mat laid out on the gold linoleum floor, feels its coolness.

She notices that men above her hover, carrying Uzis. More guards stalk the perimeter, none of them showing any countenance of worship. How hard it must be for them to stay alert for danger in the midst of joy. A light flashes against the gun barrel, and she looks up. Someone's fired? No, the strobe light reflects off binoculars. An officer scans the crowd from one of the high catwalks, where the steel bridges offer his stony face a bird's-eye view of the Bhagwan's altar and his followers, too.

What is there to fear here? Outside, there is plenty, but not here. Waleed told her that National Guardsmen have amassed in ravines outside the ranch, ready to move in. The first waves of homeless remain quarantined in a remote ravine. Waleed's been assigned to help patrol that area, and several others aren't worshiping here this evening because they deliver food and bedding to the new recruits. Residents. They're to call them residents.

The music stops, and a loudspeaker blares out, "There is no reason to be alarmed. Our peace force is in full control. No one from the outside will be permitted to harm anyone in this incorporated city. There is no reason to be alarmed." The standard announcement began last week, and Razi hears it while eating breakfast, again at lunch, and even at the break people take after the Bhagwan drives his Rolls-Royce out to Willowdale for his soda pop. "There is no reason to be alarmed."

If there is no reason, then why mention it? Razi never heard an order at the morning meetings to announce these warnings. But perhaps she missed it. Other comments fly over her head. Once, several people came from the tunnel beneath Sheela's home and entered the meeting late without explanation, without even a glare from Sheela. Another time she heard talk about a Sannyasin needing a "hysterectomy" followed by a giggle and the suggestion that the Sannyasin needed a longer "rest" to benefit from her Haldol cocktail. To refer to Haldol as a cocktail minimizes its power, its lethal potential. Razi worked with physicians in her former life who prescribed the powerful drug for those who might be dangerously psychotic. She considered it for the broken-tooth recruit who is a part of her crew, especially when he spoke about "voices" telling him to do dangerous things, like throw rocks at people's backs or use his feet to protest. But the good food and structure of the decontamination camp seem to have calmed him a bit.

When a coordinator spoke of the results of an AIDS study, Razi was surprised; she hadn't known of this specialized research. Perhaps there are other meetings that don't include her. She is an underling, someone noticed by one of the coordinators and brought to Sheela's attention.

Razi recalls talk of the elections, and Ma Anand Sheela's catlike stare at a new coordinator, who worried aloud that they cannot get enough people registered to win with a write-in candidate. They are seven hundred people short.

Razi stared at the picture of Bhagwan hanging to the left of Sheela, eyes dark and cavelike.

"You worry overmuch," Sheela told the worried Sannyasin. "Your computers simulate an election on paper. We control the one at the ballot box."

Razi closes her eyes, shuts out the guards and worrisome memories, pushes away the warnings. She hears moans of joy around her. Sheela's in control. This is all that matters, this and her faithfulness to Bhagwan. Here in the meditation center, all is well. They are protected. Razi's mother is wrong about her being blind. It's neglect that causes her troubles. She's neglected her worship. Like the landscape here, it always needs tending.

The loudspeakers blare out another warning. She wishes the Bhagwan would make them stop. Then she chastises herself. What right does she have to criticize Bhagwan? He's a deity. He can do no wrong. He has knowledge none of the others have. She's the one with poor spirit, unsettled by her mother's old secrets. Razi is too attached still to her daughter and her past. A worthless Sannyasin, she can't give up her daughter for the funds, yet she can't convince her mother of any other choice.

After the Bhagwan's message, Razi feels refreshed. The extra guards are a necessity, given the small minds of the Oregonians bent on hurting them. She needs to relieve herself of worrisome things. They must all work harder to prepare for disasters ahead that can be foreseen only by Bhagwan.

Outside the meditation center, several Sannyasins gather in small clusters. It's a scene Razi loves, the temple with its banks of floor-to-ceiling windows set at the end of a lush valley that subirrigates naturally. An underground spring keeps it green even when rain hasn't fallen for more than a month. Something beneath it nourishes. Beyond the temple rise the banks of the John Day River, rounded ridges arching like flower petals on top of each other into the night sky. The moon's so bright tonight she has no need for a flashlight, and she takes a moment or two to hug various men and women, breathe in their perfumes, feel the silk of their sarongs against her cheek. Like her, they're thrilled with the beauty of this place and the wisdom of Bhagwan.

"Want to join us at the casino?" one of the men asks.

Razi adjusts her rolled mat beneath her arm. "My mother still visits."

"Poor you," several say in unison and then giggle.

"Yes, poor me," Razi says, not adding that time with her mother of late has held more promise than long hours at the casino or the shared beds of others.

They murmur encouragement as they separate.

The air cools quickly this September night. Razi pulls her pink sarong around her to ward off the chill as she makes her way back through the moonlight to the condo. It's a joy to hear Bhagwan reminding them to give up the things of this world and to cling only to the emptiness of experience, for within that space rests true enlightenment. It is different than Zen, Razi thinks. To reach Zen, one becomes enlightened just as Bhagwan proposes, but then chooses to remain behind on this earth to help alleviate the suffering. The Bhagwan urges enlightenment as a separation from the suffering, a leaving of worldly things completely. Even their own bodies, if called on.

Her mother would say that God, her God, doesn't want us to detach from a suffering world, nor assume responsibility alone for all that's left undone within it. "We are not alone," her mother says. "Faith is about a relationship between humans, and between humans and their Creator. I never understood that until I came here and discovered how much I'd neglected these relationships, and how much time I spent hoping they'd get better without doing a single thing to make that happen."

Her mother has tried to improve her relationship with Razi. She does act as though she has genuine concern not just for Charity but for Razi as well. She notices things. She asked Razi about her bruise. She's listened to her talk about her meditative sessions. She expressed opinions without pounding Razi in judgment. Maybe in time they will find common ground. Still, those efforts are things of this world, things that keep her attached, things the Bhagwan says she should set free.

She can see lights at the Bhagwan's fenced compound. He has a healing pool to help with his very bad back and a dental chair with piped-in nitrous oxide so he can vanish pain whenever he wishes. His private doctor stays with him, and lately she hears the Hollywood group has easier access to him too. Razi's pleased he's speaking again, that she's here at this ranch now, when he is here surrounded by the comfort of friends.

Her mother's bedroom light is on in the condo. Charita must be asleep in Razi's room. It must be very late. Razi hasn't worn a watch for years, her life a schedule of the sun and moon, the hungers of her stomach and her heart.

"There is no reason to be alarmed." Razi startles at the blaring voice that fills the canyon.

For some reason she's reminded of a sociology class she took at the University of Wisconsin, and a book by a longshoreman named Eric Hoffer called *The True Believer.* He explained how groups keep members chained together by identifying outside threats so they hold each other close. Blame for problems links not to the organization but to those outside said to be harming the community of faithful. True believers know how to do this, to maintain their groups, to keep them from splintering or tiring or disappearing into disillusionment. They withdraw. They control the information and resources. They bait the outside threat, then poke at it so trouble escalates, proving their need to all stay together to protect each other and the group. "We will protect you," the loudspeaker blares.

How odd she should think of that book now.

Waleed walks up behind her. "A special meeting. At Sheela's," he whispers. "Come now."

Razi sees her bedroom light come on. Charita must have been awakened by the loudspeakers. She should go there to offer comfort, catch up with Waleed and Sheela later.

Let go of the things of this world. Her mother is there for Charita. She turns to follow Waleed into the night.

26

PAIN

"You, Ma Prem Razi. You borrow from your mother," Sheela says from her living room in Jesus Grove. "She'll like that, your wanting to wear her clothes. You want to please her, yes?" Razi nods. "Yes. Perhaps it will improve her disposition and she will be less stingy. You will all do what is asked." Razi nods. She's been chosen for something unique, something important. "I did this myself. A week ago," Sheela says. "We did not achieve the necessary results, so we have prepared better this time. Three of you will go. You will wear street clothes so you will not be noticed."

"Who else?" Razi asks.

"You will know when you are picked up."

"What are we to do?"

"Leave a little delight for the ignorant Oregonians," Sheela purrs. "We are a generous people, are we not?" Puja laughs. Razi finds the words a contradiction. Then she remembers: The Bhagwan tells them that all life is a contradiction. One can't know the answers or the questions. One's only hope is to detach.

"Of course you can borrow my stirrup pants. Take the turtleneck and blazer, too. It could be chilly…where did you say you were going?" Cora's pleased to see her daughter dressing in civilian clothes.

"I didn't."

"You look scary, Mama," Charita says. The child lies on the bed sucking on a sucker, watching her mother dress in what Cora calls "civilian clothes."

"Everything new is a little scary at first," Rachel tells her.

"Zahir tries to scare me," Charita says. "All the kids will have to go to Leeds without their parents pretty soon. I won't go without you, Mama."

"What's the occasion?" Cora asks her daughter. She'll come back later to the unnerving words of Charita. "Are you doing something for the Share-a-Home project? Your computer work or your therapy groups?"

"Just work, Mother."

"They're having you take an outside job to fill the commune's coffers, that's it, isn't it?"

She hasn't meant to be sarcastic, but her daughter is a blend of secrecy and something else, a wariness Cora sees as her hands shake at the buttons of her blouse.

"Here," Cora says, "let me help you do that." Her daughter allows it.

"Can we go with you?" Charita asks.

"No. I'm going with others. I'm not sure when I'll be back."

"And your homeless group, they won't feel neglected?"

"We share the effort here, Mother. Someone else will tend to them."

Waleed and another woman whom Razi has seen once before in the back at a meeting are already in the car when they pick her up that morning. They drive through Antelope—Rajneesh—with red-clad Sannyasins waving greetings as they pass. They head toward the sign for The Dalles, listening to the news about the upcoming national election with Ronald Reagan said to be in the lead. Waleed switches to a music station, stops on Bruce Springsteen singing a throbbing ballad to inspire the oppressed.

"We'll have lunch here," Waleed says. He parks the car in front of a crowded restaurant overlooking the Columbia River.

Inside, mothers fill their children's plates with carrots and Jell-O from the salad bar. A pregnant woman leans in, brushes a bit of grated cheese from her stomach as she steps back from the serving island. The variety of color and Muzak sounds rattle against Razi's mind as she follows Waleed and slides into a booth. "Go ahead and go through the buffet," he tells them. "Later, we'll talk."

Back in the car, Waleed hands each of the two women a palm-sized mister of clear liquid. "At the next restaurant, make sure you are alone at the salad bar, then squirt a small amount on the lettuce as you walk along. Be creative, but lettuce is good."

Razi turns the tiny tube over in her palm.

"What's in it?" Razi says.

"It's better if you don't know."

"What will it do?" the other woman asks. She's a tiny brunette with a soft voice.

"You ask too many questions. Perhaps you need a longer rest," he says.

The woman's shoulders sink.

"I wonder too," Razi says.

"It disables them," Waleed snaps. "For a short time. That's all."

"We should know what it is," Razi says. "If we are privileged to be given this task, we should know that much."

Waleed looks at her, runs his finger down her cheek. "Detach, love," he says, "just detach."

Cora calls Olaf and tells him to contact Buckle. "Rachel's been sent on some assignment, and I'm worried. These loudspeaker warnings keep Charita awake, and they're alarming me. Plus, Charita has heard some nonsense about the children being sent away soon."

"There's a lawsuit I read of in the paper about neglect of the children," Olaf says. "Maybe they're moving them so there is nothing to investigate."

"We have to get out."

"Ya. I'll tell him to be ready at a moment's notice. Do I find two or three tickets?"

"Two," Cora tells him. "I don't think there's any hope I'll get Rachel to leave."

"When do I make the tickets for?"

"I don't know," Cora says. "I don't know."

Razi's in the bathroom of the restaurant, throwing up. The mister in her mother's blazer feels as heavy as a .357 in her pocket. She has to go back out there and do what Waleed's ordered. She reenters the dining area. Another pregnant woman sits at a table while a family celebrates a toddler's birthday. *Babies.* Ranchers and their wives and children fill their plates at salad bars. She's never noticed salad bars before, never thought the lettuce might be lethal.

"It's time," the other woman tells her.

"I don't know if I can," Razi says.

Razi opens the door as Cora reaches for the knob in her nightdress, holding a glass of water. "I was worried about you," Cora says. "It's so late. Charita woke up twice, but she's sleeping now. Those warnings keep us all awake." Her daughter's face is pale. "So, how did it feel to be dressed in civilian clothes and out in the world?"

"I need to go to bed."

"Are you ill?"

"I'm tired." She pushes past her mother, steps into her bedroom, and watches the sleeping child. She looks back over her shoulder at her mother.

Something's wrong. Rachel never just stands and watches Charita sleep, not even when she stays late at the casino and Charita is sleeping with Cora. "Rachel…Razi. What's wrong, dear?"

Her daughter takes off her mother's jacket, hangs it on the stairwell banister.

"Would you like to talk? You look upset."

"Can't you leave me alone? Please, Mother. Go," Rachel says, shaking her head. Her voice has taken on a thin quality, wispy, without cadence. She sighs, blinks back tears. "It's late. Much, much too late." She reaches up to touch her mother's cheek. Her hands are freezing cold. "Go," she says. Then she closes the bedroom door, shutting her mother out.

Cora stares at the door. She shakes. Something eerie and unspoken has slithered between them and moved out.

Is Rachel telling her to leave then? She lifts her blazer from the banister. It smells of cigarette smoke. The server will pick it up for cleaning. Out of habit, she pats the pockets, pulls out tissues, gum wrappers. And an empty mister. *When did Rachel ever care about misting plants?*

"Your husband contacted me, Mrs. S.," Buckle says. "Brought the newspaper for you." It's the third week of September, and he opens it to a headline. Five restaurants in the little town of The Dalles, population eleven thousand, have been hit with massive illnesses. Again. Three had been hit the week before. "More than seven hundred people are either hospitalized or being treated by family docs. That don't count those traveling through who don't even know where or why they got sick."

Cora lifts the paper and keeps rereading, the paragraphs not making sense. A child has been born prematurely from an infected mother, and his life hangs in the balance. A teenager may die.

"Food handlers?" Cora says weakly, lifting her eyes to Buckle.

"No connection yet."

"But what else could it be?"

"Health officials believe it came from the salad bars," Buckle says.

The article reports a local congressman has requested help from the Centers for Disease Control. "It's one of the largest biological outbreaks of its kind in the United States," the congressman is quoted. He complains that he gets little attention for his cries. The report says the county health department suspects salmonella poisoning.

"Salmonella," Cora says, looking up from the paper. "Didn't you tell me they were doing something with that strain to reduce egg-production problems? Or was that a Twinkie on the tour who said that?"

"There are lots of strains of salmonella," Buckle says.

"But salmonella so close to a town hit twice in three weeks? Can that be a coincidence?" It must be. No one would intentionally poison innocent people. What would be the point?

Still, seven hundred people are ill, with no common food worker to link the restaurants, all in The Dalles, the county seat of Wasco County, and an election looms...

The phone line crackles as the call goes out to Olaf. The machine picks up, and she tells him she's bringing Charita home. "Something bad has happened here, Olaf. I wish you were there." More clicks. "I'll call you later."

Cora paces the small room. The choice has been made. All that remains is deciding whether to say it aloud so Charita can tell her mother good-bye. But perhaps they should just leave, in case Rachel tries to stop them. Cora doesn't think she will. She's too listless since her trip off the commune. She must somehow be involved. The strange plant mister suggests it. Maybe she's working at the greenhouse? No. Those poisonings. She has to tell herself the truth. It isn't safe here anymore.

"We'll get tickets at the airport," she tells Olaf later that afternoon.

"Maybe you can talk Rachel into coming for a vacation, tell her she can go back there," Olaf says.

Once out, Olaf says they'll take her to one of those deprogramming places where people who've been brainwashed can start to think again. Patty Hearst used one of those after she was rescued.

"They might try to poison people here," Buckle says when she hangs up with Olaf.

"I didn't want to say that to him, but I agree. Who knows what's next? I'll get packing."

"Whatchya doing, Nana?" Charita says. She stands in the doorway, her eyes still thick with sleep.

"Packing. We're going to go to Milwaukee," she says.

"Me and Mama, too?"

"If all goes well, yes. But for sure, you and me. It's a surprise, so don't say anything to Mama until I tell her."

The child hesitates before padding toward the small refrigerator. "Can I have an apple?"

She reaches in, and Cora rushes to her, takes it from her.

"Nana," Charita protests.

She's overreacting. Surely things in the condo are safe. They wouldn't try to hurt this child. *But there were children ill at the restaurants.* "Maybe it is a coincidence," she says to Buckle as she takes the apple to the bathroom sink and scrubs it. She hands it back to Charita, who looks at her from the corner of her eye.

"Mama will come later? To 'Waukee?"

"I hope so, I do."

"Yes. Good, you're here," Ma Anand Sheela says when Razi steps up on the wooden deck at Jesus Grove. She's been called from the Share-a-Home site. "Let us begin then."

Again, coordinators give reports. The legal staff discusses the current status of cases. Someone talks about the number of new recruits and who has been promised return bus tickets should they be displeased with the arrangements. "The first groups get return tickets after the election. The new ones will not," Sheela says. "And we should stop taking the buses through Madras. They're counting how many get dropped off there," she says. "I didn't think those people could count, but they can." Everyone laughs. "We will send only those we reject to Madras now." More laughter as the Sannyasin in charge of finances says, "There are now over three thousand new people, and the estimated cost thus far is over $207,000." The plan was to stop at four thousand recruits, get them registered to vote, hold the election, and weed out the chaff from the straw, as Sheela put it. "With those four thousand and our residents, we will win the election by well over seven hundred votes," Sheela says. "You see? The same number who are ill from eating poor restaurant food. I, too, know how to count." This time the man running the election simulation says nothing, and the others nod their heads, smiling in praise of Sheela.

Two hundred thousand dollars! Seven hundred people ill.

When the meeting adjourns to laughter and joyous talk, Razi unfolds her legs from the pillow wondering why she'd been summoned from a work site for this meeting.

"We will talk more," Sheela says. She pats the pillow next to her, and Razi sits. "You see our needs," Sheela says, staring into Razi's eyes. "The Master knows of your wish to give your all to the work here. You gave us good work in The Dalles, I'm told. You can be trusted."

Razi swallows. "The Bhagwan knows of this?"

"You have been given great privileges."

"I've tried to give back, to honor all that the Bhagwan has done for me," Razi says.

"Don't sound so whipped," Sheela tells her.

Razi worries she will vomit again.

Sheela places her small hand over Razi's, causing her to notice her fingernails dirtied from her morning's work in the ravine. Razi curls her fingers under. "Your mother leaves soon," Sheela says. "She takes your child with her."

"How would you know that?"

"We have ways. We can help your mother decide to leave something behind. She has an illness we discovered from her blood taken at her physical. Puja notes this lapse in our protection of people here. All should have been followed up. There is a cost for her treatment. And then it is often a good time to arrange for wills and legal settlements of trusts when one is facing a harsh illness with a long recovery, if at all." Sheela pulls papers from a paisley folder.

"My mother doesn't need medical attention."

"We have knowledge. We have what she needs to treat her here. She will need rest. Perhaps a Haldol cocktail."

"She can be treated back in Milwaukee."

"Her getting treatment here is not negotiable." Sheela smiles. "Barely negotiable." She hands her the papers. "You decide. Meditate upon it."

Sheela leaves the room. Razi stares at the Bhagwan's picture on the wall. She keeps rereading the papers. She's attempting to detach, but the heaviness weighing on her keeps her rooted.

The plane will leave at 7:00 a.m. tomorrow, and they'll stay at the Hilton in Portland this very night. Can Cora leave without saying good-bye to her daughter, without making one last attempt to get her to leave for a safe place? But she can't promise Rachel safety in the world of Milwaukee either, she supposes. No, it isn't for her safety Cora wants her daughter with her, it's because she loves Rachel, and having discovered that, Cora doesn't want to leave her to the afflictions here.

The scent of juniper and sage enliven her as she carries the luggage out to Buckle's Bronco. She'll remember this scent, the lessons learned.

Charita stands at the window. "We won't go without saying good-bye to Mama, will we?"

"We have a plane to catch," Cora says, holding back tears. "They won't wait for us."

"Here she comes!"

A dusty car pulls up next to the Bronco, and two burly Sannyasins follow Rachel toward the deck. Charita rushes out to hug her mother. "We're going to 'Waukee. You're coming too?"

"I'd like a word with my mother alone, please," Rachel tells the Sannyasins as they move to stand on either side of Cora. Something in their stance, their closeness, and their rubber gloves makes Cora's hands begin to sweat. "Charita, you stay out here with Buckle and talk about horses, all right?"

"Okay," she says "But you're going with us, aren't you?"

"We'll talk about that later."

Inside the condo, Cora is hyperalert to sounds, to smells, to the way her daughter bites her lip. She sends up prayers, asks for direction, patience, help, all in the space of one pounding heartbeat.

"They've come to take you for that physical you never had, Mother."

"I had it. They drew blood and everything."

"It's been ordered. Treatment's been ordered. They say you're ...ill."

"I'll see my own doctors about that."

"You're a contaminant, Mother. They need to isolate you. The only way I can hold it off...and let Charita go with you, is if you're willing to free up the trust."

A contaminant? It's come to this? "You'd let them take me—"

"It's the only way she can leave, Mother. Your only way out." Rachel's voice sounds plaintive. She's crying. "Even if I authorized it, they wouldn't let you out with her, without the money. It's too late now. Too much has happened. I've—"

"It's never too late, Rachel. You could come with us. You could. Charita wants you to. Olaf and I want you to. Your father's lawyers can protest this. I admit, I came here to get Charita, but now I want you both. Safe and sound, away from this...place. Come with us.

Buckle will help. We'll find another time to leave. I'll even pretend to go with—"

Razi steps away from Cora's advance, blinks away tears. "Sign the money over, please, Mother. I don't know what they might do. People …people are unaccounted for here. There's a holding place. Haldol cocktails…" She looks up at the light fixture. "Please, sign these papers so you can leave with Charita. Don't haggle over the money, or me. This is what I've chosen. Do this now, for Charita. Please."

Defeat and desperation write their names on her daughter's face.

"How do we do this then?" Cora says.

"Just sign this statement saying you'll hand over the trust. The Sannyasins can witness it. I'll radio that it's finished, and then you can go. Do it now before Sheela changes her mind and decides even five hundred thousand dollars is not enough to redeem my daughter and my mother."

"You'll go back, won't you, Buckle? After you see us off? Go back and check on her. Then call, please," her mother tells him.

"Yes, Mrs. S."

"Nana will take care of you," Rachel says to Charita as she buckles her child into the backseat.

"I don't want to go without you, Mama, I don't!" She's crying now. "You're selfish. You don't care about me!"

"I do, Charita, I do, I do. I haven't done a good job of it, I know, but Nana will. You can trust her. And you write to me. I'll write back. You'll know I'm all right. You're a big girl."

"But who'll take care of you? I have to be here to take care of you." She pulls at the seat belt, and Rachel leans over her, wrapping her arms around her child. Charita's screaming and not able to take a breath.

"No, no, no. Oh, baby, please. Mama needs to learn to take care of herself. Go now, please," Rachel says, turning, her eyes red and swollen and pleading to Buckle. "Take them and go."

She watches the Bronco peel out, her heart a stone, easily tossed away.

Finally, the Sannyasin at the last checkpoint waves them on. As they drive the narrow road, Cora lets the knot of emotions begin to untangle. She has Buckle pull over so she can get into the backseat to be closer to Charita, who hasn't stopped crying. "I'm here, Charita. I know it must hurt so very much." She pulls the child to her.

"More. Than. When. My foot. Hurt. Nana," she says between sobs.

"Your foot got better, remember? And your heart will get better too, I promise."

Eventually, Charita sleeps.

Cora looks back to watch the moonlight splay across the landscape, illuminating the rope of road. They drive past the distribution warehouses, the last sign of this wicked place. She's been given another chance, another opportunity to give love to a child, to raise a child up in the way she should go, so she will not depart from it. A chance to do it differently this time.

She'd provided Rachel with a set of rules and obligations, dos and don'ts. Religion without passion. Secrets. Separation and distances. Neglect. Cora won't make the same mistakes twice. They'll learn together, she and Olaf and Charita. They won't just recite the liturgy. They'll speak of risks that lead to loving, and the commitments that sustain relationships like that. They'll pay attention, find joy for this child and in this child. They'll find it in the shelter of God's love.

Behold what God has done in the strangest of places. Cora holds the child tight to her. This is still the age of miracles, despite what the skeptics say. She'll never stop putting out her hand to draw Rachel back. She kisses the top of Charita's head. Who knows what other miracles might be wrestled from this Muddy land?

27

Confidence

Razi speaks on the phone to her daughter, her mother, and her daddy, too. The county clerk has foiled Sheela's brilliant election plan by requiring an interview with every new registrant to ensure they really intend to live in the incorporated city of Rajneeshpuram. Dozens of lawyers make themselves available for the interviews. Sheela's furious. She allows no interviews and boycotts the election.

Razi and others are ordered to begin "dumping" the recruits onto the nearby cities if they won't take a bus ticket back to where they came from. Razi is no longer invited to Sheela's morning meetings. A few Sannyasins seek dynamic therapy, the way the Bhagwan's taught, hoping to restore some sense of joy in the midst of politics and chaos. Razi leads the sessions, but beyond that, she joins others sipping tea at the mall. Gray plastic wristbands of the Share-a-Home people litter the dust where they were tossed as the homeless left their A-frames. She sees little of her friend Mayor Deepa, who she hears is busy mending fences with Antelope neighbors. Waleed is distant. She hears the Bhagwan's doctor has taken ill. Construction of the underground facilities has halted. Everyone detaches from one another.

The child finally believes that the toys she's been given, the books and paper dolls, belong to her. She may share them if she likes, and Cora tells her she hopes she will one day. "Grandpa doesn't like to share his BMW, either," Cora says. "It isn't required. But it's nice to make a loan sometimes of precious things. To people you trust and to people you love."

The crying after the phone calls to her mother lessens; Charita even gets to speak to Buckle once. "I think they're going to start serving beef at the Zorba the Buddha Café," he tells her. "Your mama's promised to buy me a hamburger after we come back from an afternoon of riding."

"Are you taking care of my mama?"

"As she lets me," Buckle says. The words cheer Cora when Charita tells her.

The *Rajneesh Times* reports through the winter months about the lawsuits. That land-use group, 1000 Friends of Oregon, creates the biggest challenge as they insist the city was built on farm-use-only land and therefore violated the law. The commune faces a fine of more than one million dollars for having electricity run into the winterized tents and A-frames without permits. Hardly anyone stays in them now. Razi knows this. What a waste of government workers' time and money to pursue such a suit. Pure harassment, that's all it is. But somehow Razi can't garner energy to protest. Joy has vanished; uncertainty fills its space. Even the nights of warmth she shares with Waleed, or others whose names she barely knows, leave her empty. She's lost her center, even with the Bhagwan looking healthier when he speaks at Mandir.

In January, the *Rajneesh Times* carries a story about a fire at the Wasco County Planner's Office. Razi hears a Sannyasin joke that the county will have a hard time collecting fines without evidence of wrongdoing. She doesn't understand the joke. She doesn't want to. She hears a rumor that Bhagwan's doctor has grown sicker.

The attorney general's opposition to the incorporation makes its way through the courts, and all the Rajneesh lawyers are busy, busy taking commune vehicles out to Portland and The Dalles and north to Seattle. One headline exposes the effort of the INS to deport the Bhagwan. Another story tells of Sheela's conciliatory remarks to the Antelope people. She even suggests that the street names be returned to their originals, Maupin and Main and College instead of Buddha and Tao. Even the Hitler Recycling Center site will be renamed. Sannyasins stop work on the huge trailer park begun last summer at the edge of Antelope.

No children stay at the ranch now. Someone filed a child-neglect case, and all children were flown to ashrams in other states or countries. Razi remembers what Billy's sister shouted her first day, about the strangeness of a place without the sound of children to echo against the rocks. Razi hears the sound of their absence, of Charita's vacant place.

The gardening work continues, and the calf barns produce along with the dairy. But few work crews go out. Razi likens it to that time of sultry pause that promises a storm. So far, the storm seems to have moved beyond the Muddy to courtrooms in Portland and Seattle. No one speaks of preparing for cataclysmic possibilities. Or maybe Razi's excluded from those meetings.

Buckle shows up now and then. They ride horses together. He describes places he hunted as a boy, where he's camped, where his grandmothers dug for roots. For the first time, Razi notices the land beyond the building sites, sees what it might have looked like when Buckle's people roamed it. He points to flowers, says the black-eyed daisy ones had names written down by Lewis and Clark, who called them blanket flowers for their abundance. Once they watch a herd of elk browse; another time, mustangs—wild horses—run free across the grassy ridge, their manes flowing. "They say when God wanted to contain the wind, he gave it the name *horse.*" Buckle says. "My grandfather told me that."

"That's a story told by Islamic people, too," Razi says.

"Over there is where we spent our praying day," Buckle tells her. They're on a ridge overlooking all that Bhagwan's followers built.

"You still hope for that boys' ranch?" Razi asks.

"You never know what miracles are sheltered in the promise of this Muddy," Buckle says.

Razi doesn't hope for miracles. She's but an insect on this landscape, these sixty-four thousand acres, her time like a worker bee now spent in the communications center as they continue to solicit funds, hoping to make sense of what their duties mean. It's the only work as worship that goes on daily. She seeks meaning in a disintegrating place.

In the spring, the riding horses are put up for sale, and the sawdust and dried manure blow in the gusty whirlwinds that form in the empty corral. One day, something happens with the water system, and no one's sure either how to fix it or where to purchase parts. The trees they planted the year before dry up as the Sannyasins conserve water. Razi hasn't officiated at a marriage since the fall. She notices that people go to be "at rest" for a month or so. When they return, they never talk about where they've been.

At least she protected her mother from that.

Razi is told to allow others to move into the bedroom of the condo occupied by her mother. She shares a smaller room with two others, a man and a woman. Others use the upstairs ones. Everyone seems ready to leave. "We can practice what the Bhagwan teaches in San Francisco," they say. "It'll be warmer in the winter, and there are more restaurants to choose from."

Razi still lives for the times when the Bhagwan speaks. She is blessed to be listening at his feet. It's calmer now that Waleed and the peace force no longer patrol the catwalks. They spend most of their time keeping curiosity seekers from winding down the road, or helping people going in and out for legal meetings change the flat tires on the commune cars.

In June, the aviary operation is closed down, and all the emus are placed in huge trucks, sold, taken somewhere else. The drip irrigation system watering the massive vineyards no longer works, the filters clogged. The black plastic's wound into piles like black bracelets, the vines allowed to die.

No festival is planned for the summer at all.

"Charita misses you," her mother tells her when she calls. "Come home."

But Razi harbors a memory, a secret, as her name suggests, that affirms for her she can't come home, and that Charita's better off with her nana than with her.

On a September evening, nearly a year after her mother and daughter left the commune, Razi learns that Sheela and Puja are gone too. In the dead of night they jetted out. Within a day, so does the head of financial services, the vice president of the medical corporation, the treasurer of the Rajneesh Foundation International, and several other leaders. All gone, all flown off in jets that disappeared beyond the purple hills like morning mist.

The next day, the Bhagwan calls a news conference. Surrounded by the Hollywood people who look after him now, he denounces what these leaders have done, charging them with attempting to poison his physician, bugging his living quarters, drugging people, embezzling millions of dollars. As she listens, Razi knows her money has flown out with Sheela. The Bhagwan continues at the news conference, claiming he had no religion here, that his commune was not a violation of religion and state, that Ma Anand Sheela is responsible for all of this messy religious legal business. He orders the burning of all copies of *The Book of Rajneeshism.* The malas aren't needed anymore, he says, the sunset colors can be put away, and a new name is not necessary to be on "the way" of achieving enlightenment. To find out what "Sheela and her gang" have done, he opens the doors to federal investigative teams, who swarm in like flies to a rotting feast.

"This commune is an experiment to provoke God," Razi remembers the Bhagwan had written. "You do not know what will happen here."

You do not know, he said. Her child is gone. Her money is gone. But at least the Bhagwan is still here.

"You need to come home now," Cora says over the phone. "We've seen it on the news. The largest wiretapping operation in the country, all the way to the governor's office. And the poisonings at those salad bars! People have confessed. Oh, Rachel, you weren't involved in that, were you? They found the same salmonella strain in a secret lab, underneath Sheela's compound. Someone named Puja's been indicted. And the tunnels with the wiretapping lead right out to the middle of the horse corral. We were riding right on top of all that when Charita had her riding lessons. Oh, Rachel, please. I'm so glad you've called. No one's keeping you there, are they? You wouldn't be stopped if you wanted to leave. Who's in charge anyway?"

"The Bhagwan, Mother. He's always been in charge. As long as he's here, I'll be here. I called to let you know that I am all right. I thought you might worry."

"We do worry. Here, talk with Charita for a bit." Cora puts the phone to her granddaughter's ear, and the child happily chats.

"Olaf, she still won't leave there. What's in it for her? I don't understand, I don't. You've got to talk to her. She always listened to you."

"Loyalty," Olaf says. "If she leaves now, she admits the futility of the past five years of her life, ya? Our memories drive us to our futures."

"But how can she turn her back on her family?"

Olaf pats Cora's shoulder. "The Bhagwan is her family." He

reaches for her hand. "Stop your pacing, now. Good things have come of this. You remember your psalm, ya? No evil on your dwelling. Keep your hand out to her. Keep writing your letters. She may eventually believe through you that there is more to life than what she has. That being part of this family is not so bad, maybe. We must wait, ya? She called."

Cora allows herself to be still. "Yes, you're right." Olaf's been a rock these months, with Charita, with her own journey back to a relationship with him, within their own community of Episcopalians. Everything's been transformed since her time of going western.

Cora takes the phone back. "If you need anything, anything at all, Rachel, you call, all right? Maybe come for a visit. For the winter. It'll be lonely there. How many are left?"

"A hundred or so," Rachel says. "That's about it. But we're looking after each other."

"You can't run that place with so few people through the winter. What if the heating system breaks down? Or the pipes freeze? You're so far from anything. Oh, Rachel..."

"I'll call again, Mother. Thanks for letting me talk to Charita."

"Anytime. I love you, you know, no matter where you are."

The immigration investigator is the one who tells Razi about the Bhagwan's departure and arrest. The Bhagwan's been stopped on his way to a "rest" in North Carolina and is being held on immigration charges. He shares the news during a break in Razi's deposition, where she's answering questions about her duties and activities over the past three years.

"He's gone? The Bhagwan?"

"Flew out with lots of cash and jewelry, but he says he went for his health. We have reason to believe otherwise," he tells her. "Several charges are pending. Sheela's been located and indicted for attempted murder of the county commissioners who collapsed at the reception center. We'll get her for the poisonings, too, even if she didn't do it directly." Razi feels her stomach tighten. "There are electronic-eavesdropping conspiracy charges. Twenty-five people will get that on their record. I suspect you know about that one, having worked in the communications division." Razi shakes her head. *Will I be indicted for something I know nothing about yet get overlooked for my part in the poisonings?* "Now about your charges." Razi swallows. "The marriages you performed are a violation of the INS. You were aware of this when you performed them?"

Razi hesitates. "Shouldn't I have a lawyer or something?"

"Will they provide you with one?"

She isn't sure any lawyers remain, not with Sheela and now the Bhagwan gone. If they do, they'll be wrapped up in the Bhagwan's case or Sheela's, not with underlings like her. Some of them might be indicted too. She could ask her parents for money. Ask her father to serve as her lawyer. "I think I'll need a public defender."

They decide that the few remaining Sannyasins should all move into the old ranch house city hall, or maybe one condo, and let the other buildings go unheated. Snow falls soft as butterfly landings across the wooden decks, dusts the weeds and sagebrush growing up around the ranch house porch.

Waleed faces electronic-eavesdropping conspiracy charges and "other things" he doesn't care to discuss. He suggests they have a big garage sale of everything not nailed down so they can put the money into the commune's operating funds. "We can buy food and pay our phone bills and purchase bus tickets to wherever it is people want to go to. Before the bankruptcy court forbids it. We've got rugs and plants and tire chains and all the hand tools and pipes and irrigation equipment."

"And Uzis and carbines," someone else says, looking at Waleed.

"Haven't you heard the rumor, that we dumped all those in the lake?"

"Did you?" Razi asks.

"No money for ammunition and no enemies right now," he says, evading. "Might as well sell what we can."

"The weapons were bought for a city police force," Razi says. "Can we sell any of this stuff legally if it was bought with state or federal money?"

Waleed looks at her. "No one has answers. We have to do what we can to survive."

It doesn't seem right to take them, but Razi knows selling them wouldn't be right either. The rolls of paper have handwritten notations. If all the work they've done here has any meaning at all, if they want to start over again one day, these designs and plans and the computer disks connected to them might mean the difference between failure and success. Others might see the possibilities of this place. The Bhagwan might return to remake it. They'd be lost without the information of these drawings.

FBI agents and other investigators have pawed through everything and taken what they need to support their charges. Razi's sure this material has no bearing on any cases, but it's vital to her.

She looks out the window at the communications center as snow falls. Three inches already, and Waleed says he heard a weather report predicting six inches more. Most of the Sannyasins plan to be gone by the New Year. She isn't sure where she'll go. She has to stay close for hearings; most Sannyasins have gone to the Portland area until those issues are resolved. She's hoping for probation.

But what to do with all of these architectural and engineering drawings in the meantime, where to store them, until when? Until someone comes and finds the promise in this Muddy place. She thinks of Buckle.

Buckle carries box after box of drawings out to his truck, while Razi copies computer files onto disks. Waleed stops by once, gets a radio call that takes him away, and when they're finished it's dark. Buckle throws a blue plastic tarp over the top and ties it down with a rope. Ice builds up in the corners of his truck bed. It won't melt soon with the icy wind and cold racing down the ridges.

"What will you do now?" Buckle asks when the load's secured. Gusts of wind lift the tarp's edges now and then. He drapes his hands over the pickup bed as they talk.

"I don't really know. Stay around until the immigration authorities are finished with me. I'll have a record," she says. "Imagine that. For saying words to bring people together in a marriage ceremony. It could have been much worse. Maybe it should be."

"Words are powerful."

"Yes, they are. Actions, too. Or lack of them."

She feels tears pool. She looks away, not deserving the kindness in his eyes.

"Everything you've known for the past four years is melting away," he says. "And I'd guess you miss that Charita, too. I do. My mama always said that being separated from your tribe's a misery." She nods. "Holidays are coming up. Would you consider spending time with another tribe for a time? My grandma's got an extra bed." He wipes her cheeks with the end of his purple head scarf.

"The Bhagwan said this place was an experiment to provoke God, that people had no idea what was going to happen here," Razi says.

"If he could have predicted this, I bet he'd a done something different."

"He thought this would be the last place he'd ever be on this earth. I know he did. And now, he's in a cold jail cell in Oklahoma somewhere, and the rest of us aren't far behind him."

"Will you keep me posted about where you are?" Buckle says. "So I can let you know how this stuff is weathering in my grandma's shed." They crawl inside his cab, and the heater blasts away at them. Snow falls harder, building up on the windshield. Razi rubs her hands together inside her mittens. She doesn't want him to leave, at least not yet. She'll be alone at the condo. Her two roommates are spending the holidays in California. Maybe she'll move into the ranch house.

"I'll let you know where I am. You never know. Things might pick up here again, and I can come back."

"Really believe that?"

Does she? "No. But I can hope, can't I?"

"I know all about hope," Buckle says. "That's an Indian's middle name." He smiles at her, then looks away. "Snow's starting to come down pretty hard. Where can I take you?"

Here is a good man, a friend almost. Not that she's asked very much from him, but whatever she asks, he delivers. Where can he take her? Where is her future, her hope? She came here to give gifts that might help the world, to find meaning in the giving, but this was not the Bhagwan's vision. He wanted her to detach, to separate. But people gave her meaning. The people she committed to here have failed her, and she's neglected the people who love her most. She doesn't deserve her parents' welcoming arms, or her daughter's. What arms are open to her now?

"How about if I ride out with you to get these 'promising papers' settled into your grandma's shed? I've never had Christmas on a reservation."

"Aay," Buckle says, "you'll be good company along the way, especially if I need help changing a tire."

"That's one thing I'm still pretty good at."

Buckle drives past the ranch house, then on up the grade through the now-empty checkpoints and past the warehouses. Snow gathers at a rock cairn some old sheepherder built years before. Razi doesn't know what her future holds, but she knows that this Muddy road is not one to drive on alone.

WILDHORSE CANYON
AT YOUNG LIFE'S WASHINGTON FAMILY RANCH
1997–1999

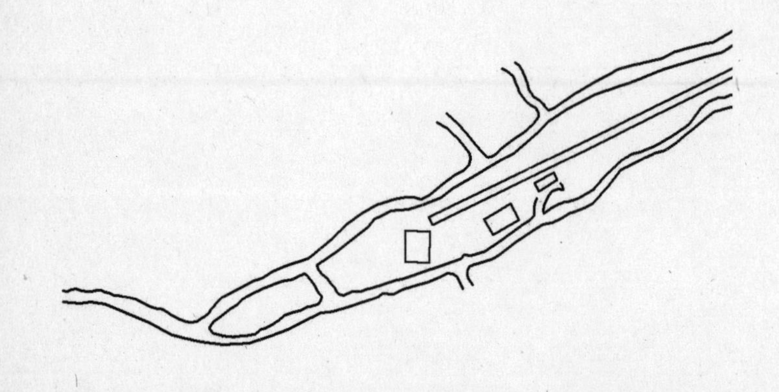

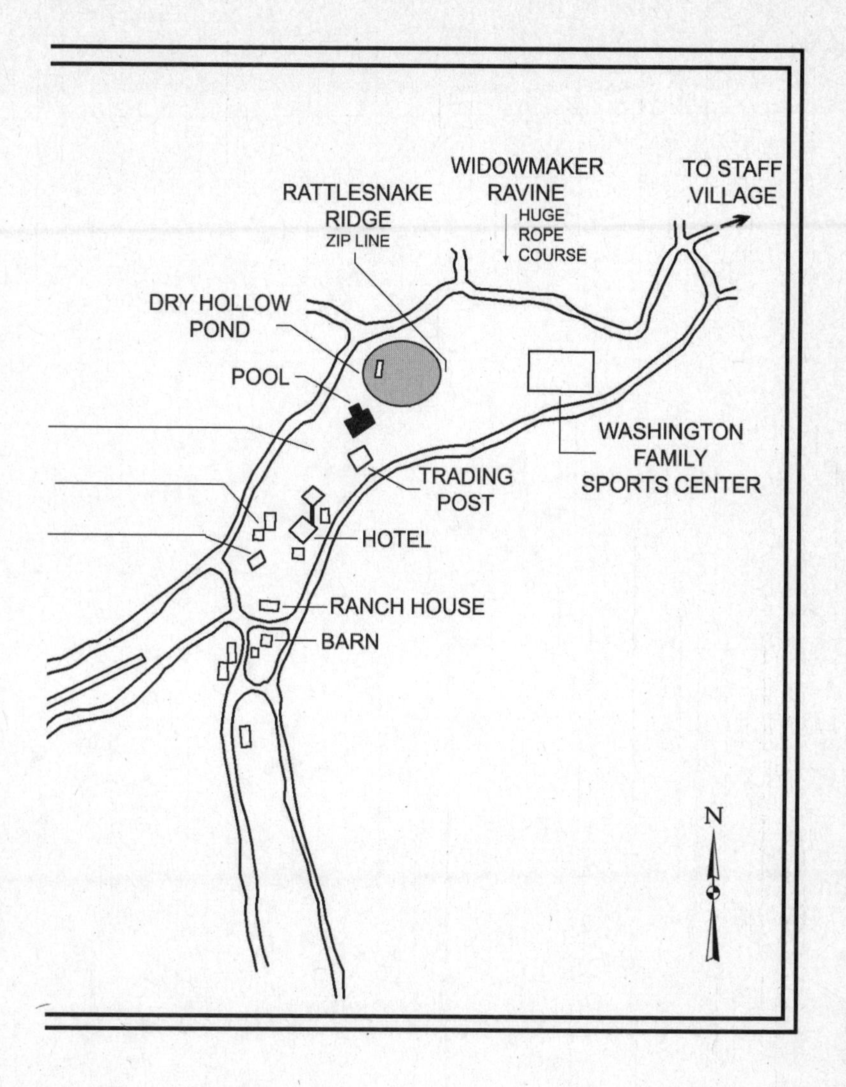
WIDOWMAKER RAVINE
TO STAFF VILLAGE
RATTLESNAKE RIDGE
ZIP LINE
HUGE ROPE COURSE
DRY HOLLOW POND
POOL
WASHINGTON FAMILY SPORTS CENTER
TRADING POST
HOTEL
RANCH HOUSE
BARN
N

A Land Deposit

The women move with quick steps, leaving shallow footprints in the crusty mud. They tie their head scarves tight beneath their chins to ward against the wind. They're grandmothers now, survivors of a turbulent time. They've left their husbands home in Antelope, watching distant battles on a tiny screen while a roasting chicken sends promise to their noses. The women come to treasure and to witness and to claim their own promise from the psalmist: *The LORD remembers us and will bless us.* They give what they can give: their time, their prayers, their confidence that warm breezes follow bitter blasts if one but persists and waits.

Through the years, each building on this Muddy Ranch, each room, each path, and even rocks and hills have heard the rhythm of these women's words, the drumming of their hearts, following a calling, a faith, a hope. Renewal. *Bring the whole tithe.... Test me in this...and see if I will not throw open the floodgates of heaven and pour out so much blessing that you will not have room enough for it.* The women trust Malachi's words, believe that love multiplies when given away.

This day in November—though the land looks abandoned to empty buildings, cobwebs, and hibernating snakes; though it appears to some as long forgotten, left to herds of elk and deer and bovine grazing—the women see something more: a transforming earthly place where holy encompasses human. Their prayers take on new strength.

Later, their gifts of time and petition given, a silver cross left hanging on a wall, they head back home. They've done what they can do. Lost in thought, they watch a vehicle approaching on the road. They sense a change, an answering, as though the rocks and hills that hold this land will soon give up their promise, bring it out from shelter into sun.

The car's license plate is out-of-state. There's a child inside. His eyes are smiling, and he waves at them as they drive by.

Part III

Charity

To the man who pleases him, God gives
wisdom, knowledge and happiness,
but to the sinner he gives the task of
gathering and storing up wealth to hand
it over to the one who pleases God.

Ecclesiastes 2:26, NIV

28

Dreams

November 1995

Jill Hartley searches for something familiar in the landscape, something not formidable she can cling to. She tightens the purple woolen neck scarf, hiding the strawberry mark that stains her neck, and shakes free her coffee-colored hair. She wishes she were home in Portland, finishing her paper, preparing for interviews with her senior subjects, "Romeo and Juliet," as she calls them. Her husband, Tom, will want some "tender time" this Thanksgiving weekend, when she allows herself to be pulled from her regimented schedule to be intimate and close. That time's a little frightening too, but not as much as this, sitting in the backseat with Tom, flinching as the car approaches tight knots of tumbleweeds like a cue ball to billiards.

"It's like the parting of the Red Sea," Gail Bartlett says as the car presses forward on the twisting road, separating the dead Russian thistles torn loose from their shallow roots. There are no shoulders here. Ravines beside the road are steep. Jill forces a deep breath.

If anyone but the Bartletts had invited them, Jill would have made Tom decline. But Gail and Isaac Bartlett are like parents to this big-bear husband of hers. But, oh, how she wishes she were sipping Starbucks in Portland instead of getting carsick in central Oregon.

Isaac maneuvers the new Chrysler around a hole nearly big enough for the car itself. Overhead, dark clouds heavy with snow billow like mushrooms shadowing the landscape. Spotted horses suffer the wind beside the road, their long tails separated by the gusts. Jill feels certain that only wild horses can inhabit this desolate country, then sees calves nearly as big as their mothers, nursing. Another blast of wind pushes the car, sends tumbleweeds over the side of a deep ravine. The car swerves. Isaac keeps control.

Gail grins. "Isn't this landscape grand?"

Gail could take a bucket of manure left on her doorstep as a prank and squeal in delight that someone brought fertilizer for her garden. Isaac's no better, indulging his wife of forty years in her impulsive schemes. "I have the most interesting life with Gail," he often says as she blushes like a bride.

From the backseat, Jill watches Gail and Isaac chat happily together as Gail points at a deer and marvels at the landscape's "grandeur." Jill sees nothing grand. They're miles from any town. The weather threatens. She's heard of people being lost for days out here, their cars run off the road in winter isolation.

"I'm so glad you two decided to come this weekend," Gail says, the brown curls of her hair peeking out from beneath her fur hat. "I've been so eager to see what's left of that mystic's commune."

"I thought you wanted to drive the old stage route from Antelope to Prineville and take pictures of winter scenes?" Jill says. She's wary.

"Oh, that, too. But we can make two loaves with one fish because that old road sweeps right through the Muddy Ranch."

"You're scouting some new property for a youth camp, right?" Tom asks.

"Aren't we always?"

The Bartletts spend their free time involved with a nondenominational Christian group called Young Life that serves kids throughout the world. "Kids learn best when they're safe, respected, and having fun. That's why they love camps," Gail says.

Jill thinks of a camp she attended as a kid. She could see tall pines through the loose chinking in the cabin walls. No heat, no lights except flashlights, and beds with old springs that shot up through mattresses as thin as a prospector's long johns. She was cold most of the time, and the leaders bored them with Scripture readings. Jill didn't feel respected or joyful or safe at all, especially when she trudged at night to the outhouse. She was not moved by the experience, except to decide to never go again.

Jill stares out the car window at sagebrush and craggy juniper trees. Who would want to come to a camp out here? She looks at her husband's handsome face, his gray eyes shining. He winks at her, smiling his isn't-this-amazing smile. She's having trouble breathing.

They descend a steep grade, and Gail reads the road sign: "Essentially a one-lane road." Jill hopes it's not also a one-way road. Abandoned long buildings, the kind one might see at a state fair, lie beyond.

"Must be their old warehouses and distribution centers," Tom says.

"I imagine they didn't want people coming any closer than they had to. They had armed guards," Isaac says. "And they probably didn't want big delivery trucks trying to figure out how to turn around on these narrow roads."

"Armed guards?" Jill asks.

"It was a difficult time, especially for locals," Gail says. "The ranch gained notoriety in the 1980s for hatching the first bioterrorism attack in the United States. Well, first attack if you don't count deliberate smallpox exposure to Indians. But in 1984 seven hundred people in The Dalles got sick. Mothers miscarried, teens and elderly were hospitalized, and many had complications for months, maybe even years afterward. Salmonella. There were attempted murders, too, right here. And before that, this place knew sheepherder wars, and before that, Indians were hunted down and killed here. Maupin, the town, is named for the man who killed a Paiute chief before there even was a Prineville Land and Livestock Company that became this Muddy Ranch. Those folks developed more than 124,000 acres of this land, but they crowded out small homesteaders in the landgrabs."

"You've done research," Tom says.

"I've always been intrigued by places that attract such extremes."

"Extreme misery, it sounds like," Jill says. "Even the landscape's uninviting."

"Is it? I see it as a place of struggle between good and evil. The land itself becomes part of the trial," Gail says.

"But didn't the commune eventually disintegrate? It's a cattle ranch now, right?" Jill asks. "You called it the Muddy Ranch."

Gail shrugs. "Who's to say that what the people of Antelope endured with the Rajneeshees' occupation was the end of something? Maybe it was the beginning of an amazing time. We might be driving into a place that will one day celebrate God's faithfulness and love in unimaginable ways." She sighs happily. "We're such a drop in the bucket of time."

"But what a splash you make," Isaac tells her. She laughs.

Now that Isaac's retired, Jill supposes the Bartletts can afford to indulge in trips that use up a lot of gas. And in this instance, tires, too. The snow-packed road felt smooth as glass, but the snow's melted at the lower elevations, and the rough black gravel grabs at their tires. One suddenly deflates like an old plastic bag.

The women stomp their boots to keep warm while the men put on the little doughnut that Jill hopes holds up.

Gail isn't the least distressed.

"We'll pray on that," she says when Jill mentions maybe the tire won't survive the old stage road. Gail's pet phrase discomforts Jill, even though Gail says it without the least bit of presumption that anyone need agree with her or that she thinks less of those who don't. The tire changed, they climb back in, and the car soon rounds a bend, the view opening to purple hills surrounding a narrow valley. Now the landscape intimidates with its high rocks and twisted trees.

"Whatever made you think of this place as a camp?" Jill asks.

"A woman in my walking group suggested it," Gail says. "We need one hundred thousand campsites by 2006 if we're to meet the needs of all the kids."

"I told her the ranch was too big, that it wouldn't be a smart move," Isaac says. "Not even worth the trip out to see it."

That surprises Jill, Isaac disagreeing with his wife. Still, here they are, making a steep descent down a twisting road, so he obviously doesn't disagree much.

They turn off the main road and head east, still on gravel. Rocks stacked like blocks are dusted white at the top, burnt-red at the bottom. In places, the towering stones lean out almost over the road. As though he knows she's beginning to feel anxious in this isolation, Tom lifts Jill's hand and kisses the back of her gloved knuckles. With his other arm he pulls her closer. A shock of his brown hair falls forward as he kisses her forehead. They've been married a year, but he's still attentive, kind. Maybe she's been squeezing his hand too tightly. "It'll be all right," he says. "Still feeling sick to your stomach?" She shakes her head.

After a few more miles following a stream on the right and ridges on the left that spill boulders toward the roadbed, they pass a lake untouched by the wind, a walking bridge across one end. A coyote waits near the broken-down dock on the far side, staring at them as they pass.

"The Rajneeshees built this earthen dam. They imported black swans to glide across it," Isaac says.

"Pretty impressive," Tom says. He's an engineer by training, and Jill sees in the light of his eyes that he's running figures on the slide rule of his mind, assessing the lake's size and construction.

They pass a building with a "Mandir Reception Center" sign hanging by one end. "This is where visitors got their colored identification bracelets," Isaac says. Another structure sits on an airstrip with a half-open door gaping like a mouth with a broken tooth. Grass spears through the tarmac. The two-story buildings are all stained a blood red. Tumbleweeds cluster between them.

Jill pushes her glasses up on her nose and tightens the scarf around her throat.

"All these buildings were abandoned after the Bhagwan's disciples sold what they could to go home or get on with their lives," Gail says.

"We heard that when people asked the Bhagwan if he couldn't

provide some help to those who were left here with no means of getting home, he merely said, 'All I care about are my cars and my jewelry.'"

"Isn't that sad?" Gail says. "After all they gave to him. A loving god he wasn't."

Isaac stops then next to the gatepost with a big beam arched over the entranceway. Jill has seen those posts in John Wayne movies and that television show *Dallas.* "It probably marked the original Muddy Station," Gail says. "This was a stage stop once."

They all stare at the "No Trespassing" sign nailed to the gatepost now.

"So we'll be turning around?" Jill asks. All she can think of is that they've driven nearly twenty miles beyond Antelope, and they have at least that many more before they return to a major thoroughfare where AAA Assist could ever find them. Surely even Gail won't press the legality of a "No Trespassing" sign.

Jill looks at her watch. Already 2:00 p.m. She starts counting. It'll be five at the earliest before they get back to the Bartletts' vacation home at Black Butte Ranch, and another three hours of driving over the mountain pass in the dark before she and Tom arrive home in Portland. She has a dozen things to do before her class on Monday morning. Tom fails to understand her need to be both organized and rested. Spontaneity is one of his gifts, he tells her; he doesn't seem to care it isn't hers. She has a final paper due next week in her major, geriatric studies, and she volunteers several hours each week at the retirement center steadying toothless men as they walk and smile at elderly women wearing scents of lavender soap. She hopes the project and paper will be the seed of her doctorate, once she finishes her undergraduate term.

Gail says, "Let's go ahead. This is a public road, even through this gate."

Gail, pressing the legality of something? Jill bets Gail's weight on her driver's license is actually correct, she's so honest. And funny. And adventurous. And loving. She supposes that's one of the reasons Tom gravitates to this couple. Visiting the Bartletts, he says, is like coming home to the family he never had. "Their lives are the stories I read first," he told Jill. The Bartletts are the family he's chosen, especially now, his own parents dead of heart attacks and intense living.

Tom visited with the Bartletts more than with his parents even before he was an orphan. He spent every Tuesday evening through high school with them at "Club," they called it, talking about life and dating and issues of faith he said weren't boring at all. On weekends, too, he hung out in their huge family room with two freezers and two gigantic refrigerators chock-full of soda pop and hot dogs and ice cream and whatever else growing teenagers grazed on. Sometimes a hundred kids would gravitate to the Bartletts' basement. Summers meant excursions on rivers and lakes, over to the coast for sand-dune buggy racing. Winter brought skiing and ice-skating, always with packs of kids. But the greatness of it wasn't in the fun stuff, Tom told her. It was in the people, the way they made him feel: wanted, respected, and worthy. Tom said the Bartletts and their brood transformed him from an isolated boy to one who found things to love. They'd even paid his way to a camp called Malibu up in British Columbia one summer—"the greatest week of my life," he told Jill.

Being an hour away from civilization by boat in some wilderness campsite conjures up an entirely different word than *great* for Jill.

"Come on, Jill. You're up for a little hike, aren't you?" Gail says as Isaac drives the car under the John Wayne arches toward a large ranch house and turns right. They pass a barn on their left, and Isaac pulls to a stop in front of a two-story red building with a deck out front and bay windows that break up its rectangular shape.

Tom opens the door, and Jill leans forward to look up at the sky. The storm that threatened on the heights has rolled on over the layers of hills. Though the wind gusts still play tag with the tumbleweeds, it's warmer here. It smells of wet earth.

"Aren't there snakes in this country?" Jill asks. "I'd better stay here."

"Not around in the winter," Tom says. "Relax, honey."

Gail says, "I can use a good stretch, can't you?"

Something heavy presses down on Jill's heart. She's a woman who tunes in the radio as soon as she starts her car, rides her bike in the summer, and opens the window to the flower-potted porch of their flat so she can hear the stereo while she studies. She likes the sound of barking dogs, of children playing in the distance, of traffic and buses. Sounds to fill silence. The sounds of the city bring comfort, let her observe life safely from a distance.

This place, this vast silent landscape, reminds her of a cemetery, a witness to bad things. A loose door hinge on the red structure clangs when the wind hits it. Jill shivers. What can Gail possibly see here that is potentially good? Tom is grinning. Jill feels small and scared and all alone.

Gail walks toward the reddish two-story building trying to see it as a board member might. Run down. Desolate. They'll have a hard time convincing the board to invest in the site. Even she can see its dauntingness; still, she sees more potential. Ever since her friend put the thought of this place into her head, Gail's turned a curious eye toward this landscape. Remote? Yes. Challenging? Yes. Too big? Perhaps Isaac is right. But think of the possibilities! She can't stop!

Earlier this year near Bend, they almost purchased land for a new northwest camp. Then Isaac, on an early morning excursion taking pictures, heard the neighbors close by, the highway sounds. Urban sounds. He came back to their vacation home, his face fallen, telling her it wouldn't work. "Our neighbors will hate us and rightly so. Kids'll be laughing and playing the music loud. Not isolated enough," he said. She didn't worry. God always tends to details, and if that spot wasn't right, there'd be another. Like this place, where isolation is its music.

"Look at that old barn," Gail says. "If only it could talk."

"It would say, 'Paint me,'" Jill says.

Gail takes Jill's hand. "We've done our share of painting over the years. It's one of the fun things about renovating sites for campers.

Especially since painting means all the other hard work has been done, and all that's left is…the artistic part."

"So many buildings, Gail," Isaac says. He pushes his fur hat back on his high forehead, stands with his hands in his London Fog coat pockets. "It might not be possible to put this Humpty Dumpty back together."

"We wouldn't be trying to put it back together," Gail says. "God's going to remake it into something totally new. Out of the dust, so to speak." Isaac nods his here-we-go-again nod. He's a good man, her husband, and as much a hopeless romantic as she. She trusts his judgment. If he thinks it can't work, they'll have a difficult time convincing the rest of the property committee that it can. *That isn't my role anyway. If this is to be a camp for kids, then God will make the way, not me, not the board, not anyone of this earth.* Her passion has always been to give what she can and let God do with that what He will.

"Who owns it now?" Tom asks.

"A Texas company bought it in the bankruptcy," Gail says. "Now a businessman in Montana has it. Dennis and Phyllis Washington." She squeezes Jill's hand. "This is a place with God's fingerprints all over it."

"Ouch!" Jill says pulling her hand free and reaching for her foot.

"Are you all right?"

"Those little stickers worked right through my boot!" Jill pulls her glove off.

"Goat heads," Tom says.

Before he can help her, Jill pulls at the tiny spiny seed stuck in the seam of her boot. "It looks like a baby sputnik," she says. Then, "Ow!" The spine pokes at the webbing of her hand.

"I've got a first-aid kit back at the car," Isaac says, heading for it.

Gail holds Jill's hand to look at the puncture wound. "You're so cold."

"Cold hands, warm heart," Tom says.

"Then you picked the right girl," Isaac says.

"She says she'll stay with me through thick or thin. 'Whither thou goest' and all that."

Isaac hands Tom the ointment, and he squeezes it onto Jill's wound.

"Ready?" Gail asks. "Let's look inside."

"Gail…" Isaac says. "The signs…"

"I can't read any signs, can you, Jill? Read? No, I can't read." She smiles at her husband. "I won't touch anything, but I want to see how much room there might be for a clubhouse or bunk beds."

"Might not be structurally safe," Tom says. "How long have these been empty? Ten, twelve years? Doors could fall off right in your hand."

Jill holds back, but Gail's already on the deck, cupped hands against the windows, nose pressed close. What she sees inside takes away her breath. Two huge rooms, large enough to have three hundred kids or more clustered in there for Club. The other side opens into another vast room where kids could eat. This could work, it absolutely could!

"Hey!" a man shouts from the direction of the ranch house. Gail turns. Pulling on his jacket, he takes long steps toward them. "What do you think you're doing? This is private property." His cowboy boots thaw deep footprints in the snowy mud.

"We were just leaving," Jill tells him as she heads for the car.

"You're right, of course," Gail says. "We should have asked. We're interested in potentially—"

"You can't be here," the man barks. He frowns and stands, resolute as a boulder. "We've had lots of vandalism. You need to get out now." He watches them, his arms crossed over his chest, while they pad their way back to the car and clamber inside.

"Do you get kicked out of places often?" Jill asks.

"I've been asked to leave some of the finest establishments in the country," Gail says cheerfully.

"This doesn't qualify," Jill says.

"I can't say I agree," Gail says. "I'm not sure how God'll work this out, but I believe that one day we won't have to leave."

"You're pretty quiet," Tom says on the drive back to Portland. At least she'll have Sunday afternoon to work on the paper while Tom watches football. Those games consume his afternoons, but they free her up to work without feeling guilty that she's neglecting him.

"Thinking about my paper."

"I'm thinking about that ranch."

"It was overwhelming, wasn't it? Like a ghost town with so many empty buildings that look almost...lonely. Even the rocks and the trees felt oppressed. It was a scary place."

"Huh," Tom says. He clears his throat. "I didn't feel that at all." He turns down the radio. "Isaac told me there's more than a good chance that the property could become Young Life's, just as Gail says. The owner's tried giving it to the state of Oregon for a college or a prison, but not successfully. Too many problems negotiating costs of redevelopment or even staffing it. Since the owner is willing to donate it to the state, Isaac thinks he might be approached to donate to Young Life. Apparently he offered it to Bob Schuller's ministry at one time too, but they would have sold it to someone else and used the funds for their ministry."

"Someone would 'give' away property worth millions?" Jill says. The idea is ludicrous. Then, "Oh, a tax break."

"Sure, but the owner really wants it to be used for something that would benefit kids, from what Isaac's heard."

"I wouldn't want to be the one who had to fix it up," she says.

"Isaac says they'll need people to live there while dealing with permits and land-use hearings and all that. And then to help develop it."

"If you ever tried to make me live there, my heart would freeze right up along with my thumbs," Jill says.

"What a challenge," Tom says. "Imagine being a part of making that place into something worthy."

"Now, that's scary," Jill says.

Tom turns to her, his hazel eyes reflecting the dash lights. He reaches for her now-gloveless hand and lifts her palm as he continues to drive, his eyes back on the road. "If we get the chance, I won't be able to say no to it, Jill." He holds her fingers before his mouth and breathes warm air on her thumb. Then he wraps her fingers into the middle of his palm. "But I promise to always keep that thumb warm—and your heart—no matter where we are."

Tom's a dreamer. Always a dreamer. Live there, in that isolation? And for what? He said, "If *we* get the chance, *I* won't be able to say no," stepping from "we" to "I" in the blink of his eye, as though what she wants in her life or what the "we" of their marriage means could be stepped over for this…this crazy idea of a camp. Jill pulls on her gloves. She has a paper to think about. Maybe this is just another of Tom's dreams he'll wake up from. But she takes a deep breath as though she's about to begin a steep climb.

29

COMMITMENT

"The Bartletts want us to drive down for dinner," Tom says. He's cautious, never quite sure how to bring up things that aren't written on Jill's calendar. She doesn't like surprises. He drops his briefcase on the bookcase of their second-floor apartment, stretching his arms over his head to take out the kinks of his commute. His eyes catch the pansies already blooming yellow and deep purple in the pots out on the porch. Jill grows them from seed all winter in the back bedroom, then sets them out, a sure sign of spring and that she's been contemplating something. That's what her gardening time is, she tells him, a chance to let her mind rest while her hands work out the academic issues. She never rests completely.

"This weekend?"

"Tonight."

She looks up from her books. Her glasses have slipped down her nose. "But you just got back from Salem. Do you really want to turn around and drive that same trip again?"

"It's not the same trip if you're with me."

His wife stands, smiles, kisses his forehead. "You go," she says. "I've got studying."

"It's Friday, Jillie. You'll have all of spring break to work." He gently pushes her glasses up. Vivaldi's *Four Seasons* plays softly in the background.

"I like your hair short," he says, brushing the smoothness at her temples with his fingertips. She cut it to conserve time, he knows that. She schedules every minute, fills the time she once needed to dry her hair with a longer stay at the retirement center. She makes little time for socializing. She carries full class loads and even now, though Tom works with an engineering firm, she still works part time at the coffee shop where he met her two years before. "I never want to be dependent," she told him, which he translates: "I never want to need anyone, not really." *Not even me,* Tom sometimes thinks. He likes being married to an independent woman, but he also wishes she'd let him take care of her. Maybe once she's out of school she will. Maybe when she realizes he won't go away she will.

Sometimes he wonders how he ever talked her into marriage. He believes in miracles, and their marriage is truly that.

"I've got a little more work to do," she tells him. "And I wanted to run back over to the center later. They're having a Home Fires gathering tonight, telling stories of when they were younger. I want to record it."

"Can't the director?"

"She will, but Romeo and Juliet are so sweet together, so attached to each other, I want to hear them tell the story of their meeting again."

"Are those their real names?"

"I can't remember real names." Jill laughs. "So nicknames help me remember."

He supposes the time she spends with the elderly isn't really work, just as his engineering isn't work for him. He loves what he does too, seeing the possibility of a landscape, reading it, then merging his vision with what a client wants, whether a golf course or water-treatment plant.

Jill's work gives her an added bonus: The people she studies remind her of her grandmother, a woman who died when Jill was in junior high. She raised Jill after her father died and her mother "disengaged by getting married over and over," she told Tom. Jill misses her grandmother still. "The people you love go away," she has said more than once. She has no girlfriends to speak of, no one she goes shopping with, and most of his associates who are married have wives who don't join them for Sunday-afternoon football. The couples at church are mere acquaintances to her. One or two other couples they met at Portland State and went to movies with a time or two are already separated. Transitions from school to the outside world take their toll.

"How about if I go with you to the Home Fires thing and we can drive to the Bartletts' later?"

"It'll bore you, won't it?"

"I like stories."

Jill sighs. "What do Isaac and Gail have up their sleeves that they need us back there tonight?"

"They don't need us, Jill." He hesitates. "They've got some news about the Muddy, and I wanted to hear about it, that's all."

Her shoulders stiffen like a brush. "They're still chasing that dog?"

"It's not a dog." She frowns at him. "Or if it is, it's a greyhound speeding along. Or no, it's a German shepherd, sniffing out the possibilities. Or better, it's a Great Dane, preparing the way for kings and noblemen to take over a landscape of remarkable challenge, converting it into—"

She punches him lightly on the shoulder. "You and your dogs. I know you'd like to have one someday."

"They're good companions."

"But not in a small apartment like this. Second floor, too. You'd have to get up in the night and take one out—"

"Nicc diversion," Tom says, holding up his hand to stop her. Jill smiles, and he pulls her to him. "We'll compromise: a Home Fires gathering with your folks tonight and then a trip south tomorrow to mine?"

"You make Salem sound exotic." Tom sees her calculating her schedule. They're as different as ballet and basketball in some things, spontaneity being one. "Get up early? Be back here by one?" Tom nods agreement. He would like to sleep in, have a leisurely breakfast, then drive on down, but if this is what it will take to get Jill to go with him, it's worth it. Compromise. Adaptation. Marriage vows ought to mention those.

"All right," she says. "Let me just—"

"No more studying, Jillie. I'm calling the Bartletts, then let's go."

"I wasn't going to study. I thought I'd take some pansies along for the center. " She steps onto the porch, then hands him the terra-cotta pots. She grabs her purse and pulls a paisley scarf around her neck. "I don't know anyone who doesn't like flower surprises, do you?"

His wife's a generous woman. If only she'd let him do more for her. Well, maybe that's for another stage of marriage.

Jill watches and she listens at the Home Fires. Romeo is in his nineties, tall with silver hair. He stands erect beside his Juliet, a woman whose white hair barely brushes his ribs. "We were different as bee and buffalo knees," Romeo says. "But we were well matched when we needed to be. She picked up my spirits, and I picked her up soon as I could and carried her across the threshold." His wife pokes him playfully. "Married sixty years. Strongest time was when I fought the cancer. She never left my side. We never needed anyone else so long as we had each other." The two gaze into each others' eyes as though just married.

"They're friends as well as lovers," Tom says afterward, when Jill asks for his impressions. They find a parking place on the street but need to walk two blocks before they're home.

"I like that they've never needed anyone else," Jill says. "They're a complete relationship." She runs her arm through Tom's.

"Marriage should be exclusive," Tom says, "but friends enrich us. They never mentioned anything about friends. Or faith. That's important too."

"I guess," Jill says. She's never asked her senior subjects about their spiritual lives. They've talked of education, family history, occupations, health, but not much about friends or faith. "My mom had lots of friends, and she went to church all the time. But she still ended up being married four times."

"Maybe she never stopped grieving over your dad, and her difficulties stem from that."

"Maybe. I don't know. She never seemed really committed to those marriages. Did I ever tell you she kept a 'divorce fund,' so she could get out anytime she needed to?"

Tom's eyebrows go up. "Well, Romeo and Juliet still like being with each other. That's what I like. A goal to shoot for when we've been married sixty years."

"You think we'll make that?"

"Absolutely." He curls her fingers over his arm. "It's a commitment. And neither one of us can afford a divorce fund."

"I don't remember much about the place," Charita Swensen tells Jill. The two women sit drinking coffee between classes. When Jill posted a request for volunteers to help interview elderly people living near student housing, Charita, a freshman, responded. Part of Jill's study examines how the elderly are affected by a changing neighborhood.

It's April 1996, and a spring rain falls through streaks of sunlight outside Portland State University's commons in the heart of downtown. Jill wears a yellow scarf her mother gave her before her mother's third—no, her fourth—marriage last year.

"I see you found one of the Bhagwan's books." Charita nods to a used title Jill bought at Powell's bookstore.

"It's all about detachment, as far as I can tell," Jill says.

"My nana, Cora Swensen, she told me about a sixth-century monk who said detachment wasn't a bad thing if it allowed us to be free of 'the wants,' she called it. Wanting things to happen in a certain way, instead of allowing ourselves to attach to what really matters. Like believing that what's happening at the moment is what we want and trusting that it's what God wants for us."

"You sound like a philosophy major," Jill says.

Charita shrugs. "My nana took religion classes after she spent a summer at that commune. It really inspired her toward deeper things, she said."

"You mentioned you lived there. I didn't know your grandmother did too."

"One summer. Nineteen eighty-four. I left when I was seven," Charita says. "I lived with my grandparents after that. Why the interest?"

Jill's not sure how much she wants to share. "My husband knows some people who think it would make a great kids' camp. We drove out there last year, and now the owner is considering donating it to the Young Life organization." Charita hasn't heard of the group, so Jill fills her in on what she knows.

Charita laughs, brushing auburn-streaked blond hair from her eyes. "Wouldn't that be ironic? Children were *persona non grata* in that place. Too much freedom for a kid is as harmful as too little. The place was so big it was hard to find my way around. I felt lost a lot. Creepy sometimes too, with older kids crowding my space, if you know what I mean." She looks away, embarrassed. "I couldn't always find an adult when I needed one. My mom told me to think of myself as having lots of mothers, but I didn't. We had 'carers,' but for them it was work. I hated being separated from my mom. The summer my nana came out was the best, because I lived with them both then. I didn't have to sleep in the kids' hut or share my toys." Charita smiles, two dimples forming in her cheeks.

"Did you ever meet him, the Bhagwan? Maybe when he drove by in his Rolls-Royce?"

"I do remember that," Charita says. "My mother and her friends clapped their hands and looked happy." Charita stirs her coffee, then adds, "She always looked happy, I guess, except when I left. But even that had nothing to do with me."

"Your leaving?"

"Her looking happy."

Jill looks at her reflection in the window behind Charita. She has her mother's same high forehead, the same black hair and dark eyes that peer out through big-rimmed glasses. Jill's mother doesn't smile much, ever, and now that she thinks of it, *somber* is a term she could use to describe herself.

"Where's your mom now?" Jill asks.

"In Canada, working for her Club Med." Jill raises an eyebrow, and Charita explains. "Not really, though it isn't so far removed from Rancho Rajneeshpuram as you might think. She works as a social director for executives on retreats. She's still involved in the Bhagwan's meditation centers. Nothing religious, she says. Just a way of teaching businesspeople how to manage stress. My mom was a therapist once. She also served five years of probation, for immigration charges."

Charita doesn't seem embarrassed by her mother's felony arrest or probation. "She's part of the Osho practice. That's what a lot of the Bhagwan's followers became, renaming the Bhagwan *Osho*."

"But not you?" Jill asks.

"It was never my way." Charita licks her red swizzle stick, stares into the swirl of the dark coffee oils. Now she looks uncomfortable, and Jill wishes she hadn't pried. It's none of her business. That's why she doesn't ask questions about personal philosophy or faith. "My grandmother changed my life when she took me out of there. But she says I changed her life too, for the better, hers and my grandfather's, for as long as he lived."

Jill considers pursuing the discussion, but Charita's eyes pool and spill over. If she isn't careful, Jill might have to share something personal in return. One thing she likes about interviewing older people is that they don't expect her to share anything about herself. They want a good listener. "Have you ever gone back to the ranch?" Jill asks.

"What's left to see?" Charita wipes at her eyes.

Jill describes the barn, the old ranch house, and the large boarded-up building where they'd been asked to leave.

"Sheela's place was in a ravine they named Jesus Grove. Calling it that always bugged my nana. There were fruit trees all around."

"We didn't see that," Jill says.

"If you take another road trip out there, let me know. Maybe I'll join you. They say a place is always smaller when you go back to it. I'd like that. Maybe it would help me understand why my mom chose it over me."

They share a pleasant meal of lasagna and garlic bread, speak of news from far-off Kuwait, and scandal in Washington, DC. They play the latest version of Trivial Pursuit. Tom wows them with his grasp of detail, and Jill laughs a tinkling laugh, looking at her husband in admiration. Then they take tea and coffee in the Bartletts' living room.

"There were people out at the Muddy the weekend we were," Gail says. Jill knows this is what Tom lives for, this update on the Muddy. "A Young Lifer and his son. They fished and felt the same way we did about the possibilities for a camp. He had permission to be there. I take it as a sign that someone else sensed the call to be there at the same time we did." She fills them in on Oregon State's decision not to accept the Washington family's offer of the site for a college or a prison.

"We'll have to get a land-use change through, remember," Isaac says. "And write new legislation to allow for recreational use on a farm. The hearings in Antelope about the Washingtons giving it to the state got pretty heated. This is not going to be easy even if the property does come to us."

Isaac tells them that after the *Oregonian*'s Steve Duin ran a column titled "Church or State," the "fisherman" visited the ranch the same week they had made contact with the columnist. The article mentioned an Antelope rancher, Jon Bowerman, who'd been interviewed for a *Frontline* documentary about the Rajneesh era. His words led them to think he was a man of faith who'd like to see something good come from all that turmoil. They hoped to introduce him to the ideas of Young Life, to see if he might become an ally. Several board members came to the site in the spring, according to Gail. Practical-minded businessmen stood in the spitting snow and wind and had trouble seeing possibilities. They announced the Muddy "a dog."

But another staff member drove from the coast, visited the property, saw its spires of rock, the dramatic ravines and vistas, the possibilities of preexisting water, sewer, electricity, and structures, and thought that even with its history—maybe even because of it—the site could prove a special place. He quoted Colossians at that meeting, and his words touched a chord. *For God was pleased to have all his fullness dwell in [Christ Jesus], and through him to reconcile to himself all things, whether things on earth or things in heaven.*

"Christ's love can reconcile what has gone before," Isaac says.

"Isn't that something, Jillie?" Tom says, inviting his wife into the discussion. "All these indicators that the camp is meant to be?"

Jill ties a tight knot in her scarf. "The terrain there challenges my thinking that it could be a camp at all," Jill says. "Those lava rocks look...foreboding to me. Totally unwelcoming, like garbage deposited there."

"Did you know that the word *commitment* comes from an old banking term that meant *deposit?*" Gail asks. "A deposit was like a promise against which one could later draw. I like to think of all those geological deposits, and all the things deposited there by the Rajneeshees, as commitments God made to the land. It's as if He's made a promise against which there could be a draw, sometime in the future."

"But what do you think we can do now?" Tom asks. "While we're waiting for the Washingtons to decide one way or the other."

"You know about change, Jill," Isaac says. "What do your sociological studies tell you about how we could proceed? What would help local people know that we just want to be good neighbors?"

"I imagine the Rajneeshees told them the same thing."

Tom reaches a hand out to his wife, his eyes calming. She's spoken more harshly than intended.

"Time. It'll take time for the neighbors to trust your intentions.

They'll want to see you, feel you, touch you, and not just read about you in the paper or through lawyers' letters."

"We have to let them see that we're the non-gun-toting religious group," Isaac says.

Jill nods. "And that you're not rigid with rules and requirements, as cults are. They profess freedom, but they really aren't. Ultimately, real change happens through personal interactions."

"That's exactly the Young Life philosophy," Isaac says. He leans forward, pushes back a strand of gray hair. "Kids don't need to be preached to or pushed. They just need information and the chance to see how people who say they're Christians live."

Jill says, "Often when we dislike a group, it's because we don't see them as individuals, just as a group, as though they're all alike." She sounds like she's answering a final exam, she knows. "We forget that they're people with families and favorite football teams, hobbies, aches and pains, and disappointments. We don't like to spend time with people we don't know, so we rarely greet them and then never discover anything we have in common with them. We avoid each other. Detach, I suppose you could say. Stand back."

"You're brilliant, Jillie," Tom says. "We need to have people living out there now, engaging in conversations, being good neighbors." Jill raises her eyebrows. "Any chance the Washingtons would let Young Life people move onto the property? To provide security maybe?"

Gail lowers her eyes. "The truth is, no one from our organization has had contact with Dennis Washington yet. The latest we heard is that he might just bulldoze the buildings and let cattle remain. Those hearings and negotiations with the state left a bad taste in his mouth. He might just want out. Period."

"No one's approached this potential donor, and yet you're all thinking of the possibilities of living there? Having a camp?" Jill asks.

Tom seems not to have heard. "I can go up there weekends. Maybe another Young Lifer and I could do it together."

"You'd give up Sunday football, for a pipe dream."

"There's still Monday-night football," Tom says. He's serious. "I'll do whatever it takes to be a part of this."

"You actually think this will go through then?" Jill asks.

"We're praying about it," Tom says.

"Uh-huh," *When did he start using that phrase?* Jill wishes she wasn't such a skeptic, but she questions the motives of people who pray before they get in their car or before they put up new drapes, who have "conversations" with God as though God's someone who chats over the back fence with them like a neighbor. That kind of intimacy seems…unbalanced, makes God small. She wonders when Tom will start having "intimate conversations" before meals instead of the familiar words of "Come, Lord Jesus, be our guest" that she grew up with. She loves her husband more than anyone else in her world, but she doesn't want him becoming a religious fanatic.

Tom says, "We're told to give what we have and then to ask for what we need. God will return the gifts in ways we can't imagine. So bountiful it'll be 'pressed down, shaken together.' Those are the words."

"Give to get," Jill says, her anger rising. "Why are there so many hungry people in the world then? Why can't we cure cancer? Lots of people give to those causes." She wishes they were not having this conversation in front of others. He's an intelligent man. How can he hold a belief so bare of sound reason? "Surely good people have given and waited, prayed for relief and believed it would come. And it didn't."

"Maybe it's the timing," Tom says. His hazel eyes sparkle. "We have to trust. We have to still go forward 'as if,' trusting that God is larger than our imagination."

"Oh yes, that's always the out, isn't it? 'God will answer the prayer in due time. Meanwhile, ignore that growling in your stomach. God's busy putting together a youth camp on a desolate ranch in Oregon. He'll be around later to tend to you.' How can you believe in a God like that?"

Gail and Isaac exchange a look. Tom tries to touch her hand, but she brushes him off.

"*Belief* means giving your heart to something or someone. And there's always something mysterious about love, don't you think? Come to Antelope with me next weekend, Jillie," Tom says.

"There's nothing in that landscape for me." *How can he be so blind?* She lifts her eyes to his, gets up to put the Spode china dessert plate on the Bartletts' sideboard. She's shaking. *Maybe there's nothing here for me either.*

A Land Deposit

Lightning starts the Ashwood fire in August. It licks the ridges, burning hot and fast, spitting at the sage and greasewood, gobbling up the twisted juniper. Volunteers from Antelope, the ranchers, and residents of surrounding areas bring their pickups filled with water tanks and slap at the flames. The local rule requires saving houses and buildings; move animals, but don't risk people for the sake of fences or haystacks or the like. People and occupied structures, that's what matters.

Structures on the Muddy ranch are numerous, too many. All wooden. Old. There'll be no way to save them if the fire races down those ravines. The ranch manager might smell the smoke hours before the flames expose themselves, unveil their avarice. Not much anyone can do but warn the ranch, point to an exit route, wait to see what way the fire will take.

Range fires burn hot and fast, the old-timers say, seeking fuel. Three hundred buildings on the Muddy Ranch mean good eating for a fire.

A private pilot skirts his way around the fire as he flies across the Muddy. He watches as a finger of flame moves down a far ravine and pulls into its palm one single structure, engulfing it with fire. It leaves standing only stone pillars and the fence that is the boundary of the former Bhagwan's compound.

Of three hundred unoccupied buildings on the ranch, only the mystic leader's home is consumed by flames. Beyond the building, the fire burns on until the region accepts the offer of rain, and the two move out with each other.

30

Examination

Jill and Tom settle into a routine taking them to the spring of 1997. Jill signs up for seminars with titles such as "Pharmacology and the Geriatric Physiology" and "History of the Social Welfare Movement, Emphasis on Geriatric Philosophy and Legislation." The titles sound stimulating to Jill, though Tom wrinkles his nose when she reads the syllabus to him aloud. She'll graduate in June and begin taking courses toward her doctorate.

"Someday you'll be old and glad I've had these courses," she tells him.

By day, Tom designs intricate systems to transform landscapes into golf courses. But he's found new interests now. Twice a month on Saturdays he drives to Antelope, then back. Twice a week, evenings, he works with a group of teenagers he's gathered, neighborhood kids he's met while shooting baskets or at the launderette. He collects them like precious shells along the beach. Jill notices when he talks of them that he sees each as unique. With a senior member of the Young Life staff, Brad Jones, Tom starts their own "club," his theology "buttressed," Tom says, by more regular attendance at church. Jill even goes with him, and once or twice experiences what was pleasant those years before with her grandmother holding her hand, singing songs, and listening to stories. But more often, the people look to the altar and to each other, and Jill feels she's an outsider, that she's a hypocrite to be present, to enjoy, when she harbors so many questions of belief. She's a skeptic, one who doesn't so much doubt as examine. She's accustomed to examinations.

Some days after school two or three of the kids stop at their flat. They play foosball set up in the second bedroom while Jill's plants look on, or drink soda pop as they lounge on floor pillows Tom bought. She hears them laughing behind the door, boys and girls, while she reads, examines data she's collected. They always invite her to join them; she declines. They call her Mrs. H.

Tom's days and nights are full, weekends, too. He comes home inflamed as he talks of trials these young kids face: the alcoholic parent, the rich kid left alone for weeks while his parents travel, getting himself to school. The kids speak of sex and drugs and school bullies and the pressures to conform in ways that could "eclipse their lives and souls," Tom tells her.

She and Tom lie together in their bed, the sounds of traffic drifting through the open porch door, city streetlights highlighting Jill's pots of rhododendron.

"But I never realized how invigorating kids are, how much they give back. They make me think and laugh."

"They tolerate your bad jokes," Jill teases.

"That, too."

She lets her husband hold her, revels in the warmth of his chest, the safety of his arms. She feels herself relax, though only for a moment. Her mind wanders to things she should be doing.

"My time with them's worthwhile, Jillie; I'm reinvesting something I was given, giving it back. We've raised enough money in our car wash for three of them to go to camp in Malibu this summer. I hope it's okay if I plan to go along."

"Using a week of your vacation?"

"It'll be great. You could come too. You're good with kids. I've seen you."

She doesn't mean to stiffen, but she does. His enthusiasm makes her wistful. She wishes she knew why.

So many details, Gail thinks. A project this large has more details than cats have capillaries. But at least now they can roam the property without fear of being kicked out. Forrest Reinhardt, who came fishing with his son the same weekend they'd first visited the Muddy, turned out to know someone who knew the Washingtons! Mick Humphreys, that friend, made contact, and of all things, Mrs. Washington had been to a church camp once as a teen. From there, the puzzle pieces just seemed to fall into place as Gail had faith they would.

Today, Gail's hoping to meet Antelope neighbors at a picnic Young Life is sponsoring beneath the locust trees in the backyard of the Antelope community church. Members of the Catholic church a block down have stayed to eat and visit with their neighbors too. Brad Jones and Tom and others are here today from their organization. Gail hopes they won't overwhelm the people they mean to befriend.

Brad has been making a five-hour drive each week; Tom drives over three hours for his Saturday connections. Both have told Isaac they'll apply for the construction manager position when that time comes. Yet both seem not the least competitive about the outcome.

Brad and Tom begin the task of greeting Antelope neighbors, hoping to reduce the mistrust that might be engendered by "another religious group" moving in. Gail knows that some people struggle to understand the differences between a ministry and a cult. That local rancher, Jon Bowerman, appears to warm to the camp idea. Gail wonders if it's because Brad and Tom so easily admit knowing absolutely nothing about ranching or cattle or sheep. Admitting ignorance might be endearing to a community still reeling at the hands of people who claimed to know everything. The Rajneeshees robbed these people of their hospitality, that's how Gail sees it. Or maybe Antelope residents will set aside their mistrust in hopes that the new owners of the Muddy will lease some of the sixty-four thousand acres for grazing, or allow neighbors to fill their deer and elk and antelope tags on the property each autumn.

One man, whose ancestor owned the Silvertooth Saloon years

before, resists their outreach. Gail hopes he might attend the picnic, where home-baked bread and berry pies serve as sacraments, Christ appearing wherever two or three are gathered in His name, making friends of strangers. Mr. Silvertooth's been writing letters asserting that the Big Muddy should never be anything but a cattle and sheep ranch, the way it's "always been."

Of course, it hasn't always been a ranch. Gail's read the history. The landscape once knew natives who did not till the soil or move sheep across it to Summit Prairie in the spring. Some even say the Anasazis roamed this far north. Their chiefs might have asked that it remain "as it's always been" when men named Hahn and Fried laid claim. But the Silvertooth descendant says he'll resist any zoning changes making the Muddy into something recreational, Christian camp or not. He and 1000 Friends of Oregon, the land-use watchdog group that doesn't want productive farmland reassigned to other purposes, can kill the project with land-use appeals.

Gail sighs. She wishes she could ease the local residents' worries with words, but after what they've been through, words won't be sufficient. They'll need to see for themselves whether these newcomers can be trusted. Relationships will make the difference. She has faith in that. The word made flesh.

They've hired a fine lawyer, a woman, who has already contacted the planning commission to write new legislation and zoning laws to permit the camp. She's told the board to expect resistance, however, even with the backing of a former U.S. senator from Oregon and other influential parties who know people "who know people."

Gail knows there are hundreds of people in the network praying that if this is meant to be, then it will be.

She sets the anxiety of Mr. Silvertooth aside. Here is a breaking of bread together, sharing food and conversation with the residents of Antelope and local ranchers who would be neighbors. She wants to take it in, enjoy.

She notices a family with several Indian children seated at the long table, and when Gail asks, she's told the children are foster children raised by an Antelope family reaching out to others. They'll be good neighbors, Gail thinks, people who've learned to give, to care for more than themselves even when they felt abandoned and abused.

Brad's exchanging fishing stories with a big man wearing a cowboy hat that he adjusts with a guffaw at each punch line. Tom's bent close chatting with a teenage boy. He brought along some of the Portland kids. She hears the *cachink* of horseshoes against iron rods and a shout of triumph. Young Life volunteers from Seattle, Bend, and Portland have joined this day too.

Jill hasn't come. "She's getting ready to write her master's thesis," Tom says when Gail asks. He looks away, the way a son might who doesn't want to share something he knows his mother will disapprove of.

"Tell her she was missed," Gail says.

Jill sitting beside Tom, his eyes bright with enthusiasm, that's one important detail Gail was hoping to see.

"Dennis Washington will give us the property if the zoning change is approved, new legislation accepted, and we raise ten million dollars within five years and put the money into development to make this a camp for kids," Brad says. He's stopped at Tom and Jill's flat.

"Ten million dollars?" Jill's stunned by the amount.

"The property's worth nearly that much, and the Washingtons don't want to give us title to something that we can't develop and maintain. It'll ultimately take more money than that, but ten million would allow us to maybe be self-supporting within five years."

"You actually think you can raise that? I mean, if investors see the property, they'll never contribute those kinds of dollars."

"We already have a commitment of a million from a board member; another million, potentially, from a relative of a board member. They've both seen it."

"Maybe you should come back out, Jill," Tom says. "You were

there on a terrible day, and you haven't been back since. Spring, summer, and fall, it's beautiful."

"Uh-huh." Jill wonders if all engineers see the world as clay for their creative hands. Tom's never met a project he didn't like, never looked at a client's landscape and said it can't be done. A realist he isn't. Jill balances that in their marriage, and once Brad leaves, she intends to let Tom know just how unrealistic a crowd he's gotten attached to. Maybe this is how cults garner disciples, making innocents think they can create something from nothing, blinding them to realities. It does fit with her understanding of cultist communities. And Tom's so enthusiastic. The thought unsettles.

"What the Rajneeshees have already put into this place is invaluable," Brad says. "We'll have until 1999 to open the first camp. That's a little more than eighteen months away, so we'll have to raise the operating money first. Create staff housing out of the condos and some of the better A-frames, and use Sheela's Inn for the clubhouse and dining hall. Until we can build. Every building's going to have to be reconstructed. There're broken pipes in walls, broken water lines, and electrical's a mess. We don't even know where the underground lines are. No one seems to know where the schematics for the infrastructure have gone."

"We never even got to see Sheela's Inn when you were there. Jesus Grove they called it," Tom reminds Jill. "And there's a huge building, the worship center, or maybe it was a greenhouse. It's all glass, eighty-eight thousand square feet. We're thinking sports complex. There's room enough for four basketball courts, two soccer fields, rock climbing, a skateboard park, a restaurant—"

"All under one roof?"

"Incredible, isn't it?" Brad says.

"What are all these play things really good for?" Jill wonders aloud. "Isn't it supposed to be a religious camp? For kids to learn things about Christ and stuff like that?"

"But that's the fun part," Tom tells her. "Kids do learn. We involve them in activities and programs that people plan years for, so the whole experience becomes a…a metaphor for our relationship with God. A zip-line experience is like stepping into the unknown and flying across the sky, just trusting. The ropes course is about learning to rely on your team and doing something you don't think you can do, something you might *not* do without others to support you. Having kids jump into a pool at 10:00 p.m. with their clothes on says you can plunge in, do interesting things that don't hurt you or others but give you joy. It's about spontaneity and trust."

"Zip line?" asks Jill. Then, "Never mind. I don't think I want to know any more."

"It's going to be the most amazing adventure ever, to see how this will all come together," Brad says.

Jill can see the fire in her husband's eyes. He often gets excited about his ideas. Before the Muddy—his other passion—came into their lives, he'd drive her to various sites on Sunday afternoons to show her a golf course he designed, or the industrial centers constructed by skilled engineers. His enthusiasm for his work was one of the things that first attracted Jill to him. That and his enthusiasm for her, his willingness to care for her.

Now his wide and handsome face is awash with nearly luminous joy, a joy she's rarely seen. Maybe on the day they married. Maybe.

She watches the men lean against the kitchen sink with their soda pops in their hands, laughing about the possibilities, drawing designs for "zip lines" and "clubhouses" on the backs of envelopes, each detail making them more excited than the one before, each dream a claim and a promise. She pulls the paisley scarf hanging loosely around her neck into a gentle knot.

Tom looks up from the table to catch her staring. She looks into her husband's eyes. He winks. Jill Hartley knows her life's about to change.

A car honking outside the window and a distant fire siren sing a comforting duet, drowning out Jill's heart pounding in her ears. Her breathing is shallow. She hears the dog's breath beside the bed. A break-in in the flat below earlier in the summer prompted her and Tom to visit the pound, even though they don't really have the space. Gideon, they name him, and Jill has grown to love the German shepherd who demands so little of her. He's old and he drools a bit, so she's given him a red neckerchief to wear.

"You can drive back once a week for your one class, and spend the night if you have to use the library," Tom says. "But you'd have quiet time there to write. It'll be perfect."

"Perfect? Far from it." What could be perfect about driving that twisted essentially-a-one-lane-road alone? She's never changed a flat tire on her own. She doesn't know anyone well enough to invite herself to stay with them one night each week in Portland. She doesn't want to be discussing this. She's tired and overscheduled, and she's done it to herself. Juliet is ill and may not make it. She hasn't heard from her mother in months.

"*Perfect* doesn't mean it meets the impossible goal, you know, Jillie. It means to be complete. Full-grown, like your mature rhododendron. You with me, the two of us doing what will make a real difference in people's lives, that's what's perfect. 'Perfect love drives out fear.' "

"Who said I was afraid?" Jill snaps.

She knew this was coming, knew it would be the conversation that defined their future together. That ranch has become a goat head in the heel of their marriage. The dog whimpers. She reaches down to pat his head, straightens his neckerchief.

"On that ranch, we can contribute—"

"Nothing. I can't. There's nothing I can give there and nothing there for me to receive. Nothing. Here I can at least get employment. I will have to make ends meet if you give up your position."

"It's the chance of a lifetime. To help assess the infrastructure, how that place all worked. It's worthy work, Jillie. It's an engineer's dream. We'll raise the support we need—"

"The people at the retirement center expect me."

Tom waits before he says, "But mostly you go there because of the research, right? You're not really…invested."

"I have relationships with them," she defends, wondering as she says it if they will miss her or if another bright-eyed graduate student visiting them each week can easily replace her.

"You don't even know their real names." Jill glares. Tom looks away.

"We could work on *our* relationship out there, Jillie. We'd be our own best friends, the way we thought we'd be when we got married. The way you say Romeo and Juliet are for each other."

"Only because the nearest other human being would be, what, twenty miles away?"

"People live within two hundred feet of us here, and we're not friends with them, Jill. Besides, the ranch manager will stay on until the zoning changes are complete and the Washingtons sign the property over to Young Life. There'll be other human voices near by. They're going to call it Wildhorse Canyon. Isn't that a great name?"

"You mean it isn't even final?"

"Think of it as an adventure. We can tell our kids we lived in a ghost town that was once a commune and became a celebration place. 'A thin place,'" Tom says. "That's what the Celts called places where something mysterious and holy comes down to earth."

She scoffs at that. "What kids? You can't expect anything romantic to happen in the midst of spiders and snakes."

"Sheela's place, now the Orchard Inn, is perfect for us. Fruit trees around it. You love helping things grow. It could be ready to live in without much work. It'd be like vacationing in an exclusive resort, Jillie."

Jill grunts her disgust. Orchard Inn. Wildhorse Canyon. He's already renaming places, something people do when they fall in love.

To name is to love, she's read that somewhere. *Tom calls me "Jillie." Why don't I have a pet name for him?*

"You deserve some time off. You don't know how to rest. I worry about you sometimes."

"But you'd go there without me, right?" Her posture dares his answer.

He hesitates. "No," he says. "If you won't come with me, I won't go. We already have so little time together, I don't know how far we could drift without breaking the anchor."

"Oh, Tom. Do you really want to live in an inn where people engineered death plots? Sounds to me like selling your soul."

"Don't say no until we go back there at least once. We'll make it an end-of-the-summer-term celebration. For a week. Just you and me and Gideon. We'll sit on the deck, I'll read the Sunday paper to you. We'll explore together. I'll even grill steaks. Polish your toenails." Jill laughs at that. She has the builder's hands, wide palms; Tom is graced with expressive, long fingers that more easily hold the nail-polish brush than a shovel. "Give it a try, please?"

Jill sighs. Going there for a week will prolong the ultimate pain of telling him she cannot do this, cannot leave what she knows to step into this wilderness he offers. Yet maybe giving him one hundred percent of her attention for a time is the way to douse the fire fueled by the huge, unknowable, inhospitable Muddy.

31

Closeness

She promises a week, no more. Tom hopes it'll be enough to help her see as he sees. He's reminded of the Christmas song, "Do You See What I See?" He wants her sight to match his own. He wonders if anything less than such a dramatic change as coming here for the next year or two will ever bring them closer. Her mother's been divorced three times; his parents, too. Each had another spouse before they died. He feels a weight in the bottom of his belly.

Their three-year-old marriage has unfolded differently than he imagined. He met Jill in a coffee shop while he studied for an exam. He engaged her in conversation, her sable eyes soft and inviting him to sink. They shared a love of music and the arts, read Rilke poems together, and before long he anticipated his study time only because she joined him. He watched her with customers, kids and parents, other students. She was kind and respectful, engaging them in conversations about themselves. She was steady, reliable, a good listener. He shared things with her in those early days he hadn't shared with anyone. Weeks passed before he even noticed the sea urchin–shaped birthmark on her neck, and then only when she consented to go to the coast with him, where the wind whipped off her protective scarf.

He'd always been a good promoter, someone who could close a deal, and so he had, asking her to marry him often enough she finally consented. He found a good job. He thought they'd have time together with only one of them in school. He thought she'd quit her job at the coffee shop and let him support them both. She had other ideas.

They didn't even take a honeymoon.

He's had only brief glimpses of Jill when she comes up for air. That's how he sees it, her coming up for a quick breath before she sinks back into studying and work and separation from him. This is not what he imagined for them, for him, and most of all not for her. How to make her life better, that's what he's always wanted. It's what marriage should be, what love looks like in his mind.

At least she's agreed to go with him. It's their first real break from routine.

A pair of golden eagles circle above them when they arrive. "The presence of eagles is considered good fortune by the Indians," Tom says, directing his wife's eyes upward. Jill nods, but she doesn't appear cheered. He's never seen a sky so blue.

They enter the Orchard Inn, a single-story building a short distance from the ranch house. The building's nestled among overgrown peach and pear trees, possibly a quince. Two large meeting rooms occupy most of the L-shaped building, where Ma Anand Sheela once held press conferences. Another room might have been a kitchen, but holds only a deep sink. The whole building's stripped of furniture, but not of the mauve and gold carpet, which reminds him of the eagles' wings. Their voices echo in the vastness.

They choose a room looking out onto the ridge toward the entry gate. They've brought an air mattress, folding chairs, sleeping bags, and a small propane stove that Tom sets up on the deck. None of the many bathrooms in the motel-like inn works. They're all rusted, stained, and full of spider webs. They'll make themselves a latrine for the week with a shovel.

"Outside? Just do it…outside?"

"Maybe we can ask the ranch manager to use his—"

"No! That's fine. I'll adapt," Jill tells him. "Can we drink the water?"

"The water we brought with us. But I've got biodegradable soap for our daily baths in the river," Tom tells her with a grin. There's no power. The Rajneesh generators aren't working, so they have lanterns and flashlights to light their nights.

Tom sets up the chairs, inflates the mattress, and fixes supper. He whistles while he works, and the dog's ears stand alert. "You're glad we came, aren't you, boy?"

"I'm glad," Jill says, but she looks undressed without her books, without her schedule. She holds her arms around herself. She startles at the sounds of birds. She coughs at the dust. Her hands clasp tightly as though one reaches out to pull the other from a turbulent sea. Her neck scarf is in a knot.

"I think I'll clean the bathroom," she tells Tom.

"You don't have to be filling every minute, do you?"

She sinks back into the plastic chair and sighs. "I wonder how some of the elderly at the care center sit all day long and do nothing," Jill says.

"They're not working all the time. They're resting." A sizzle from the steaks draws the dog closer. He's salivating. "I bet those card players, or the ones who sing in the chorus are healthier," Tom says.

"It's the ones who play the bells, we call them the 'ding-a-lings,' who laugh the most," Jill says.

"I bet they're the oldest," Tom says.

Jill looks thoughtful. "I wonder sometimes if music does contribute to longevity."

"Laughing makes you live longer."

"Then I'll probably die young," Jill says. "Except that only the good die young."

"Hey," he says, leaning over to lift her chin. He loves that pointy chin. "Don't go talking about my best friend in that kind of tone." He kisses her, steps back to turn the steaks.

"I didn't think I was your best friend anymore." He turns to look at her, spatula still in hand. "All those kids you spend time with, even this place, have replaced me. Young Life is 'the other woman.' "

"You think that? Nothing will replace you, Jillie, as long as you don't want it to. As long as we don't let it."

That night, the dog pads into the bedroom and lies beside them, giving out a soft whine. Jill reaches over to pat his neck. "Good boy," she says. "It's all right." Tom holds Jill as they lie together like spoons. He sees the rounded ridge, a silhouette under the star-dotted sky, and an old juniper that looks like a riderless horse, all bent over. He wants to express his gratitude that she's come with him, to win her to his passion, to make this vast acreage a place small enough for her to know it. How to help her discover the intimacy of something so big, that's his challenge. Maybe the secret is in the details, breaking it down into smaller pieces that she can find joy in.

Tomorrow he'll take her for a drive. Then he'll inflate inner tubes and pull her down the river, float lazily together in the warm pools of the John Day. Midweek, they can hike up into the hills to look for fossils in the pink and purple rocks. Wildflowers still dribble the ravines, wide black-eyed Susan–like blooms. Jill loves cultivated flowers. Maybe the wild ones will also speak to her. He'll give her an armful, help her relax, feel the bounty of this place and not just its challenge. Maybe if she sees the good things the land gives up, it won't be so fearful.

Gideon nuzzles Jill; his wet nose touches Tom's hand draped over his wife's shoulder. Tom can't remember when he felt so at ease.

"Gideon's nervous here," Jill says.

"Most new things make a body nervous at first," Tom groans as he turns to face her. "We have to stay engaged long enough for things to become familiar. He knows where to get comfort, don't you, boy?"

"Engaged," Jill says. "That's a funny word to use."

Tom thinks about his choice, confirms it. "It means a pledge, a promise, and a commitment even when you don't know the outcome. An engagement marks a choice. That's what coming here with you will mean to me, Jillie. To engage in a challenge I think I'm called to." He feels her stiffen. "I know you're uncomfortable with that idea, that someone can be called, but that's how I feel. Remember the Rilke poem, about being called by name and sent out into the world? God whispers, 'you, sent out beyond your recall, go, to the limits of your longing, embody me'? I hear that whispering here. And I want so much for you to be engaged in this adventure with me."

"People stop being engaged, though. They turn pledges into marriages that require very different things than engagements. A marriage is something...more enduring between lovers."

"Only if they remain engaged, Jillie. Only if we stay engaged."

The week surprises Jill. She and Tom have laughed and talked in ways they haven't for months. Maybe even years. By Thursday, she feels like a honeymooner. She's even stopped opposing when he talks of what this place might be one day, where kids might come to know the love of Jesus Christ. She tries to see it as he does. She remembers a quote from Marcel Proust that the "real journey of discovery is not in seeking new landscapes but in seeing with new eyes." She tries to see with Tom's eyes.

They walk past the building Gail looked into during Jill's first visit. "I think we could redo that. It's huge and wide open," Tom says as they go toward the corrals. Jill does feel safer this trip, leaning on her husband's wisdom. They've looked inside condos that remind Jill of strings of Monopoly game hotels and walked through the worship center, where Gideon stared at the stone altar and barked warnings. They drove past the place that must have been a sort of cafeteria. Remnants of hydroponics lie next to a greenhouse, covered by shifting sand. They walk slowly past the Bhagwan's compound, a burned-out pool still surrounded by its high fence and stone pillars, one with a singed edge. Gideon lowers his tail, hair rising on his neck. He growls low.

At each site, Tom paints a picture of how he thinks it could be most easily converted for the kids. He's so optimistic.

Still, there are places the dog refuses to go at all, even in the daylight. He won't enter the modular buildings attached by a long hall to the Orchard Inn. The dog starts into a room, then with a high-pitched whine, pushes his way out, backward. The room is empty; the dog distrusts what's there.

"He's sniffing history," Tom tells Jill.

"Didn't they have a crematorium somewhere too? Who knows how many people ended up there."

"That'll be one of the first things we dismantle," Tom tells her. "We've already decided that. Any place that gives an eerie feel."

"The whole place feels that way to me," Jill says. They whistle at Gideon and let him run beneath the orchard trees.

"People are praying about which sites need dismantling and which sites can be…redeemed." He hesitates on the last word. "An outreach group from Portland. Young Life has called on others. I'll let them know how Gideon reacted in Sheela's place."

"But that's so…woo-woo," Jill says. Her breath feels shallow, and she ties her light scarf into a loose knot that hangs on her chest.

"No one's going to mess with your head and make *you* feel a certain way, Jillie. This place is marked by geologic turmoil and spiritual turmoil, by people who did evil things here. Attempted murders. Actual murders if you go back far enough. But now there's something new. It's like light coming through cracks. It's nothing to be afraid of. To me, it's a gift that Gideon notices strange things, or that strangers come here to pray. It's as though we're not alone, because we aren't. How I see it is in Psalm 27. 'I am still confident of this: I will see the goodness of the LORD in the land of the living.' We'll live in this land, Jillie, and through all of us, God'll do amazing things."

"I just don't think God can do anything through me," she says, wishing the good feelings from the beginning of the week could extinguish her anxieties.

"There's an old saying from the Ojibwa people," Tom tells her. "'The grandmothers and grandfathers are in the children. Teach them well.'"

They sit on the back deck of the inn, looking at what appears to be a quince tree. "So my geriatric interests can be fed by caring about children," she says.

"Generational giving," Tom says. "We're all connected. You get things from your time with those old people, and I get my kicks out of kids."

"Future old people," she says.

"Be selfish about it," Tom tells her. "Those kids will make decisions one day about our social security, so we might want them to have fond memories of people with white hair and canes who treat them well." She laughs. Tom sighs. "I love it here, Jill. I've never felt more at home."

She believes Tom is somehow meant to be here. She supposes she envies his confidence in knowing where he's to apply his passion. But what about her? There's nothing here for her. She'll be throwing away her education to join him in this adventure. How will they pay for food and basics? He's said something about raising support, which means they'd be like those people who came to her grandmother's Methodist church every few years on furlough, they called it, as though they were in the army or something and home on leave. They'd share their mission work with those who'd contributed through the years. She can't imagine asking others for money; she can't imagine accepting their gifts.

There'll be no enduring community here, even with the volunteers Tom says will come, even with additional staff who'll prepare the camp for kids, then leave. She majored in sociology rather than political science because she's an observer, not an engager, a word whose meaning gives her pause in light of Tom's definition. What would there be to observe here? The disintegration of her marriage? It's on the verge of that. What will she engage with at this Muddy? The landscape is so large and unknowable it could almost be a metaphor for God.

Still, this past week has been peaceful most of the time, eating picnic lunches, lying in the arms of her husband, taking walks with a dog happy to be out of a small city apartment. This is their last night. Jill asks herself whether she's done what she set out to do when she agreed to spend the week with her husband. She fixed breakfasts. She massaged his feet. She shaved him once before he decided to let his beard grow. She listened to him, tried to see the dilapidated buildings through his eyes; that's been perhaps her greatest gift, trying to see with his eyes.

Yet he's most pleased when she lets him give to her, when she accepts what he offers, when she takes the time to notice that he does. When she engages.

Jill lies on the bed on this last night looking out at the sky. Tom snores beside her. What will she do when he asks for her commitment? He's so anxious to be here that he's willing to come for the interim, will wait to see who will be hired for the construction manager position. He would probably stay on for free if they could find a way to do it.

She hears coyotes howling, close. Gideon sits up quickly, jangling his collar and tags. Tom doesn't hear it, but Jill hears everything in this silence. Wind shifting. A mouse scratching. A coyote wail, closer this time. Jill gets up, opens the door into the hallway. The dog takes a hesitant step with her, pausing, then a few more steps, finally leading her to the french doors. She opens one and steps out into the night. "I don't know how I got here, Gideon," she tells the dog aloud. She isn't usually so brave. Gideon shakes his head, his leash tugging at her fingers. She sees the gold eyes of coyotes, and she shouts, "Out of here!" They scurry away, but Gideon continues to bark short warnings long after they are gone. She listens for a porcupine or perhaps one of those wild boars that Tom says root in the weeds beside the Muddy Creek. Instead, she hears silence.

What's bothering the dog?

Gideon looks up at the north sky. Jill does too, then. She catches her breath. A ball of light like a Christmas ornament with a tinsel tail shimmers in the night sky. "Hale-Bopp," Jill whispers. She's forgotten about the comet's scheduled appearance. But this is an early sighting, surely. So far away, so removed, and yet here it is: a phenomenon proclaiming the predictability of the universe. She feels tears spring to her eyes at this mystery, a pledge of order and routine, reaching her right in the middle of a godforsaken landscape. *Perhaps God hasn't forsaken it. Perhaps this is indeed a thin place, a spiritual place.* She shivers. She doesn't want to experience this alone. "Let's go wake up Tom," she tells the dog.

"I'm already here," Tom says behind her. She didn't hear him approach. She startles, but he reaches his arms around her. His rough beard feels good against her cheek. "Have you ever seen anything so beautiful?"

"So far away," Jill says.

"I was talking about you," Tom says.

"So was I."

Tom stays silent. Then, "I've felt like we are closer than ever before this week. Have I misread things? Again?"

Jill leans back into him. "It has been nice. I…almost hate to leave." She can't believe she's said those words.

He turns her to face him, his features barely visible in darkness. "Do you mean that?"

"I don't know." The words are a desperate whisper.

"I feel like my whole life has been preparing me for this place at this time. And I can't imagine it without you here too."

Could she deny the one person who loved her unconditionally the very essence of his heart? Was she being asked to give him that? Was the sighting of Hale-Bopp a reminder that there is an order, a powerful God caring enough to give this gift of love to someone as unworthy as her?

"It would only be for a year, right? And it would be the two of us, like we've been this week? But with running water? Electricity? And furniture? Acting as caretakers until the land transaction is complete?"

Tom nods. "Unless they hire me for the construction manager's job. Then we'd stay until the first camp is ready. That'd be two years at the most."

She doesn't even want to think about that. "Let's take it one year at a time."

"I yield to your better sense of timing," Tom says. "*Yield.* Always liked that word. Makes me think of a harvest."

Jill remembers the yield sign way back in the city. To her, *yield* means to wait, to let another go first. But the one who yields has a goal too.

"I could take one class, fall term, or spring," she says.

"Antelope has lots of people with stories to tell. You could interview them for your research."

Her hands feel sweaty, and her neck grows warm. She touches the birthmark, exposed. "All right," she whispers.

Tom puts his strong fingers to the back of her head and gently pulls her to his chest. "I can't do a thing about Hale-Bopp's distance from this earth, but my pledge to you is to bring you closer to the things that matter to me most."

"And I promise to stay engaged," she says. It's the first time she's truly felt married.

32

Comfort

Tom says it's good to be certain in the beginning, because events that follow often make one wonder, make one want to turn around, even wish one hadn't started on the trail. The first months at Big Muddy prove this. Jill and Tom's move goes smoothly once the board selects them as caretakers, the job of construction manager to be decided later when the property becomes Young Life's. No one now says "if," just "when." Gail and Isaac, Brad, and a few of Tom's teens help them move to the Orchard Inn, combining picnics on the steam-cleaned carpet with laughter over breakfast. It's their new "home," though Jill thinks that living in a motel without furniture hardly qualifies.

Trouble begins within days of Jill's attempts to create a routine.

She drives twenty miles to get the mail from Antelope. The water company tells them they won't deliver anymore because of all the flat tires. There are over one hundred capped wells on the property promising abundant water, but the reservoir leaks, and all the water pipes that once delivered water to thousands are cracked. All have to be replaced, so in the meantime, someone needs to drive seventy miles one way for drinking water. They drive with four extra tires in their car. Only the ranch house sports reliable plumbing, but the ranch manager hasn't made any noises about sharing water with them. He'll have to move if the land-use changes are approved, and Jill thinks he's not too happy about that prospect. The generator Tom gets running for their power shuts off at will with a cannonlike blast. Tom starts it manually, often in the middle of the night. He makes repairs often in his underwear. Jill can't repair a thing. She sweeps out cobwebs and kills cockroaches, but each day, twenty more come for the wake. Cleanup is futile.

No one understands how hard this is, Jill writes in the journal she decides to keep. *I feel like a homeless person wondering what'll happen from day to day. I can't even think about taking a graduate course. Driving that far every week...I must have been crazy. We've been here three weeks. It feels like a year. The grumpy ranch manager's decision to leave is the only high point this month.*

Metal chairs cluster at a card table, the only furniture besides their bed. They've set up a stove and refrigerator in what Jill says is her "dysfunctional kitchen." The sink's deep enough to wash a pig and lose it in the suds; the appliances stand so far apart she should skate between them.

Then visitors begin to come through. A young couple from Bellevue arrives with a toddler in tow, and Jill thinks they judge her insane. They "camp" the night (there are no other beds), serenaded by the coyotes and the cannon blast of the generator. They're pleasant, but Jill figures they won't be back.

Government people come. County planners. Tax people. Architects. Zoning checkers. Electricians. *I don't think the Young Life office has any idea what it's like to be here all the time. People fly in to assess, evaluate, examine the property. Those who drive don't arrive when they say they will, so Tom drives out to find them, changes their tires. Volunteers show up to clean up weeds or paint, and Tom's not sure what to let them do. They're so kind and giving. They stay the weekend; they have to eat; we have to feed them. There's no budget. So many people.*

All Jill can do is count on Tom's assurances that this is but the muddle in the middle of the moment. Their lives remind her of homesteader stories in which one hundred things must be done at once: Clear ground. Dig wells. Build houses. Plant fields. Raise chickens. Have babies. Put up food...and all within five years, or lose the whole investment. Somehow, enough people survived, though Jill notes that many pioneer women died young.

"I've brought along a set of dishes," Gail says on their first visit since Tom and Jill assumed the caretaker role. "I figured there were lots of people coming. That usually happens with a new camp. People like to donate their time. This place is so far out, though, we thought fewer would." She scans the room. "Not the most homelike atmosphere, is it?" Rolls of sleeping bags line the walls; more sit outside for those who prefer a canopy of stars.

At least Gail acknowledges the realities. Sometimes Jill wonders if these Young Life people really see the world the way normal people do. She knows they're not "abnormal," but their Pollyanna assumptions that all will work out because God's in control annoy her.

True, resources for this transition time have come from surprising places. A few more people have increased pledged funds by another million dollars; after their visit, Gail and Isaac agree to furnish the Orchard Inn with couches and tables and beds for the motel-like rooms, even pots and pans for the kitchen.

A group of women from eastern Washington sweep out the cobwebs in Sheela's house and find a tiny silver cross. Tom suggests this is a sign of blessing on their work. Jill's still uncomfortable with Tom characterizing God as one who cares enough to intervene with such details. "It's how we're changed," Tom says.

"Do I need to be changed?"

"You're perfect the way you are, Jillie." He kisses her nose. "Unless you think otherwise."

Tom and the property management staff who visit target a square building out by the airport and make plans to move it closer to the sports complex to become the clubhouse or a trading post. The design to convert the commune's worship facility to a sports complex begins to take shape, but all agree that doing anything before they have staff housing is futile. Doing anything permanent before they have possession of the land is foolhardy in Jill's opinion, not that anyone's asking her.

Maybe if it all falls through, she and Tom will go home.

Sheela's modular home will not be converted to staff housing. It has no kitchen and a modular can't really be revamped. The property team decides it needs to be dismantled and discarded. "What it needs," Jill says over breakfast one morning, "is to go to a home that already has a kitchen and just needs bedrooms."

"A rather unique need," Tom says, stuffing oatmeal into his mouth.

"Didn't Gail mention a family with a bunch of foster kids that lives outside of Antelope?" Jill wonders aloud. "They came to that picnic."

Tom asks her to check it out, which she does by talking to the postmaster.

"They could use it," Jill says after she's met them. The board approves the family's having the modulars, as soon as the property is really Young Life's, and if they're willing to move the buildings out. She's surprised at the lightness she feels at this news.

"The only bad thing is that now they have to wait on those planning meetings too."

"It's what life is, Jill, living with ambivalence."

The volunteers keep coming. Jill cooks now, making stews and hamburgers, taxing their meager food budget. She learns to buy in bulk and to set mousetraps to save the bags of flour from the rodents' greedy teeth. People from all over give up their weekends to work, even without assurance that the camp will ever really become a camp. It doesn't seem to matter. They gain by giving, from what Jill sees. Some call it worship.

"I don't see how it's worship," Jill says to Tom one night. They're taking the dog for a walk, watching as he runs through brown and yellow leaves. Jill's removed his red kerchief so it won't get tangled in the brush. The weekend "worshipers" have returned to Seattle and Boise and places beyond. "I wish they wouldn't say that. It's not liturgy and hymns and keeping eyes forward—that's what I think worship is. They even laugh."

"You put worship into too small a box, Jillie. Did you know *liturgy* actually comes from a word that means 'work of the people'? Everyday work, the things someone has to do to make a home and to feel at home. Doing that together is a kind of worship. You've always worked hard, but you haven't laughed much in doing it. Maybe instead of your staying inside and cooking when people come, you could join us. Weed whacking has its moments. You might enjoy yourself."

Weed whacking as worship. Something more to add to the muddle of her mind.

"This room," Jill says. It's at the top of the stairs at the ranch house and looks out onto the hillside with a view of a bent juniper tree.

"If we took a downstairs bedroom, we wouldn't have to haul this mattress all the way upstairs. Putting Gideon out at night would be easier," Tom tells her.

He has a point. "What was it you said about treating me like a queen?" Jill asks. "Wait. Let me get the dirt and cobwebs from my ears so I can listen to those sweet words of subversion you used to get me here in the first place."

Tom smiles. "There's furniture now at the inn. Sure you don't want to stay on there? No more sleeping bags."

"At least that new consultant Young Life sent has a nicer place to stay. But I need something that feels more like a home. I didn't realize how much privacy we had in our flat. I miss it."

Jill sweeps, then washes the bedroom wall, a faint flower scent making her wonder if perhaps an older woman lived here once, wearing lavender and lace. She paints the woodwork. In the upstairs bath, she sets candles in brass holders and brings a fern to soak up the steam from the claw-foot tub. Both the ranch house and the inn now have running water and bathrooms that work.

On the allotted day, she and Tom carry the headboard and slats up the stairs and lay the mattress. She makes up the bed, and while Tom goes downstairs to get water bottles, Jill rests, really rests, on her lily pad of comfort floating in this reservoir of chaos.

She lies back, arms outstretched on the bedspread. A robin on the roof's break trills outside the window. It is good work to see a beginning, a middle, and an end. It's a rare afternoon when no one's here. No volunteers. A phone's been hooked up, but it's silent this afternoon. It's the first time she's rested during the day in weeks. She never napped in Portland. What she wants to do is to spend this afternoon reading, napping, maybe loving her husband. It amazes her that she would think of such a lazy day. More amazing that she can make it happen. It fits into the schedule because there isn't one. Who knew what nice surprises await when one takes the time to let life happen.

Jill rolls onto her side. She's forgotten until then about the small door nearly hidden by the maroon wallpaper of roses. Jill gets up, pushes the door, discovers darkness beyond. She gathers a flashlight, turns it on, and follows the light, making her way through cobwebs on her hands and knees. She spits out dust and brushes off the webs sticking to the beaded sweat on her arms. She moves the light, and an unusual shadow forms at the end of the closet. Jill investigates, discovers a sharp corner, and around it, a small forgotten table with thin, spindly legs. She drags it out, inch by inch, sweat and dirt mingling in the October heat.

In the sunlight she sees that it's the perfect size to hold a lamp beside the bed. She dusts it off, pulls out the drawer, and turns it over. No markings. She pushes the drawer back in but it jams. It has to fit. Jill wiggles and shoves the drawer, then reaches into the open space for the obstacle and there finds a gift, a bundle of letters tied with a ribbon of blue. The penmanship is distinguished by a hand so precise it looks almost printed. No postmarks. She opens a letter of yellowed paper. The words read like prayers written by a woman named Eva Bruner.

The planning commission's held one meeting at the Maupin School and another in Antelope. Jill stands in the back listening to the pained voices of the Antelope neighbors. They've been through a war that no one outside understands even after all this time. They were a community united in caring before the Rajneeshees came; now they're cautious, one or two even callous. For the land to become anything but a cattle ranch again appears to resurrect their sense of powerlessness. One gentleman in particular persists. "No, no, no!" he says. "They're gone, all of them, and we don't need any new cult coming in there."

"If Young Life were a cult," their lawyer says, "I'd be nervous too." She speaks evenly, simply, without judgment or condescension. Her blend of professionalism and compassion might ease the residents' anxiety, Jill thinks. After all, these people had never heard of Young Life before Tom and Brad and others began making connections to their world, engaging them.

"Are there secret handshakes and whatnot? No one wears a picture around their neck?" a woman asks. She fans herself in the jampacked room.

"Our only requirement is that campers be willing to hear the gospel message while having a great time and being treated with dignity and respect," Tom says. "Most of the people involved in our camps around the country are kids who aren't affiliated with church. They haven't been brought to faith by a parent or grandparent, as you've done for your kids and grandkids. They meet in clubs during the school year, at people's homes. And in the summer, after they've helped raise money to pay their way, they attend camps designed to make every child feel important, loved beyond measure." An Antelope man scoffs. "It's how we feel about kids, that each is unique in God's sight. The people who volunteer or work for Young Life, your future neighbors, want to be a part of demonstrating that love to kids, that's all."

Jon Bowerman, the local rancher won to their vision, speaks on their behalf. Others express support. One woman says she's gone to the ranch regularly through the years since the Rajneeshees left asking for blessings and the formation of a camp. "We even left a little cross in one of Sheela's rooms."

"You weren't supposed to tell that," her friend says, tugging on her sleeve.

"Will you get street kids? We had our share of street people brought in and then dumped on us," the man complains.

"Anyone connected to their local club can come, but we bring adults they know along with them. One adult is involved for every six to eight campers. Adults stay in the bunkhouses with them. They have relationships with the kids that continue when they go back home. Relationships are what we're about. We're a noisy group—we like to laugh and play our music loud—but we're good neighbors." The attorney urges the residents to talk with neighbors near other camps around the country.

See what others say about us. People's lives are the stories others read first, Jill thinks. *We're being asked to tell the story of this camp by the story of our lives.* The neighbors' fears will only be calmed by volunteers who drive through town or stop for coffee or join her or Tom when they come into town to pick up the mail. Jon Bowerman or Brad or Gail or Isaac will earn trust by taking the time to meet their neighbors and treat them well. This will be about how they engage.

In her sociology courses, her professors minimized the importance of that one-to-one experience with another person over time. None suggested that's what changes lives, maybe even societies.

Jill looks around the room. Most of these Antelope people are different from her. They find comfort in the silence of this vast landscape, where she feels small and as easily trampled as a weed. But they've had more time with the land. They're invigorated by the remoteness. Would they feel as small and easily trampled if they tried to live in Portland or Seattle? When she sits beside them on the hard wooden pews at the little Antelope church on Sunday evenings, they can't know how she's struggling to feel at home here. They can't know that she feels as frightened as they do about change.

With one complaint filed before the planning commission's deadline, one person can thwart everything. They have until 5:00 p.m., forty-five days after the planning commission meeting. One Antelope resident, or any other group like the 1000 Friends of Oregon, can write a check for five hundred dollars to begin an appeal and stop it all. It would delay the project and bring gift-giving to a halt. Then she and Tom will leave. They'll go back to Portland. She'll take that class. Tom's dream will end. She can't describe what she feels.

Forty-five days later Brad and his wife, Molly, the Bartletts, and Jill and Tom walk out of the courthouse in The Dalles. The vote to rezone 1,360 acres of the Big Muddy Ranch for recreational purposes is unanimous. No appeals are presented. Their lawyer says it's a record, maybe even a miracle, for a land-use change in Oregon to go through without protest.

Tom says, "This reminds me of the psalm: 'What is man that you are mindful of him?' "

Jill feels small again. This camp is small in the scheme of things. Yet here is another amazement she can't explain away.

"All the little capillaries of God's heart for kids came together today," Gail says.

"Look there." Brad points toward Mount Hood and the glowing tail of the Hale-Bopp comet. Jill looks at it with a measure of sadness now, the news having reported the suicides of those who believed the comet hailed the end of the world.

"It's like a signature, isn't it?" Gail says. "A reassurance that God's been writing this story through the ages, sending heavenly things as signs of the order of the universe. Things may seem chaotic, but there is a plan. We are but the pages he's chosen to write this chapter on."

For Jill, the comet's brilliance is a reminder she's needed, a reminder of a night when she felt loved enough to make a change. Tom still says his prayer was answered that night when she agreed to make that muddy place a home by being in it with him.

33

GIFTS

"Go ahead and sign up," Tom says. "Things will be slow until spring." They've left Christmas decorations up, taken down the tree. Snow swirls around the ranch house as the old wood stove pumps out heat mixed with the scent of apple pie Jill's baked. The little orchard gave up fruit last fall. Once, when Jill accepted the offer of using her washing machine instead of driving into Madras, an Antelope woman told her how to freeze apples by adding lemon to the slices, so when she pops them into the pie, they taste fresh.

"I'll probably have to go alone," Jill says. She wants Tom to volunteer to drive with her to Portland but won't ask directly.

"The neighbors aren't too happy with us at the moment with our cows wandering around." Tom is still embarrassed by a rancher's visit before Christmas. They didn't know how to feed the large round bales of hay lined up like Tootsie Rolls in the pasture, left there by the ranch manager. The neighbor took a roll of toilet paper and furled it out. "Like that," the rancher said. "The cows'll know how to follow along and eat and stay out of my fields." Tom has been preoccupied by how much he doesn't know, including how to handle the two hundred head of black baldy cows that came with the Washingtons' gift of the ranch. The new calves need to be branded, tended. The Washingtons also donated two million dollars to begin creating the sports complex with the hope that it might be ready when the camp opens eighteen months from now.

"Are you praying about cows?" Jill teases.

"This week it's fences," Tom says.

At least she's become more comfortable with these "spiritual realms," as Jill thinks of them. She must admit: Unexplainable things are happening here. The cows might be a questionable gift, but an elk hunter who filled his tag on the Muddy expressed his gratitude by writing out a check for one million dollars to be put toward the camp's development. They're more than halfway to the goal of raising the ten million dollars they need. Already people willing to relocate their families have applied from other states, seeking carpentry and remodeling positions. The decision about the construction manager hasn't yet been made, but Tom and Jill expect carpenters by the end of the month.

"Would you pray for me, Jill?"

"What? You want me to—"

"Just think of me. These cows, the fencing, they're a distraction from the bigger picture here, and I'm not real happy about this part of the gift." Tom's neck looks red, and she's sure it's not all due to windburn.

"I… Yes, of course I can ask things for you," Jill says. She won't ask Tom to pray for her trip. It feels too much like begging. She's afraid to pray for herself for fear her uncertainty will just negate her request, maybe make life worse. "About the position, too? That you'll get the job?"

"That I'll accept whatever happens as being what I want."

Jill drives the four hours it takes for the first class. She knows she'll have a long day traveling over and back. The weather holds. The pass over Mount Hood is sanded, and she doesn't need the car chains or the sleeping bag and survival kit Tom assembled for her. At the university, she attends her two-hour class, speaks to her adviser, explains her lack of progress on her thesis. She speaks to former classmates, acquaintances. After class Jill drives to the retirement center where she once spent long hours. She visits with a woman who climbed a

Cascade mountain with her husband for her seventy-fifth birthday. She looks for Romeo and Juliet. She finds the tiny woman merely sitting and staring. She doesn't respond to Jill's invitations to play checkers or take a walk. Her memory's faded. She doesn't remember who Jill is. When Jill asks about Romeo, she turns away.

"He died right after Thanksgiving," the director tells Jill. "And Irene's just drifted since. She's grieving. We're trying to keep her connected, but you know she never had any other friend but him, no community to speak of. And she has no faith to draw on." Jill asks about her "ding-a-ling" women. Both have passed away.

Jill thanks the director and makes her way to the car. She finds herself examining her relationship with Juliet—Irene. It couldn't have been much support for Irene, as she didn't recognize Jill. Jill left her address with the couple before she left, telling them if she needed anything at all, to ask. Jill's edgy. She ties and reties her woolen scarf. She wishes she'd brought Gideon along for company.

She drives back, leaving at dusk. She maneuvers the little Nissan through the traffic, out toward Gresham, and up over Mount Hood. Four hours over, two hours of class, and four hours back. Can she do this every week for "The Sociology of Aging"? It'll age her. Slush on the road slows her. She concentrates, breathing easier when she reaches the long flat of Agency Plains near the reservation, thinking that route, though longer, will have the roads plowed of snow. Only a few more hours between here and home. She leaves the radio off, thinks of Tom, hopes he's had a good day. She speaks his name aloud, then swallows and says, "You know what he needs. Me too. Thanks."

In Madras, she picks up groceries, saving a trip later in the week. It's nearly 10:00 p.m. She's tired, not energized as she thought she'd be, having been back in "civilization," wearing "civilian clothes" instead of the jeans and sweatshirt that's become her uniform. She waits at the crosswalk for a man with a cane to make his way to his car. As she watches him shuffle along, she blinks back tears. She didn't cry when she heard of her ding-a-lings' deaths or observed Juliet's painful mourning. Irene. But then she hadn't cried over the death of her grandmother, a woman who held her close, nursed her through illnesses, whispered kindnesses to her on lonely days more often than her mother. *Her mother.* A woman of wealth and impulsivity who spent her husbands' money on remaking her eyelids and chin. The rough skin of Jill's birthmark itches beneath her woolen muffler.

Maybe Jill doesn't know how to truly be attached or engaged, to people or a landscape. Maybe she's not capable of deep feeling. She's never felt connected to her family. What business does she have thinking she can earn a doctorate and prepare others for their senior years? She doesn't know how to prepare for her own.

Her neck is wet beneath her wool scarf. Tears have seeped there while she's sat, waiting at the crosswalk. *Please, please,* she whispers, wondering if Tom has a survival kit for grief.

Jill begins by taking morning walks with Gideon, extending herself farther from the ranch house and the buildings along the airstrip where Tom works with other property staff to wire an office with electricity. She and the dog kick up skiffs of snow. The sky is blue as bachelor's buttons, and the castle points of rock jut into it like purple spears. She walks out to the empty corral, listens to the silence. She sees no coyotes. The snakes are dormant, Tom assures her. It feels so vast. But she's taking action. The image of Irene wasting away in mourning galvanizes Jill to reject isolation.

Eva's letters say that's what she chose also, to both wait and participate. This landscape is where Jill is, it's her home. She needs to get to know it. She sets a goal of exploring some new ravine each day, of listening without expectation to whatever she might hear. She'll write each day on her thesis too, and add to her idea to examine the role of friendship in longevity, and maybe even faith.

April 1998

The gravel road takes Gail and Isaac to the ranch without a flat this time. They stop in front of the old ranch house, its split-rail fence in bad need of repair. A patch of dirty snow peeks out from beneath the porch as the car stops.

Gail surveys the arched entry, a slight flutter in her heart. "Wild-horse Canyon" the sign reads now, below "Big Muddy Ranch." Now they can also add the Washington name and Young Life to that sign. Everything has been signed, sealed, and nearly delivered. " 'God had planned something better for us so that only together with us would they be made perfect.' Hebrews 11:40," Gail says aloud. She knows that verse by heart. "I think that verse isn't only about his plans, but about us being made more perfect."

"Could be," Isaac says.

She gets out of the car. Isaac stands on the other side. She hears a rustle in the tall sage near a streambed. New sounds, new demands, new hopes. That's why they've come here as seniors, having been asked to contribute their experience with camp development and staff and volunteer support, all needed before busloads of kids can come down that same road.

"Looks like a party," Isaac says, nodding toward the dozen or more pickup trucks with horse trailers parked by the slope-roofed barn.

"Well, it is a wild-horse canyon," Gail says.

Jill steps out onto the porch, wiping her hands on her jeans. She's wearing a red neckerchief today, cowboy style. She smiles in greeting and, with the dog following, steps off the porch to receive Gail's out-stretched arms.

"Tom and the consultant are in the barn. They're trying to sort out the cattle with a cowboy organization. I just came from there myself. They'll be coming in to eat soon."

"So we have ourselves a working cattle ranch," Gail says.

"*Working* is a debatable word," Jill says, but she smiles. Gail doesn't remember the woman's smile being so full or her greeting so warm. "The cowboys tell us fencing is a full-time job by itself, with these sixty-four thousand acres and miles of river frontage. We have to have the fences in good order to keep the government leases, and we have to rotate our cows each season so they don't overgraze. But at the same time, we need them to eat down the high grass so it doesn't choke out and die." She catches her breath. "They haven't been managed for years, so bulls have gotten in with young heifers that aren't ready for calving. We had to separate the bulls. Guess where we put them?" Gail shakes her head. "Inside the security fence of the Bhagwan's compound! Where his hot tubs used to be."

"You're becoming quite the cowgirl," Isaac says.

"I seem to have a knack for it." She blushes. "We'll be branding later this month with the Washingtons' Flying W brand. Cowboys showed up. Christian Cowboys of Eugene, they call themselves. Tom says they were willed here by an Antelope neighbor tired of our cows in his pasture." She laughs. "One of them helped round up wild horses years ago on this place. I need to finish fixing lunch, but afterward we'll sit and catch up. Come on in."

"Let me help you," Gail says.

"You're a guest," Jill says. She reaches her hand to Gail's. "I need to serve you. I've never had that privilege before."

"But we're not guests. We've come here to live," Isaac says. "Didn't anyone tell you?"

That evening, the Bartletts and Tom and Jill sit around the old kitchen table with cups of coffee. Starbucks coffee. Gail and Isaac carried in large boxes of it donated by the Seattle-based company. Enough for a year. Jill still shakes her head at how these contributions arrive.

It isn't clear what role the Bartletts will play or how hers might change now, but Jill's feeling flexible. Fencing with the cowboys has helped. She likes the boundaries fencing offers, the straight lines, the security of the barbed wire and the symmetry. She's learned the fence's strength is in the corner posts, how deeply they've been set, how strong the wood, how well they're anchored. Where the soil is shallow, rock cribs or jack braces hold the posts sturdy and the wires tight. And every so many feet, an H-brace is put between the long lines to help keep them taut. The H-brace makes her think of people bound together by that stability Tom says is Jesus Christ. "Even in a blizzard, a fence line can keep you grounded," Chuck, one of the cowboy's told her. "Might take you awhile, but you've got something to hang on to while you're walking toward home."

Jill's walked the fence line up by the warehouse buildings, near the reservoir, down ravines hiding little A-frame houses. Each trip she makes in safety fills her reservoir of strength.

During the so-called slow time of winter, she and Tom read books she picked up at the library in Madras, several aloud to each other. They have no television. A newsmagazine arrives monthly, putting the outside world's challenges and disappointments into a manageable perspective. Watching daily news reports robs her of a sense of humor, she realizes, something she needs to deal with life. She rubs Tom's feet and trims his new mustache, which makes him look like Tom Selleck. They even take a bubble bath together in the old claw-foot tub. She writes more on her thesis while coyotes sing and Tom and Gideon snore. Bawling calves serenade her sometimes. The cowboys say they cry because they've been weaned from their mothers.

"You made orphans of them," she says.

"No, ma'am," a cowboy tells her. "They got mothers. Always will have. But they got to move on to grow up." He hadn't intended it, but Jill wonders if he speaks of her as well.

Tonight she's let her mind wander, inhaling Starbucks coffee.

She looks at Isaac and Gail now, their eyes shining with anticipation of what lies ahead. Here sits an experienced couple still vibrant and involved. What's in this for them, giving a year or more of their lives to this cause? Gideon lies at Jill's feet. He gets along with everyone. How will it be, living so close to Gail and Isaac? Older people can either be hardy or cranky, rigid or adapting. She isn't sure which these two might be, or how closer contact will change her relationship with them. They're like in-laws, she realizes.

The wind whistles through the walls, and the house creaks. She hates the thought of leaving it tomorrow to drive over the pass to class. She's looking forward to spring break so she can spend it lazing around at home. There'll be branding to do too. Something new.

"That's how we see it," Isaac says.

"What do you think, Jill?" Tom asks. His hazel eyes look wary.

Jill's hands are warm around the Starbucks coffee. "I'm sorry. I was enjoying my leisure." She pushes up the glasses on her nose. The turtleneck sweater she's wearing feels suddenly too warm.

"Well deserved, I might add," Gail says. Her curls are blends of brown and gray and cap her face. "I'm amazed you're taking a PSU class. You leave at 5:00 a.m.?"

"I won't during spring or summer term. Try to write more," Jill says.

"The Bartletts will act as hosts and give tours and help coordinate volunteer requests," Tom says.

"That sounds great. I'm really not much of an extrovert. But I'm good at giving people directions about things to do, once I know what task the property people have in mind."

"I won't be alone in figuring such," Tom says. He clears his throat. "They've selected Brad for the construction manager position. He can't get here until July though."

"Why? I mean, they did?"

"And they think that things would work best if Gail and Isaac move into the ranch house," Tom says, "and we move back into the inn." His eyes hold sympathy. Can he see how disappointed she is? Will he protest on her behalf?

"It's the first place people will stop," Gail says. "It would save you from having to deal with all that. The inn has plenty of room for sleeping and cooking, but the phone's hooked up here. The carpenters and their families can stay at the inn until condos are ready. There'll be more contractors each week now."

Jill's trying to sort this all out. "But if Brad's the construction manager, will we even need to be here? Would we have to move now and then move again in July?"

"I wonder if we could sleep on this," Tom says, "and discuss it further in the morning."

Jill lies under the comforter while Tom offers up petitions. She still struggles with her right to do the same. She can pray for world peace, even for Tom a little, but not for something so meaningless as to sleep under that old wallpaper on the second floor of the ranch house. Prayers like that belong on behaviorist charts listing goals and steps to get there. Such charts seem too far beneath so mysterious a God.

Tom says *Jesus* without hesitation. *What is it about that name that catches in her throat?* It seems so personal, so raw. The soft ache of saying it makes her feel pleading, wounded.

She wants to comfort her husband, being overlooked for the position. He must be so disappointed. Had all those thoughts she'd had about not wanting to be here, about giving him just a year, had those been silent prayers answered over his? Why would God listen to her over someone so faithful as Tom?

"I'm so sorry," Jill says. She strokes his thick mustache, makes a mental note to buy a sharper pair of scissors so she can trim it better for him. "I know you wanted that job more than anything. Did Isaac say why the board picked Brad over you?"

"He's had more development experience with big projects. He worked for Howard Hughes for a time, and he's been involved as a leader with Young Life, running camps. They have to go with the best all-around man, Jill."

"But—"

"I'm sorry we'll have to leave. I really wanted to be a part of all this."

She feels her heart lurch. "What would you do here if we stayed?"

"Apply for a carpenter's job. Drive the backhoe, dig ditches," Tom says. "Whatever they need."

"But you have so much more to offer somewhere else."

Tom snuggles against her. "Don't you feel something moving on this land, bringing peace and sheltered promise? People giving so generously, from their time to their coffee? I want to be part of something bigger than us."

Tom holds her close. "I'm sorry my prayers didn't work," she says. Tears trail down her cheeks.

"But they were answered, Jillie. I wanted the best person for the job to have it. The board's chosen. I trust that. And I wanted for us to be closer. That's happened too."

She listens to the coyotes crying in the distance. Eva Bruner's letters spoke of waiting, but of acting, too.

She waits, wants to say this right without misleading him. "To be honest, I hate to think of leaving too." She can't believe those words come from her mouth. "I love this old ranch house. I have an idea," Jill says. "It may not work, but…"

She waits for him to encourage her to finish. Tom remains silent. "Don't you want to hear it? Tom?" Her husband starts to snore.

What had Eva Bruner quoted in her letter? *I will both lay me down in peace, and sleep: for thou, LORD, only makest me dwell in safety.* A psalm. Jill will start reading those as Eva did, memorize them as words of comfort she can call on in a time of trial. Maybe they'll explain how her husband can sleep so easily on the board's decision, and on leaving this place he says he loves so much.

Jill isn't looking forward to breakfast, and at first she thinks it must be her anxiety that causes her to mishear Gail.

"No, we discussed it. Even after a night sleeping on the bunk beds, we feel absolutely that you two should stay in the ranch house, and we'll move into the inn." Gail's voice is low and strong, and Jill loves her for the words she says.

"Maybe we could all live in the house together," Tom says. "It is pretty big."

Gail grins. "You have no idea about kitchens with two women," she says. "No. This will work out well. If you don't mind, Jill, I'll do breakfasts at the inn."

"Mind?" Jill says. "It's a miracle!"

"And if you'll do dinners, except on your class day, we can still serve the contractors at the inn."

When Tom leaves to help the cowboys, Jill considers talking with Gail about the idea Tom slept through; she doesn't. She considers placing a phone call to her mother, to take action. She doesn't. She decides instead to read a psalm, then take her walk and wait. Eva waited until she knew for certain how to proceed.

The consultant says the engineers' drawings would help beyond measure in establishing decent power grids and repairing the water system. No one seems to know what's happened to them or the building blueprints or the architectural designs. The notes could explain why the Rajneeshees set a sewage pool where they did, or where the underground utilities run. They'd know where the electrical circuits were inside the walls of the condos and hotels and learn where phone boxes were buried.

"Would those plans tell where the secret passageways are?" Gail asks as they drink decaf after supper.

Tom laughs. "We filled one in when the family with the foster kids took Sheela's modular home out."

"Did you go down there?" Isaac asks.

Tom looks like a small boy caught in a prank. "I found what

looked like a laboratory of some sort, and a hot tub full of mice droppings. Oh, and a snake skin. The tunnel came out at Muddy Creek. Guess maybe it was at a distance enough to escape immigration or something."

"A hot tub would be a nice way to wait out the authorities," Gail says.

"There are a bunch of them in the courtyard of the one hotel," the consultant says. "That's one of the big projects: After we convert the hotel rooms into bunkrooms, we'll have to get the hot tubs out and replace them with ponds so the kids can have a nice place to sit and relax."

Isaac says, "We've got a volunteer to provide all the landscaping once we start on the hotels, but we can't even begin that until the staff housing's in place. It would sure be good to know where pipes and electrical lines are before we start excavating for the lake and pool."

"Why would anyone take them, the designs and drawings?" Jill asks.

"They had a big garage sale," Isaac says. "Sold everything not tied down."

"Maybe we could put an ad in the paper," Jill says. "Say we're seeking the architectural designs from old Rajneeshpuram. Give our phone number. See what happens."

"Great idea," Gail says.

Jill feels her face grow warm, surprised how much this older woman's friendship brings her comfort. It's such a pleasant feeling, and all she had to do to get it was participate.

34

Details

The first response to the newspaper ad comes from Jill's former class volunteer, Charita Swensen.

"You said if you went back out there you'd tell me," Charita says when the two realize their connection.

"Things changed kind of quickly," Jill says. "So what do you know about the plans?"

"Nothing, really. But I figured if someone's looking for the plans, something must be happening down there. I thought maybe I'd drive out. I never dreamed I'd get to talk with you again. Do they still have horses there?" Charita tells her she once took riding lessons there. "I haven't thought of Buckle in years. Anyway, I'd like to visit. Would it be a trouble?" *She needs to come soon, or Tom and I will be gone.* Jill suggests a date, then asks Charita if she thinks her mother might know what happened to the plans, as she'd been one of the last to leave. "I could ask her if you'd like. Do you have e-mail down there?"

Jill laughs. "We're lucky to have a working phone."

"I know they had phones there. Lots of them. They had wiretaps."

"All managed underneath the horse pasture in a little cement shed. A terrible mess of phone lines. That's one of the reasons we need the plans," Jill says. "Most of the work was done internally, not by outside contractors, so we have no way of knowing what they actually did or how they did it. Phone boxes and lines included."

"Maybe my mom will help," Charita says. "At least I can ask. She's still involved with them, though."

"Didn't the Bhagwan die?"

"That fact hasn't lessened her loyalty."

The call comes late at night. Tom stumbles to the phone. "Yes?" He listens, then hangs up.

"Who was it?" Jill asks.

"Someone who says she has all the architectural drawings and disks and blueprints and even the engineers' notes."

"That's great!"

"Not so great. She wants seventy-five thousand dollars, or she'll destroy them."

He must be in his seventies, Jill thinks, maybe even eighty gauging by the fragile way he walks. His name is Arnold, and he's worked for years for a neighboring spread, the Imperial Stock Ranch. His wife has recently died. His employers introduce him. "I can repair tack, work on furniture, fix things," he says. "I understand you need volunteers." He pats Gideon, who leans into the man's bowed legs. Arnold stands with his cowboy hat in one hand. He wears a plaid shirt and Levi's, Western boots.

"Who decides this sort of thing?" Jill asks Tom. The operational questions are tricky as Brad doesn't yet live on the ranch to make decisions. Young Life's main office is in Colorado, and there are regional offices with decision makers in between. Fund-raising happens long distance, while fund-expending happens close to home. Arnold sports an ivory mustache and a full head of white hair. He has kind blue eyes. He tugs on Gideon's neckerchief to straighten it.

"I guess you could stay in the bunkhouse," Tom says. Isaac concurs.

"We should check with someone." Jill doesn't want to argue. She's set a goal for herself of finding ways to build Tom up each day; disagreeing with him in front of others isn't one. But some things require immediate answers. *Who'll cook for him? What about if he's injured or needs medical care? Can someone his age have a role in such a demanding place?*

"I think we're all right with the decision," Tom says. He sounds annoyed. "You can eat with us, Arnold. And I bet you know a thing or two about cattle."

"That I do, sir," Arnold says. He's soft-spoken. "And I'm pretty good at fencing. One of my favorite things to do. And I've always liked kids. My kids live far away, so I don't see my grandkids much. Making this into a camp'll be good for me."

The contractors working on the first condos in the Staff Village take their coffee and breakfast at the Orchard Inn and are pounding nails by seven. Isaac and Gail offer grace over the meals and without hesitation reach for hands around the table. Gail steps over any discomfort that might arise by a carpenter's callused hands holding the palm of his buddy's, or Isaac's or Tom's, but each follows suit, and none appears to object to the practice. Over evening meals at the ranch house, many of them linger before moving to their bunk beds at the inn. Sometimes Arnold tells stories about the old ways of the region. Jill listens most attentively, Gail notices, especially when Arnold speaks of the killing of the sheepherder and the young man who'd been convicted.

"Course I wasn't born when that happened," Arnold says. "It was back in '01. I came along thirteen years after. The fellow's wife was just a child herself, having to deal with such trouble. Quite a story, that one. Word is she lived here in this old house. I like being a part of a place that has such an interestin' history. Even what the Rajneeshees did here is interestin'."

Jill opens her mouth to speak, but one of the contractors interrupts. He talks of being a lapsed Catholic and wondering if Catholic kids can come to this camp when it's finished. He's part of the crew whose labor's been donated by an excavating firm from Bend.

"Sure," Isaac says. "And Baptists and Lutherans and every other branch of the Christian faith…or of no faith at all."

Jill winces.

Gail watches Jill. The young woman fidgets whenever words of faith are spoken aloud. She's seen that before in the journey of young people. Raised in the church, then disappointed, even hostile. Sometimes she wonders if people who say they're atheists aren't really so disbelieving of God as angry with Him. Angry about a hope not met, about a mystery they want unraveled. Maybe years later they're trying to make their way back, and they stumble over the words that carry painful memories. Even the words have to be transformed, she supposes, when one turns around. She's had a journey like that herself. Her own child's involvement in Young Life turned her life around.

"The opening date's been courageously set for June of 1999, a year from now," Isaac says. "Your hours of volunteer time and the donations, they all add up as tithes that God multiplies, just as He did the loaves and fishes."

"The fish I'm interested in are the ones in the John Day River," one of the men says, and they all laugh. "Even if it is late for steelhead."

"We'll claim divine intervention if we catch one," his colleague says.

"You're doing a great job cooking for everyone, Jill," Gail says after the others have gone. "But I think we ought to get ourselves a set of pots and pans and furnish this Orchard Inn kitchen so you and I don't have to keep running back and forth. This morning there were fourteen people for breakfast, not counting us. We're going out on a limb here, but we'll just go ahead and start ordering supplies out of Portland and Bend. Maybe even get deliveries. We'll get reimbursed later. I know the VPs will understand. Planners and implementers often march to different drummers. We can make our own music knowing we'd all sing the same tune if everyone were here."

Gail watches her, wondering what the girl's thinking. Tom told them of Jill's initial reluctance to come here and of her hopes to stay here only a year, which is fast approaching. But she looked disappointed by the board's hiring of Brad and by the talk of their leaving once Brad and his wife, Molly, arrive. "Maybe you can get a tire-repair shop set up out here too," Jill says. "One of the volunteers says the rocks the Rajneeshees put on the road are made of tiny slivers of obsidian—that's why there are so many flats during the summer without the protection of packed snow. Remember that first day we came here? We're lucky we had only one."

"Now that's divine intervention," Gail says and is pleased when Jill laughs.

That evening on the ranch, prayers are lifted for the delivery of the blueprints. Jill listens, and she hopes for them, for Tom, for the others who put their faith in the filling of such details.

"I wonder if that woman who called was my friend's mother," Jill says later. She tells the others what she knows of Charita's connections to this place. Jill didn't take her phone number, but Charita's to be there within the week.

"We'll just trust that what we need will be provided," Isaac says.

The pickup truck rolls in with a blue tarp strapped across the back. Charita steps out. "Meet my riding instructor," she tells Jill, introducing her to a man wearing a big black hat with a red bandanna wrapped around it as a hatband. He sports a silver rodeo buckle; says his name is Buckle.

"How did you find him?" Jill asks. She turns to Buckle. "Did you live here?"

Charita's sunset-streaked curls bounce as she answers for him. "I reached my mom, and she told me his name. He lives at Warm Springs."

"We Indian guys like living with our moms," Buckle says and grins.

"We heard...from a woman wanting money for them," Jill says.

"You did?" Charita looks confused. "But she told me where they were and to bring them out. That's strange." She unties the blue tarp as she talks.

"It's everything we carried out of here," Buckle says.

The entire pickup bed is filled with cardboard boxes wrapped with yellowed tape.

"It couldn't have been my mother who called," Charita says after they unload the material. "She felt so bad about what she did here." They carry it to the second floor above what Charita says was the Devateerth Mall. A casino once rocked with music at one end. Charita points out the dumbwaiter where she said she once hid all night after the casino closed. At the other end were the banks of phones soliciting money for the commune.

"What did you say she was arrested for?" Jill asks.

"Immigration-law violations. She married people in order to help them remain here. But her worst deed was that she was there when the salmonella poisonings happened. She even went inside some restaurants, but she said she couldn't do it. She got sick instead. But she never stopped the others from doing it, and she says she'll pay dearly her whole life for that."

They stack boxes on carpet that smells of mildew and dust. Leaves blown in when the door opened litter the room.

"Did someone else know you had them?" Tom asks as he sets another boxful down. The consultant keeps shaking his head in wonder.

Buckle says, "One of the peace officers knew where Razi took these. He might have seen the ad and had someone approach us."

Charita seems relieved. "I didn't want to believe it might have been my mom."

"My grandmother was making soap once," Buckle says, surveying the boxes. He hikes up his jeans and straightens his belt buckle, hands on his hips. "They made it the old way, swirling lye and ashes, and it never would set up. She pressed a prayer—that's what she called it—saying, 'Send me what I need to make this soap set up.' Well, along comes this old dog dragging an old greasy leg bone from some poor unfortunate deer." He tipped his hat back from his forehead. "She picked up that bone and tossed it into the pot. 'What're you doing, Grandma?' I asked her. 'Using what the Lord delivered,' she says. 'It don't matter who brung it. It was the Lord provided it.' The soap set up just fine."

Within days, the consultant is called away to some other project, abandoning the plans in disorganized boxes spilled onto the leaf-laden carpet. Tom and Isaac spend a day matching numbers. "Page 3 of 15"…but there are a dozen marked the same. They paw through stacks of blueprints. Even Jill puts in long hours, making little progress. "I'm beginning to think that God has a sense of humor," Jill tells Tom. "Maybe we should have asked not only for the plans but for someone to organize them."

Tom tells Jill on a June evening they'd best begin to pack. They're walking to the dairy fields to set up irrigation pipes to water the fields.

"Are we leaving?"

"Here's our option." He's holding her hand as they walk. "Molly will be here soon. Brad and she need to live near the phone and to be closer to where the contractors stay. So we need to move out to a condo, if we stay on. But you didn't agree to that if I didn't get the construction manager's job. So...we can pack up now and only move once. Head on to that next place, wherever that is."

So this is her out. They can leave now.

She knows without knowing that she doesn't want to leave, not yet. Maybe it's her time with Arnold that's been such a gift. The man points out the names of weeds and wildflowers, telling her the abundant ones, the black-eyed Susans, as Jill knows them, are known locally as blanket-flowers. "Indians called 'em that. My wife loved seeing those in the summer," he tells her. He shows Jill roping tricks at the corrals, and one day they even saddle up two horses and ride partway up the old stage road that once took travelers to Prineville. "I bet that young girl whose husband went on trial took this route," Arnold says as they ride. "She musta felt so alone. Something we don't have to worry about, living here," he says. Back at the ranch house, he offers to sand the porch bench. "Keeps me busy and keeps those slivers out."

Arnold is always giving.

Maybe it's her study that has taken on new dimensions since she's been here. After witnessing Juliet's/Irene's grief, Jill hopes to show the effects of friendships on longevity. The more friends one has, perhaps, the longer one lives. That's her theory. But watching the Bartletts and Arnold makes her think generosity, too, is as important as one's friendships, maybe even more important than one's health. Or perhaps true friendships, even true love, are composed of generosity, of both giving and receiving in life's small and bigger things.

Maybe her reticence has to do with watching her husband at work with others. She'd never been privileged before coming here to watch him interact with men who shared his vision and his interests. Single men—some taking paid positions, some under contract, and some volunteers—have arrived to work here now too. A California builder who took a wrong turn in Prineville while vacationing with his father ended up as a visitor to the ranch, then phoned his pregnant wife to say he'll be back home to help her pack the three kids up and bring the family north. The Bellevue couple who Jill was sure must have thought her crazy are coming too, toddler and infant in tow.

Tom pounds a stake into the ground to bolster the irrigation pipes so they won't fall over with the surge of water. Into Jill's silence he talks. "The Bellevue people raised their own support to be here," Tom tells her, "because there wasn't a paid position for someone of his skills. He'll handle the building of the swimming pool and the excavation of the lake. He's a civil engineer, and we're fortunate to get him."

"They seem like reasonable people to me," Jill says. "Yet they're *volunteering* to be here? Gail and Isaac, they had comfortable lives before choosing this place, but they at least have retirement income to rely on. The engineer…he's making a donation of his life, his family, too. It's a…curiosity what makes them come."

"You came."

"I didn't want to live alone."

Tom's quiet. "Maybe. But I don't think that's all." He turns on the irrigation pump, and they begin to hear the *shuck, shuck, shuck* sound of water sprinkling the fields. "These people's lives were changed years ago by giving their hearts to what they love. What happens when you love someone that much is that you want to keep giving it away."

"You could do those things," Jill says. "Landscaping or building bunk beds."

"Yeah. There's a carpentry job open. I could remodel condos and work on the hotels."

"Would you really want to take a carpenter's job when you could do so much more engineering somewhere else?"

"I would." He doesn't hesitate. "But not at the expense of us. You said you'd only give this a second year if I got the construction manager's job, and I didn't. A deal's a deal."

The setting sun casts a pink glow against the rocks, washes the hayfield. A lone blue heron lifts from the river, its legs reluctant, trails against the sky. They work together to move the long steel pipes, signal each other when the line is staked and ready to accept the surge of water.

"I'm going to miss this place, Jillie, I am. Just when it's getting going too."

"I love the look in your eyes right now. I suppose I envy what inspires it. You're the closest thing I ever gave my heart to, the best thing I believe in."

Tom takes her hand, and they walk slowly back to their home. "You inspire that look too," he says.

"No, I don't. But I'm closer to having that happen than I ever was in Portland."

He squeezes her hand. "We'll look back and say, 'That was quite a year.' "

Jill watches the sunset change the colors of the ridges, feels the firmness of her husband's hand. She can't remember if she ever had this before they came here, this connection to her husband. She looks up at the rugged hills. She can't recall a time before the Muddy when she felt humble but not broken by such a grand and mysterious place. Maybe being changed doesn't mean being broken so much as letting herself turn around. She hasn't been gobbled up by some televangelist by following her husband here. She hasn't lost her mind. Instead, she's begun to find herself. The qualities that define her—her goal-setting, her love of the elderly, her tendency to examine before she engages—are traits God can transform and use in her life and maybe others, if she lets that happen.

"Why not look back and say, 'It was quite a couple years'?" Jill says.

Tom stops, stands in front of her. "You mean it, Jillie?"

"I did come to please you, Tom. But now I want to stay here not only for you but for myself. I'm finding something here that maybe I could find in Portland, but in a different way. These rocks, this place intimidates me. But there's a comfort too, and I want more of that before I turn my back and walk away."

"We can only do it if I get hired as a carpenter," Tom says. "Unless you went back to work somewhere, maybe came here on weekends. But that doesn't seem fair, not really."

"There's always another way," Jill says. "I have a plan if you're not hired. But I believe you will be."

"You're not going to tell me your 'plan'?"

"Let me surprise you. Be spontaneous."

"You're amazing, Jillie."

"So are you, Tommy Boy."

"Tommy Boy. I think I like that," he says and soundly kisses his wife.

Tom is hired, and Jill is not surprised.

After Brad's arrival, the contractors and carpenters and their wives begin meeting for morning devotions and work assignments. Brad's wife, Molly, will follow in a month. Other new people come too. They spend one week at the Orchard Inn and after that move into a condo that may or may not have appliances beyond a toaster, microwave, and refrigerator. Stoves aren't considered essential. A hot plate is. Jill lets newcomers know about the used appliance place in Madras. She's taken back a condo from the spiders, and Gideon approves, moves easily onto his pillow set in the laundry area near the condo's back door.

On Brad's first day, Tom tells him about the blueprints stacked at the former Devateerth Mall. "Jill's offered to keep working on the disarray."

"I pale at the thought," Brad says, "but it has to be done. As soon as I'm back from Portland, that's where I'll be spending the next ten days or so. Thanks for the offer, Jill. I'll take it."

Before he can leave for his meeting, the phone rings. It's a man from San Diego flying into Portland for a water-quality conference. He wants to know if he can come back with Brad to visit. When he hangs up, Brad's narrow face looks flushed. "This guy who called, he knows all about the infrastructure here. He can walk the property and tell us where things are. He knows the organization of the plans. He was the chief architect when the Rajneeshees were here."

The group gathered stands silent. "How amazing is that?" Isaac finally says. "That he should just happen to call now, when we need him the most."

"Abundance," Tom says. "Pressed down and shaken together, overflowing."

"We're such a drop in the bucket of time," Gail says.

Jill wonders at such timing. She joked that they should have prayed with more specificity, but they didn't need to. What they needed has been provided. Even she names it a miracle when the man returns with Brad, spends five days organizing the blueprints, his experience a gift happily received. He refuses any offer to compensate his time.

Generosity, overflowing, over time.

35

PENTIMENTO

By August the new carpenter from San Francisco has spent three weeks, wins the hearts of Brad and Tom, and travels south to bring his wife and three children north. Brad's wife, Molly, comes down the dusty road too, an aging cocker spaniel lying on the seat beside her.

Jill wonders if the families will stay, though they appear undeterred by dust or daunting duties. No one earns large salaries. Jill expects differences to emerge quickly, as they do when strong-willed people gather in one place. Instead, a cautious camaraderie forms. At first, Jill gives the women nicknames in her mind. Pretty Baby is the woman with the infant at her breast and two younger ones beside her. They look Scandinavian, with creamy skin and blond hair wispy in the wind. Blanket Flower from Bellevue has two dark-haired children. She nods her head whenever anyone talks, indicates her attentiveness and interest. Blanket flowers, with their brown centers and yellow leaves, bob along the roadside, bringing cheer as they grow wild. Each time Jill sees them when she takes her morning walks, she thinks of this young mother. Molly Jones is Molly Jones. She hates the sight of snakes. Gail stays as Gail. She's solid, never faltering, like stone.

The women spend long hours together. She has even less time with Tom, who dives into condo renovation. She's never lived this close to other people, where all share the work, many meals, and downtimes.

"Snakes," Molly says one morning after the men leave for their work sites. They're at the Orchard Inn. "I'm phobic. I mean really, really phobic. And I'm not accustomed to…this distance from everything." She grew up in Houston. "This is so…primitive." She waves her hands to take in the landscape. "I'll run into those snaky slimes, and I really cannot stand even the thought of that."

Gail picks up the Bible on the kitchen table, turns to Psalm 91: " 'He is my refuge and my fortress.' And this part is for you, Molly. Verse eleven and on. 'He will command his angels concerning you to guard you in all your ways;… You will tread upon the lion and the cobra; you will trample the great lion and the serpent.' " She finishes with, " ' "Because he loves me," says the Lord, "I will rescue him; I will protect him, for he acknowledges my name." ' You just need to ask for protection."

"It actually says that about the serpents?" Jill asks, leaning over Gail's Bible.

"It's not really my style to shout out anything when I see a snake except, 'Help!' " Molly says, endearing herself to Jill. "I'm not your usual Scripture-quoting soul."

" 'No harm will befall you, no disaster will come near your tent,' " Gail continues. "That suggests a sheltered place."

"But bad things do happen, even in a shelter or a tent," Jill says. She carries dishes to the sink, wonders if the group will disagree. If they do, no one says so. Instead, Gail speaks.

"God doesn't promise we'll have no trouble, only that He'll be with us through it. Goodness can come out of trouble, though we may not see it. Even in our lifetime. We endure those times with each other's help, and with the certainty that we're not alone."

Pretty Baby says, "There's an artist's term, *pentimento.* It means someone is penitent or that they've changed their mind. In a painting, you can sometimes see the original, ghostly lines where the artist made corrections, became 'penitent.' It's a way of knowing the painting is authentic, because you can see the master's hand in it, including the corrections."

Jill wonders if this place shows marks of the Master's hands. The geologic landforms that natives walked across. Sheep and cattle arriving to tear at grasses. The wars that followed even Eva Bruner's tragedy, and what the Rajneeshees did here that now serves another purpose. Perhaps those are ghostly marks left by the Master's hand.

"Psalm 91 will have to be my song," Molly says. "I'll be singing it day and night and in the shower too. As soon as the condos get showers." Jill thinks Molly's Texas drawl makes her sound happy no matter what she says. "I don't usually say this sort of thing," Molly says. "I came here because my husband wanted to more than anything. But I think I'm supposed to learn something here too. Maybe how to give up control and leave my grown kids to themselves." She shivers. "Scarrry."

"Perhaps our lives get corrected when we find ourselves in settings where we have to see things differently," Jill says.

Someday perhaps Jill will tell these women of her first fears and of what still troubles her, but not now. They're too different from her, much more spiritual.

"When do you think they'll get the water system hooked up?" Blanket Flower asks. Jill can see why it matters to this woman with kids still in diapers.

"Remember that day, Jill, when they sent the new delivery boy with the water?" Gail says. "He looked so confused. He thought he'd walked into a Rod Serling *Twilight Zone.*"

"The ranch does have that quality," Molly says. "We probably seem like aliens to our friends." The women affirm her experience, and they all laugh, even Jill. They all share uncertainties about being here. Yet they've come. Maybe they'll be friends one day, these people gathered as though from different planets, seeking something they hope this land will offer up.

"You remind me of her, when she was young," Arnold says.

"Who?" Jill pours him a second cup of coffee. He lingers after the morning work gathering, and for the first time that Jill can remember, she and Arnold are the only ones still at the Orchard Inn. Even Gail is gone.

"My wife. She was as strong a woman as you'd ever want to meet, and sweet as sugared coffee."

"Why, thank you," Jill says. "If I didn't know you better, I'd think you were flirting with me, Arnold."

Arnold laughs. He rubs his white mustache. "Just because I'm on a diet don't mean I can't look at the menu," he says. "Martha used to hate that saying. Didn't like being compared to a menu item."

"I can see why." Jill wants to keep him talking. She likes the lilt of his voice and the comfort of his words. She thinks maybe he'll share some stories of his cowboy years.

"She was shy, too," he says then, heading in a different direction. "Afraid someone might see who she really was and find fault. Amazing thing was that everyone who met her thought her brave and wonderful. She never saw herself that way, though. Always tried to prove to others how strong she was. Stayed up nights tending bummer lambs. Sleep deprived, I think they call it now. Running on empty, it seems to me. Thin as a rein, like you. Never wanted to ask for help, either."

"I need lots of help," Jill says.

"Yeah, but you don't like to accept it," Arnold says. "That's like me now too. Old age creeping up. Hardest thing in the world for me to let people bring me here and ask if folks could find a place for me."

"But you're loved here. The children adore you."

Arnold nods. "I feel that. But I didn't know what purpose I could serve. We all want to have a reason for living, not just take up space."

"Have you found that here? Your reason?"

"I'm a grateful man. I pray every day for the work here. For the kids who'll be coming. That things go well. Sometimes I'm somebody else's answer to prayer. They say that when I fix a wheel on a stroller for one of the kids. 'You're an answer to prayer, Arnold,' they say."

"That is a nice thing to be, isn't it?"

"Lately, I've been praying for you, Miss Jill."

"Me?"

"Today, I'm your answer to prayer."

"Because you gave me that nice compliment comparing me with your wife, I'd say you are." She smiles at him. He's a sweet, good man.

"No, because you've got something on your mind, something big."

Jill feels her neck grow warm and blotchy, her breath get short. "Do I?"

"I believe you do. You're just supposed to trust your heart, Miss Jill. Don't do so much worrying over it. Just step in there and see what happens."

"There's only an eighteen-inch crawlspace," Tom says over dinner. "And it'll be infested with black widows and snakes."

"Will you have to do it?" Jill's skin crawls with the thought of him under the condos, covered in cobwebs and dirt.

"It's got to be done if we're to get the permits."

"Are you still okay that you're not part of the big decisions now?" Jill asks. Tom looks puzzled. "You've always done the creative parts, design and overseeing. I just wondered if this more...basic work is as satisfying."

"It's all good work," he says, then smiles. "But I'm not looking forward to dismantling the spider condos, I can tell you that."

Within days, two Seattle volunteers arrive. One's employed by the Sonics basketball team. Tom tells her that evening that they never hesitated when given a list of tasks to choose from. They chose snake-and-spider detail and the hot work of welding steel beams to braces in order to secure the condos and the permits. They promised to return each weekend until their work is done.

"There really isn't a hierarchy of work here," Tom tells her that night. The window's open to the evening breezes, and she hears a pheasant crow. Quail chatter just outside. "I'm still part of something bigger, we all are. I'm not saying there aren't irritations and disagreements about how to go about a thing, but it's never personal. It's like the goal is always out there, that we're doing this for the kids. Brad's good at keeping that the focus. Better than I'd have been."

"You're good at whatever you set your heart on," Jill tells him. She realizes it's a truth she never noticed when they lived away from here, or if she did, she failed to say so. Tom has always built her up; she's rarely commented on his work.

The smell of smoke one morning pushes work aside as men meet with their Antelope neighbors to fight a lightning fire. The women make extra sandwiches and deliveries to the fire lines. Brad notes in the morning meeting that they need to consider how to establish fire protection on this ranch. Again without running any ad, just putting out their needs, they hear from the Portland Fire Chief, who arranges for a pumper truck to be available on loan, and from another firefighter, who makes a personal gift of buying up used equipment and donating it to the camp. He provides training for its use.

Jill takes the training, likes being able to haul the long hose, discovers that she's stronger than she looks.

Susan (whom Jill once only thought of by her nickname Blanket Flower) suggests planting flowerpots in the old greenhouse so when the swimming pool is finished—it hasn't even been started—and the trading post moved and the camp actually ready, there'll be flowers there too. They take turns becoming the "watering moms," with Jill claiming the plants as her babies. No easy feat, this watering, considering they have to use a generator to run the pump that brings water from Muddy Creek. Once, electricity had run to the greenhouse, but not now. Jill negotiates with the men for an hour's use of the eighty-pound generator. Then she and Susan, with children underfoot, water the tubs of plants. The next day, Betty (once known as Pretty Baby) and Gail say they'll watch the children during watering, since it's a demanding task. The women coordinate their efforts. Jill thinks of them as friends.

It's nothing like her porch garden back in Portland, but for Jill to have her hands in dirt again is gratifying. *Who plants a seed beneath the sod and waits to see believes in God.* Jill saw that on a wall plaque once. The saying takes on deeper meaning as she drags the garden hose to the creek to pull up water and keep the flowers alive. *Wait to see.* She wonders if Arnold's gift wasn't to tell her not to worry, but to work with flowers and simply wait and see them grow.

Volunteers show up to pull weeds, to install toilets, and to move walls. Weekends bring laughing young lives. Molly volunteers to answer phones, arranges for the visiting groups, helps Brad and property staff decide where to house them and, with Jill and Gail, how to feed them. There are daily meetings now to set up and report on projects, sometimes at the Orchard Inn, sometimes at the ranch house. Donations arrive to pay staff. The women decide to have a Bible study in the mornings. Jill considers sitting that out. She doesn't, though, remembering Tom's word *engagement* and Arnold's prayer for her to just step in.

Once during the gathering time following their Bible study, Molly comments that she's never understood how the Rajneeshees accomplished so much in so short a time. "It's so hard to see the progress here."

"I saw videotapes with the architectural materials," Jill says. "People worked twenty-four hours a day here, with big power lights."

"Sounds like slave labor to me," Betty says.

"On the blueprints for the crematorium, someone noted that that's what they were here, slaves who gave up their money and time and then didn't even have a choice about their deaths."

"Is it still here?" Molly asks. She wears her big hair pulled up into a bun at the top of her head.

"It was dismantled pretty early," Gail says. "The Washingtons had several areas bulldozed, including the old medical clinic out past the corrals."

"We aren't slaves here anyway," Betty says. "People are paid and are free to come and go."

"And we don't carry Uzis or eavesdrop on phone calls," Gail says.

"We're working below minimum wage, though," Susan jests. Aside from health benefits and housing, she and her husband are volunteering. Even so, she says they're getting much more than they're giving. "We take our wages in kids," Susan says. "When we open up the camp, their joy will be our reward."

No one coerces. No one says, "You must" or "You should." Jill finds it increasingly easy to say what she thinks or feels. Their actions are a response to need, to seeing work that needs doing while upholding the community. Perhaps even more than generosity their gathering together sustains, Jill thinks.

The Bible study turns to personal matters. Molly argues with her husband and wishes she didn't. Betty wants more help with the kids from her spouse at night. Susan doesn't always bob her head in agreement. She was once a teacher, and she misses her profession. The missing makes her feel ungrateful that she has so much, and yet… Even Gail wonders at times how long she and Isaac are supposed to stay here. Their son no longer goes to church, a pain that grieves her. No one claims perfection or certainty, qualities Jill applied to them that none possesses.

The group grows as more volunteers arrive. They expose warts and worries and ask each other for support. Jill never had sisters. These women make her think of what good sisters would be. Molly's hanging on to the old dog that should probably be put down, but she can't bear to be without it. Susan wishes she could better comfort her husband when his workday troubles. Someone in addition to Jill struggles with her mother and questions of belief. No one pressures anyone to speak; they just accept. None of them has all the answers, not even Gail. Why has Jill thought this was the case, that these are people who do not struggle?

One morning, she tells them of her birthmark, the jokes and gibes it's garnered through the years.

"I didn't even notice," one of the women says, another new person added to the group. She's quilting as they linger after their study.

"That's why you always wear a scarf," Susan says.

"That, and so I can keep dust out of my nose when Arnold's showing me how to rope and ride," Jill says. They laugh with her, as she wants. "I've never talked about this with anyone, except my mother. She wanted me to have it removed." No one speaks. "She's ashamed of me. That's why she wants it off. But it's a part of who I am."

"I bet if you didn't cover it up, people wouldn't even notice." Susan says.

"Maybe your mom was trying to keep you from being hurt," Gail says. "People can be so unkind to children. Maybe that's why she wanted you to have it removed."

"Why didn't she have it taken off when I was a child then? She had the money. She was too distracted with her...husbands." Jill wishes she didn't sound so bitter.

"Maybe doctors couldn't. Maybe they still can't."

Jill sits back in her chair. It never occurred to her that her mother's wanting surgery could be an act of love. She thinks of Betty's pentimento story, seeing through history, making corrections in the present. She looks at the faces of these women, sees their struggles, and admires the support they give their families and each other. She covets their willingness to be vulnerable and to grow. She's never had a family quite like this.

Jill's observation skills are keen, she knows this. Her professors sang praises of her insights. But the interpretation of what Jill sees needs work. Perhaps this is Arnold's prayer, that she accept there's more than one way to see this world, more than one way to experience the divine.

36

Provision

Jill must decide if she's going to renew the trip back and forth to Portland in the winter term. She doesn't want to stay away from the university setting for too long. Professors might forget who she is and not think of her when grants come up. She's gotten good references for her Guggenheim application, which she submitted October 1. Winning such a major award is a long shot. They only gave out 158 the previous year, all across the country. She believes her idea holds merit: exploring the role of generosity, friendships, and work as determining factors of longevity and quality of life. She doesn't tell Tom she's applied, but she does discuss the term.

"It's the worst time of year for you to travel over the pass," Tom tells her. "Do what you think's best, but I'd worry less if you waited until spring term."

"I just wonder if I can stand not going to Portland every week. We'll get cabin fever here."

"I don't know. Darkness falls earlier, and we won't be able to work such long hours. We'll be home together more, and I can beat you in Trivial Pursuit."

"Or not."

"Then we'll fill the time with other things," Tom says and winks.

"I think I'll stay on home this term," Jill says and twirls her neck scarf as she bats her eyelashes at her husband.

New full-time arrivals pepper the fall months of 1998. By October, nearly twenty full-time residents and their families live at the ranch. Their repair of the water system can't be more welcome. Each new staff family follows the routine of staying a week in the Orchard Inn with meals. Then they move into the condos with semikitchens. They earn salaries; they pay rent. Jill helps others find stoves at a secondhand store in Madras, but like most of the staff, they live on anything that can be boiled. Eggs are good. They buy these from the Antelope neighbors. Acquiring staples at the closest grocery requires a two-hour trip, possibly longer when factoring in flat tires. Betty's family carries six extra tires in their van, and they buy nine gallons of milk at a time because that's how much their freezer holds. Carpooling is difficult, with bulk groceries and supplies consuming all available space. The families live at the Staff Village, and as more couples join the property, bringing young children with them, this village becomes a community where residents often take meals together even when they no longer need to.

"I had no idea how excited I could get about a garbage disposal," one of the new women says at the morning gathering. Jill smiles. They celebrate and share each little amenity.

Jill prepares meals for the new arrivals for their week in the Orchard Inn. She offers little extras, cuts the fruit into flowers, uses cloth napkins. Giving comes easier for some reason. Jill's never met so many new people. Yet she even remembers their names.

The men resurface the runway—a necessity for medical emergencies and to move the old Mandir Reception Center building closer to what will be the sports complex. It will be the trading post for kids to get their smoothies and their soda pops. It's October, a month that can easily bring freezing weather as well as heavy rains.

"We need five days with temperatures over seventy degrees and no rain in order for this surface to set up correctly," the contractor tells them. They pray that the rain or snow will hold off. A dozen extra volunteers are on hand. It's a perfect pour. Two hours after the five days end, a cool rain begins.

Hunting season brings fresh game, including deer and elk. Another couple with a special interest in outdoor activities, game management, and land use, joins the team. Jill goes out with them and sees the landscape differently in the company of those who read the hills. They point out signs of deer or elk, identify springs they might fence off for cattle. The horse Arnold's matched her up with is a gentle paint. As she gets to know him and the land, she rides the trails alone, above the camp one day. She overlooks it.

The vastness doesn't oppress. Instead, she recognizes familiar places, places she has walked, places where she's sat and let the world surround her, places where she's learned to feel at home.

She hears a sound like tiny rocks sliding down a hillside, and her heart catches. Her horse steps sideways but Jill holds the reins, stays mounted. The whole hillside appears to move, not from rocks, but from hundreds of chukar game birds, flushing. A blush of red stains their wing edge as the gray birds lift against the autumn sky. Jill pats the horse's neck. He holds steady. "I thought it was a rockslide," Jill tells Tom later, "but I misinterpreted. I got to see something frightening turn into something grand."

The game guys harvest a wild boar one afternoon, one of the pigs let loose some years before that now root their three hundred pounds through gardens and fencing. "That's the noise I heard in the bushes the first day I got here," Gail tells Isaac. Steelhead trout swim up the river, and Tom and the others catch one or two. They invite the Antelope neighbors for surf-and-turf barbeque, decide to make it an annual event, spreading the bounty of this place.

In the morning, when the whole group meets to discuss the day's duties, someone names some needs: Lumber. Paint. Within days a call comes offering up the necessary amount of two-by-fours, including cost of shipment and delivery. Dozens of gallons of paint are donated. The paint arrives, but no one can schedule painting into their workload. Within the week another volunteer phones: Can they can use a crew of painters who want to devote part of their vacation to the ranch?

"You can't deny these, can you Jill?" Tom says to her one evening. It's well after dark, but he's been at the workshop building bunk beds. Jill warms his dinner on a hot plate. Cassette music floats through the condo. The acoustics between buildings are superb. No one ever hears his neighbor. Tomorrow Tom will help finish laying propane pipes so they'll have more consistent heat this winter.

"It does seem...miraculous," Jill says. Her memory of the morning prayers and their quick fulfillment scoops Jill up into the arms of wonder, bringing her closer to give her heart to something she can't quite explain.

Thirty kids arrive in late October for a trial run at a camp. "We'll hold club at the Orchard Inn and eat there, sleep at the East Village on mats," Brad tells them. "Staff from regional and other places will give the usual Young Life welcome with cheers and applause and funny noisemakers. The Bend group has worked hours on program planning to share a message in a happy way. Our trial run should make quite a ruckus ringing out against the rimrocks."

A doctor is present as required, volunteering his time. One adult for every six to eight campers pushes the population to about thirty-five, most arrived from Bend. When the power goes out, they serve cold dinner and build a huge bonfire and roast marshmallows, then let the kids spread shaving cream and oatmeal on one another and run through the sports complex, sliding on the gold linoleum.

"What do you think of all this?" Jill asks the volunteer doctor as he leaves the complex lit with spots of flashlights and laughing kids.

"I think I'd better make sure we have enough first-aid supplies," he says, shaking his head.

Jill's never heard the gospel message told this way, woven among laughter, songs, and food. At club, she looks around at Tom and Arnold and many of the others. This is what they live for, this part in telling the story of God's grace to kids. *The grandmothers and grandfathers live inside the children. Teach them well.* Tears spill easily at this place, Jill notices, and not just from the kids' eyes.

Visitors come, and Jill assumes duties as a tour guide, a task she finds she likes. Some add their own remarks: a comment on the former worship center or where Noah's Ark Boutique once stood. "We called our tour guides Twinkies." Afterward, they acknowledge they once lived here, and Jill asks if they'd care to characterize their time. It's a sociologist's kind of question. To a one they say they wish it hadn't ended, that it was the best years of their lives.

"What about the poisonings, the violations, and the attempted murders—"

"We weren't a part of that," they're quick to explain. "That was Sheela and her gang. We wanted to live peacefully, and we're sorry that part happened. This land was good to us." They often sigh.

Jill understands their longing for past pleasures. Isn't that what humans do, try to reclaim the past because they've made it better in their memory than what it really was? She brings this up the next morning following their study. Gail says, "There is a proverb that says desire realized is a sweetness to the soul. That suggests we can attain the desires of our hearts. It's not all lost longing."

How will Jill remember this journey after she and Tom are gone? Like those Rajneeshees who visit, will she remember it as the best time of her life, a place she hated to leave? *Perhaps we never will.*

"This isn't like me at all," Molly tells Jill as they walk one morning out near the reservoir. "But some of the things here…they bother me. Like that rock." She points to a reddish block balanced on one rounded edge, crisp against the morning skyline. "When I pass by it, it feels like eyes are watching." Jill can't see it, but she's less skeptical now of those who do. "The men have got so much work with the housing I don't think we can bother them with pulling down rocks."

"You think they might have something evil attached to them?" Jill remembers Gideon's refusal to enter certain rooms. And the other day her horse wouldn't go through the security fence surrounding the Bhagwan's old compound.

"Whoever thought I'd be Dale Evans in my fifties, riding for justice," Molly says. Jill laughs. "But something about this..." They walk a bit farther, Molly whispering Psalm 91 under her breath.

"I'm surprised you notice anything up high, you're so busy looking for snakes at your feet," Jill says.

"I haven't seen any yet," Molly sings.

"I'm almost certain none are out in December."

They confer at the morning gathering. The next time someone returns from Portland, they're asked to bring hyssop and oil. "Hyssop," Gail tells the group, "was used in the Old Testament to purify the leprous houses. It makes things new. 'Cleanse me with hyssop, and I will be clean,' the psalmist wrote. Solomon had quite an understanding of botany, and he often spoke of cedars and the lowly hyssop. We use the humblest reed as a way of healing."

"Some native Americans burn sage to purify a place," Jill says. "Arnold told me that."

Molly, who again says this isn't like her at all, asks aloud then for the healing of this rock. They seek other healings: Betty, with her blond infant at her breast, prays that her baby's cough will go away, and they dot her head with oil. One of the newest carpenter's wives asks that her pregnancy go smoothly. There are four women pregnant here. Jill touches her hand to her neck where her birthmark stains. They all need hyssop.

"I still want that rock down," Molly says, even though they've stood below it, sprinkled it with their hyssop-scented oil. "It looks like some ancient sentry standing guard at a pharaoh's palace."

Jill says, "Rajneeshee women ran all the heavy equipment when they were here. Why not us?"

But Tom and Brad and the other men say they'll manage the equipment, and secretly, Jill's relieved. She's never even started up a backhoe, and Arnold tells her starting diesel tractors in the winter can be tricky. "Those men will do anything if they get to play with tractors and chains," Jill says. On a Sunday before church that evening, they make a party of it, all bundled up in mittens and hats. Brad rides up in the backhoe bucket and wraps the rock with chains; Tom operates the machinery, and all of them stand well out of the way as the odd-shaped rock plunges to the roadway.

"It does have kind of a face, doesn't it?" one of the women notes.

Tom scoops it from the roadway, then hauls it to a section of the property where the road often sags in spring rains. He dumps it there not far from Currant Creek, with plans to drop the bucket on it two or three times to break it into smaller pieces. When he releases it, a chunk breaks off and tumbles toward a pile of weeds. Even over the engine noise they hear a different sound: *Cachunk, cachunk, cachunk.*

"There must be another pile of rocks over that way," Tom says. Jill walks in that direction.

"Careful of the snakes," Molly shouts from the safety of Brad's truck.

Through the bulrushes dusted with snow, Jill follows the trail of the boulder.

"There's a rock cairn in here," she shouts back. "It's been built up to mark something." With shovels, they dig around the rock wall, knocking down sage and grass, clearing it of debris. It's a circle of rock. "I wonder who put it here. And why," she says.

"Looks like an old tipi ring," Arnold says, "'Cept that it wouldn't be so high if it was that. Maybe a burial site?"

Jill's shovel clinks against something just below the surface. She digs deeper and finds an old Folgers coffee can, rusted to a dirty red, flattened and poked full of orderly holes.

"Somebody used it for target practice," one of the men says.

Jill shakes her head. "The holes are in a pattern. I'll take it back and see if I can figure out what it says." Something about it makes her think of Eva Bruner's letters.

"Brad's having nightmares," Molly tells the women. "He shouts aloud. Wakes the dog and me, not that the dog's been sleeping all that well either. Poor thing can hardly breathe."

"Brad's having trouble breathing too?" Betty asks. She pats the baby at her shoulder.

"No, the dog. Brad's breathing loud enough to wake the dead with his night screams."

"He's worried," Jill says.

Molly nods. "About meeting the needs for the camp. Here it is, January, and we've hardly begun the camp facilities. Everyone keeps saying, 'June 13. We can't disappoint all those kids who've already signed up to come here June 13.' He's gotten approval to order a stainless steel swimming pool. From Italy. Because we can't dig the hole for it until it thaws, and by then getting cement trucks down here will be troublesome. He's just worried that everything won't come together. And he wants it to so much."

"Is there anything we can do?" Betty asks. She tucks her blond hair behind her ears, then signals for her four-year-old playing in the corner to use a quiet voice.

"Be understanding when our guys increase their long hours," Molly says.

"No more late-night duets in the tub, I guess," Jill says.

"You have a tub large enough for two?" Susan asks.

"Our tub fits three," one of the women says. "Children," she adds quickly.

"I thought everyone was so sure that the plans would fall into place. Tom says that all the time. Like Murphy's Law in reverse."

"Our guys want God to be lauded through all this. Like all of us, they wonder if they'll be enough to do the job," Molly says.

"It's not up to us," Jill says. Gail looks surprised.

More people join them: plumbers, women who make signs, a camp cook. With each new addition, the group changes. But for Jill, each newcomer fits in like a missing puzzle piece. They close the gatherings now by praying for each child who will someday come to Wildhorse Canyon. Jill wonders if anyone long years before prayed for her that way. Maybe she should call her mother.

March 1999

Four trucks filled with concrete wind down the serpentine road from Madras through Antelope and onto what the new sign says is now "Wildhorse Canyon at Young Life's Washington Family Ranch." Snow clusters along the road at higher altitudes, and the dirt road grows slick where the ice turns into thaw. Brad meets the first trucks, breathing in relief that so far none has slipped off the road. Now if only they can keep the concrete from freezing at night while they pour new concrete pillars inside the sports complex, then lay hardwood on the floor. They'll need 150 loads of concrete.

They've had to get permits, then remove every structural pillar in the complex and replace them with stronger headers to bear the weight in the 88,000-thousand-square-foot structure. They've dug out six inches of dirt across the entire floor to prepare it for the pour.

The women prevail in a portion of the renovation: Molly with her "this isn't like me" feeling says the altar must come down. "The hyssop oil's not enough," she says.

"There've been snakes around there, that's for sure," one of the men says. "But we can rename the altar 'the sports snack shop,' and in time, it'll take on a whole new form."

"Molly's got a good feel for things," Jill says. "Even though I don't see it—and I've never seen a rattlesnake there—I vote to take it down."

Prayers spoken, they concur. And when the contractor from Bend pulls out the altar rocks, he finds a tunnel underneath—and rattlesnake skins marking it as a place that once drew reptiles to squirm and crawl beneath the Bhagwan's preaching.

They cover it with concrete. Molly sighs relief.

"It helps," Tom tells Jill, "to know you're thinking of me. I like it when you bring me lunch and dinner on site. Sometimes I just can't quit what I'm doing at the lake and pool excavation. Before long they'll put me back on the hotel renovation while we wait for the pool insert that's coming from Italy. And we can work all night with the lights now."

"Can they use painters, or people to clean up the work site at the end of the day?"

"You'd do that?"

"To be a part of things."

"They'll need help building the zip-line platforms. Or the blob tower."

Jill doesn't know what these things are, but those involved with camps find joy in telling her, describing, too, the ropes course and the climbing walls and the go-cart tracks.

"Feeling the wind on your face when you come down that zip line, flying across the trees and into the lake—it's just a great rush," Tom tells her.

"Sounds like you've done it."

"I have. You will too. And that's what we want kids to know, the rush of living, making choices that build them up to be the people God wants them to be. Overcoming their fears with the support of others, that's what this is about, Jill. Celebrating being a kid and preparing them for the relationships in life that truly matter."

"'Unless you come to me as a child...'" Jill says.

"Exactly," Tom tells her. "You do remember a little from your past."

Everyone turns out to help move the reception center to a site across from where the lake and pool are being built, where they'll convert it to the trading post. The moving company has one week available to lift the sixty-foot-wide building onto its truck, take it down the runway, then across the fields and creek, while men on backhoes and volunteers with shovels gouge out sections of the bank where it's too narrow for the building. Blasts of spring wind swirl around them.

The move's completed without a hitch. Now begin the Sheetrocking, woodworking, painting, shelve building, and even the stocking of the shelves with soda pop and snacks and books and clothes for kids to buy to remember their visits. They build a deck, and Jill imagines for the first time kids there, sitting, laughing. Maybe those kids who called her Mrs. H. back in Portland. Tom's dream—and the dream of so many others—becomes real to her. This is what it's all about, giving a gift to kids.

Being a part of making it happen is a gift to herself. She's glad she didn't sign up for any spring classes either.

April. They've begun meeting in the ranch house; the kitchen in the Orchard Inn is being redone so kids can eat there and hold club there at the first big camp. The Bellevue engineer reports that the lake bed is giving them trouble: It has a shallow water table and a layer of mud like blue goo at the bottom. So they'll line it. Every man, woman, and child arrives, prepared to walk in mud while pulling black plastic across the lakebed. Each has to watch the one beside him and offer help as needed when someone stumbles or sinks into goo. The work moves as fast as the slowest person, slow and steady, each waiting for the others to do their part. For Jill, there's something metaphorical about community in their efforts. No gain is made until even the slowest person has come along beside.

Beach sand's needed and can be purchased several hours away. But Jill recalls a pile of white sand she saw when out riding a few weeks ago. "I think we could drive there. We might have to take a few fences out." Brad and Tom make a foray to Jill's site, decide it'll work, marvel at what a pile of beach sand's doing in the middle of a field. On the way back they take a different route, and right beside the road they spy another pile of white sand. They need nine hundred cubic yards; this closer pile looks like six hundred. Brad says they'll start here. "We can take the fence out and dig into the other pile if we need to." When they finish, they've moved exactly nine hundred cubic yards, just the amount needed for the lake's perfect sandy beach, and they never touched the other pile.

The stainless-steel pool arrives but must be put together with wrenches and bolts. The directions are in Italian. Brad makes contact with the manufacturer and discovers an Italian engineer should be arriving soon. He does, by taxicab; the first and only one transport by cab anyone can remember. Unfortunately, the pool engineer only speaks Italian. But the language of dreamers and builders finds a way to communicate, and the work of assembly begins.

Each new challenge and its unusual solution reenergizes Tom. "It can't be explained in any other way," he tells Jill. "There is a hand here tending to each detail. Even finding out that the spring we're pumping out beneath the pool has exactly the amount of water we need to keep the pH in the lake balanced. The spring gives up fifty gallons a minute; we need fifty gallons a minute to keep the lake clear of moss. They're right beside each other. Perfect engineering. Everything we need has been provided."

"Is it this place?" Jill asks. "Or the purpose, or...?"

"I've never known anything like this. Nor have the other guys. I'm not sure I'll ever find this kind of experience again in my life. Thank you, Jillie."

"For what?"

"For coming here. For allowing me to stay as one of the carpenters and do this for however long we're allowed."

"I don't think I gave you anything."

Tom holds her to him. She feels wetness on her cheeks. *From Tom?* "You heard me dream a thing and didn't squelch it. You listened and sacrificed"—she starts to correct him, but he puts his fingers to her lips—"you changed your life for me, Jillie. There's no greater love than to lay down your life for a friend."

"I don't think that's what that verse means," Jill says. "I didn't die."

"You have, though, to a lot of things. Your schedule. Your goal to stay in school. Your fear of being around people who pray like they breathe." Jill smiles. "That's what I'll remember about this place after we're gone. Not just God's keeping a promise to the land and to the kids who will come, but how He filled our pledges to each other, how He's worked in our lives. I never dreamed of a gift like that."

Neither has Jill.

37

Wonder

Men work longer hours, while women wonder what's happened to their family lives. Except for worship every Sunday and brief stops for meals, the men are on the work sites. When they can, women join the effort by painting, sweeping, cleaning, planting. The stroller moms take walks to show their husbands to their children. "Daddy's working for the campers. Daddy's working for the campers." They repeat it like a chant they tell themselves, knowing ritual can comfort, knowing that mommies are working for the campers too.

Suppers are ready at 8:00 p.m. Because the sunset hesitates now above the rounded hills, it's still daylight at ten. Each man stays out until it's dark. There are sinks to set, walls to erect, all those hotel rooms waiting to be transformed into dorms. Arnold's old wagons are set in place to make the landscape look like what it once was: a sheep and cattle ranch, a place where stage coaches transported a young wife to her husband and then back to this place, where her faith lifted and settled and lifted again against her spiritual landscape.

The trading post isn't finished. Sarsaparilla-drinking teens sitting on the deck are yet a distant dream.

The zip line's completed, however. Given the proposed height and distance, a quarter mile from the top of the ridge with the crooked juniper to mark it, the term "prayer-a-chute" is coined for whoever is the first to try it. "Will you go on it?" Molly asks Jill one day as they water flowers.

"I'm afraid of heights," Jill says.

"You won't be that high for long."

"Arnold says he'll go. And when he turns ninety in a couple of years, he wants to hold the record for the oldest one to take the zip."

They send a pile of rocks down the cable first. It hits the lake at fifty miles an hour. They go back to the drawing board to reconfigure. Afterward, Tom goes down. Gail does too. "You've inspired me, Gail," Jill says, and she commits.

"You wear this harnesslike thing." Tom shows Jill as they walk the steep hill to the platform. "It can hold three hundred pounds, so don't worry."

"How will I hit the lake? Should I leave my glasses here?"

"Maybe. Yeah. I'll take them."

Jill can feel her heart pound. She's never been this impulsive. "Arnold says I should just participate," she says.

"Good for him. He's going next."

Tom hooks her contraption to a cable that extends out over the ridge, out over the road, across Muddy Creek and the newly planted greenery beside the pool, over the sandy beach, and right into the lake.

"I'm not a very good swimmer."

"You're going to end up on the shallow side. Molly and Brad are there waiting. You go ahead. Just step off now."

Jill steps to the edge, moves back. She steps again, looks down, steps back. "You're sure it's safe?"

"I wouldn't risk your life for anything. Just trust," he says.

And so she does, stepping off into the unknown, feeling her weight against the cable picking up speed, soaring through the air, the wind in her face, the blur of rocks like wrinkled faces smiling up at her. A cheer rises from her throat. "Wheeee!" She's a kid again. She plunges to the lake, the very touch of her body turning her around so she splash-sinks in with her back to her friends reaching around to hold her, her eyes lifted to the hills where Tom waves wildly. The scarf she's wearing peels off in the landing and floats away. She doesn't try to bring it back.

Several dozen volunteers descend on Memorial Day weekend. They sand and paint, check on the three thousand trees being tended for use in landscaping. Orchard Inn trees, the quince, apples, pears, and peaches, sport tiny fruits forming on the branches once pruned by volunteers. Poles for the ropes course have been delivered, and the Wasco Electric Company said they'll stand the poles since "they have to be in the area anyway." *The electric company just happens to be passing by?* Everything that can go right does.

Jill sees a faith here, beholds the mystery of her seeking thoughts and acts of love. Many acts of love. They're almost finished here. But she's not. Perhaps it's time to make her call.

When was the last time they talked? At Jill and Tom's wedding five years before. Her mother had flown in from Santa Fe, brought a gorgeous Acoma wedding pot, even though Jill had written on the invitation, "Please, no gifts." She approved of Jill's white turtleneck wedding dress. "It highlights your eyes," her mother said. "One of my wedding dresses had a turtleneck. My favorite, though, had a V neck." She fingered Jill's wispy hair hanging down on either side of her cheeks then. "A scoop neck would look lovely on your long neck. I wish you'd get that birthmark removed. I don't know why you won't let me help you. I'd pay for it, you know."

"Because you want it removed so I don't embarrass you. I am who I am, Mother. With or without it."

Her mother sighed, shook her head as if to say, *Must something always come between us?*

"Besides, Tom doesn't mind."

Her mother said that Tom's blind eye spoke well of her new son-in-law, though she barely got to meet him before taking the next flight back to New Mexico.

Jill expects a machine to answer and nearly hangs up when her mother's voice greets her. Her voice catches, and she clears her throat, her fingers lingering on the stain at her neck. She tells her mother of the ranch, calms her mother's alarm that she's dropped out of school. "It's temporary, Mother. I'll finish, but this is something we decided to do together."

Jill asks about her mother's husband, about their latest trip, a golf tournament they played in, raising money for a cancer unit. Finally Jill shares the reason for her call.

"Would you consider loaning me money, Mother?"

"You'll have the surgery? Oh yes, Jill."

"I'm really not interested in having that, but we could use the money right now for something else."

"You're pregnant! That's wonderful."

She tells her no, she's not, and finally finds the wherewithal to say what her emerging faith has been taking her to say. Her mother hesitates, comments on how long it's been since they've talked. "I won't loan it, but I'll give it. It's the first time since your father died you've asked me for anything. I do hope it won't be the last."

Jill turns to the clock: 4:00 a.m. It'll be dawn soon. Could the men still be working? Might something have happened to Tom? She thinks of the open trenches from the irrigation pipes, the propane lines. Maybe he hurt himself making his way home.

There are too many details, too many unfinished things yet to accomplish before the kids arrive tomorrow. No, today! It's already today. The program staff's here, as are dozens of other volunteers geared to implement the "construction" theme. Adult leaders have traveled from as far away as South Carolina. Jill wonders what they think as they enter this twilight zone.

It's June 13. Why should Jill wonder about something as minor as finishing the floor of the trading post in time when God's provided so much more than that? The sports complex has a new floor of bird's-eye maple; the hotels are ready with bunk beds and linens. Food handlers and chefs have been working for weeks on the menu and preparations. Tom says the kids will be "served" as though they were at a banquet at each meal. Volunteers have even arrived for that. So much has been attended to, why does she worry?

Gideon makes barking sounds in his sleep. Maybe she'll dress and walk down the hill and help the property intern stock the store shelves at the trading post. Jill gets up, turns the light on, then stops at the table to look again at Eva's letters, now in a scrapbook that Susan decorated. Why did Eva leave the letters behind? It's still a mystery.

She turns to Eva's letter about her husband's trial. How hard that must have been for a young girl. Her mother wasted away. Eva never got to know her mother. She knew tragedy, this Eva Bruner, but she persevered despite it. She made a life for herself. She forgave Dee for being who he was; she forgave herself for withdrawing her love from him. She brought her child into this world and accepted the kindness of family and friends. She participated in living even when she imagined she had little to live for.

It does not matter whether he responds to me or not. It is what I can do to continue the relationship, to know him better, Eva wrote. Faith as trust, attentiveness, participation.

Jill thinks Eva was writing about her husband; but what if Eva was writing of her spiritual relationship? What if she was speaking of staying engaged despite the lack of ready answers? Perhaps questioning is a sign not of unbelief but of a deepening faith.

If only he would answer, Eva wrote. *But no, he withholds his words of comfort and assurance. Instead he holds accountable my lack of loving him enough. Me, who trusted when he said that he would never leave me nor desert me. I go to see him, and he stares across the room, the spider on the wall behind me holding greater interest than his own wife's countenance. I counted on him. He turned away. Why should I stay, then, in this man's life, he who would listen to an inner darkness despite the pleading of my voice?*

Eva wrote nothing after learning of her husband's pardon. Perhaps she took Gillette and they all stayed with his father until her husband's death. What had happened then? Jill will never know. The piece of tin they found that day suggested a letter *D* or *G* but no date that might have marked a death. Had the tin been secured to a wooden cross that marked a grave? She wishes Eva had written of that.

But she didn't. Some things, like the rock deposits layered over time, mark a depth of mystery, require waiting to find answers, may keep them hidden for several lifetimes.

"I actually got dressed and went looking for him," Susan says. " 'Have you seen my husband?' It reminded me of that children's book *Are You My Mother?*" She laughs. "They probably thought I was nuts. Good thing my mom's here to stay with the kids."

"I thought about doing that. I had visions of Brad falling into trenches, or a wild boar attacking, or him stepping on a snake. Psalm 91!" They all laugh. They're in the Orchard Inn for worship. They've taken time to gather, even while old toilets recently pulled out of the hotels litter the grass. Weeds still triumph next to the welcoming signs. The kids are due within hours.

Music begins; a few guitar players pluck their strings. Tambourines flash a beat, but mostly it's the voices that fill this room that soon, very soon, will have campers singing in it. Jill spies Tom, and he moves over so she can stand beside him. He puts his arm around her shoulder. Could there be anything as comforting as being held by one's best earthly friend while singing songs extolling God's sovereignty and splendor?

Jill's agreed to run a couple of the pool contractors—who speak English—to the airstrip, where they'll be flown out to Portland. The pool's been approved to hold eight hundred thousand gallons. The well has started pumping. She slips out of worship, drives the contractors in the old Nissan. As their plane takes off, she notices a van on the dusty road. Inside ride a man and a boy.

It can't be a camper already! They're to arrive on big buses, and the program staff will greet them wearing funny false teeth and wild hats and cheering and acting rowdy.

"Can I help you?" Jill says.

"We're looking for the pool. I'm the state inspector."

The pool isn't even filled! How can he check the pH level, the chlorine level? Hadn't they thought of that? They'll never have it open for the kids. They'll have to wait until tomorrow or the next day or the day after that. *What's he doing here on a Sunday with his son?*

"Follow me," she says.

She finds Tom, tells him who's waiting outside. The pool crew heads for the door while inside they raise their voices higher to the hills.

Jill sees the inspector later, having coffee, sitting on the deck. He shakes his head no in response to something Tom says, then listens, talks more while the water slowly rises. The Rajneeshees challenged dozens of inspectors, often not letting them even enter. This inspector can make or break the joy of the first group of campers. There'll be long faces if they can see that pool but not be allowed to enter.

They'll survive, Jill decides. The kids will adjust, because what will happen for them here is not about the size of the pool or the ropes course or the basketball court in the sports complex. It's about the relationships that have already begun, relationships between adults that will help make the Word real in kids' lives. The camp's success rests on the prayers of people like Gail and Isaac, on what was begun years before in the hearts of people these kids will never meet, at least not in this lifetime.

An eagle dips its wings above the pool, and Jill thinks of the chain of time. She hopes some Indian kids might be coming to this camp to see a place their grandparents knew as fruitful.

The inspector accepts Brad's word that they won't let kids in until the pH level's safe, then grants them permission to open the pool. A call from Antelope announces the buses of kids will be an hour late—just enough time to finish filling the pool, stocking the shelves, and preparing their service for 150 kids.

At four o'clock, Jill hears the rumble of diesels coming down the reptile road, and she wonders what they must be thinking, all those kids from city places like Columbus or Seattle having never been in land like this. Do they wonder if they've tumbled into a Stephen King novel?

Many, O LORD my God, are the wonders you have done. The things you planned for us no one can recount to you; were I to speak and tell of them, they would be too many to declare. The words of Psalm 40:5 come to her unbidden. Jill smiles as the buses lumber across the Muddy Creek bridge. She'll claim that psalm as a personal one.

"It was terrific," Tom says as he holds Jill in his arms that night. "The God I know loves to surprise. He tells us to delight in the Lord, and that's what we did today, what those kids did. We made sure the first kid off the bus was someone who'd never been to a Young Life camp before." Leaders in Antelope who were meeting the kids and putting them on buses assured them they'd do their best to make that happen. "We even hoped it would be a kid who doesn't believe," Tom says. "And then we prayed for that kid, that this would be the best week of his life, and he'd come to have a personal relationship with Christ. We all agreed to pray for him when he got off the bus."

"Or her," Jill says.

"Or her. Down the road they came, the buses stopping in front of the hotels. Kids stood up in their seats, and then one young guy stumbled off, his eyes wide with the surprise of it, the bigness of it. He spun around looking at these rocks and the lake and the adults and the college kids here to serve them. And I don't know, Jill, it's like everything we've been working for all came together. I started to bawl, and I forgot to pray for that kid when he stepped off. The speaker got his name, but I remember what he looks like. I couldn't believe I forgot to pray right then."

"I don't think that'll matter," Jill says. "I don't think you were asked to bring that child into Christ's net. You were just told to throw the net out. And you have."

By the end of the week they are, all of them, joyously exhausted. Team leaders have met early every morning to support each other, to identify special requests for individual kids, to pray for them and each other, to fix glitches in activities for the day. Jill observes with curiosity the flexibility they built into the schedule, keeping it unexpected from day to day. They're impractical, Jill thinks, having kids in the pool—in their clothes—at 11:00 p.m. playing water volleyball, and yet the laughter filled her up when she heard it. "Those are some of the moments they'll remember most," she's told when she asks why they do such unusual things. The schedule is renewed each morning so kids don't get bored and can't predict what will happen when. Meals are staggered. At 11:30 each night, they still play music on the grass outside the Sarsaparilla. Kids sip soda pop and munch popcorn beneath a night sky thick with stars like fireflies.

"Hey, Mrs. H!" Jill hears her name called and accepts a patting hug from a teen who once participated in club at their Portland flat. They chat; the blond-haired girl introduces her to other friends. "She got me interested in Young Life," she tells the girls.

"I did?" Jill says.

"Sure. Your house always smelled so good, and you had all those plants, and I felt, you know, at home there."

And then they're gone, bouncing to the music as they walk toward the sports complex, leaving Jill behind, standing there in awe.

Jill thinks this might be a perfect picture of life: one never knows when the joys or challenges will appear. Love surprises. "We're a part of the romance," Tom repeats, "helping them see that this is a place where they're called to respond in love to the One who loves them most."

Jill attends all the club meetings, the one structured hour of each day when the kids hear the gospel message through skits and story and song. Arnold sits beside her laughing at the program staff's antics, blinks back tears as the stories move to message—unique depictions of separation and sin, confession and redemption. These words have troubled Jill throughout her life. Here, she hears them new, the stories bypassing her critical side, moving directly to her heart.

Jill pulls on her jeans and sweatshirt. It's chilly for a June morning. Tom's gone to tend to a leaky faucet in the hotel. They'll meet for breakfast at the Orchard Inn with all the kids and staff, then join that final "say so."

"This morning," Molly tells Jill the day before the kids load back up into the buses, "the kids have a chance to stand up for the 'say so.' If they've had a changed relationship with Christ this week, they can stand up and 'say so' in front of others. No details, just their name and their willingness to stand for Him."

Tom's gone on ahead, and Jill helps clean up after breakfast, then slips into the adult guest seats, a few folding chairs set behind the floor space where the 150 or so kids sit cross-legged or lean against each other, singing along with the crazily dressed program staff. It's always a happy time and a sad time, Tom tells her, when the last morning arrives, because the kids are leaving. "Grieving." All love requires giving one's heart, then grieving when the recipient leaves. Jill thinks of Romeo leaving Juliet behind with no one to sustain her, no arms of a friend or a faith to hold her in her crying. Maybe she'll drive over to visit Juliet—Irene—bring her here for a week. They've plenty of room in their condo.

The speaker for the camp shares final words, and then he describes the 'say so' part. Jill watches as a few hesitant kids begin to stand, hating to be the first, hating to bring attention to themselves, and yet willing to announce to others that something is different about them now. Something's changed.

The leader hands the microphone to the first camper, who speaks his name out clear and then suddenly—in a way that had never happened at any Young Life camp before, Tom tells her later—he takes the microphone back. His voice breaks. "This young man, he was the first camper to set foot on Wildhorse Canyon."

Tom's prayers have been answered, along with a legion of others sent up through time. Someone was faithful to this child. Eva's prayers, Cora's, Gail's and Isaac's, Molly's and Brad's, Tom's, and yes, Jill's, and hundreds of volunteers throughout the country, theirs too, have brought this child this moment. Jill stands prepared to say so.

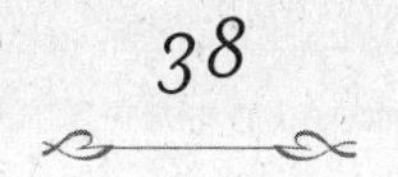

LIFE

"You have to look at the scrapbooks," Molly tells one of the new women. "It gives you such a sense of history in this place." Molly lifts the collection of Eva's letters. "She waited for a good thing to happen and had faith it would, and it did."

"I still wonder why Eva left these letters behind," Jill says. "You'd think she'd want to keep a chronicle of her journey with her, especially one that ends with her husband's pardon. At the very least, I bet her daughter Gillette would want them."

"Gillette would have her own version of what happened," Molly says. "We have to do this too. I've got to get Brad to write down his story of this place, and I'll write mine before we leave. About the dog getting better and never seeing a single snake the entire time I've been here, Psalm 91. I've graduated from phobic to merely hating them. Now that's a healing." They all laugh. "Others who come here years from now should know about this time, about the wonders that happened here."

"I'm not much of a writer," Gail says.

"It's the story that matters, and you're the only one who can write your part. Look at this. Did you see this? Eva's quoting a verse in John. 'And many other signs truly did Jesus in the presence of his disciples, which are not written in this book: But these are written, that ye might believe that Jesus is the Christ, the Son of God; and that believing ye might have life through his name.' "

Jill can name the miracles of this story, and understands now how they have moved her to believe, to love with new dimension.

The Bhagwan once boasted, "This commune is not an ordinary commune; this is an experiment to provoke God. You may not be aware of what is going to happen." He had no way of knowing how prophetic his statement would be. Charita told her that his followers believed something amazing would happen at the turn of the century. It is June 1999. Something already has.

"How would you like to stay on here?" Jill asks Tom. They sit on the porch looking down on the garages that once held the Bhagwan's Rolls-Royces and now offer a secure place for storage. They're eating homemade ice cream.

"I'm not sure they'll have that many positions once we finish up. And we're not so independently wealthy we can afford to volunteer."

"Maybe we are," Jill says.

"You've become a dreamer after all this time?"

"It's what you want, isn't it? To continue being a part of making this happen?" She tells him then of her mother's willingness to loan her money. "Actually, she wants me to take it as a gift, but I think we can find a way to pay it back in time, when we rejoin civilization. If we do." Until then, if they live frugally and Jill doesn't take a classes, they can remain another year at least. Volunteer their labor.

"Not finish your degree? I couldn't—"

"Hear me out, Tommy Boy. I know I can drive over there every week. I've done it. I know I can get a doctorate, but now I also know I don't have to. At least right now. I can yield and take the harvest that's here. I read these letters of Eva Bruner; they're prayers actually. But they speak of giving, something I'm learning to do, and they speak of taking in. Charity is a coin with two sides; the giver needs a receiver. Eva had to let her father-in-law help. My mother's always wanted to help. She wanted me to have the birthmark removed." Jill swallows. "I wouldn't let her. But she's willing to give us the money for other things. This is her gift to me, to us. I can give it to you. And through it, we can both give to the kids."

"What about using the money for the surgery? Wouldn't you like that?"

She reaches for her neck. She doesn't bother with a scarf anymore. "It's just a part of who I am. What I have is what I want."

Coming here set her on a journey as it had Eva Bruner, as it did Cora Swensen. No human being could meet their needs. Had she not taken the journey, she might never have learned that accepting the charity of others isn't a sign of weakness. It's a requirement of relationship—to risk, to wait, to pay attention, to trust that being filled comes not from Tom or even from these women who will remain her friends forever, but from something larger. *Someone* larger, who has brought about this magnificent place where even silent prayers are heard and answered.

Jill reads Eva's letters repeatedly. *They have come to assist us with the building of the cabin. I hesitate to wonder how they knew of this need. Mildred, I imagine. But neighbors farther out near Donneybrook and Ashwood, Antelope, too, arrive in wagons, their children and their lunch baskets tucked in the back. Why would they do this thing, assist a woman and her child? Gillette and I are but strangers to them. A couple I believe were jurors, my eyes keen to see the faces once again of those who sent my Dee away. Yet Dee sent himself away. Now he keeps himself away from me, his child, his father. But I have found a way here, through these words, to make sense of this. Today will be a day I treasure always, men and women gathered in a common task, to raise a house, a home, for someone they know so little of. "You will pass it on," Mildred tells me. "That is what we do here. We live. We grieve. We give, receive. We pass love on so they will know we are Christians, by our love. This land demands it, then makes it so."*

Jill drives the dusty road from Antelope to pick up the mail. It's September. They've had eight camps, all successful, if not without glitches. She and an Antelope woman are going to Madras later, to the Juniper Family Finders office to see if they can locate information about Gillette Bruner. Maybe her descendants still live and might like Eva's letters. Jill has set up interviews with some of the former cowboys Arnold told her helped round up wild horses on the ranch. She thinks she's located a descendant of the man killed by Eva Bruner's husband. She's intrigued by the stories of this land, wants to write them down.

She eases out of the car, runs inside while the Nissan hums. She picks up the clump of mail from the postmaster. Jill once called her the "postmistress" and was corrected. "They don't pay me enough to be a mistress," she said and then laughed. "You won't be hopping like that in a few months," the postmaster tells her today.

"Sure I will. I know people who've run marathons in their eighth month of pregnancy."

"You kids," she says, waving Jill away with good humor.

Jill looks at the letters. Advertisements, mostly. A phone bill. One envelope from her mother. Jill pauses at that; she's been writing to her mother these past three months without a reply. But Eva did it, kept writing, not sure what might happen. Jill tears it open and reads. She can hardly wait to tell Tom. Her mother and stepfather want to come for a visit, after the baby arrives.

Then Jill spies the Guggenheim letter. She takes a deep breath, not sure how she'll take this news. If she's awarded the grant, she and Tom will face big decisions; if she's denied it, she's not sure how she'll feel. A failure? Out of habit, she reaches for a scarf that isn't there.

We regret to inform you that your application for funding has been denied.

Jill's not disappointed, she's relieved. Another miracle.

A Land Deposit

Jill watches as Buckle's grandmother bends over her *kapn,* her digging stick. An April sky is filled with wispy clouds; hawks dip their wings above the cliffs, then down. Children laugh, making swords of their digging sticks. The grandmother admonishes. "Hey, hey, now. This is sacred time honoring first fruits of the Creator." The old woman wears a colored scarf tied at the back of her neck. She might be a Russian grandmother, or Jill's own. Jill feels linked to her, to all women serving their families through the ages from the land.

The children settle down as their grandmother shows them how to identify the plant. She pushes the pointed stick, then bends and lifts the root out. "We clean them here," she tells the children, "so the husks will replenish the earth and there will be more next year. We give back a portion of what we're given."

Tom has his arm draped around Jill. Next week, Charita plans to bring her grandmother, Cora, for a visit. Irene stands with her sweater blown open in the breeze. She holds a young boy's hand. Jill reaches out to take her other hand, and the woman smiles.

"Next year at this time, we'll have a little one to nurture out here with these root diggers." Tom pats Jill's belly.

"If it's a girl," Jill says. "Girls do the root digging and gathering. If it's a boy, we'll have to wait until August and go huckleberry picking with him. Boys get to do that."

"And hunt," Tom says. He winks.

They move toward the old tipi ring, a perfect circle. The grandmother points with her chin. "There," she tells the children, "right in the middle one grows." The hills offer protection from the wind.

Jill sees a sheltered circle with Tom, friends, her future child, all surrounding. She can look across to those on the other side. She can reach out and hold hands with two beside her. God at the center, Jill thinks, with those in the circle moving always toward Him while holding on to each other. This landscape's large but can be known, in part, some mystery always remaining. So she must wait and yet engage. It's what faithful living is.

"Salvation," Gail reminded them that morning at the Bible study, "really means 'to make wide or sufficient' in Hebrew. And in Greek, when Jesus says that one's faith has saved them, it means their faith has made them well. They've been rescued from a harm."

Just beyond the grandmother's bent head, Jill spies a flash of red. "Oh look!" she says. "It's a blooming barrel cactus! Isn't that amazing?"

She stands in awe on this land of sheltered promise; a land that now knows salvation, too.

Author's Notes and Acknowledgments

I've long been interested in early histories of the West, how women in particular endured, and what allowed them not only to persist on harsh landscapes but to triumph. The landscape of eastern Oregon in particular makes one marvel, as it appears at first to be so daunting. Geologist and professor Ellen Morris Bishop in her book *In Search of Ancient Oregon: A Geological and Natural History* describes the Muddy Ranch terrain like this:

> Shattered by volcanic explosions and baked by lava, this vent eroded into...a kingdom of 100-foot cliffs and coagulated spires. It is a hostile place whose landscape seems to remember its eruptive ferocity.... The mind flips into fast forward, then to reverse, merging images, sounds of destruction, and chaos like a digital video cut. The past is present. The present is past. Time is circular. Process continues.

The land knew violent geological eruptions, followed by human settlement eons later that produced its own violence and demand. Indians died there. Sheepherders and cattlemen fought there. Women wept when their husbands or sons failed to come home from these wars; some participated in them. But they also exercised hope and faith amid that landscape, and discovered lessons of love.

In 1998, while speaking to a community group in Salem, Oregon, I mentioned the "Essentially a one-lane road" sign I'd seen on my way to visit the commune in 1982. I suggested I might like a similar sign for our own homestead driveway, eleven miles from pavement. I'd heard that the former Rancho Rajneeshpuram commune would soon become a Young Life camp. I thought it fascinating that a place that had known such trial and turmoil over time should now find itself in this context. Gwen Barrett, a board member of Young

Life, attended that gathering. She later planted the seed, as only Gwen can do. "You should write the history of the Muddy," she told me. But I knew if I did, it would not be a history so much as an exploration of three eras through the eyes of three women.

Theologian Frederick Buechner uses the term *upthrusts* to describe examples of God pushing up through the ages to reveal something of God's nature. The development and existence of this nondenominational camp on the unlikely site of a murder in the early 1900s and the bioterrorism of the 1980s is to me an upthrust of the most interesting kind.

Over the next six years, the Barretts invited my husband and me to what is now Wildhorse Canyon at Young Life's Washington Family Ranch. There I listened to the stories of the Washington family's generosity, of renewal, and of slow healing for the Antelope neighbors and the land. I heard of gifts given—materials, supplies, thousands of volunteer hours, and more—and amazing stories of how the camp was raised out of ruins. I am forever grateful to the Barretts for their encouragement and assistance in the writing of this story, and for their early contact with the Young Life board, which willingly provided me with resources and encouragement throughout my research.

By 2003 the story had me in its grip. This would be a different novel from my previous ten, not a historical novel in the usual sense. It is my hope, however, that this story is history to nurture your soul.

Part 1, the story of Eva Thompson Bruner and her husband D.L. (Dee), is based on a true account. The press recorded the murder trial as volatile and political in nature. Eva, Dee's "child-wife," and her father-in-law testified. Dee was found guilty and sentenced to life. My thanks to the Crook County Historical Society (Gordon Gillespie and researcher Jim Zimmerlee) and to Gale Ontko's series for details about the Prineville, Oregon, trial and the history of Central Oregon. Probate and other circuit court records revealed the question of Dee's mother's sanity, Dee's siblings, and his detachment from his family. State archivists found not only a copy of Dee's sentencing but his mug shot as well, and I'm grateful.

Henry Hahn and Leo Fried were real men who ran a mercantile in Prineville, brought jobs to wranglers and sheepherders, and managed a spread unequaled in size at the time (nearly 124,000 acres) running thousands of cattle and sheep and wild horses. It became known as the Muddy Ranch. The stage stopped at the ranch house where cooks served meals often to forty wranglers at a time. Hahn and Fried were influential men who many at the time believed had at least sanctioned Reilly's killing, if not ordered it. They didn't like crowding, and they had the power and influence to effect what they didn't like. The murder of Tom Reilly represents the beginning of another era when people bathed the land in blood.

I could not verify whether Eva and Dee had children or remained on the Muddy, despite the excellent efforts of Joanne Ward, librarian at the Columbia Gorge Discovery Center in The Dalles, and Beth Crow and others at the Juniper Family Finders in Madras, Oregon. But there was a Morrison Thompson who lived in Dufur believed to be Eva's uncle, and there was a John Thompson convicted of a murder at the Silvertooth Saloon in Antelope, who was later pardoned. Dee's outcome, too, is verified by prison records.

Art Campbell's book *Antelope: The Saga of a Western Town* is a fine resource for this era and this particular event, as is the Martha Stranahan article about the specific history of the Prineville Land and Livestock Company. (See suggested reading list.) An unpublished history by Judy Straalsund titled "History of the Big Muddy Ranch" also provided valuable information. Contacts at the Warm Springs Indian Reservation offered details about the land as ceded ground, given up by natives at the time of the treaty of 1855, but still used for hunting and digging roots.

The ranch continued in the hands of the Hahn family for many years. Les Aldrich's reminiscences in a 1999 Young Life *Communicator,* as well as other memories shared through the Jefferson County Historical Society, provided details about early ranch life. Well into the 1990s, wranglers still looked for wild horses on Black Rock. One of the last rides my horsewoman sister Judy Hurtley took before she died was with former wrangler Sonny Bain, rounding up wild horses for the Muddy.

The old stage road Eva took to Prineville still runs as an unimproved public road through the ranch. I did indeed find barrel cacti blooming on the property when we drove that rutted passage.

My personal experience with part 2 and the Bhagwan's commune began in 1982, when a visiting Wisconsin friend and I awoke to the news of an election held in Antelope, Oregon, where an East Indian mystic had gained control of that little Western town. The newly elected mayor was a woman my friend and I had known before she became a Sannyasin, a follower of the Bhagwan. On impulse, we drove two hours to see her. (My husband and I would soon become distant neighbors of the commune when we established our own remote homestead downriver from Rancho Rajneeshpuram in north-central Oregon.) That November day, we were checked in at the Antelope/Rajneesh reception center, cleared for travel on the road, waved through at security points by armed guards, then met by our friend. She served as our tour guide and shared the three points of vision included in this story. We ate at Magdalena Cafeteria (a site where, according to former resident Tim Guest's account, hundreds of tubs of lettuce were once thrown out because the salmonella test pans had not been properly separated). We were shown Rajneesh Mandir, where the celebrations were held and the peace force patrolled the catwalks with Uzis. She took us to her and Ma Anand Sheela's quarters in Jesus Grove. The commune managed nearly sixty-four thousand acres of land at the time and faced numerous lawsuits filed by the state of Oregon and 1000 Friends of Oregon, a land-use watchdog group, and Antelope residents. I left intrigued and saddened by the changes on the property, in the surrounding communities, and in our friend.

Many of the observations in part 2 stem from this visit as well as later visits, numerous verbal accounts of those on the receiving end of the destructiveness later attributed to the Bhagwan's leadership, newspaper accounts, and even television documentaries about the commune. The collections at the Columbia Gorge Discovery Center in The Dalles, Oregon, and at the Wasco County Library were especially helpful. Special thanks go to Margaret Hill, former Antelope mayor, and Ralph Bently for personal recollections shared with me. The Bently collection donated to the Discovery Center, including videotapes, was invaluable.

These were difficult times for people of Antelope, Madras, and The Dalles. They endured scorn from those who accused them of religious intolerance, even up to the day the community and elected officials were poisoned, and in the days that followed, when communities were asked to provide care to hundreds of homeless people abandoned by the commune. In 1985, the commune began to disintegrate, exposing the intricate complexities of the foundation, the commune, Rajneesh (Antelope), the religious division, and myriad corporations —including the trust for the Bhagwan's ninety-four Rolls-Royces. Charges of and later indictments for attempted murder, electronic eavesdropping conspiracy, immigration conspiracy, lying to federal officials, burglary, harboring a fugitive, racketeering, first-degree arson, and first- and second-degree assault followed. My friend the Rajneeshpuram mayor was among those indicted on the lesser charges.

During the bankruptcy sale, my husband and I made trips to the ranch to purchase irrigation pumps and black plastic tubing that once served the commune's vineyards. We put these to use on our own ranch. Later we bought rugs and other furnishings, and at Christmastime we shared peanut brittle with pleasant Sannyasins who helped us put chains on our truck's tires. Many of them were troubled by what had happened to their neighbors under the direction of Ma Anand Sheela and Ma Anand Puja, and by what they believed their Bhagwan had tolerated, if not condoned. Their newspaper carried stories of their betrayal.

Articles by Win McCormack and Bill Driver in The Dalles *Weekly Reminder* and *Oregon Magazine* early on raised an alarm discounted by many at the time. Detailed accounts of these years can be found in the *Oregonian* July 5, 1985, article "For Love and Money" by Scotta

Callister, James Long, and Leslie L. Zaitz; *Charisma and Control in Rajneeshpuram* by Lewis F. Carter is another valued resource. Carter attributes the "legitimate use" of the salmonella as coming from a Warm Springs laboratory; other sources cited an eastern seaboard lab. All attribute the "destructive use" of it to the commune's leaders. University of Oregon Professor Marion Goldman's book *Passionate Journeys: Why Successful Women Joined a Cult;* Lewis and Clark professor Frances Fitzgerald's work *Cities on a Hill;* and from a child's perspective, Tim Guest's *My Life in Orange* were especially helpful. I am especially indebted to my friend Blair Fredstrom, for her Web-site searches on my behalf, and to the Sherman Public School Library in Moro, whose librarians, Arla Melzer, Jeanney McArthur, and Judy Harmon, not only found and purchased a copy of the Carter book but checked it out to me for as long as I needed it for research.

There was no real Cora Swensen or Razi or Charita. But there were children at the commune, though few. Their stories have remained largely silent, despite a lawsuit against the commune charging possible neglect and abuse at the ranch. Shortly after the charge, it's believed that most of the children were sent to other communes around the world, making investigation impossible. An account by Tim Guest published in 2004 in the United Kingdom and scheduled for printing in the U.S. in late 2004 chronicles one child's life growing up in the Rajneeshees' communes around the world, and specifically his feelings of abandonment and fear while attending the Master's Day Festival of 1984, when this story takes place. He also notes the danger for children there. "That year, the summer of 1984 at the Ranch, many of the Medina kids lost their virginity; boys and girls, ten years old, eight years old, in sweaty tents and A-frames, late at night and midafternoon, with adults and other children.... I had just turned nine years old" (pages 198-199).

Ma Anand Sheela was found guilty of attempted murder, sentenced to fifteen years, and fined $469,000. She served less than five, paid $200,000, and was deported to Europe. At this writing, she goes by the name of Dr. Sheela Birnstiel and lives in Maisprach, Switzerland, where she operates a self-established senior residence for the care of mentally and bodily handicapped people. The Bhagwan died in 1991. Members of the former commune are scattered throughout the world and follow the teachings of Osho but have largely discontinued the dynamic meditations and the aggressive rhetoric of the Bhagwan's era. Some members of the inner circle pleaded guilty to their charges and are part of the Federal Witness Protection Program. Only a small portion of the five-million-dollar settlement of lawsuits, some of which was meant for victims of the salmonella outbreaks, has ever been collected or made available as restitution to the victims.

A bronze plaque on the post-office flagpole in Antelope stands as both a witness and memorial to the trials of those citizens. "Dedicated to those of this community who throughout the Rajneesh invasion and occupation on 1981–1985 remained, resisted and remembered… 'The only thing necessary for the triumph of evil is for good men to do nothing.' Edmund Burke."

Part 3, Charity, owes much gratitude again to the Barretts. I am grateful for their sharing and for putting me in contact with needed resources. Serendipitously, at another book group in Bend, I mentioned my interest in this story and met Doris Gillet from Seattle. She and her husband, Al, were early residents of the ranch in 1998 shortly after the approval of the zoning ordinances (which did indeed pass through without an appeal). Their son and daughter-in-law, Dana and Pam Gillet, arranged for early interviews with the senior Gillets; with Jay and Tiffany Taylor, the earliest residents who arrived in late 1997; and with Gordon Hecker, a Young Life engineering consultant hired to assess how to transform the property into a camp. He left in early 1998. Their insights about those first months provided the foundation for this story, and I am grateful for their permission to make composites of their stories. None of them, by the way, was a skeptic like Jill. They came to Wildhorse Canyon with various degrees of enthusiasm, and all who participated in the actual building of the camp gave their hearts fully to the cause. I am especially grateful to Pam Gillet for her wisdom and encouragement in my writing of this story, and for late-night conversations at the ranch that added richness to my life.

I am also grateful to the following people for their phone-interview time and for the copies of papers and reports they provided to me: Denny Rydberg, Young Life national president, and Jim Eney, northwest divisional director, and his wife, Janet. Janet Eney, in a conversation, offered the idea that the camps "serve the orphan in us all," a concept that came to frame this story. I am indebted to her. Jim Eney was named by many I interviewed as the vision behind the impossible task of bringing the dream for this camp into reality. The liaison he provided between the Young Life leadership in Colorado Springs and the field staff (such as Steve Fox, who brought the first group of teens to the camp) was considered instrumental in the success of the project. Planners and implementers sometimes do not talk well with each other; this appears not to have been the case due to Jim Eney's leadership and collaboration.

Rex Baird, first project manager of the camp and his wife, Jane (who never saw a rattlesnake the entire time she was there—Psalm 91—and who brought with her an ailing dog she eventually took home for more years together) provided insights not only about their time on the ranch but about the philosophy of Young Life. Both had been active in the organization for years and felt called to this ministry of transition. Most volunteers and staff reported to Rex during the construction phase. The Bairds' gracious recounting of the miracles Jill experiences and their humility regarding their part in the development of the ranch are appreciated and admired.

The miracles Jill relates in the story are actual events, including the disappearance of the property schematics, their mysterious return and organization, the lake construction, the beach sand, and on and on. A Christian Cowboy of Eugene did have a dream to come to the ranch and pray for its use as a kids' camp. I'm grateful to the many volunteers who shared their stories in the scrapbook, including the story of the first boy off the bus. There are now one hundred full-time staff and volunteers living at the Washington Family Ranch. Many shared their stories, and I'm grateful.

Ben Herr, property manager at Wildhorse Canyon and an early believer in the possibility of the site for a camp, gave both touring time and the loan of scrapbooks and photo albums. He served briefly on site at Wildhorse and returned later to the position of property manager that he now holds. I'm especially grateful to him for his time, his accounts of the Young Life story, of early visits to meet residents. I am also grateful for Ben's support of my storytelling.

Jay McAlonen turned his love of flying into charitable activities for Young Life during the early months. He made himself and his airplane available to project and board people, greatly enhancing the communication needed for complex negotiations and rapid decision making. He was later appointed by Dave Carlson, vice president in camping, as the first property manager serving with Rex Baird until the opening of the first camp. Mick Humphreys shared his remembrances of making the connection with the Washington Family; Mike Higgs described early prayer support for the project and for efforts at reconciliation with native peoples who once roamed the land. I thank him for sharing his spiritual history of the ranch.

Doug and Dana Kuhn, the engineer in charge of the pool and lake development who raised their own support to be a part of this project, and who grieved the loss of a father they loved at the same time, graciously gave me their time and memories. I thank them. I'm grateful to have spoken with Lance and Jan Wagner, who arrived from San Francisco never having heard of Young Life, but who followed their hearts to that landscape and who, with their towheaded children, remain there still.

Forrest Reinhardt did come to the ranch with his son the same weekend as the Barretts in 1995, dreaming the same dream. Kevin Bryant of the Young Life staff headed the fund-raising for the Washington Family Ranch. With the help of additional contributions from the Washingtons and numerous donors, the match was met within the time limit, and the camp became self-supporting within three years instead of the expected five.

There were many others—readers, people in different settings, acquaintances at conferences unrelated to Young Life (or so I thought) —who, when learning of my interest in the story, shared experiences of painting or fighting cockroaches and spiders while volunteering at Wildhorse. All describe their time as healing and transforming despite the challenging terrain. A list of over eight hundred volunteers continues to grow, people giving of their time and talents on behalf of children. Today, a game-management program operates on the ranch. Most of the grazing is leased to local neighbors, as the camp no longer runs cattle. Efforts to reclaim portions of the land that were overgrazed by cattle and sheep continue, as do attempts to reengage native people in the Young Life story. A scholarship has been created to assist native children who want to participate at Wildhorse Canyon, securing another link in the chain of time on the land.

Because the story ends with the first camp, I did not explore the range and contribution of the program staff, or the coordination between property and program, relationships that are hallmarks of the Young Life camps worldwide. Interested people are welcome to visit, take tours, and discover for themselves the heart of Wildhorse Canyon.

I thank the staff at WaterBrook Press who take a story and make it a reality. Thanks also to my agents Joyce Hart and Terry Porter. And thanks to Carol Tedder, my prayer partner. Finally, I once again thank my family, my nieces Arlene and Michelle Hurtley for their efforts, and our granddaughter Mariah, who lived with us through the writing of this book. She brought the importance of children out of a historical novel and into our home. Jerry, your map-making is extraordinary, your encouragement without equal, and your personification of faith, hope, and charity a welcome promised shelter in my life. Thank you.

Arnold Dalke did come to Wildhorse Canyon as a man in his eighties. On his ninetieth birthday in 2004, he rode the zip line and set the record as the oldest to have done it, just as he hoped.

Jane Kirkpatrick, www.jkbooks.com

A scholarship fund has been established to encourage the camping experience at Wildhorse Canyon for Native American youth. Tax-deductible contributions can be made to the fund in care of Young Life's Washington Family Ranch at Wildhorse Canyon, P.O. Box 220, Antelope, Oregon 97001. A portion of royalties for this book will be donated by the author and her husband for this purpose in honor of their deceased son, Kevin, a descendant of the Choctaw nation.

Author Discussion and Questions for Reflection

I chose *Pentimento* as a working title for *A Land of Sheltered Promise.* I was struck by the adjustments and changes on one remote section of land that, at first glance, appeared to harbor meaningless trials and pain. *Pentimento,* with its translation of "turning around" as in "repenting," suggests that an artist with a master plan, a vision clear, often makes shifts and adjustments while working toward completion. A viewer can often see these adjustments in faint, ghostly lines. Only in the end product can one see how important the earlier revisions were to the outcome. Such a looking back allows the authenticity and intention of the master to shine through.

I was also intrigued by this landscape, which drew such extremes in belief and behavior. Was this remote Oregon high-desert ranch a place that the Celts might call a "thin place," or a place Native Americans refer to as sacred ground, where heaven and humanity merge?

In 1901, a woman must struggle with what it means to remain loyal to a convicted killer who is her husband; she later witnesses a miracle. During the Rajneesh occupation of the ranch—in the wake of murders and attempted murders, the manipulation of legal systems and land-use laws, and the crowding and terrorizing of innocents—an outside observer is left to conclude that no good thing came of what the Bhagwan called "an experiment to provoke God." His followers lived remotely, in many instances abdicated personal responsibility, disappeared from the lives of their children, and challenged their neighbors in profoundly disturbing ways. Yet even in the midst of chaos, faith did flourish, and those in the surrounding towns hoped good things might one day rise from the bad.

At the end of the century, generosity, charity, and love—not deception—marked the landscape and relationships of the people drawn to that dramatic land of rocky spires and purple hills. The Sannyasins who came before may not have intended it, but love converted their efforts into a stable foundation for the Young Life enthusiasts. Water, electricity, housing, the land itself, and the generosity of Montana's Dennis and Phyllis Washington and their family prompted others to give, to demonstrate their passion for bringing young people to their Christian faith. Their efforts, their commitments, lifted people to a place of grace.

In this story, Eva, Cora, and Jill are asked to wait, to trust, to hope before the promise of the land unfolds, revealing a landscape of laughter, healing, and retreat. It just took time. And a few adjustments.

1. For the author, this is a story about landscape and loyalties. What loyalties are explored in each of the three sections of Faith, Hope, and Charity? Are any of these loyalties threaded together from one section to the other? Do those threads ring true to you as a reader?
2. As you think of your own generational stories, do you recall any loyalties that troubled your ancestors, or did their loyalties offer them sustenance over time? Do you recognize any of those struggles and/or loyalties within your life today? Does this story of faithfulness over time bring you hope or frustration? Why?
3. Following her husband's conviction, Eva Bruner came to the conclusion that it did not matter how her husband responded to her efforts to engage him. She chose to be clear about what mattered in her life and found the courage to act on that. What other choices did she make in an effort to come to terms with the changed relationship brought about by her husband's actions? Do you have a predictable response to the uncertainties and disappointments of life? Describe it. Is your response helpful, or does it prevent you from finding resolution so you can move forward? Does Eva's decision suggest an alternative for you?
4. Mildred and the Muddy crew offered help to Eva. Her aunt and uncle offered assistance, as did her father-in-law. Cora and Jill also had offers of help they struggled to accept. Why

is it so difficult for strong women to ask for or receive help from others? What is it about accepting the generosity of others that compels so many women (and men) to spurn these offers? Is this an area of your life that challenges you?

5. In part 2, why did Cora Swensen struggle with her right to remove her granddaughter from life with her mother on the commune? How did her assessment of her own love and parenting history undermine the certainty she sought in order to act on behalf of her granddaughter? How was Cora's faith changed by attempting to understand it in the midst of the communal demands and the religious fervor at Rancho Rajneeshpuram? How were her relationships with her daughter and husband affected by her time on the ranch?
6. What enabled the Bhagwan to engage Rachel/Razi when the faith of her mother did not? How well did the author succeed in creating a three-dimensional character presented as a composite of many of the women at the commune who were well-educated, compassionate, and wanting to serve, and who found themselves in a landscape they would otherwise never have chosen without the influence of the Bhagwan in their lives? What ultimately kept Rachel/Razi from participating in the salmonella poisonings? Is it consistent with her character that she would have given up the engineering drawings those many years later?
7. Jill Hartley came to the landscape reluctantly, unlike Eva and Rachel, and even Cora. What or who helped Jill decide to go with her husband to the Muddy Ranch? How was her tendency to "stand back and watch" challenged at the Young Life camp? What happened when she took the risk of entering into something unfamiliar? Can you remember a time when you stepped into a "wilderness" and discovered not the fears you imagined but refreshment, like the rush of a zip line carrying you into something satisfying and new?

8. What does the term *engagement* come to mean to each of the women in this story? Within one's faith life, are we asked to "engage," that is, to trust God's promise despite outward signs that perhaps the promise has been forgotten or compromised by leaders, laws, trouble, and sorrow? How does a faithful person sustain belief when outside evidence in support of that faith appears to be lacking?
9. French writer Charles Saint-Beauve noted that a skeptic is "not one who doubts but one who examines." What did Jill Hartley examine? How did her examination lead her to a *conversion,* a word that comes from the Latin word meaning "to turn around"? What did she face in herself as she learned to see others and her circumstances differently? What was Jill looking for? Do we seek on our spiritual journeys, or are we being sought?
10. What role did the legal system play in the lives of these three women and their journeys? How was "crowding" affected by the justice system in each of the three eras?
11. Is religious conversion, as writer Kathleen Norris suggests, a "lifelong process" or a once-in-a-lifetime act of commitment, or both? What role did the community of believers play in the turnarounds of Eva, of Cora, of Jill?
12. Each of the women experienced changed hearts despite the conflicts within their relationships with their husbands and their mothers. What else did the women hold in common? Can you identify a time when you accepted an outcome even though it was not what you'd prepared for? What permitted you to make this adjustment?
13. Novelist Willa Cather once noted that where there is great love, there are always miracles. What miracles occurred in these stories? (Or do you think these events lacked the significance to be called miracles? Why or why not?)
14. What signs of pentimento are evident in the lives of Eva, Cora, and Jill? What signs of pentimento are evident in your

life? In what ways has God kept Scriptural promises to you, sheltering you in the land of your own life?

15. In 1 Corinthians 13:13 Paul wrote, "And now these three remain: faith, hope and love. But the greatest of these is love." Which of these three emerges as "greatest" in *A Land of Sheltered Promise?*

If your reading group would like to schedule a half-hour visit with the author via speakerphone or e-mail, please visit her Web site at www.jkbooks.com and click on Book Groups for additional information.

Recommended Reading

Part I: Faith
Prineville Land and Livestock Company Era

Brogran, Phil F. *East of the Cascades.* Portland: Binfort & Mort, 1964.

Campbell, Arthur. *Antelope: The Saga of a Western Town.* Bend, OR: Maverick, 1990.

Crook County Journal. Prineville, OR, 1901.

Hands, Mary. *Jefferson County Reminiscences.* Portland: Binfort & Mort, 1957.

Harris, Bruce. *The History of Wasco County.* The Dalles, OR: Wasco County Historical Society, Limited Edition, 1983.

Marion County Probate Records, 1880, 1886.

McNeal, William H. *History of Wasco County, Oregon.* The Dalles, OR: William McNeal, Limited Edition, 1954.

Nielsen, Lawrence E. *In the Ruts of the Wagon Wheels: Pioneer Roads in Eastern Oregon.* Bend, OR: Maverick, 1987.

Nielsen, Lawrence E., Doug Newman, and George McCart. *Pioneer Roads in Central Oregon.* Bend, OR: Maverick, 1985.

Ontko, Gale. *Thunder Over the Ochoco, vol. 5: And the Juniper Trees Bore Fruit.* Bend, OR: Maverick, 1999.

Oregon State Prison records. Secretary of State Archives Division. Salem, Oregon, 1905.

Rees, Helen. *Shaniko People.* Bend, OR: Maverick, 1983.

Stranahan, Martha. "Prineville Merchants Henry Hahn and Leo Fried Begin Developing Muddy Ranch in 1882." *Spokesman.* Redmond, OR, date unknown.

United States Census Records, 1880.

Part II: Hope
The Rajneesh Era

Bently, Ralph. Personal interview and review of extensive Bently Collection held by the Columbia Gorge Discovery Center, The Dalles, Oregon. The Collection includes issues of *The Dalles Chronicle, The Dalles Weekly Reminder, The Oregonian, Oregon Magazine,* and *Rajneesh Times,* and *Willamette Week* articles from 1981 through 1987 in addition to other items, such as personal correspondence to and from Laura Bently, former mayor of Antelope; audiotapes and videotapes of city council meetings, Concerned Oregonian meetings; television news clips including *60 Minutes* and *Frontline* programs related to the years of volatile change for the Antelope residents; court documents related to land-use appeals; letters to the editor; county-court hearing minutes and recordings; Antelope flag dedication and "Freedom Memorial Dedication" placed following the dismantling of Rajneeshpuram and Rajneesh and to honor the perseverance of the Antelope residents.

Bharti, Ma Satya. *Drunk on the Divine: An Account of Life in the Ashram of Bhagwan Shree Rajneesh.* New York: Rajneesh Foundation, Grove Press, 1980.

Callister, Scotta, James Long, and Leslie L. Zeitz, "For Love and Money." *The Oregonian,* July 5, 1985.

Carter, Lewis F. *Charisma and Control in Rajneeshpuram: The Role of Shared Values in the Creation of a Community.* New York: Cambridge University Press, 1990.

Fitzgerald, Frances. *Cities on a Hill: A Journey Through Contemporary American Cultures.* New York: Touchstone, 1987.

Goldman, Marion S. *Passionate Journeys: Why Successful Women Joined a Cult.* Ann Arbor: University of Michigan Press, 1999.

Guest, Tim. *My Life in Orange.* London: Granta, 2004.

McCormack, Win, and Bill Driver. "Bhagwan's Child-Rearing." *Oregon Magazine,* May 1985, 72-74.

Webber, Bert. *The Rajneesh and the U.S. Postal Service.* Medford, OR: The Webb Research Group, 1988.

Part III: Charity
The Young Life Era

Aldrich, Les. "The Big Muddy Ranch to Cult to Camp." *Young Life Communicator,* March/April 1999.

Higgs, Mike. "Prayer Mobilization for the Ministry of the Big Muddy Ranch" and "Proposal for the Spiritual Cleansing and Reconciliation of the Big Muddy Ranch." Portland, OR: LINC Ministries (privately published), 1996.

Duin, Steve. "Church or State." *The Oregonian.* Portland, December 24, 1995.

Rayburn III, Jim. *From Bondage to Liberty: Dance, Children, Dance, The Story of Jim Rayburn Jr., the Founder of Young Life.* Colorado Springs: Morningstar, 2000.

Straalsund, Judy. "History of the Big Muddy Ranch." Young Life's Wildhorse Canyon, Oregon (privately published), 1999.